LUKE'S

ABSOLUTION

THE COLLOWAY BROTHERS #3

K.L. KREIG

To the wonderful bloggers
who work tirelessly to spread the word about
great books simply out their sheer love of them.

I've gotten to know so many of you personally.
I appreciate and thank you for bringing my words
and stories to your followers.

Prologue

December 27th

LUKE

Enjoying the view of her toned bare thigh with each step she takes, courtesy of that nice high slit in her dress, I watch her sashay over to where I'm leaning against the bar. She orders a Corona Light from the bartender, tapping her perfectly manicured pink nails against the cool granite while she waits.

I've been watching her with that jackass photographer for the last hour, getting progressively angrier by the minute, not quite understanding why. She's smokin' hot, yes, but I have absolutely no claim on her. Not that I wouldn't mind a little sample. Or fifty.

Confusingly, it's the same reaction I had when I saw her in his arms last Friday night. The urge to introduce his face to a cement wall was so great, had she not been drunk off her ass, I may not have been able to resist.

She'd be a handful for any man to juggle, no doubt in bed and out, and picture boy, Cooper Jensen, isn't even close to enough man for her. It will take a strong hand to control her, make her submit, and God himself help me, that's all I've thought of since I laid eyes on her for the first time months ago. I want to hear her raw voice sobbing my name while I have her pinned helplessly underneath me. Who knew that Eric's sister was so fucking sexy? Probably why he kept her under wraps all those years ago.

Addy Monroe is like a wild horse. Untamed, full of fire, even feral if you get her riled up enough. I had a small taste of that last weekend after Gray's bachelor party when we stopped by the bar where the girls were having their own celebration. I saved her from herself by confiscating their almost-empty bottle of Patron. Every heated word she spat tugged straight on my cock, and by the time I left with her passed out in my arms, I was rock hard. Let's just say it was a long fucking night all around.

I want her. Not that I *deserve* her. She's untainted, unlike me. I have so many fucking stains, industrial-strength cleaner couldn't remove them all. But I'm not looking for a relationship; I'm looking for a good fuck. I'm looking for oblivion.

Liar, my conscience loudly whispers.

Fuck off, I tell him, even louder.

I discreetly adjust my hardening dick. "No tequila tonight?" I feel the smirk on my face, but don't know if she sees it or not. I'm trying to refrain from looking at her as I will my own body into submission.

"Unrequited love sucks, doesn't it?" she replies with a bite before taking a sip of her beer straight from the bottle. I love a woman who isn't too prissy to drink her alcohol from the actual container it's served in. More than that, I love a woman with a smart, feisty mouth.

"I have no idea what you're talking about, sweetheart."

I flick my eyes over to see hers stray to Gray and Livia across the ballroom and her lips upturn in a sly smirk. "Whatever you say. I'm pretty much the subject matter expert on that shit."

She turns and leans her back against the bar, mirroring my stance. We're both silent, watching the happy newly married couple with drinks in our hands. The more I think about what she said, the more it plain pisses me off.

Yes, I care deeply for Livia. I have for years. No one can possibly understand what I watched her go through and what I had to suffer through myself. How that bonds two people on a totally different plane.

But even if Livia could have been mine, I know her heart will always belong to Gray. I could never interfere with that. Wouldn't. Besides, I've done enough to my family without intentionally trying to steal my brother's girl. I do have a few shreds of decency left that I'm trying desperately to hold on to. They're wound so tightly around my fingers, they're cutting off the circulation, but I'll be damned if I'll let them go.

Regardless of what Addy may think, I'm

genuinely thrilled for them both. After what she's been through, *no one* deserves happiness more than Livia. But fuck, I won't deny watching them get married today was hard. Harder than I thought it would be, and it's not because I still want her. I gave up on that notion years ago, even if my heart didn't quite get the memo.

No...it was hard because the love that hovers above them like a bright golden halo is sickening. What's even more sickening is that as I watch them, I'm envious. I want *that*, only the logical part of me knows I'll never have it. I push those feelings of optimism that keep bubbling to the surface down deep into the muck again. I may have moved past the worst times of my life, but in no way do I kid myself that I'm worthy of a woman's love or acceptance of who I am and the things I've done.

So tonight I need to forget.

About Livia.

About my tainted past.

About all the things I now want but will never get.

And I think Addy Monroe is just the woman to do that, even if it can only be for a few minutes. My dick hardens painfully whenever I set eyes on Livia's best friend, the little sister of *my* best friend Eric, and I have to be honest...she's the only one who's stirred it for quite some time now. I've wanted this spitfire since the minute I saw her shaking the tits and ass God so graciously blessed her with at the bar when I first came back to Chicago in September to protect Livia from our sordid past.

"Maybe fifteen minutes in the back will wipe that smirk off your face," I whisper as I lean sideways toward her. In my peripheral, I see her head turn to me.

"Wow, a whole fifteen minutes, huh? I think I'll have to take a rain check on that offer, Rico Suave." She spins on her heels to walk away from me.

Oh, hell no.

Next thing I know, her body is pressed against mine, held in place by a firm palm to her neck and another circled around the trim waist I've wanted to squeeze all night.

Sweet Jesus and Mary, she feels fantastic. I have to suppress the groan that wants to escape from somewhere deep inside—it would give her too much power over me and control is what I need to wrestle from her, inch by agonizing inch. My lips are at her ear, grazing the tender flesh with each word I rasp.

"Sweetheart, I can spend the next fifteen *hours* lavishing untold pleasure and blissful pain all over and inside every single inch of your delectable body until you beg for me, *cry* for me, to stop."

The way her breath hitches has my cock pleading to ram into her over and over. Uncaring who may see, I release her waist and grab her hand, bringing it between our bodies, forcing it to my shaft with my hand on top. Guiding her, I squeeze, moving our twined fingers up and down the length of me. She moans and my eyes close at the image of sinking my cock slowly between her red-glossed clever lips.

Nipping her lobe harshly, I grate, "Let's start with that smart mouth of yours, shall we?"

Chapter 1

Mid-March, two and a half months later

Addy

"Wow, Cara, that's really good," I tell the cutie as she puts the finishing touches on the oval plate she's painting. This is the third time her dad has brought her into my studio this week where she's worked painstakingly to create the perfect birthday present for her mom.

"Thank you, Miss Monroe. Do you think my mommy will like it?" Her excited eyes latch onto mine, seeking my approval.

"How could she not, sweetie? You have talent, you know that?"

The ten-year-old beauty beams from ear to ear at my compliment. "You really think so?"

I lean down and whisper in her ear like we have some sort of special secret. "I don't think so. I *know* so."

My gaze lifts to find her dad watching me, a smile on his face as he mouths *thank you*. Cara gets back to work on the plate she's painting and I stand there probably a little longer than appropriate just adoring the spunky little girl.

At twenty-eight, I thought by now I'd be married and have the requisite two kids. Unfortunately, that hasn't panned out so well for me. I have no boyfriend, no prospects, and right now, no intention to have either. Don't get me wrong. I believe in the concept of true love. I believe in marriage. I watched my best friend marry the love of her life a few months ago and I know they will be happy until the day they die. I want that. I want true love. I just haven't found it with the right guy yet.

A pang of sadness, or loneliness, tries to pull me under her doom and gloom hex, so I shove that bitch out the door. I don't have time for such stupid emotions. I have a great life and good friends. Who cares that they're all dropping like flies into the wedded pool of bliss and I'm left standing on the sidelines to witness their happiness? Alone.

I sound bitter; I'm truly not, though. I learned a long time ago I don't need a man to make me happy—that's all on me. And I'm happy with my life. That's not to say I wouldn't mind a guy to keep my bed warm, but I'm not on the prowl to get one to put a ring on it either.

Besides, I have too much on my plate to worry about a relationship. As the owner of All Things Painting, I have almost two years under my belt as a small business owner and it's doing surprisingly well. Late last year, I expanded from my basic pottery painting and glass into more of the adult space, adding weekly canvas painting classes called Sip and Dip. It's true what they say: wine really does go with anything.

And last month, I secured several contracts with local aftercare programs and daycares for summer fun field trips where I'll have some of my experts onsite for an afternoon of fun. I also have several proposals in to some of the larger Chicago businesses, pushing my studio for team building activities.

Yet, as I gaze at Cara, there's no denying my favorite part of this job is seeing the kids come in and create their own masterpieces. Masterpieces they will give to their mothers or fathers or grandparents or that they'll proudly display in their rooms until they're fourteen and don't think elementary art is cool anymore. Then it will get packed into a box and stored in the garage or basement or attic because their parents can't bear to get rid of something made by the hands of their children, and that piece will end up being given back to them twenty years from now as a Christmas present. Or maybe given to *their* own children when Grandma cleans out her closet.

I may sound old, but it's a sad day when kids are more interested in the next new video game or traveling competitive sports teams than on exercising the creative side of their brains.

"Thanks, Jeff," I finally tell Cara's dad before forcing myself away from them. "Just leave it here and I'll take it to the kiln when it's dry." I move along the line of tables to see if other customers are in need of assistance with their various projects.

I stop to help one woman with some detail work, getting her a size zero spotter brush instead of the size six she was trying to use. I assist another with selecting and mixing just the right shades of blue to replicate the choppy waters she's trying to paint from a Hawaiian vacation picture. After I ensure everyone else is doing fine on their own, I head to the back where Julia is pulling out a fresh batch of glazed pottery from the kiln.

"Everything come out okay?" I ask. Unfortunately, when you fire pottery, sometimes the tiny fissures in the clay cause the piece to break. It doesn't happen often, and when it does, it's devastating not only to me but to the person who invested so much time painting the piece. It's even worse when it's a child who's so proud of their accomplishment. It's a tragedy, at least in the world I live, yet also unavoidable.

"Yep. We're all good."

"Great. Did you hear anything about the pottery delivery from Smith's?"

"Finally. It's supposed to be here on Thursday." Only two weeks late. With Easter right around the corner that hasn't been good for business as I'm completely out of some of the more popular pieces.

"Good. Thanks, Julia. I'm headed to the back to do some paperwork."

Just as I settle into my comfy, padded desk chair, my cell buzzes. When I catch a glimpse of the caller, I smile. I may have overexaggerated when I said I didn't have any prospects in the men category. I do...just not the one I *really* want. The one I really want is like most of the others who have come before him. The type of man I'm always drawn to. The type of man who has broken my heart time and again.

An undeniably hot, mouthwateringly sexy, tatted badass with a powerful motorcycle planted between his firm thighs.

And just like my last two relationships, this one is in love with someone else. A 'someone else' who happens to be my now-married best friend. He can try to deny it all he wants. I've seen the way he looks at her, holds her, and takes care of her like she was his. I wasted almost a year and a half on Aiden, the last man who never got over his previous girlfriend, and within three days of our breakup, he was back with her.

Talk about a giant black eye to a girl's psyche.

So as much as my body, and possibly even my heart, hasn't willingly climbed on board the whole 'forget about Luke Colloway' train, my mind certainly has. He's exactly the type I need to steer clear of. The love 'em and leave 'em Harley-riding bad boy who dissolves women's panties with his wicked words and wolfish smile.

It's irrelevant anyway—I haven't heard a peep out of Luke since Livia's wedding in December when he oh-so-artfully propositioned me for what would have undoubtedly been the best, most carnal night of my entire life. I think the thick length of him is still embedded into the palm of my hand. Every time I remember it, which, okay let's admit is several agonizing times a day, my body burns hot with want.

I may have stupidly turned down a night of uninhibited sex with a man whose weighty gaze I could feel on me the entire night...a man who's walked straight out of the mist of my fantasies, but I'm not about to be a man's second choice ever again, even if only for a night. I want to be someone's first. Hell, I *deserve* that.

Pushing Luke to the back of my mind where he belongs, I answer my phone before I miss the call. "Hello, Mr. Jensen."

"Mr. Jensen, huh?" he quips. "Are you always so formal, Ms. Monroe?"

Cooper Jensen has been calling me for nearly the last three months, using every technique under the sun to get me to agree to go out with him. I have to give him credit; he's almost worn me down. The reason I've been begging off is because I don't want to do the same thing to him that's been done to me. He's my second choice, which is foolish. He's an insanely handsome masculine specimen who should be every woman's first.

Cooper is a straitlaced, genuinely nice guy who drives a Camry and doesn't have a single spot of ink on his finely honed body. At least, that's what he tells me; I don't know that from my own personal inspection. And while Cooper makes the right girly parts tingle with his chiseled cheeks, sandy hair that curls around the bottom of his ears, and his piercing, soulful green eyes, he's not my typical type.

Which is exactly why you should say yes, Addy. You need atypical.

"Only when I don't know a person well enough," I answer.

"Oh, Addy," he grates, his voice low and smoky, making those certain parts that are tingling quiver in a bit of angst. "Your lips are very familiar to me."

I suck in a sharp breath at my vague drunken memory of being in Cooper's arms the night of Livia's bachelorette party. "Well they don't remember you," I reply saucily and a little more breathlessly than I want.

"They would if you said yes."

"I don't know..."

"Addy, just one date. We're attracted to each other."

"Speak for yourself."

"Tsk, tsk, tsk, you're a terrible liar, Ms. Monroe, even over the phone. Come on, you've got nothing to lose and I'll be a perfect gentleman. You have my solemn vow."

"What if I don't want a perfect gentleman," I tease, having no idea why the hell I just said that.

It takes him a few seconds to respond and when he does, his gravelly voice drops low. "I think that's exactly what you want, Addy Monroe. A gentleman who will worship you the way you deserve."

I let his words sink in, testing them out. While he's right, I want someone to worship me, I'm not at all sure I want it to be a gentleman. Perhaps it is time to branch out into unknown territory and date an *actual* gentleman, so I know for sure. I'm silent for such a long time as I contemplate his offer he calls my name, asking if I'm still on the line.

"Yes," I finally reply quietly.

"Yes, you'll go out with me?" he asks, his voice threaded with excitement.

"Yes, I'll go out with you."

"Does Saturday night work?" Wow, he's wasting no time.

"I already have plans this Saturday night." Kamryn and I have had a girl's night planned for weeks. I haven't seen her much and I miss her. I need time with my girl.

"Not another hot date, I hope?"

"What if I said yes?"

"Then I have to be honest, I'd be a little jealous."

I laugh. "No jealousy needed, Mr. Jensen."

"Good to know, Ms. Monroe. Then how about next Saturday?"

I mentally check my social calendar. Not that it's at full capacity lately. Sadly. "That works."

"Perfect. How about I pick you up at seven? Maybe we can have a predinner cocktail somewhere."

"That sounds great."

"Okay then. Text me your address and I'll see you next Saturday."

"I'll see you then. Bye, Mr. Jensen." I'm just about hang up when I hear my name. "Yeah?"

"I think it's only fair to tell you up front that I plan on making it impossible for you to say no to a second date."

I chuckle. "Game on, then."

"Oh, but this isn't a game to me, Addy," he responds in a deep, sultry voice. "Until Saturday."

"Bye," I say, completely breathless again.

I hang up and stare at my phone for long minutes, excited to spend an evening with an attractive man who obviously wants to spend it with me. Yet, a small part of me feels a twinge of guilt, as arresting green eyes laden with promises that no doubt can be fulfilled, morph into guileless hazel ones that swirl with heady desire but hold no promises at all.

Chapter 2

LUKE

"Thanks again, man," I tell Bigs, picking up an end of the king-sized mattress and walking backward out of the U-Haul in tandem with him. Moving is a bitch, and doing it by yourself just plain sucks ass. We stop and close up the vehicle, not wanting the rest of my shit stolen. It may not be much, but it's mine. I'd just as soon keep it that way.

"No problem. She know you're movin' in yet?"

I let a ghost of a smile turn my mouth. "What? And ruin the surprise? Not a chance in hell."

We walk right through the 'secured' outer apartment doors that any idiot could prop open, leaving all the occupants of this fine twenty-eight-unit building vulnerable the minute they step foot into what's theoretically to be their safe haven. The alarm that's supposed to be attached to the outer door appears not to be working. My first order of business is to call the supe and get the damn alarm fixed, along with securing our apartment with locks that would keep even the most sophisticated burglar out, instead of the current ones any amateur could pick.

I've never liked where Addy and Livia lived. It's not exactly in the nicest part of south Chicago, but when I moved Livia here, I wasn't about to let her live alone. I needed to get away from her so she could heal. I couldn't leave her completely alone either, so when I found out Eric's sister lived in Chicago and was in need of a roommate, it seemed like the fates were on our side for fucking once.

"Somehow, I don't think this is the type of surprise a woman likes."

Somehow, I don't think Addy Monroe would like *any* kind of surprise. She seems to have her little world in tip-top organized shape. Or so she wants everyone to believe. She needs it shaken up just a bit. And I'm a goddamned walking earthquake.

"She'll deal."

We navigate the flimsy piece up three flights of stairs, into my new digs and to the bedroom I'll now be occupying. Flopping it onto the springs that sit on the floor because the bed frame sits in pieces in the corner, I take a look around at my new "home." Unwelcome memories cause a little pang of hurt in the middle of my chest.

It's been almost six months now that I was in this very room, holding Livia in my arms when she was such a goddamn mess over my twin that she couldn't even function. I look toward the bathroom, where I can still envision her bubble-covered body. It was the first time I'd seen it without bruises or blood or broken bones. I remember the restraint it took to hold back from pulling her to my mouth, begging her to choose me instead.

I did the right thing, though. Livia clearly belongs with Gray, not with a man like me who has so many fucking ghosts in his closet, I'm surprised people can't hear them howling.

My selflessness with regard to Livia is one of the only things in my life I'm truly proud of. I care enough about her to walk away and that was a damn hard thing to do.

Maybe moving in here was a bad idea. The shit of it is, I've actually been making progress in getting over Livia, too. Gray and I have been spending more time together, especially since I moved my business to Chicago six weeks ago, and our relationship is slowly improving. With each new story he tells me about Livia and the babies, strangely, the easier it gets to accept it, *them*, and the further I can put Livia in my taillights. God knows I don't want her in my brights anymore.

Even though I've been quietly paying the rent on this place every month, I've struggled for the last few weeks with my decision. Is moving in here the right thing to do? Not only do I not need any reminders of Livia Kingsley/Colloway, I haven't been able to get the mahogany-haired, hazel-eyed knockout—who will be sleeping in the other bedroom just feet away from me—out of my fucking head. All I've thought about is how she rebuffed me the night of the Livia and Gray's wedding and how much I want to change her mind.

I want to tame the untamable.

And I shouldn't, because Addy Monroe is the type of woman you marry, not the type of woman you just fuck and chuck, and husband material, I am not. Regardless of that fact, am I backing off? No. I'm not. I *can't*. I can't explain what I don't even understand myself, but I'm irrationally drawn to her.

"How about a beer, then we'll get the rest of the stuff?" I ask Bigs, needing to get my mind off what a stupid decision I've just made. I should have just cut bait and found a place of my own that held neither memories nor the woman I want to throw up against the closest wall and fuck into submission. But what can I say? I'm a poster child for self-destruction. Always have been.

"Thought you'd never fucking ask," he replies, already headed toward the kitchen where I've stocked the fridge with a case of Heineken. Handing me one and taking one for himself, we pop the tops and clink before each taking a nice long gulp.

"You sure this is a good idea, boss?"

Ben "Bigs" Briggs is an old friend of mine and an employee I've had on the payroll of my private investigation company for two and a half years strong now. He's also the one I sent to Chicago to keep an eye on Livia for a month until I could figure out the shit with the video that was leaked. We've been through hell and back together and I'd trust the man with my life. He's my closest confidant and knows *almost* everything about my past with Livia, and in one drunken night a couple weeks ago, I guess I mentioned my unholy attraction to her best friend. My new roomie.

"I'm sure I'm tired of listening to you and Hattie's moaning every fucking night, so yeah."

His grin is wide and shameless. "Walls are thin, what can I say."

"Oh, I've heard plenty of what you've had to say. Even through the Kleenex I shoved in my ears. I now know things about you I would rather go to my grave not knowing."

That draws a loud laugh from Ben. "Probably taught your sorry ass a few new things."

"Yeah, a few new things *not* to say."

"Asshole. Say, I got a tip earlier on the bail jumper. I'm headed to Kankakee tomorrow to check out a lead."

"Take Stucky with you. This guy's bad news."

"Lucky for him I'm his worst fucking nightmare."

"Bigs, I mean it."

"Worried about lil' ol' me, are you?"

"No, I just want Stucky out of my hair." I laugh, taking a long pull of the bitter hops.

"I don't want to be stuck with that whiny bitch any more than you do, LC." Hence, why we call my newest employee, Jason Stark "Stucky." He's proven to be a brilliant investigator, but he's a bitch baby no one wants to be around for long.

"When you own your own business, then you get to make the assignments."

"Fucker." He slams the rest of his beer and sets down the empty bottle on the pristine counter before heading toward the front door. "I'm going to grab the last couple of boxes."

"Thanks, man."

I look at the clock to see it's after eight and I wonder when the hellcat will be home. I know she owns her own painting studio, although I have no idea what hours she keeps. I have to imagine owning her own business like I do, means she puts in a lot of time. I half expected her to be here when I pulled up in the truck but was kind of relieved when she wasn't. I didn't want to get into a pissing match in front of Bigs. He'd never let me live that shit down since he tried talking me out of moving in with Addy in the first place.

"Never shit where you eat, man."

But I already had one father, thank you very much, and God knows I've lived under the boot of too many people for too many fucking years, so I'm not about to let anyone hold me back from doing what I want to do when I want to do it.

And, right or wrong, over these last few months what I've decided I want to do is Addy Monroe. Repeatedly and wickedly until I've had my fill of her. Wooing a woman like that from afar will never work. She's going to need constant, daily convincing of the reasons she needs me to explore every inch of her sexy temple.

21

I inanely wonder if she's dating anyone. Guess maybe I should have thought about that before I moved in. Oh well, far as I know, she's got no ring on her finger and until she does she's fair game.

I'm just finishing my beer when I hear a commotion in the hallway. I step out of the kitchen into the living room to a shrill voice yelling, "What the hell?"

I don't see her because Bigs takes up the entire doorway with his bulk; I sure do *hear* her, though. Bigs catches my eye. With a shit-eating grin on his face, he shakes his head and steps to the side, heading down the hallway with two big boxes in hand.

Watching the space Bigs just vacated, I lock eyes with the woman I've ached to see for nearly three long months.

"Are you fucking kidding me right now?" she shrieks. "What in the hell do you think you're doing here, Luke?" I'm sure her arms would be flailing if they weren't filled with folders. I almost wish they weren't; I'd love to watch her indignant display.

She opens and closes her mouth several times, no more acidic words falling. The barely leashed fire shooting from her eyes would singe me if I actually gave a shit. As it is, I don't, so I lean against the counter and drink in my fill of the stunning spitfire I *cannot* stop thinking about. I let my gaze slowly roam down her tight body, which is sadly hidden underneath a light pink spring jacket.

Jesus, she is something else. No wonder she's

haunting me. Addy Monroe is the only woman I've met in the last five and a half years who has eclipsed all thoughts of Livia, so if I'm honest with myself, that's the main reason I need to be here with her. She does so many things to my body, to my emotions, but giving my heart and soul a little bit of peace is probably the single biggest one. And while I feel like a rat bastard taking something that she's not freely offering me, I fucking *need* that peace like I need air. If only for a little while.

When my eyes finally collide with hers again, I let a broad, cocky smile turn my lips, as fury further turns down hers. It's quite apropos, I think. For some reason, we seem to bring out the worst in each other. All that fire will make for one hell of a good fuck, though. She can say otherwise, but she wants me. Plain as day.

Bigs was probably right. Never shit where you eat. But hell if I care at this particular moment. All I'm doing is planning the hundred ways I'm going to make her moan, scream, and sob my name in pleasure...and maybe even a little in pain. I do keep my promises, after all.

"Hello, dear. How was your day?" I finally retort sweetly.

Her eyes light in fury.

Yeah.

This is gonna be fun.

Chapter 3

Addy

"Hello, dear. How was your day?" he says with so much false sweetness I swear I was just dipped in a vat of melted sugar.

"You'd better explain yourself," I grit. I have had one hell of a long day and all I've thought about for the last hour is sinking into a hot bath with a bottle of beer before falling into bed. Carla still has the flu, so that means I'll have to open the store at 10:30 instead of going in at 1:00 as I usually do on Fridays. The last thing I need is to come home to some pompous ass invading my personal space. Even if he is the best looking pompous ass I've ever laid eyes on.

When I struck up a conversation with the intimidating but good-looking big dude named Ben, who's now walking toward me from what used to be Livia's bedroom, and he told me he was helping a buddy move in, I have to confess I was excited at the prospect of a younger guy living in this building. It's mostly filled with low-income families and senior citizens on a fixed budget. I admit this isn't the greatest place to live, however, the price is right. Cheap. And, while I'm now finally making a decent profit, a good part of what I make is still going right back into my business.

So I was excited, until big and handsome walked right into *my* apartment, that is. He was all chatty on the three flights up, but once we walked through my open door, he completely clammed up. Could have been my screeching or it could have been the knowing look Luke Colloway was giving him.

"I'm waiting."

"Not really sure I owe you an explanation, sweetheart." Luke picks up the two empty beer bottles on the counter and opens the garbage, tossing them in. Ben is standing at the mouth of the hallway taking us in, trying hard to contain his smile. Unsuccessfully, I might add.

"What?" I breathe, unable to believe what I'm hearing. "You pick the lock and move your shit in here without my knowledge and you don't think you owe me an explanation?"

"Name's on the lease, doll, so just taking what I'm paying for."

I set down the tax files I need to sort through this weekend and walk into the kitchen until I'm toe to toe with the most gorgeous and infuriating man I have ever met. I have to try hard not to drag in a long breath, filling my lungs with his impossibly intoxicating scent. And I most definitely have to push all thoughts of how good it is to set my starved eyes on his sexiness again

25

after ten weeks (but who's counting?). Jesus, the things he does to my body without even a touch should be illegal.

"What do you mean *your* name is on the lease?"

"I don't think I stuttered, fireball."

"Fireball?" I spit incredulously. "You do realize that's a character on *Rudolph the Red-Nosed Reindeer*, don't you?"

His eyes darken like a sudden storm swept in. "God, Addy, you're so fucking sexy when you get all riled up," he rasps. His warm breath, which smells faintly of beer, showers over my face and drizzles slowly south. Then, oblivious to the fact his friend is standing twenty feet away, he grabs my hand and brashly brings it to his stiff erection just like he did at Livia's wedding. "This is what your smart mouth does to me, fireball."

My thighs clench against the flood that just left my va-jay-jay. Curse this denim. I want to pull my hand away as much as I want to unzip his faded jeans and slip inside to feel the silky hardness my fingers are currently wrapped around. I've daydreamed about his cock a hundred times in the last few months wondering what his velvety skin would feel like against me, *in* me. Hell, I've daydreamed about it *a lot* longer than just three months.

But I am not about to give Mr. I've-got-the-biggest-ego-of-the-century-going any more satisfaction of doing either. So, holding his eyes, I let a smirk tip my lips and let him hold fast to me, secretly relishing in the fact that I have remembered his impressive length accurately all this time.

"Sounds like more of a Luke problem than it does mine."

A mirrored smile lifts the corner of his mouth, his hand tightening on mine. I have to fight my lids not to close in ecstasy. *Oh God.*

"I think you'd like it to be an Addy *solution*, sweetheart."

I bristle. "Don't flatter yourself."

"Don't lie to yourself," he retorts smugly.

He holds us in this position for several long seconds, our eyes sparring. When he lets my hand go and it drops to my side, I almost whimper at the loss, the warmth of him still radiating in my palm. Neither of us moves a muscle, except for my heart, which is currently beating almost out of my chest in both rage and excitement. I can't remember the last time I was this turned on.

Uh...that would be never.

"How is your name on the lease, Luke?" I ask, lowering my voice.

"I signed it when I helped Livia move here."

"Why?"

"That's not your business, Addy."

"Show me."

He barks a laugh. "Show you? What...don't believe me, sweetheart?"

"I'm not sure you're trustworthy." His eyes flare with hurt so fast I almost miss it, but I don't. Then I immediately feel bad. Livia apparently trusted Luke, and I have no reason to think he would lie to me about something like this. "What if I don't want you here?"

"What if I don't want *you* here?" he retorts, his hazel depths dancing with mirth.

At five feet eight inches when I wear flats, I'm only about seven inches shorter than Luke. Today, I'm wearing three-inch heels, which brings my mouth in line with his scruffy jawline. The urge to lean in and take a long lick is almost overpowering. My hands curl into fists as I fight the itch to sink my fingers into his long dark locks and pull his mouth to mine.

I lean up so our lips are a hairsbreadth away. They brush slightly when I whisper, "Liar."

Then before I can do something stupid, like close the millimeter that separates us, taking everything I want, I take a giant step back along with a deep cleansing breath. Except with every inhale I catch a lungful of Luke.

Damn. Shit. Fuck.

This is bad. So very bad. I *cannot* live with Luke Colloway. If I thought I had a hard time resisting him before, that will be nothing compared to living with the sensual, irresistible, walking, talking sex-on-a-stick twenty-fours a day.

Gah!

"I want you gone by morning," I demand, turning to gather my stuff.

"Not gonna happen, sweetheart," he calls behind me.

I resist the overwhelming impulse to stomp out of the room like a five-year-old and quietly gather my files and purse before walking calmly toward my bedroom.

"Pleasure to meet you, Ben," I mumble when I skirt past his hulky frame.

"Pleasure's all mine, Addy." He smiles when our eyes catch. Big and intimidating is actually not so much when he smiles. He's quite attractive, really. I stop, giving him my full attention, an idea forming in my head.

"Say, what are you doing tonight?"

"Ah..." The smile drops from his face in a hot second and his eyes dart back and forth between Luke and me. I don't look at Luke, certain he's twenty kinds of pissed at my invitation. I can practically feel the waves of anger wafting across the small space, crashing into me. Well, tough shit. Two can play this little game, *fireball*. I smile but keep it inside.

"He's busy," Luke barks and now I do slide my gaze his way.

"Well, see...I didn't ask you and Ben here is a big boy, so he can answer for himself."

"Bigs, leave." Luke's volcanic eyes never leave mine and now I let my smile out, giving my attention back to the man in front of me. *Bigs*. The man I'm irresponsibly and selfishly using to get under Luke's skin. I turn up the flirt another notch...or ten.

What the hell is wrong with me?

Resting a hand on his forearm, I ask, "Ben, I've had a long day. How about a drink or two at the little bar down the street?"

"Like hell," Luke bellows.

Ben's eyes have been volleying between Luke and me in amusement. Gently, he places a hand over mine, removing it with the utmost care, like I might break if he moves too fast. "Sorry, doll. Love to, but I'm pretty attached to my balls. And my manhood." He strides for the door, long legs eating the short distance. "Later, man. I'll return the rental," he calls behind him before sealing Luke and me in this tiny space alone.

We have another silent face-off before I huff and spin on my heels. Heading down the hallway, I shut myself into the safety of my sanctuary and take a deep breath for the first time in minutes, pissed I didn't grab a beer, or twelve, on my way. I need one now more than ever, but there's no way I'm about to step foot outside my locked door for the rest of the night.

Great, I'm now a prisoner in my own home.

I close my eyes, wondering what in the hell I'm going to do no. No matter how much screaming, yelling, or protesting I do, I already know Luke Colloway is as stubborn as the day is long.

If he wants to live here, he will...and there's not a damn thing I can do about it.

Chapter 4

LUKE

I watch her tight ass disappear into her room, my mouth watering for a taste.

Well, that went better than I thought, I think, pulling another beer from the fridge.

Far better, actually.

Balls are aching, but I'm not choking on them.

Not a mark on me, although under the right circumstances, they'd be most welcome.

And I still have two functioning eyes, which I thought for a few seconds she was gonna scratch out.

She does a number on me, that's for sure. I could pound nails I'm so fucking hard. I'll definitely be jerkin' the gherkin tonight, but I don't plan on doing that for any extended period of time.

Now that I've seen my fireball again, I am more determined than ever to get everything I want.

Which, in case you haven't figured it out yet...is her underneath me, hot and needy, while I kiss her slow and bring her up fast, her throaty pants spurning me on as I lavish unparalleled pleasure all over her body.

In other words: I want to fuck her raw and fuck her hard. And I don't plan on waiting long to do just that.

Chapter 5

Addy

Leaning against the door, I tell myself...*think, think, think*. There has to be some way out of this. Dumping my stuff on my dresser, I sift through my purse until I find my cell, calling the one person I know will have answers. Quickly, punching a series of buttons, the phone rings.

Once.

Twice.

Three times.

"Hello," a tired voice answers. I look at the clock and note that it's not quite nine yet.

"I'm sorry, were you sleeping?"

She chuckles. "Not quite, but close. I know, I know, I'm a loser."

"You're not a loser. You're six months pregnant with twins. I'm sorry. I can talk to you tomorrow."

"No, no, it's fine, Addy. What's wrong?"

"Why do you think something's wrong? Can't I just call and talk to my best friend because I miss her?" Oh, something's wrong, all right. Very, very, *very* fucking wrong.

"Because you sound…off."

"Is your portion of the lease in Luke's name?" I blurt. *Way to ease into it, Addy.*

"Uh…why do you ask?"

"When I got home from the studio tonight, he was moving all his shit into *your* unoccupied bedroom, that's why."

"Oh." She sighs.

"Oh? That's all you have to say?"

"Yes?" she answers sheepishly.

"Yes? Is that a yes that's all you have to say or a yes to my original question?" Crickets answer me. "What the fuck, Livia?"

"Addy…it's a long story."

"Livia," I whine. "How could you do this to me?"

I knew it was too good to be true that I would actually have this whole twelve-hundred-square-foot apartment to myself when Livia moved out. All she told me was her portion of the lease was taken care of through October and I didn't need to worry about it until then, to which I was grateful. I loved having Livia as a roommate and I don't want a new one, especially a sinfully sexy one with a sharp bite and a wicked mouth. One who will likely worm his way into my pants before the month is out.

Oh my God. This is a complete disaster.

"I…I was trying to escape some things when I moved to Chicago and Luke helped me. He thought it would be best if I flew under the radar for a while and if the lease was in his name."

This is the most Livia has told me about her past in all the time we've been friends. I think back to all the secrets I know she's been carrying since I met her and for the thousandth time, I wonder what she was running from. There was no doubt she was running from something. Or someone. Yet I've never pried and I'm never going to. If she wants to tell me her secrets, she will. If she doesn't, well, then that's fine too. Not many of us are open books. I know I'm not.

"I'm sorry," I breathe. "I just...he's...unnerving. He pushes all of my goddamned buttons."

Sheer frustration.

Outright anger.

And the scariest of all? My blood burns with a raw sexual desire I haven't felt before with *anyone*, and I don't like it. What I like even less is I don't want to deny it.

"Addy, Luke's a great guy once you get to know him. He's...well, he's just a little rough around the edges."

Ya think? Somehow I think she knows a very different Luke than the one he's shown me. And I wonder why that makes the seeds of envy blossom deep within my belly. "Did you know about this?"

"No. I didn't know."

"Did Gray?"

"I don't know. If he did, he hasn't said anything. I would have at least given you a heads up."

"Ugh. I know. I'm sorry. What am I going to do?" I ask, flopping unceremoniously onto my bed.

"I don't know that there's much you can do," she replies quietly.

"Hmm," I mumble. I could move out but not until October, and that's seven months away. Christ on a crutch.

"I thought you...liked him?"

I do. Too much. That's the damn problem! "Whatever gave you that idea?"

"Come on, Addy. This is me you're talking to. Have you forgotten what happened at my bachelorette party a few months ago? I thought Luke was going to go all homicidal on Cooper for laying a finger on you."

Crap. No. No, I have not forgotten. I distinctly remember sighing in contentment when he held me tightly to him before I let the effects of the alcohol take me to oblivion. The memory is hazy, but I'm not sure I could ever forget the feel of Luke's strong, muscular arms wrapped around me or the feel of his hard chest beneath my hands or how I felt safe and, strangely, cared for. It was the first time in a very long time I'd felt that way. I swore I could feel his phantom arms around me for most of the night, although when I woke late in the morning he wasn't there, so I know I was dreaming it.

That night, I was trying hard to numb the pain and may have gone a little overboard. Earlier in the week, I'd found out that Aiden had gone and got himself engaged. Three months after our breakup. It was like a swift punch to the solar plexus. Not for the first time, I wondered why I had to fall for guys who couldn't commit themselves to *me*. Since we share many of the same friends, their happiness was like a cold glass of water thrown in my face daily through social media. *Yeah, Facebook. Yeah, Instagram. Yeah, fucking Snapchat.*

"And even I didn't miss the way he stalked you with his eyes around my wedding reception. I've seen the way you've looked at him, too, Addy."

And does that bother you? I want to ask but don't. I know Livia's madly in love with and married to Luke's twin. I also know they share a special bond, so I don't know how she would feel about her best friend hooking up with him. Happy or jealous? I don't even know why I'm thinking of hooking up with Luke in the first place because that just *cannot* happen. He is the quintessential bad boy and I just don't need that in my life for a whole host of reasons. First, being my heart is finally starting to mend from the last one. I don't wish it broken again.

Luke will absolutely break it. He might as well carry a warning sign around his neck that says, "Caution: I'll fuck you in more ways than one."

"I don't know what you're talking about, Livia. I was drunk."

She laughs. "Right. Okay, play it your way, Addy, but you and I both know the truth."

The truth?

The truth is I've wanted Luke Colloway for over ten long years, ever since I saw my brother's friend when visiting my father in Detroit. The truth is that Luke Colloway is the man who turned my tastes onto bad boys to begin with. The truth is, Luke Colloway is the man I've compared all others in my life to.

The truth? I'm screwed ten ways to tomorrow.

"I have to go." I'm tired of talking, thinking, and torturing myself with Luke.

"Say, come over for dinner tomorrow night. I miss my friend."

"I don't want to be a third wheel."

"You're not a third wheel. Asher and Alyse will be here too. Besides, I finished the nursery and I want to show you."

So I'll be a fifth wheel, instead. *Sigh.* "Okay. What time?" I could use a little time with my best friend. It's not been the same since she moved out.

"Seven-thirty?"

"All right. What can I bring?"

"Nothing. I have everything planned out." She pauses. "I'm sure everything will work out the way it's supposed to, Addy."

"Right. Sure."

"See you tomorrow?"

"Yep," I agree, hitting the disconnect button before throwing my phone down beside me. I stare at the stark white drywall ceiling that could use a fresh coat of paint and think back to the first time I laid eyes on Luke.

My parents had divorced when I was nine and Eric was eleven. My father moved to Detroit while we remained in Joliet with our mother. The day Eric turned fourteen was like the day I got a new brother. One day he was a great kid with a fun-loving, laid-back personality who got straight A's in school and had grand plans to become a vet. The next, he was hanging out with the bad crowd and started skipping school, smoking weed, and stealing. Lying became like second nature to him. By fifteen, my mom couldn't take it anymore and shipped him off to live with our dad.

Unfortunately, he didn't fare much better in Detroit, which in hindsight probably wasn't exactly the best city to send a troubled teen to.

Despite Eric's issues, we were always very close. I missed him terribly when he left me, so I visited my dad and brother as much as I could, hoping that I'd be able to be a good influence and bring him back to us. Besides, visiting my dad was a great escape from my mother and whomever she chose to warm her bed with that month.

But as much as I tried to be there for Eric, it didn't help, and the older he got, the more often he wasn't home when I visited. He tried desperately to shield me from his friends and his lifestyle, always telling me, *"You have potential, kid. Don't make the same mistakes I did."* Whenever we talked about him getting out of whatever illegal activities he'd gotten himself into, he'd tell me it wasn't that easy. I thought that was a cop-out, although it didn't make me love him any less.

The summer after I graduated high school, I

spent a month with my father and Eric. As usual, Eric wasn't around much. My dad and I had a great time anyway—he's a great man, and my mom could learn a few things from him. Sadly, she won't. Her life revolves solely around her.

One evening, Dad and I went to a free blues concert at Memorial Park on the shores of Lake St. Clair, which was one of my favorite things to do in the summer there. It was after eleven when we arrived home and I went straight to bed, but I woke up in the middle of the night with insomnia—a pretty common occurrence for me. I've always had a hard time sleeping, even when I was a baby, according to my mother.

I was almost three-quarters of the way down the stairs, headed to the kitchen to get a glass of water when I heard his deep timbre for the first time. Even before I saw him, there was something about his voice that drew me in. The quiet rumble sent phantom fingers of pleasure feathering all over my body, settling heavily between the dark junction of my thighs.

I backed up two steps so I was hidden by the wall and quietly sank down, certain that if I set a foot into the kitchen, my brother would freak out. I absolutely *had* to see the face attached to that sinful voice, because in my mind I already knew the visual would be far, far better.

I leaned forward and from my vantage point through the banisters, caught my first glimpse of Luke Colloway. I held my breath for fear of making a noise, ruining the ruse. I was sure they'd be able to hear the quick cadence of my heart, which was beating double time as I drank in the Adonis sitting in my father's house.

Holy mother of perfection, he was stunningly beautiful. Unlike any man I had ever laid eyes on, not that there were a lot of them in Joliet, Illinois. You could immediately tell he was rough, brooding, and intimidating. A predator of sorts. Not someone you'd want to meet in a dark alleyway, but definitely, someone you'd want to show you his dark side in the bedroom.

He was lounging at the kitchen table, his right arm slung casually over the empty chair beside him and one ankle thrown on the opposite leg. His light grey T-shirt wasn't too tight, but taut enough so I could see the honed muscles underneath, rippling with every slight movement he made. Tats decorated the arm he rested on his thigh and more peeked out the top of his shirt. Faded, ripped jeans molded to his powerful thighs and even from that distance, I could see he had been gifted in all the right places. The outline of his impressive package was visibly evident, and I still distinctly remember how it made my girly parts throb.

Long, enviable lashes, a wicked eyebrow ring and shiny chestnut hair tied at the nape of his neck rounded out the sexy as sin package. He was the very definition of bad boy and had me breathlessly enthralled.

I sat there for over an hour while he talked to my brother and another man, neither of whom I could see from my angle. I don't remember a single word that was said, my entire focus solely on him. A million questions ran through my head, both then and now. I wanted to know anything and everything about Luke Colloway.

I quietly made my way back up the stairs only when he headed for the front door, slipping back into bed and falling into dreams of a man who'd made my blood sing and my body a live wire of desire without a single look or touch. I saw Luke three more times before I went back to Joliet, each time as I hid in the shadows like a love-struck stalker.

A few days before I left, I got up the courage to ask Eric about his "friends" in a general way, not letting on I knew anything about Luke in particular. He was short and terse and told me to mind my own business, which only fueled my intense interest in the man even further.

I've often thought about Luke over the years, wondering if he ended up in jail, like Eric. And wondering if he straightened his life out, like Eric. I still don't know about the first part, but it seems like the latter is true. At least I hope it is—I don't need to invite trouble to my doorstep.

As I watched Luke interact with his friends back then, I could tell he was an enigma and in my few interactions with him over these past few months, I see he hasn't changed a bit. In fact, he's even more so.

When he showed up at Firefly last September, I recognized him immediately. When Livia called him Grant, however, I was utterly confused. Once you see a perfect male specimen like Luke Colloway, you never forget him. He'd aged, of course, and time only made him sexier and darker, but I would recognize him anywhere.

After a few stolen moments alone with Luke, I asked him why Livia called him Grant. All he would offer was "it's a nickname." But after the blowup in the hospital when Livia was admitted, it was very evident something underlying was going on that I'd likely never be privy to. When I pressed Livia once, she would only say they had a complicated history. I even tried asking Eric; he swore he didn't know anything either. I'm not sure I believe him.

Luke Colloway is a mystery, a conundrum. And I hate puzzles or riddles of any kind. I'm a logical, straightforward thinker. I have no patience for the mysterious. Typically, there's a very good reason people try to hide behind their shrouds and if you go prying, you'll regret it. So I don't. But in Luke's case, I find myself wanting to decipher him for some stupid, unknown reason.

Only, if I crack his code, I have no doubt regret won't be the emotion taking up residence in my heart. He will consume me, use me, then ruin me. I'm not naïve enough to understand the only way Luke and I could ever end is in heartbreak.

Which is exactly why I have to find a way to squelch this burning inside me and avoid Luke Colloway as much as possible until I can find a way out of this fucking mess.

Chapter 6

LUKE

"Run into something?" I ask taking in the shiner Bigs is now sportin'.

He shrugs, sliding into the seat across from me. I'm always in awe of how graceful he is for a six-foot-five, two hundred-and-forty-pound beast. "Trust me, he looks far worse."

"He in custody then I take it?"

"Yep." And that's all I'll get from Bigs. He does his job, he does it well, and he's tight-lipped about giving details. Not that I generally care. I'm not that big of a talker anyway. "So, how'd it go with your new roomie after I left?" Bigs cajoles, a full-on grin eating his face. Fucker. He knows exactly how it went. He could see the steam pouring out of Addy's ears as well as I could.

"We're besties now."

"Umm hmm."

I have to admit I waited two hours for Addy to come back out of her room, my cock throbbing the entire time, before finally giving up. I heard her talking on the phone shortly after she shut me out and have to imagine she called Livia to confirm my story. I never took her for one to avoid conflict, but in all fairness, it was a shitty move on my part to just blindside her like that. I also know that asking permission from the woman who damn near matches me in the stubbornness department would get me nowhere, so I don't regret the choice I made.

I need a place to live, a place I'm already paying for, even though I could easily afford to move somewhere else. Somewhere nicer. But I don't want anyplace else. I want her and I can already tell she's going to fight me, fight this magnetic pull between us every step of the way.

I didn't miss the way her eyes dilated in sweet desire the second they landed on me. She was pissed, yes. She also wants me and won't let herself have me. I plan on making it very fucking hard for her to resist me for long, even though I know I can't give her everything she needs.

Addy's an incredible woman and she deserves better than the likes of me, but fuck if I can resist anymore what I've been trying to fight for months. Her draw is too powerful. It's selfish and an asshole thing to do, yet I want her so damn much, I can't make myself do the right thing and just walk away.

"Couch is still open if you need help moving out," he smirks.

"I'd rather slit my wrists."

"Jesus man, that's a little melodramatic."

"Just being honest." Besides, there's not a damn thing in the world that would keep me away from Addy now that I've laid eyes on her again. I'd be lying if I said I could concentrate on a damn thing all day today, not being able to see her face this morning before I left. I may have even tested her door on my way by so I could take a peek. Locked, of course. Smart woman, that.

Bigs shakes his head, chuckling. "So, do you have anything else for me over the weekend or are you good 'til Monday?"

"Nah. I have two asset search requests that came in earlier and a few tracing requests. Those can wait until next week."

"You get that contract signed with Warnf and Hardy?"

Warnf and Hardy is a local law firm and I recently negotiated an exclusive contract with them. My firm will handle anything and everything from insurance investigation to anything divorce related, like adultery and child custody, locating assets, marital property disputes, and everything else they want to throw at me. I've been working on that deal for months now. It's a gig that helped me secure my move to Chicago, so it's a big coup. It also means I need to add another body or two to keep up with the expanding workload.

"Had Melinda courier it over this morning. I have two interviews set up for next week. I want you to sit in."

"You got it. So, are we hitting the bar tonight or what?"

"What? Your ball and chain going to cut the

rope she's tightly wrapped around your dick for the night?"

"Hey, fuck off. That's not true."

It so is. In all the years I've known Bigs, I've never seen him act like this with a single woman. He met Haddie just a few short weeks ago and he's been dating her since. Although she still has her own place, I'm not sure why. They practically live together at his. He's whipped and I may give him shit 'til the cows come home, but I'm happy for him. He deserves happiness. "Can't. Family thing."

Bigs studies me for a few seconds.

"Christ, spit it out," I bark.

"Just wondering how things are going with your family, now that you're reunited and shit."

I sit a little dumbfounded at Bigs' question. I've been friends with him since I was sixteen. He knows the rocky history between my family and me and he's one of two people who knows what caused me to spiral out of control. If not for him and Eric Monroe, I'd probably be six feet under. Hell, I'm not sure I would have made it to my twentieth birthday. Bigs single-handedly saved me from myself and the drugs that took over my life at that confusing time. Too bad he couldn't save me from so many other things, Peter Wilder included. But as I look back, I was where I was meant to be: saving my brother's wife, even if it cost me a huge part of my own soul in the process. I would do it over and over again. For Livia. And for Gray.

I look at my watch before answering. "Confession was last week, Bigs."

"I think you missed church last week." He grins, settling back in his chair for a nice long chit-fucking-chat.

I smirk. I don't miss church. Not anymore. I need all the absolution I can get and on a very regular basis. I have so many sins to atone for, I could go to church daily and it still wouldn't be enough. It will never be enough.

Once again, my conscience whispers at me to leave Addy Monroe alone. *She's too pure for you. Too good for you.* And he's right. Once again, I tell him to fuck off and take a flying leap off a short bridge. I *need* her. For some absurd reason, she quiets my demons and I'm so tired of them clamoring all the fucking time. I need a respite.

"You're not gonna leave until I give you something, are you?"

"Ah, you know me so well."

I glare at my friend, knowing he won't back down. "It's getting better," I confess, giving him as little as possible but hopefully enough that he'll leave it alone.

"Have you told your brothers or your mom about your dad?"

Guess not.

My sigh is deep and long. "No."

"Will you ever?"

"No. It's water under the bridge, man. All it would do is churn shit up that's better buried with him. Why would I intentionally hurt them?"

"So they understand what the fuck happened, Luke. Your dad's gone and you're here. They

48

deserve to know. I don't know why you've shouldered a burden by yourself that's not even yours to fucking carry, man."

Bigs' passionate plea hits me someplace deep. He's a good friend, a good man, and it's not very often he expresses his brotherly affection for me. He's been telling me for years to come clean to my family about what I know. I just can't do that to them.

They all think my dad was some kind of fucking saint, a hero, father of the year, but he was far from it. He fell off that white horse when I was sixteen. Who am I to tarnish their view of a man they're all trying to emulate? Who am I to destroy the woman who loved him more than she did herself?

I can't. I won't. Like I said, I do have some honor I'm trying to hold onto, so by all that's holy, I will take this secret to my grave.

My dad's actions may have been the catalyst to my own martyrdom, but I've long accepted the bad choices I made were all mine. I own every single one of them. I was young and stupid and handled things badly, heading a hundred miles an hour blindly down the path of self-destruction.

By the time I did my penance, in walked Livia Kingsley. And so started three years of hell the likes of which I still can't comprehend some days. Peter Wilder was a thug, an evil malevolent human being who deserves a special place in hell. He did a lot of vile and unforgivable things for the five years I was with him, but his indiscriminate and inhumane torture of an innocent could not go unpunished.

"I made my own decisions, Bigs."

"Fourteen years is long enough. You deserve to put your demons behind you, Luke." Bigs only calls me Luke when he means business. He's serious as fuck right now.

He holds my eyes, silently challenging me to disagree. I do, but I don't voice it. I'm done talking about shit that can't be changed. Instead, I nod once, sharply.

"Right," he replies, pushing himself to stand. He knows I'm done talking and he knows how this story ends. "See you Monday."

A glance at the wall clock shows it's after six. My office is about twenty minutes away from my new apartment. I have a family dinner I need to attend in little more than an hour so that gives me about fifteen minutes to shower and change before I need to head to Gray's.

It takes me just a few minutes to straighten my desk and secure my files before I head out, locking the front door. As my bike roars to life, I find myself wondering what plans Addy has for tonight, wishing like hell I'd said I was busy when Gray called yesterday morning, so I could spend a night sparring with her. As it is, I already agreed. There's no backing out now.

Oh well...there's always tomorrow. And the day after that, and the day after that, and the day after that. I let a big smile curl my lips just thinking of the many ways I plan to break down Addy's steely resolve to keep me from her bed.

LUKE'S ABSOLUTION

She may be hardheaded and tenacious, but my picture is in good ol' *Webster's* next to those two definitions, so even her "A" game won't be good enough to best me.

I always get what I want. Eventually. And I definitely don't play fair.

Chapter 7

Addy

"Shit, shit, shit," I mutter under my breath. It's already almost a quarter to seven. I want to shower before I have to head to Livia's for dinner, but there'll barely be time to change and freshen up before I have to leave. With Friday night traffic, it will likely be a forty-five minute drive into the city, so as it is, I'm already late.

I barrel through the front door, slamming it shut in my haste, and practically run to my bedroom. A quick scan of the living room shows no sign of Luke. Good. The last thing I'm in the mood for is a run-in with the man who's vying for "asshole of the year" award. At least, Livia didn't say Luke was attending dinner tonight. For that I'm thankful. It would have been a big fat no-go otherwise.

Today, I decided since I'll never be able to bully Luke into moving out, I'm just going to make the best of it until October and find another place. In the meantime, I'm going to keep myself busy, so I have to spend as little time here as possible. It sounds good, in theory, yet in reality, I'm kind of a homebody and the thought of having to work late every night or find some other fake reason not to be in my own home makes me angry.

My sanctuary has been poisoned by a living, breathing, erotic walking piece of art. While most women would die to have Luke Colloway as a roommate, I am not most women. But I am most definitely *female*, and even I know I'm in trouble when it comes to resisting his somewhat unconventional charms. Avoidance is my only option, though, if I'm going to make it out emotionally unscathed.

I drop my purse on my bed and start stripping out of my paint-splattered shirt and jeans. Today I helped a customer on the wheel and let's just say I spent the next hour cleaning up paint that had sprayed twenty feet across the studio. I got most of it off of my skin, I think, and if I didn't, oh well. Livia will have to deal. It's not like I'm out to impress anyone tonight, anyway.

Deciding I should let Livia know I'll be late, I whip out my phone to text her when my skin begins to prickle. My eyes lift from my fingered frenzy only to land on the man who's irritatingly preoccupied my every thought all goddamn day.

Standing proudly in my open doorway, Luke looks good enough to eat (literally), in his black molded jeans, scuffed black boots, and tight V-neck charcoal T-shirt. His face is scruffy and his unruly dark locks look freshly showered, combed with only his fingers.

Jesus, every time I look at him, I'm stunned breathless anew. His face looks like that of an avenging angel, but you know underneath he's the devil incarnate. And I yearn for him to lavish his wickedness over every part of my body, even though I know he will taint me for all others.

Too late, I realize two things.

One: I didn't think Luke was home, so I didn't bother closing my bedroom door. I've lived alone now for months, and neither Livia nor I needed a lot of privacy before, so that's a bad habit I'll have to break immediately.

Two: I never got any further than *removing* my clothes, which now lie in a heap at my feet, so I'm facing my nemesis in my bright pink, practically see-through lacy bra and matching thong.

The look of blatant hunger on his face as his heated eyes rake slowly over my body weakens my knees...and my resolve. Damn him and the unnatural effect he has on me.

"Fuuuuck." His impassioned drawl reaches my ears and holds a tone of awe I don't think I've ever heard from a man before. Involuntary chills break out. I try to suppress the shiver they create but fail.

Damn. Damn. Damn.

When his lustful gaze finally reaches mine, my traitorous sex readies herself for him to fulfill the silently declared promises I see swirling like thunderclouds in his hooded eyes.

Untold pleasures.

Blissful pain.

Yes. I remember word for word what he said months ago.

Word. For. Word.

We stand there lost in each other for I don't know how long until logic finally trumps lust.

Wow. That took a long time.

"What the fuck, Luke?" I yell, stomping to slam my door in his face. Of course, he anticipates my move, stepping inside before I have the pleasure of trying to break his damn nose with the heavy wood.

"Big plans tonight, fireball?"

I stop, unwilling to move any closer, even though my body is being drawn to his like an invisible magnet. He's struggling to keep his eyes on my face and I inwardly smile. "Yes," I retort smartly. "Very big."

"With who?" he demands. As if in slow motion, I watch the lust evaporate in an instant, replaced immediately with anger. *How dare he?*

I raise my chin a little. "Not your business, big guy," I snip, throwing his words from yesterday back in his face.

We both stand our ground, once again locked in an age-old battle of wills until Luke's phone dings. He takes it out of his jeans, not breaking eye contact. When he finally looks away to read his message, I breathe a sigh of relief, wondering why the hell I'm still standing here in my underwear, giving the man a free show.

I see a sly smile curve his mouth before he pockets his phone again. Before he turns to exit, his eyes deliberately drop one last time to my chest, which I've so readily put on display. They linger so long, I know he's zeroed in on my beaded nipples poking through. "You have a good night, fireball."

"Stop calling me that!" I yell childishly, pissed at myself for admiring the flex of his ass as he leaves. As soon as he clears the door, I shut and lock it for good measure. Although, I'm sure if Luke wants into my bedroom, he'll just help himself, lock or not. Just like he helped himself to my apartment.

Egotistical asshole.

For a full minute, I let my inner child out, stomping around my room and muttering wildly under my breath as I pull a fresh pair of jeans from my drawer and throw on a light, three-quarter-sleeve lavender sweater. I pull on a pair of cognac-colored Frye riding boots that I splurged on over the winter and take in my appearance in the full-length floor mirror. Satisfied, I spend the next ten minutes in the bathroom brushing up my makeup and throwing a few curls in my long hair.

When I emerge, I assume Luke has also left. All the lights are off except for a lamp throwing a soft glow in the living room. Even though it's a warm spring day, I grab a heavy brown leather jacket from the coat closet and, pulling my keys from my purse, head out the front door and down the three flights of stairs.

Our apartment doesn't have garages; there's a small parking lot in the back that holds enough spaces for about half the tenants. The good news is I can generally get a spot relatively easily because the average age of our building is about seventy and a lot of the elderly don't have cars. Sometimes, on Sundays, I will help a couple of them run errands, to the grocery store or the pharmacy to pick up their meds. They have no one else and I'm a sucker for old people.

Just like bad boys.

Absently pushing the back door open, I'm preoccupied with finishing my forgotten text to Livia when I hear the distinct rumble of a motorcycle coming to life. I freeze and slowly raise my head, knowing exactly who that roll belongs to. Not many seventy-year-olds or single mothers driving a bike where I live.

There in all his glory, watching me like I'm his next meal, sits Luke on his Ducati Diavel. The titanium beauty is absolutely stunning, but by all that is holy, if I thought Luke was like a sex god before, he is unequivocally the King of Kings with a 500-pound, 160-horsepower machine sitting between his long legs. I want nothing more than to lie down on that magnificent contraption and selflessly offer myself up for his pleasure. It would be a hardship. It's a sacrifice I'm willing to make for all of womankind, though. I'm noble like that.

Trying not to let him know he's getting to me, and pushing down my disappointment that his black leather jacket now covers up his sexy tats, I look away and head to my car. But that vindictive bitch called Murphy's Law apparently has it out for me, because as luck would have it, it's parked right beside his bike.

"Hop on," he demands as soon as I'm beside him. *Oh, I'd like to hop on, all right, but I'll be hopping on pop, not your bike.*

With a slight shake of my head and a deep breath, I gather my wits and move to fully face him. "Did you fall and hit your head as a child? In what instance do you think I'm going to follow your every command?"

"Oh, fireball," he drawls seductively, "trust me, there's a time I *know* you'll follow my every command. Each roughly whispered wicked one of them."

I suck in a sharp breath at his insinuation, the one that just landed with a loud thud straight between my legs. His deep licentious voice drips thickly with sex and promise. But not the type of promises I'm looking for.

Okay, okay I lie. I *want* those promises. Badly. I just want more than that, too.

"You walked right into that one, sweetheart." He laughs darkly. He's right. I did, however, I still want to wipe the sexy smirk off his face. With my mouth...and maybe a certain other body part. Let's just say Luke Colloway isn't the only one who knows how to ride. I'm so lost in my lascivious thoughts and trying to come up with my next snarky comeback that I almost miss his next comment.

"I'm not going to argue with you, fireball. We're already late."

"What do you mean *we're* already late?" I ask slowly. Goddamn Livia Colloway to hell. She knew exactly what she was doing. At least, I know Luke wasn't in on the ruse either until just a few minutes ago when he got a text, probably from Gray, because there was no doubt he thought I was getting ready for a date. For some reason, it makes me feel marginally better that I wasn't duped by him.

"We've been summoned to dinner, doll. Now get on."

"I can drive myself, thanks," I mutter, getting more livid by the second. There is no way I can sit with my crotch flush against Luke's ass and my palms tightly pressed against those corded chest muscles for thirty minutes. That, combined with the reverberation of the bike between my thighs, will have me coming in record time. I've been on edge for months, my own fingers not cutting it anymore.

I'm already thinking of excuses I can use to get out of this...

Flat tire.

Attempted mugging.

Bad case of mouth herpes.

...when suddenly I'm lifted off the ground and plopped unceremoniously onto the back of Luke's Ducati.

"What the hell?" I try struggling; Luke's hands hold me tight.

"I was told to bring you. That's what I'm doing."

"I am perfectly capable of taking care of myself. You'd even be surprised to know I've been doing it since I was about ten."

"Addy, we're going to the same damn place.

Why would we drive separately?" he asks with utter exasperation.

You're exasperated? Well, get in line, buddy.

"Because I want to leave when I'm ready, not when you are."

"Jesus, woman. Must you always be so goddamned stubborn about everything?"

"Me?" I screech, my blood pressure ratcheting up with each second that passes.

"Yes. You," he pipes back loudly.

"Let me tell you something, you pompous—" Before I can get another word out, his hands wind through my hair and he pulls me to his hard, unyielding mouth, effectively silencing me.

His kiss is controlling. Demanding. *God.* It's divine. It's like nothing I could have possibly imagined in my wildest, most erotic dreams. His lips are full and soft and fit perfectly to mine. I fight him for all of one and a half seconds before I melt into his dominance.

When his tongue touches mine for the first time, electricity fires like a headwind through my veins, making me hot and dizzy with longing. He swallows my unwanted moan, making a low growl of his own. At twenty-eight, I've been kissed by plenty of men before, but never like this. This is pure, animal male branding. And just like that...I am his.

Almost as fast as he descended he's pulling away. Leaning his forehead against mine, his breaths come in short harsh gasps. Mine doesn't. I'm not breathing at all. When his molten, hooded eyes meet mine, I swallow a whimper and begin thinking of a whole new litany of excuses to get out of dinner. There is no way on God's green earth I can spend an evening with Luke after being kissed like he owns me.

Or else he will. Own me. My lips already singe with his branding.

I don't want to be his. I *can't* be his.

He will break my heart.

He will destroy me.

He's right. I *would* follow every roughly whispered wicked command. God, I'm weak. So pathetically, horribly weak.

I am in so much trouble.

With a slight shake of his head, like he's as confused as I am, he silently reaches in his sidesaddle and grabs a helmet, gently putting it on me. He adjusts the strap until it's snug, but not too tight. He takes the keys and phone from my hands and throws them into my purse before sliding the strap over my head and under one arm, so it's taut against my body.

I let him handle me like a rag doll; each movement is slow and tender as if he's afraid he'll scare me away. Little does he know that each soft touch draws me in further. Putting on his own helmet, his movements are quicker and rougher now.

My eyes never leave his face, and his refuse to meet mine again. I pull my bottom lip between my teeth, chewing nervously.

I tell my legs to move, hefting me off of this bike and back to my car. They won't.

I tell my mind to stop replaying that kiss over

and over and over again. God help me, it can't. My lips still tingle, reminding me that kiss really just happened.

Luke scootches me back slightly, so he can throw a long leg over the seat. Once settled, he reaches back, pulling me snug to him. Taking my arms and placing them around his waist, he says huskily, "Hang on tight, fireball."

Then, before I reattach the pathways between my brain and mouth—which were burned away with his kiss—he revs the engine, backs us up, and winds our way carefully out of the lot. Once we hit the pavement, he takes a right and opens her up, forcing me to meld my front to his back or become road kill. Against my will, he hurtles us toward the city where I'll have to suffer a long, interminable night in the presence of Sin Incarnate himself.

Fuck me. Could my life possibly get any worse?

Chapter 8

LUKE

I'm royally fucked. Never, in a million years, did I think that a woman could taste so good. Her unique flavor still lingers in my mouth, making it water. Sugary honey mixed with a healthy dose of stubborn. Over these last several months, I've imagined a thousand times how Addy's lips would taste and what her tongue would feel like dueling with mine for the upper hand. I thought I'd have to wrestle it away from her like a goddamned alligator fight. She vehemently holds on to her reins of control, just like I do.

But feeling her sweetly melt into me after only a second was just about my undoing. My dick will be wearing the metal bite of my zipper for a week. I shit you not; I just about picked her up and carried her back into the apartment, fucking her until we both passed out in sated exhaustion. Then I'd re-nourish us and start all over again until her pussy was so swollen my cock wouldn't fit anymore. Hell, I almost didn't make it out of the apartment in the first place after seeing her barely there lingerie. That sight is still smoking in my memory banks, clouding my vision.

I'm no manwhore, although I've also never, *ever* had a serious relationship, choosing to move from bed to bed instead. It's true my door has revolved with too many women whose faces I don't even remember or care to remember. Not one of them was noteworthy. Not one of them has crossed my mind past the one or two times I fucked them. Hell, if you showed me a police lineup of women I've fucked and those I haven't, I honestly couldn't tell you which ones I wet my whistle in. That may make me sound like a rat bastard, but trust me, I was doing them a favor. It was wrong to draw a woman into my lifestyle, so I never even tried. Truth is...I've never met one I *wanted* to drag into my debauchery.

Until *her*. Christ, I want to debauch Addy in so many ways I need a goddamned journal to note them all, like a bucket list, so I can tick them off one by one after I enact each wicked fantasy currently racing through my mind. Otherwise, I'll never remember them all.

The minute I laid eyes on Eric's little sister, the chemistry between us has been arching hot under the surface, like a sleeping volcano. And with one kiss, I just woke that fucker up. The moment my lips touched hers I felt the heat rain down around us and I swear I heard a big cosmic boom. It reverberated so loudly in my chest, I felt its echo throughout my entire body. Twenty minutes later I'm still reeling as I feel its incessant pings.

LUKE'S ABSOLUTION

As we fly down I-94 toward Gray's, I let my hand drift briefly from the handlebars to curl around hers. I feel her chest expand and her palm tighten against my pec, which twitches under her hand. Before moving my hand back, I glide it from her upper thigh, close to her crotch, and down to her knee, making sure to press my thumb down the sensitive inner meat, which causes her to squeeze me tighter.

I want Addy. *Fuck*, how I want her. My balls have been in a perpetual state of tightness for months. And while I've had every intention of just getting into her pants, after only one taste I want more than that now. I'm fucked because I want *her*.

Wanting and deserving are two totally different things, though. I do not deserve her. And after that kiss, for the first time in my life, I *want* to deserve something. But I know I never will and it cuts me deep.

I'm nothing like my brothers. I have not lived a pampered adult life, running a multimillion dollar company. I didn't have family I could count on, except my mom. My mom has always been there for me even when no one else knew it. I missed dinners and holidays and birthday parties. I have a jaded view of the world that can only come from seeing its vile and depraved underbelly. I'm rough and crude and definitely on the wrong side of heaven. Damaged, at best. Ruined, at worst.

I am not husband material. I am not father material. Hell, I don't even think I'm boyfriend material. I've never wanted any of those things until I came back into the family fold. Watching Gray, Asher, and their women drown in happiness is hard to stomach when I know I'll never have the same.

As much as I loved Livia, I knew in my heart those things women dream of could never happen between us. There were so many reasons why, the least of which was I was a criminal at the time, even though that was the last thing I wanted to be and in many ways was forced to be. Hell, I thought I'd be pining away for my brother's wife for the rest of my life...that I'd be on the outside looking in, always wanting what I couldn't have.

Until I met *her*, the one woman I never expected to meet.

Mine.

Addy is like no other woman I've ever known and she continually proves that each time I'm around her. She's smart, quick-witted, and has a one-of-a-kind fiery spunk I've never run across before. I want to shut her mouth with my cock as much as I want to hear the next blistering thing she's going to say. I'm drawn to her like moths to a goddamned blue fluorescent light. I can't make myself stay away no matter how hard I've tried.

I need to just walk away before I do something I'll regret. Like hurt her. There is no doubt that will happen. It won't even be intentional; I could never hurt her on purpose. But that won't stop it from happening, anyway. I need to drop her off, turn my damn bike around, pack up my shit, and move out tonight, never laying eyes on her again.

Problem is...I fucking *can't*.

If I thought I felt at peace just being in the same vicinity as her, that's a fraction of the serenity and contentment I've found with her touch. Very simply, she's the solace to my tattered soul. Her light blinded me the first time I set eyes on her and it felt so fucking warm and good, I can't even begin to describe it.

And once the spots in my vision faded, I saw color. She's infused brilliant color back into my life. If you want honesty, she's the real reason I moved my business here. *She's* the light that drew me home. Yes, I wanted to reconnect with my brothers, but the genesis behind my move is currently sitting with her pussy pressed snugly against my ass, tits smashed to my back, holding on to me for dear life.

This sounds so clichéd, and I fucking hate clichés: she makes me want to be a better man, if for no one else but her. I don't give a shit what anyone else thinks of me. I've lived my life on my terms and if someone doesn't like it, pound fucking sand. But I *care* what she thinks. Probably too much.

God, I hate myself, some days more than others. I deserve a slot perpetually burning right alongside Peter Wilder for the pursuit I'm about to lay on her, because it can't end any other way than with both of us decimated, our hearts broken and bleeding.

Today I've stooped to a new low. I'm about to drag an innocent down with me. I'm just too selfish to give her up.

Yep. I'm a real prince.

Chapter 9

Addy

With Luke's easy maneuvering, it took less than thirty minutes to arrive at Livia's. Unfortunately, those thirty minutes felt like thirty hours. My skin burns everyplace I touched Luke. So long as I live, I'll never forget the feel of his masculine perfection pressed against me. And when he briefly caressed my hand and thigh during our cool ride, I moaned. Loudly. Thank God the rush of the wind carried it away. The last thing I need is to stroke his overinflated ego.

The minute he parks his bike, I whip off the helmet and hop off the seat like fire ants are crawling up my jeans. I don't even look back after my feet hit the ground, not caring if he's behind me or not. In fact, I pick up my pace, practically running for the front door. Once inside, I wave to Sam behind the security desk and rush to the elevator bank. Pressing the up arrow, I bounce from foot to foot while I anxiously wait. The last thing I need is to be in another closed space with Luke for a second longer.

Yet once again, the luck of the Irish has completely fucked me over; just as soon as the steel doors open and I step through, Luke is on my heels.

"Have to pee or something?" he drawls. Goddamn, he's good at that. I hate it when men talk almost condescendingly to you, but on Luke, it's not. It's as natural and instinctual as breathing and Luke wouldn't be Luke without that tone and inflection in everything he says. I love it and hate it equally.

"Or something," I mutter, trying my damnedest not to look at him and his sexiness. He laughs loudly, his deep voice echoing off the steel walls until I'm sure I'll hear it in my sleep tonight. Great, infect *all* my senses why don't you.

Damn you, Luke Colloway. *Damn you.*

As if by small favors, the elevator rises quickly to the penthouse and the doors open in short order. I exit first and almost as quickly as I knock, Livia answers. Throwing my arms around her, I curse in her ear. "I swear on my grandmother's grave, I will get you back for this, Livia Colloway."

"I don't have the slightest idea what you're talking about, Addy." Her feigned innocence grates on my nerves, so I simply glare before turning and heading into the kitchen.

I need a damn drink. A strong one. And a lot of them.

Then I need to use the bathroom to ease my sexual discomfort. Pronto.

"What's your poison tonight?" Livia asks, the

devious bitch sauntering in behind me. Luke is following her, but I don't look at him.

"Tequila if you have it. And keep 'em coming."

"No. She'll have a beer," Luke interjects leaning nonchalantly against the granite island. He sounds authoritative. Commanding. And pissed. Gray's already handed him a Heineken, which he's tipped to his lips while keenly watching me over the top of the green glass bottle.

"Are you for real?" I rant, stalking right up to him. I could give a shit that we're going to have another audience for our verbal throw down. What the hell...seems to be our thing. "I'll have whatever the fuck I want. Just because you bulldozed your way into my home does not mean you can bulldoze your way into the rest of my life, Luke Colloway. I'm a grown fucking woman and I can make my own decisions. And if I want tequila, by God, I'm going to have fucking tequila!"

"That was a lot of 'fucks,'" he drawls mockingly. I grit my teeth hard, biting my tongue in the process. Damn him, the bastard. Then he closes the small space between us, lowering his voice. "Have you forgotten what happened last time you drank tequila, fireball?"

No. No, I have not. I haven't had a two-day hangover since college, although I did have one after that night. I swore off tequila after that, but I'm so damn wound up, I need something strong to take the edge off. And a beer just won't cut it. "Stop calling me that, asshole."

"Because I haven't," he continues, unfazed. "I haven't forgotten how you passed out cold in my arms or how I held your hair as you puked into the garbage can or how your breathing was so shallow all night long I thought you had alcohol poisoning and I was going to have to take you to the hospital."

I freeze, digesting what he just said. I play it repeatedly to make sure I heard it right. Thinking back to that horrible night, I remember when I woke at almost noon on Sunday. I was in my bra and panties with an old ratty CSU Cougar T-shirt thrown over me and no idea how I'd gotten that way. I couldn't remember a thing past being lifted into Luke's arms at the bar and the safety I'd felt in them.

"You stayed?" I breathed, suddenly very uncomfortable with everything he must have witnessed that night. My teeth find my bottom lip. They always do when I'm anxious.

He gently grabs my chin between his finger and thumb, running the pad back and forth hypnotically. I want to yank away from his touch as much as I want to lean into it. But I do neither.

"Of course I stayed. I wasn't about to dump and run. I'm not as big of a prick as you make me out to be, Addy."

I'm speechless, and that doesn't happen very often. His intense gaze has me completely trapped and I'm unable to do a thing other than fall a little bit further into Luke, against my better judgment and definitely against my will.

"Please, Addy," he softly beseeches. He

LUKE'S ABSOLUTION

releases my chin, only to whisper a finger across my cheek, tucking a wayward hair behind my ear. It's intimate. Tenfold over that blistering kiss he gave me less than an hour ago.

My knees feel weak. My head, jumbled. My face burns where he just touched me. It's as if my decision on which alcoholic beverage I drink means more to him than anything else in this moment.

Holy shit. If I thought the fork-tongued Luke was impossible to resist, that doesn't hold a candle to the caring, sensitive one standing in front of me right now. This is the first time I've been personally gifted with the side of Luke that Livia regularly sees. The one I've gotten only rare glimpses of.

I like it. *Way* too much.

Danger, danger, Will Robinson. Danger!

"Okay, fine," I concede, mumbling the words.

He nods slightly, looking more relaxed than he did a minute ago. I have to fight the silly urge to wrap my arms around him. I turn to see Livia and Gray watching with looks akin to cats that swallowed a canary, particularly Gray.

Damn them.

"I need the bathroom," I announce before I slink away for a few precious moments alone to regroup.

Once I'm behind the closed door, I lean against it and let the confusion of the last hour wash over me. My emotions seesaw more with this man than with anyone else in my entire life. One minute I'm ready to set a horde of angry bees on

73

him and the next I want to throw him down and ride him until my cells are imprinted in his, so even thinking of another woman causes him to writhe in agony.

But right now? Right this minute, I just want to feel the warmth and comfort of his arms holding me like I'm his. Which is utterly ridiculous. I'm not his. I'll never be his. Men like Luke don't commit. They flit, like butterflies (or dicks), from one vagina to the next. That doesn't stop my foolish heart from wanting him regardless.

That's my problem.

I want the impossible.

I always do.

Chapter 10

LUKE

What the hell was I thinking, making a scene like that in front of my brother and his wife? I wasn't. Clearly. But the thought of Addy numbing her discomfort or whateverthefuck she's trying to do with that poison damn near had me feral.

I wasn't lying when I said I spent that entire night worried as hell. Twice I damn near packed her up in my rental car and drove her to the ER. She would wake long enough to vomit and then fall back into a deep sleep. So deep, I thought she was in a coma. Only an asshole would leave her alone in that shape, so I spent the night with her in my arms, staring at the ceiling, fighting sleep, relishing and remembering every second of how it felt to hold her. It was fucking heaven.

That's when I knew.

This woman belongs to me. The kiss we shared earlier just confirms what I already knew to be true.

No one has ever felt so right pressed against me, not that I've given a lot of women that opportunity, mind you. And she won't

75

remember—she was too blitzed, but she clung to me all night long between her bouts of throwing up. I never wanted her to know I stayed and took care of her. I knew she'd react just like she did now.

Embarrassed.

Defensive.

Closed off.

Don't lie to yourself, Colloway. You didn't want her to know because you don't want her to think you care about her, even when that's the furthest thing from the truth.

"What was that all about?" Gray inquires. Addy's fled to the safety of the bathroom; the doorbell just rang and Livia's gone to answer it. I can hear Alyse's laugh and Asher's deep voice. I know we have about sixty seconds until they're back and our privacy will be gone for the night.

"I have no fucking clue," I lie. "Why didn't you tell me you invited her to dinner?" Not that I mind spending time with Addy; I just don't want her to feel like I've ambushed her either, which is fucking crazy—I plan to ambush her every other chance I get. But I want to crumble her defenses, not her trust. *Probably not the smartest move to just barge into her apartment then, asshole.*

"I honestly didn't know until I texted you. Livvy apparently invited her last night."

Ah yes, during the infamous fact-finding mission Addy went on to see if I was telling her the truth about the lease. That accusation, while it hit too close to home, still stung sharply.

"I take it you came together?" he asks. I nod

and Gray grins. I may have overstated the truth that I was "instructed" to bring her. I desperately needed the feel of her body pressed against mine again, even if it was under false pretenses. "I bet that was a...challenge."

"You could say that." I chuckle, throwing back another swallow. "Everything with that woman is a challenge."

"I seem to remember you love a challenge, Luke."

I tip my beer in his direction. "Nothing revs my engine hotter than a good one." And if Addy has any sense about her, she'll have figured that out by now. The harder she pushes, the harder she makes me. The more she denies what's between us, the more I want her, until it's all I can think about. I've never shied away from a challenge in my life and I'm not about to start now. Especially when there's nothing I've wanted more. She's wholly consumed me.

"Hey, beer me, Gray," Asher greets as he walks into the kitchen, Alyse's hand firmly in his. Turning to his fiancée, he lowers his voice. "What do you want, baby?"

"I'll have the same thing."

Gray digs in the fridge then hands her a Molson and Asher a Heineken.

"Conn coming?" Asher asks, taking a swig.

"Nah. He's out of town. Checking into that executive recruiting firm he's looking to acquire. He said he'd swing by if he doesn't get home too late," Gray replies. He snakes an arm around

K. L. KREIG

Livia's waist, pulls her close, and places a lingering kiss on her temple. I watch, happy that not an ounce of envy has reared her ugly head. It feels nice. Real nice.

"Where's Addy?" Alyse pipes in.

"I'm right here," she calls from behind me. She's been gone for several minutes and I was about thirty seconds away from barging in on her, invited or not.

"Great, now I can show you the nursery," Livia tells her excitedly, clapping her hands in glee.

"Beer?"

Livia hands her one and I don't miss the fact that she won't look at me. In fact, she's taken position as far across the spacious kitchen as possible from where I stand. I want to stalk over there and haul her to me, kissing her senseless, staking my claim. I want to make it crystal clear to her that she's mine. I want to take her back to the bathroom and fuck her into admitting she wants this—*us*—as much as I do.

But I don't.

I just watch as the women leave in the direction of the bedrooms, presumably to get a tour of cribs and changing tables and diaper bins. How the fuck I even know that boggles the mind. Gray is definitely rubbing off on me.

And I'm not hating it. That's the scary part.

"You have it baaaad," Asher chuckles as soon as the women are out of earshot.

"I have no idea what the fuck you are talking about, Ash."

When in doubt...deny, deny, deny.

"Really? Then you'd better relay that message to your dick, brother."

I adjust myself. I'm hard as a rock after watching Addy sashay away in those tight-ass jeans that showcase her every curve to perfection. I swear she moves like that on purpose. "Fuck you."

"I don't think it's me you want to fuck," Ash quips.

"It's you I'm going to be fucking up if you say another word like that about Addy."

Asher leans against the counter, smug and happy as shit with himself that he's goaded me into reacting. That's more of a Conn move than an Asher one. Guess he's filling in for our absent sibling tonight.

"Shit." I scrub my hand over my stubble, wondering what I think I'm doing pining away for a woman like Addy anyway.

"Don't fuck this up," Gray says, nodding in the direction the women went.

"There's nothing to fuck up, Gray." Deny, deny, deny.

"Oh yeah. There definitely is."

Before I can answer, I hear the cackle of the girls right before they walk back through the living room in our direction.

"Okay, let's eat!" Livia announces. Gray jumps like he's just been tazed, pulling something from the oven. Livia's shooing us into the dining room, where the table is dressed impeccably and everyone starts taking their seats. Well, by everyone, I mean Asher and Alyse. Addy is apparently waiting to see where I'm going to sit before she chooses. No doubt she plans on sitting as far away from me as possible.

And I decide I'll let her. I pull out a chair on one of the ends and take a seat, giving her an out. Everything I do is strategic. I've chosen this particular spot because I can easily see everyone else at the table at all times, which means that Addy has chosen unwisely. Now, I'll be watching her every move throughout the meal. She would have been better off sitting beside me.

"Wow, Livia, this smells great," I compliment, taking a giant inhale of the fragrant vegetable lasagna she's set on the table.

"Thanks, Luke. It's probably not as good as yours, but..."

My gaze strays to Addy, who is watching me intently, confusion wrinkling her forehead. *Yeah, sweetheart...I have many hidden talents. All of which I'll be showing you very soon.*

The moment our gazes connect, though, her eyes shift away and I'm left feeling strangely bereft. Another emotion that's confusing as hell.

"Nah. I'm sure it's great. I don't cook much anymore."

I gave up cooking the last couple of years. Not a lot of fun when you're just cooking for one. When I look back on my childhood, my mother teaching us to cook is one of my fondest memories. It was a bonding experience every family should try.

Food is passed, silverware clatters, and everyone digs in. For the first five minutes of the meal, I hardly take my eyes off Addy, trying to catch her gaze again. It's fruitless. She's intent on ignoring me.

The minute I focus on my plate, however, I feel her weighty stare exactly the way I did ten years ago when she didn't think I knew she watched me from the stairs of her father's house. I haven't lived this long in the life I did by not honing my sixth sense and it was pretty fucking sharp even back then.

I don't react. I don't lift my eyes. I don't curl my lips in a knowing smile.

I savor it. I bathe in it. I suck it in. I relish in the fact she's as drawn to me as I am to her, even though she'll die before she admits it to me or anyone else.

All during and after dinner, the conversation is light, jovial. The guys talk about sports. The girls chatter about babies and weddings. It's nice to be with my brothers again. I've missed them more than I realized. More than I would previously admit.

I sip my second beer, conscious of the fact I have to drive us home. I rarely let go and let myself get rip-roaring drunk, the slip with Bigs a couple of weeks ago being an exception. Control and all that...I hate it slipping.

Sitting back, I look around at my family. The "couples" at the table sit next to each other, forcing Addy to take the other end. I notice Asher lean over to place a heated kiss on Alyse's lips and I can't help the unwelcome twinge of jealousy that flash fires through my blood.

I wish like hell that Addy and I could be here as a couple instead of practically archenemies. But I have no idea what the fuck I'm doing relationship wise. My brothers are tender where I'm hard. Refined where I'm rough. Boardwise to my streetwise. Would Addy even want the likes of me for more than just a roll in the sack?

I do, but somehow I know I'm going to fuck things up epically. I'm going to end up hurting her and I'll just as soon cut off my own dick before I do that. I wish I could be the man she needs, but I stopped wishing a long time ago. Put wishes in one hand and shit in the other and see which weighs more. Shit always wins.

Suddenly the hypocrisy of what I'm doing hits me like a Mack fucking truck. I have no idea why I'm trying to pull her into my world. My depravity. My tainted past may be behind me, but that doesn't make the things I've done any less real. Any less wrong.

If pure, innocent Addy ever finds out some of the downright heinous things I've done, she'll go running for the hills, and I'll help her. Hell...I'll personally drive her there.

I need to leave Addy Monroe the hell alone. She's far too good for me. For the second time in my life, I need to be a better man and do the right thing.

Problem is, the right thing is often the hardest of all.

Chapter 11

Addy

Cooper: Looking forward to tonight.

For the tenth time, I look at Cooper's text and think about cancelling. It's not fair for me to lead him on when my head is like the jumble of the day. But it's now an hour away from our first date, and I'd feel bad bailing. Besides, I already told him I was looking forward to it, too. I'd better get my head in the game and start acting like it.

Luke and I stayed at Livia's last Friday night until nearly midnight. I effectively managed to limit my interaction with him both there and when we returned home, and for the better part of the week, actually.

I admit I put my plan to stay away from Luke Colloway into full-blown action, keeping myself busy for the last eight days. I've closed almost every night. It actually worked out well, since Carla is just now getting over that bug and she's usually my closer. Luke doesn't seem to be around a lot anyway, keeping odd hours just like I do. I'm not sure if he's truly busy or trying to avoid me, too. The thought of the latter distresses me for some dumb reason.

As much as I've tried to forget it, dinner at Livia's last week has been on my mind constantly. The ride, the kiss, the confusing and intense exchange in her kitchen. The fact that Luke looked to me when declining another beer because he was driving. Why do his responsibility and concern endear me to him even more? Why should I like the fact that he considered me before responding? Ugh...why am I reading into things that aren't even there?

I learned a lot of things about Luke that night, paying more attention to the conversation the guys were having versus the one I was supposed to be engrossed in with Livia and Alyse about Alyse's upcoming wedding.

He can cook. Quite well, so I hear, although he doesn't do it much anymore. He's a huge Detroit Lions and Michigan Wolverines fan. He's allergic to shellfish. He's never been out of the country, so Asher and Alyse's wedding, which is in Turks and Caicos, will be his first time. That also means he doesn't have a felony record since felons can't get passports. Even if he did, I wouldn't really care. I know all too well how good souls can make poor decisions, just as I know they can be redeemed. My brother is a prime example.

Taking a sip of my fortification (aka Cabernet), I sigh and get back to my primping. Somewhere in the back of my mind, I feel if I need fortification for a date, I should be calling it off. *Just this one date*, I tell myself. Then I'll tell Cooper I don't have time for dating right now, which isn't really untrue. I'm too busy bobbing and weaving, avoiding another sinful man.

Which is exactly why you should give Cooper a chance.

I'm just finishing applying a second coat of mascara to my smoky eyes when my cell rings. I'm surprised to see it's my niece.

"Hi, Landyn."

Landyn is my sister, Samantha's, twenty-five-year-old daughter. Sixteen years separate my sister and me, so I've never been very close to Sam, who escaped our household before things spiraled downward with our parents. Fortunately, I am close to Landyn. She's almost like the sister I feel like I never really had.

"Hey, Auntie Ad. What are you up to? Did I interrupt a hot date or something?"

"No. That starts in T-minus forty-five minutes." I laugh.

"Ooohh. Is he hot?"

"Very." Cooper's hot all right...then why doesn't he set my blood on fire like a certain tatted, Ducati-riding sex god who's probably creeping around the apartment somewhere just waiting for me to emerge from my prison cell? I wish I knew the answer so I could fix it.

"I'm so jealous. I haven't had time to date in months."

"Guys are more trouble than they're worth. Trust me."

"Maybe. But a girl needs to get laid every once in a while to keep the dust bunnies cleared."

"Landyn," I cry. "For God sakes, I don't need to hear you talk like that." *And I don't want you to follow in your mother's footsteps. Please, let this cycle break with Sam.*

"Why? You do know I'm not a virgin, right, Ad?"

"How could I forget the detailed accounts of all your escapades?" I laugh. Landyn tends to be an over-sharer and there are some things about your sweet niece you just want to ignore. "Just...be picky, okay?"

"I always am, Ad. You're a good role model," she answers quietly. *Not hardly, however,* I don't correct her. I've fallen in love with the wrong men my entire life. I could already envision myself doing it yet again with my new roomie. I guess I'm not a quick learner.

"How's your mom?" I ask, changing the subject. I already know the answer. If I could, I would have raised Landyn myself, but being only three years older than her, that wasn't really an option. Much like me, she's an innocent caught in the crosshairs of the unfairness of life.

My mom got pregnant with Sam when she was seventeen. She married Sam's father and the relationship fizzled within two years. Good ol' Mary tried her luck twice more before finally meeting my father. By that time, Sam was already ten and because her father was absent, Bob adopted her, treating her just like she was one of his own.

LUKE'S ABSOLUTION

Three years later Eric was born. Two more, and I came along. And nine years after that, they divorced. The reason? Like all others before him, Bob Monroe was imperfect. My dad was victim number four, but he was far from the last. My mother can't be without a man any more than she can go without her daily bottle of five-dollar store-brand white zinfandel.

My feelings about our estranged mother have always been a bone of contention between my sister and me. Unfortunately, Sam has followed too closely in my mother's footsteps, so her judgment's a tad clouded. Sam's managed to maintain a good relationship with her, whereas I'm lucky if I talk to her once a year and that's only because she calls me religiously on my birthday.

I may be a horrible daughter, but the fact of the matter is...she was no PTA, cookie-baking mother of the year either. I'm not even sure she knows how to bake a cookie or work the oven for that matter.

"You know...same old, same old," her soft voice replies. It's difficult sometimes to emotionally recover from a parent who's fallen so far from the pedestal you put them on when you were a kid. Now I understand there's nowhere to go but down once you've unfairly elevated them, or anyone, to that lofty platform. I try not to do that anymore. I wish Landyn and I didn't share that camaraderie. Unfortunately, we do.

"I'm sorry, sweetie."

"Yeah, well…you know how it is."

Boy, do I ever.

"How's work going?" I ask, changing the subject to lighten the mood. I don't need to be a Debbie Downer when Cooper gets here.

"Good. That's actually the reason I was calling."

"Oh? What's up?"

Landyn finished nursing school last year, specializing in geriatrics of all things. I'm proud of her. She has the smarts to know this is an ever-expanding and growing field and she'll have job security until she wants to retire.

"I was thinking about coming up to see you sometime in the next few weeks."

"That would be awesome, Landyn."

Landyn still lives in Marion, Indiana with her mother and her mother's newest boy toy, Fabron or Fabian or some stupid thing like that. I think my sister's moved all over the country following men around. After my mother was diagnosed with severe cirrhosis of the liver a couple of years ago, she moved closer to help take care of her. Now her pool of men has dwindled considerably, but apparently, that hasn't slowed her down.

"Yeah. I'm looking into a couple of graduate programs and I'd like to check out the campuses and meet some of the faculty before I decide to officially apply. And I have a couple of interviews I'm hoping to line up. Can't very well afford school there if I don't have a job."

I don't really think that's true. I would never ask Sam, but I know Landyn has a fairly substantial trust from her birth father, whose identity Sam refuses to reveal. I don't know the whole story and neither does Landyn. Landyn and I have talked about her trying to find her biological father on her own, but she said she doesn't want to find a man who never wanted her. Whatever her decision is, I will always support her.

"Wow. That's great, Landyn. That would be amazing to have you live here." And get away from your whore of a mother.

"You still have that extra bedroom I can crash in for a few days, right?"

Uhhhhh....Shit.

"Ah...not really. But we'll work something out." Damn that Luke Colloway for moving in here without even consulting me.

"Really? You have a new roommate? Since when?"

I take a big breath and sigh. "It's a long story."

"Sounds like a cocktail's needed." She laughs.

"Or five."

"Is he your date tonight?"

"God, no! Why do you think it's a guy anyway?"

"Addy, please. The longing in your voice wasn't a dead giveaway or anything. Is he hot?"

Sinfully.

Suddenly a little bloom of envy tries to sprout. Landyn is drop-dead gorgeous, just like her mother. Long lean legs, natural blonde hair, big brown eyes with lashes that mold them perfectly. Model figure.

Men fall at her feet. *Luke* will fall at her feet. And why wouldn't he? He's got eyes and a dick and I'm trying my hardest to push him away. But once he gets a look at Landyn, any thoughts he had of me will just evaporate like mist being hit by the sun's hot rays. That thought should make me happy, yet it only stirs the dirt in my gut so those seeds root and grow.

"I'll take your silence as he's hands-off."

"I didn't say that," I argue weakly.

"You didn't have to, Ad. God, I can't wait to hear all about what man drama you have gotten yourself into! Listen, I'll let you go so you can finish getting ready for your hot date while you're thinking about your hot new roommate. I'll call you soon about the deets, okay?"

"Yeah, sure," I mumble, ignoring her "man drama" reference. It hits way too close to home. As I disconnect, I'm irritated with myself for feeling this jealous over something that hasn't even happened or that I shouldn't even care about. Luke can date or fuck whomever he wants. It's none of my business.

Oh God. But I don't want him to do it *here*. Imagining it and hearing it are two totally different things. The thought of him bringing a woman back *here* and having to listen to them as he lavishes his "untold pleasures" and "blissful pain" all over *her* body makes me physically nauseous.

Christ. This man has infected me but good.

Pushing the sickening thoughts of Luke and a faceless woman to the back of my head before I vomit, I finish my makeup and straighten my long hair. Half an hour later, I take one last look in the mirror, satisfied.

Tonight I've worn a simple curve-hugging, sleeveless little black dress that hits me just above the knees. The neckline plunges, showing a little cleavage, although nothing slutty. The most risqué part of the dress is the sheer back. I've paired it with some strappy nude three-inch open-toed heels. With a swipe of dark red lipstick, I'm good to go.

Not too shabby, Addy.

Finishing off the rest of my wine, I open my bedroom door, praying like hell Luke isn't here. Somehow, I just know there will be a testosterone brawl in my living room if he is. I wouldn't be surprised if Luke tried to throw down, staking some fictional claim on me.

When I walk into the main area, I already know he's gone. Even though I was praying he wasn't here, I suppress the stab of disappointment that he won't devour me with his hungry eyes, making my nipples pucker and my flesh prickle under his intense perusal. I don't think about the last hour I spent dressing and primping for one man and one man only.

And it's not the man it should have been.

I'm just pulling my turquoise pashmina from the coat closet when the doorbell rings. Steeling myself, I walk the short distance and open the door after verifying it's Cooper through the peephole.

"Hi." I smile. I'm surprised to find myself actually happy to see him. He looks great in his black dress pants and tan crewneck sweater.

He's silent, his eyes skating slowly over me. Cooper Jensen is handsome, successful, fit, and masculine. He's every woman's man. But all I feel, as his eyes rake my body, is a slight tingle. The smallest of warming that one may feel when they stand over a hot stove. I don't feel the scorching inferno that burns me from the inside whenever Luke sets his eyes on me.

When his gaze finally lands on mine, his emeralds sparkle with heat and appreciation and I can't help but smile.

"Wow, Ms. Monroe. You look...wow. Breathtaking."

"Why thank you, Mr. Jensen."

"How about we make a deal?" he rasps, moving into my personal space.

"Okay," I answer hesitantly, tipping my head to keep hold of his eyes.

Bringing a hand up, he runs a strand of my hair through his fingers, watching it slip all the way through before lifting his eyes to mine again. "Let's drop the formalities. I want to hear my first name roll off your lips."

Wow, the heat just turned up a notch. "Cooper..."

"Yes. Just like that," he whispers seductively.

"I thought you were going to be a gentleman?" I manage to breathe when my lungs fill again.

A smirk tilts one corner of his mouth. My God, he really is sexy. "You make that hard, Addy." He takes a slight step back, before adding, "You ready?"

I nod rapidly, breathing deep. "Let me grab my purse."

When I return to the door, with my wrap and clutch, he takes my hand in his. Closing the door behind us, he leads us down the stairs.

On the three-flight descent to Cooper's car, I decide to leave all thoughts and dreams and fantasies about Luke at the door and enjoy my first date with Cooper Jensen. We may not have the sparks that Luke and I do; maybe it's more of a slow burn instead of a raging fire.

Slow is better, right? Right.

Riiiight.

Chapter 12

LUKE

I was just pulling into the parking lot when I saw them.

I saw his hand on the small of her back.

I saw the way that dress hugged her curves like a walking wet dream.

I saw the way he looked at her like he knew he was the luckiest son-of-a-bitch alive to have such an incredibly special woman on his arm.

I saw her genuine smile as he opened the car door for her.

I saw him already falling.

Then I saw his murder in vivid detail play on a reel through my mind.

I have spent an entire week, since dinner at Gray's last Friday, avoiding her. Trying to convince myself to leave her alone. Reminding myself that I'm not nearly good enough for her. Remembering the blood on my hands and the fact I don't want to stain her with it.

But seeing her with Cooper Jensen has me seeing red. Blood red. *His* blood.

I may not be good enough for her, but the fact

of the matter is...no one is. I'm good at walking away and I'm the motherfucking master at faking shit, yet after seeing her leave on a date with another man, I'm done. I'm not walking away from her, and I'm certainly not going to stand by and watch someone else snatch what's mine out from under my nose.

Fuck that shit.

He's not taking my color.

She is *mine*. And I don't share.

I've wasted too much time pining away like a lovesick fool for this woman, pretending that I don't want her. I want nothing *but* her. I'm done pussyfooting around. It's time to up my game to a full-court press.

A better man would let her go, let her be with someone like Cooper Jensen. Hell, a better man would *push* her toward someone like him, which apparently I've unconsciously been doing.

But I'm not a better man.

And I've finally just accepted that the *only* way I can possibly be one is with her by my side.

Chapter 13

Addy

"So when was your last serious relationship?" Cooper asks, staring at me intently across the dimly lit table.

He's taken me to a very romantic Spanish restaurant on the south loop of downtown Chicago. Dim lights dangle from the ceiling at varying levels, and the large arched windows give the open space a unique ambience. He managed to finagle us a fairly private booth in a less rowdy part of the restaurant.

Cooper ordered the chef's luxury tasting menu for two, so sitting in front of us is a variety of cheeses, meats, olives, garlic shrimp, bacon-wrapped dates, some type of croquet, scallops, chorizo, and braised rabbit flatbread. It's more than I could even comprehend eating, although I've enjoyed tasting almost everything. Except the rabbit. I just can't force myself to take a bite of Peter Cottontail.

Sipping my bourbon, agave nectar, and blackberry cocktail, which contains a hint of mint and black pepper and is like sex in a glass, I think about how I'll answer, deciding on the truth.

"Eight months ago." Eight long, dry lonely months. Which is probably why I'm panting like a dog in heat every time I look at my sexy new roommate. I need to get laid. Maybe then I could forget about the fact I want to mount Luke and ride him into the sunset.

"What about you?" I ask, trying to get my mind back to the man in front of me. The man I *should* want instead of the insanely frustrating one my mind keeps drifting to.

"Two years."

"Two years? Wow. By choice?" Two years is an awfully long time for a man like Cooper Jensen to remain single.

"Until recently, yes. Did your last relationship end badly?"

How about every relationship I've had. "Don't they all?"

He chuckles, taking a sip of his own inventive concoction, which includes tequila, making me immediately think of last week and Luke's insistence that I not drink it. I admit I may not have ordered it tonight with him in mind.

Sucker. That's me.

"Most, I suppose."

"Yours?"

His expressive eyes answer before he verbally does. "Yes. Very badly."

"I'm sorry." I can relate all too well.

"Me too," he replies, the pain of that last

relationship still evident. "What happened, if you don't mind me asking?"

I look down and twirl the ice in my glass, the blackberry bits hypnotizing me. It's been five months since I found out Aiden was engaged and I should be over the sting by now, but I'm not. Our lives always look clearer in the rearview mirror. We pick up the signs we missed while staring blissfully ahead into the sunrise of our future, which only served to blind us from reality. I missed the signs Aiden gave me, some of them blatant. I missed the signs Alison tried carelessly to hide. Love didn't make me blind; it made me reckless and stupid.

I won't make that mistake again.

"Well, let's see...he told me he didn't love me and started dating his old girlfriend three days after we broke up. He's marrying her in two months."

"Holy shit. That is bad."

"Yeah. Good times."

"How long were you with him?"

"Too long," I sigh. Long enough to know that he didn't love me the way I loved him, but I tried to overlook it. He never did the little things for me, like open my car door or pull out my chair or leave me goofy notes in the morning. He never helped me on with my coat or called me during the day just to hear my voice. I tried to brush it off, telling myself he just wasn't romantic. Turns out that wasn't it at all, as I ever so painfully found out.

"He proposed to his fiancée when they were

on a getaway to Aruba. He had the hotel concierge draw a huge heart in the sand on the beach and fill it full of red and yellow and orange flower petals. The whole thing was surrounded by tiki torches. Then he took her on a long, romantic walk on the beach that night, ending there, kneeling down, and asking her to marry him. It was all graciously filmed by said concierge so it could be shared on every social media site possible."

"Ouch. God, Addy, I'm sorry."

I smile sadly, finally lifting my eyes. At least, they aren't filled with tears. "I'm not. I was never first with Aiden."

"You deserve to be first," he declares passionately, taking hold of my hand across the table.

"Yes, I do," I whisper softly. Our eyes lock and the heat that was just a hot summer's day earlier has turned into a sizzling crackle. I think if I let myself, I could eventually fall in love with the man sitting in front of me.

On paper, he has every quality I'm looking for. Outside of his insanely incredible physical characteristics, I can already tell he'll be an attentive lover, a devoted husband, a doting father. He seems mentally stable, has ambition, and owns a successful business. He's not playing the field anymore; he's looking for a mate.

Perfect in every way.

Then why does my mind keep wandering back to another man who has already penetrated my soul in ways I'll never understand? On paper, he's someone you would immediately discard and not because of the tattoos or the bike. He's cocky, infuriating, and has a sketchy past. He's aloof and uses sarcasm and deflection to protect himself from the judgment of others. He's the most mulish person I think I've ever met. Even more than I am.

But it's the glimpses of the man underneath that have me wanting more. He's passionate and deeply caring. He's sensitive, but would never admit it. He can be tender and devoted. He would protect the ones he loves to the death, if necessary. He loves his mother profoundly, as do all the Colloway brothers. Watching them together at Livia's wedding almost brought tears to my eyes.

And I have a feeling that a night in the bedroom with Luke would show me I've never experienced true sexual pleasure at the hands of a man before. As explosive as we are outside of the bedroom, I know we'd absolutely combust inside it.

Luke Colloway is imperfect in so many ways, so why do I keep thinking he may be perfect for me?

"Probably bad form to talk about exes on a first date, huh?" Cooper asks, sensing I've gone far away. I have, but not for the reasons he thinks.

"We could do better," I quip, dragging my attention back to him once again.

"So we shall."

We spend the next three hours nibbling,

chatting, and laughing. By the time we leave, it's nearly eleven.

"Home?" he asks as soon as we get in the car the valet has pulled around. I can hear the hope in his voice that I'll want to extend our date, however, I have an early morning. I've promised Mrs. Ruffalo that I'll take her to get her meds and pick up a birthday card and gift for her great-grandbaby who's turning two. Madge likes to get an early start. I'll be lucky if she lets me sleep until eight, even though I've told her repeatedly the pharmacy doesn't open until ten on Sundays.

"Yes, sorry. I have early plans tomorrow."

"I hope not a breakfast date," he teases.

"Sort of," I joke back.

"Really? Am I going to have to spend the night protecting my turf?"

I laugh, thinking of how Luke would react if I invited Cooper in and dragged him back to my bedroom. Probably about the way I would react if he did the same. Both scenarios would likely end in violence. "Unless you're worried about an eighty-five-year-old grey hair stealing me away from you, I think my virtue's safe." But my virtue is most definitely not safe with the man behind my front door.

"Eighty-five? Wow, you get around."

"Why do you think it's been eight months?"

Laughter fills his Camry. "Secret's safe with me." He crosses his heart and kisses his closed fist in promise and I chuckle at the gesture.

As we wind through the streets of downtown

Chicago to the interstate, Cooper reaches over, plucks my hand from my lap, and brings it to his lips for a light kiss. He looks over at me briefly and the longing I see in his eyes makes my heart flutter, but it also makes my guilt prick for some stupid reason.

Twenty-five minutes later we're pulling up in front of my apartment building. He rushes over to my side, opening my door. Extending a hand to help me out, I take it and find myself inches away from him once I'm fully standing. He looks like he wants to kiss me and I'm not sure if I want him to. As stupid as it is, I'm still remembering the feel of Luke's lips on mine last week and I don't want another man's to replace them quite yet, even though that's exactly what I need to do.

"I had a great time."

"I'm walking you up. This date began at your door and will end the same way. Unless you have other ideas." He winks playfully and I smile.

"I thought you were trying to be a gentleman?"

"I thought we already covered that. You make that very hard."

"How so?"

"By just being you, Addy," he says lowly.

I sigh, wondering why I can't force myself to feel the same way about him as I do Luke. I want to. Somehow I don't think Cooper Jensen will hurt me the way I know Luke Colloway could. Feeling eyes on me, I look up to my living room window to see the shades fluttering slightly as if someone was just standing there. Suddenly, I'm getting anxious for this date to end.

"I think I can make it myself, Mr. Jensen."

"Back to that, are we? I think I'm going to have to change that, Ms. Monroe," he declares under his breath. Grabbing my hand, he leads me up the walk and inside the building. I'm surprised to find the light that's been out in the entryway for months now working and wonder when Ruis, our lame-ass super, fixed it. I've complained about it no less than six times. I don't remember it working last night, but, of course, I've been otherwise occupied, what with my head mixed up and all.

When we make it to my front door, I turn toward Cooper, leaning against the cool wood for support. "Thanks for a great evening. I truly enjoyed it."

"Me too," he murmurs. Stepping closer so our bodies are almost flush, he cups my cheek. His thumb lightly strokes my jaw, making my eyes involuntarily close. "Addy...I want to kiss you." His voice is low and needy.

My heavy lids open just as his lips descend on mine. They've barely made contact before I'm falling backward through the air, crashing into a strong, unyielding male chest. Corded arms band around my middle, holding me tight and I barely notice the look of confusion on Cooper's face before I hear *him*.

"Hi, honey. I've been waiting for you," a guttural voice rumbles directly in my ear.

Chapter 14

LUKE

Keep her in your arms. Keep her in your arms. *KEEP HER IN YOUR ARMS.* Because if I don't, I'm going to fucking throw picture boy over the banister to his untimely death three flights below. If not his death, at least a severe maiming...maybe even paralysis, if I'm lucky.

My woman safe in my arms? *Check.*

Holding myself back from hard prison time? *Barely...but check.*

The look on Cooper Jensen's face right now? *Priceless.*

"You can go." If my voice could physically spit nails, Jensen would be full of two tons of unforgiving lead.

I step back, dragging a now flailing and protesting Addy in my arms with me. One touch and I'm already stone hard and I don't care to hide it, so I press her more firmly against me to show her exactly what her squirming is doing to me. That shuts her right the hell up.

"Uh, is everything okay here?" Camera man asks tentatively, his gaze moving back and forth

104

between Addy and me, concern pinching his brows together.

"Lover's spat," I answer before slamming the door in his face.

See...this is the difference between me and photo guy. I would have broken down any fucking door to get to the spitfire now in my arms, but I know he'll slink away like the douche he is. He is nowhere near man enough for Addy.

"You have officially gone insane!" she screeches so loud I'm quite sure my ears are bleeding.

I would let her go, only I know she'll just run to the door and I swear if I see that loser's face again it will never look the same. As it is, I'm fighting not to tie her to my bed so I can chase after his ass and run him off the road, making it look like an innocent mishap. I can visualize tomorrow's headline in the *Chicago Tribune*: "Tragic Accident Claims Life of Rising Photographer."

Boo-fucking-hoo.

Shaking my head to rid the murderous thoughts, I focus on the only thing that really matters.

Picking Addy up, I move to the kitchen where I can let her go and trap her in all the same. No way to get out except through me and that's not happening. The instant I loosen my arms, I brace myself, and my harpy doesn't disappoint.

Half a second later, I narrowly avoid the punch that she's wickedly aimed squarely at my jaw. Grabbing her wrists in my hands, I yank her back into me and walk backward until she's pressed against the wall, my stiff cock digging into her lower belly. Raising her trapped hands over her head, I lean down until my nose is only inches from hers.

"Are you happy with yourself?" she spits. Her eyes glow bright with anger and the threat of retribution, but fuck me, I don't think I've ever been harder in my entire fucking life than I am right now.

"Very," I grate. I take slow, measured breaths, trying to calm the raging storm that's fighting to be unleashed. I need to kill or I need to fuck. I'm not sure I'll be able to control the inferno boiling inside me if I don't do one of those within the next two minutes.

And I certainly don't plan on killing. I don't need another body count added to the tally.

"You ruined a perfectly good date!"

"I don't want you going out with him."

Her chest heaves. Christ, she's always beautiful, and when she's all fired up she's simply spellbinding. "Well, tough shit! I want a bulldog, a pair of Louboutins, and a man who will put me first for once. We don't all get what we want, do we?"

I tuck all that information she just unknowingly gave me away. If I push her enough, she gives me exactly what I want whether she knows it or not. Every morsel I learn about her will help me in my cause to win her.

Addy has become the center of my world for longer than she realizes, longer than I care to admit, and she'd better believe she'll get every fucking thing she wants and then some.

I don't know what the hell a Louboutin is, but I'll find out.

And a dog? Sounds easy enough. I like animals.

As for being first? She's the *only*. I think back to her snide comment at the wedding about unrequited love and being the subject matter expert. She thinks I'm still in love with Livia. She couldn't be more wrong. I wasn't lying when I said Addy has eclipsed all thoughts of the woman I've been trying to get over and this week, barely seeing her? It's never been more excruciatingly clear.

The pieces that make up Addy Monroe are starting to come together. Slowly but surely. Her love has gone unreciprocated. Just like mine. She's scared to try again. At least, I'm not in that damn boat alone because the devil himself knows we'll both need to bail the rising waters cooling our ankles at times.

"He's not the man for you," I tell her, lowering my voice yet not loosening my hold one iota. I'm no fool.

Exhibit A: Hands tightly secured.

Exhibit B: Body's pinned nice and snug between me and the wall so I don't end up sterile.

"Oh? And you are?" she mocks.

"Not even close, fireball. But that's not going to stop me from having you anyway."

Her eyes widen and she opens her mouth but

decides against whatever clever retort she was about to vomit. We're locked in a battle of wills. Her hazel eyes, which are rimmed with a thin ring of blue around the outer edge, bewitch me, binding me to her completely. Permanently.

My fiery gaze roams over every inch of her face, relishing in the fact her lipstick is still intact. It's the only reason her date is still breathing.

I want to gorge on her.

Brand her.

Claim her.

Fucking mark every inch of her flesh so everyone knows she's taken.

I ache for her to yield her stubborn will to me and me alone.

I have never experienced these overpowering feelings for a woman before. The thought of another man's hands or lips on her all night has turned me into some wild, uncontrolled animal. I'm not at all the man she needs, but I'll kill anyone who tries to take her from me. I am never letting her go.

"Stop."

"Stop what?" I rasp, watching her full lips move. When her eyes close on a gasp, I realize I'm rocking my hips, pushing my hardened shaft into her. I bend my knees until I'm lined up with her core and thrust harder this time. A long moan, along with a plea to our lord and savior, falls from her parted lips.

"Luke, stop." She's breathless and not convincing in the least.

The need to reach under the hem of her dress,

rip her panties to shreds, and fuck her where we stand is almost uncontrollable. I don't think I'll be able to keep from sinking into her hot pussy tonight, marking her as mine, mine, mine. Her body will only know my touch from now on.

"Stop what, fireball?" I run my nose along her cheek, nipping at her ear. Jesus fucking Christ, my entire body aches for hers. I feel like I'm burning alive.

"Looking like you want to eat me."

Somewhere in the distance, I register the ring of a cell phone. Well, well, looks like Mr. Jensen wants to be sure little Red Riding Hood didn't get *eaten* by the Big Bad Wolf.

She hasn't. *Yet.*

But she will.

I let my lips graze her lobe as I declare my intent. "Oh baby, I don't want to eat you. I want to *devour* you. Whole."

The hitch in her breath tugs straight on my pulsing dick, causing him to twitch like mad. When I pull back, her hooded eyes are dilated in heady desire.

My stalwart control snaps.

I cannot go one more second without feeling her underneath my fingertips or my mouth. Securing her wrists with one hand, I slowly trail the other down the expanse of her bare arm, enjoying the shivers my touch produces.

I continue downward, letting my thumb graze the outside of her perfect tit before I dive lower to the place I desperately want to reach. At my first stroke on her bare thigh, the breath she expels washes over my neck, down the front of my tee. Grasping the lean meat, I start working my way back up, pushing the hem of her dress along with me. When I reach the golden treasure, I run my thumb along her drenched, panty-hidden seam and I almost come in my jeans.

"Fuck, fireball," I groan. "You're so damn wet for me already."

"It's...it's not for you," she pants.

I freeze, my eyes snapping to hers. *So she's gonna play it like that, is she?* Challenge thrown, challenge fucking accepted, fireball.

"Is that so?" I rasp, my caress along the soaked silk becoming more insistent.

I briefly see the whites of her eyes before they once again lock on mine. Palpable desire flashes so fast I almost don't see it before she hardens again in defiance. My fireball...she's going to fight me tooth and nail through even the most intense pleasure I plan on heaping on her.

"That's...so."

My lips curl. Squeezing her wrists in warning before I release them, I reach behind her neck. Finding the zipper, I drag it down. She starts to lower her arms, but I reach up, firmly planting them back in place high on the wall.

"Don't move, Addy," I command, slow and deliberate, just daring her to defy me. My voice sounds like I just swallowed a load of gravel.

Her chest heaves as her body and mind no doubt war on whether to follow my demand. Her body wins, thank fuck.

Leaning down slightly, I grab the hem of her

dress and drag it up over her head, her raised hands making for easy removal. I throw it in a ball on the counter beside me, leaving her before me in only heels that would look amazing by my ears, a strapless black bra that I want burned over a roaring fire, and a very wet silky black thong that has the thinnest of threads holding it on either side to her perfectly flared hips.

"Sweet Jesus, fireball." Her stomach trembles as my finger traces the exposed, taut flesh along the top of her almost nonexistent panties. I count the moments until the rest of her is quivering beneath me. "You're the sexiest fucking thing I have ever laid eyes on."

My cock is literally ramming on the door of his metal prison, pissed as fuck he's still behind bars, but that's where he'll stay until I'm good and ready to release him.

Because once he's out, he'll ravage.

Nudging her legs apart further, I almost weep at her exquisite compliance. I know a certain throbbing part of my anatomy is weeping...big time.

Her shallow, choppy breaths are sweet music to my ears as I run my middle finger back over her cloth-covered lips, which could be wrung out now with her want. *For me.* And I'll get her to admit it, come hell or high water.

Pressing my fully clothed body against hers, I grab ahold of her wrists again and growl, "Admit you're wet for *me*, Addy."

"Never," she breathes, fisting her stubbornness tightly. Her body may have bent to my will, but it will be harder to get her mind to follow suit.

I find her opening, pushing my fabric-covered finger due north. Her hips buck at the unexpected intrusion as her head falls back against the shitty-grey-painted Sheetrock.

"Luke, God."

I let my thumb flutter over her pebbled clit. It's so fucking hard already and I've barely laid a finger on her. I can envision it peeking out from under its protective hood, waiting for my mouth, my tongue.

Mine. No one else's.

I drive up further, wishing like hell she'd acquiesce so I can rip these fucking panties from her, drop to my knees, and eat my fill of what I'm sure will be the sweetest pussy I've ever put my lips on.

"Concede."

"I won't," she pants.

But she will. She's close. To both yielding and coming.

My thumb circles the most nerve-laden spot on her body faster, harder. She's riding my hand like an expert equestrian. Fuck, I need her to submit. Now.

My fingers never losing their rhythm, I drop her wrists and fist her hair, pulling her lips to mine, groaning at the taste of her fire and tenacity. Her mouth opens willingly to the silent demand of my tongue and we begin the all too familiar clash for dominance that's become our signature.

Deciding to change tactics, I let my damp finger slide underneath the drenched material and moan loudly at the first feel of her hot, smooth pussy which is wetter than I could possibly imagine. "Fuck, Addy. Fuck...this is for *me*," I whisper against her now swollen lips. Sinking two fingers deep, she cries out and I croak, "Your body's begging only for me. I want to feel you come around my fingers. Shudder under my mouth."

I kiss her jaw, dragging my lips down her neck, over her exposed collarbone, tasting every inch of her I can as I leisurely pump my fingers in and out of her saturated channel, curling them just right. My pressure on her clit is light, not nearly enough to send her soaring.

"Give in to pleasure. Give in to *me*, baby. Admit you're soaked for *me*." I'm practically begging her to end our mutual torture when she finally fully submits.

"It's for you," she says on a light whisper. "You."

Thank fucking Christ.

I waste no time withdrawing my fingers and ripping the flimsy material from her hips. Dropping to my knees, I spread her dripping lips and dive in head first. Low curses fall between licks of my new drug of choice. I'm an instant addict. Plunging two wet digits into her tight heat, my mouth latches on to her clit and sucks.

Hard.

My scalp stings as I register her fingers are now wrapped in my hair. She holds me to her for support as her legs begin to shake. Seconds later she shatters on a loud keen, her pussy riding my face with wildness like she did my hand just seconds ago. I don't let up, forcing her to give me two more orgasms in quick succession before I gradually let her float back to earth.

Fucking hell.

A strange sensation has settled in my chest. I've never wanted to be inside of a woman more than I do Addy Monroe. While I've pleasured my lovers in the past, in the end, it was always about me. It was *my* way to get off. It was *my* need to sate. It wasn't about my partner.

I already know this is different. This is more than just fucking.

For the first time ever, I want to think about someone else. I want this night to be all about Addy. Don't get me wrong, I'll get off, but the entire time I'll be focusing on giving her the greatest pleasure she's ever known.

Everything will be with her in mind.

As I stand, I feather tiny kisses all the way up her torso. Reaching behind, I deftly undo the clasp of her bra, immediately drawing a hard pink nipple into my mouth when the fabric falls. I suck and bite, moving from one amazing tit to the other. Every part of her tastes incredible. Addy's hands are in my hair again, her back arching. She mumbles incoherently as she strains to get closer to me.

I can relate.

Unable to wait any longer, I pick her up. "Wrap your legs around me, baby," I coax softly.

This time, she easily complies without lip or hesitation.

Pressing kisses all over her face as I walk with Addy in my arms through the apartment back to my bedroom, I'm fully aware of three things.

One: This will be the first time I've *ever* made love to a woman in my entire thirty years.

Two: This coupling will unequivocally be life changing.

Three: There's no going back. She's mine now.

Chapter 15

Addy

As Luke carries me down the hallway, my orgasmic fog begins to fade, panic quickly filling the barren space. *I thought I could hold out 'til month's end before I gave up the goodies?* My God...I've made it little more than a week. I'm completely shameless. I haven't had sex in over eight months and within eight days of living with my infuriating roomie, and fresh off the heels of a date with a genuinely nice man, I'm going to let Luke fuck me blind. My sanity was clearly left in a messy ball on the kitchen counter, along with my dress. Or maybe it's still by the door, along with my purse. All I know is it's long gone and I'm not looking for it.

Once in his room, he lays me gently on his king-sized bed. Standing, his intense stare never leaves mine. Instead of the smugness I expect to find, all I see now are promises.

They're confusing.

They're thrilling.

They're intoxicating.

LUKE'S ABSOLUTION

They lure me in, making me believe they're real, making me believe there could be an *us*. But I know they're all false. These promises ride on the coattails of the powerful and inebriating pheromones he's emitting. It's a heady bouquet that erases your logic, makes you bend to its sinful will. Yearn for more.

Submit.

I should be disgusted with my surrender, and somewhere deep down I know I will be tomorrow, but all I can do is stare in flat-out awe as Luke reaches behind and grabs the neck of his black Ducati tee, pulling it over his head. It lands on the carpeted floor with a whisper, the only noise in the room outside of our heavy breathing.

I feel like a voyeur as I drink in the sight of his deft fingers. Only moments ago they were working *me*; now they're working the button and zipper of his jeans. When he drops them to the floor, the air suddenly becomes thin.

Commando. *So fucking hot.*

Luke now proudly stands in front of me, buck-ass naked. *Naked.* As in...not one stitch of clothing. You don't understand...this is something I've fantasized about thousands of times over the years, only you can't possibly envision something that's unimaginable.

Sweet.

Baby.

Jesus.

Luke Colloway is pure, untainted, masculine perfection. He exudes male dominance and power. He's a work of art that would sell for millions of dollars if he were painted onto a canvas. His ink tells a story; he's hung like a prize bull and his finely honed, rippled body begs me to trace each corded muscle with my tongue to make sure they're real. They say a picture is worth a thousand words, but I could snap one of Luke right now and there's only one word that would repeatedly come to mind whenever I looked at it.

Fuuuck.

The three orgasms Luke wrung like an expert from my body earlier should have sated me, yet desire stirs again deep in my core. My sex aches to be filled with this man and this man only.

"Now who's looking like they want to eat something?" he drawls. *That damn drawl.* That damn, *sexy* drawl would wet my panties if I had any on.

Light spills into the darkened room from the hallway, so I can't see the intricacies of Luke the way I want. I need hours to trace every tat, exploring their details, but I begrudgingly drag my gaze back to his heated one. Only for a moment, though, because he fists his impressive shaft, slowly pumping back and forth. On the third pass, he swipes his thumb over the angry, swollen head, massaging the milky pre-cum into his dark pink skin.

"God," I whimper on a breathless moan. My tongue darts out to wet my lips.

Whatever reservations I have crumble the second Luke's fervent groan reaches my ears. Fuck it. I'll worry about how I'm going to live just as roommates again tomorrow. Tonight...I want him and I'm tired of denying myself any longer.

I feel like I'm diving headfirst into the shallow end of the pool. There are warning signs posted everywhere, but I ignore them, taking the dangerous plunge anyway, praying I don't hit bottom, ending up paralyzed.

Coming to my knees, I crawl to the end of the bed, where Luke is clearly waiting for me to make the next move. His watchful gaze is filled with raw hunger and barely leashed anticipation. He's restraining himself...for *me*, and I can't help the little bit of myself that falls harder for this magnificent man in front of me.

Batting his hand away, I take his cock in my own. I never break eye contact as I lean down, running my tongue from the base of his shaft all the way to the tip. I circle his glans slowly before taking him fully into my mouth. On a growl, his hooded eyes drift shut briefly before reconnecting with mine. The need I see in them strips me raw.

"Addy, Jesus Christ." His thick voice drips with desire. I increase my pressure and pace, gently fondling his balls. I listen to the change in his breathing and the tightening of his fingers in my hair, telling me exactly what he likes.

I want to suck him to completion. I want to work his body into a frenzy the way he did mine. I want my mouth to bring this arrogant man to a state of vulnerability he'll only show to me. I also selfishly want to feel him thrusting into my needy, empty sex.

He must feel the same, because his hands cradle my head, pulling me off his cock with a pop and up to his waiting mouth. Fire spreads from where our lips and tongues frantically meet in roaring, uncontrollable waves throughout my blood: a match set to dry kindling. As our bodies fall back onto the soft mattress, he throws one arm out to keep his heavy weight from crushing me.

"Fuck, Addy. I've been desperate to feel your pussy around my cock."

Ditto. Well, you know what I mean.

His lips aggressively attack my face, my neck, my breasts. His heavy cock pulses enticingly against my inner thigh. He bites my nipple so hard, I gasp, writhing in both exquisite pleasure and blissful pain. Holy hell...I knew he could deliver on his promise.

"Yes," I beg. "Please, Luke."

"Do you ache as much as I do?" he mutters against my naked and heated flesh, his sharp teeth nipping a blazing trail down my abdomen.

"More," I admit softly. He has no clue how long I've fantasized about this moment. Over ten long years.

In one quick motion, Luke pushes himself to his knees and freezes. His hazels are alight with desire and longing and we stay in suspension like this for several moments.

Then, in a completely unexpected move, he brings a finger to the middle of my forehead and lightly feathers it down the curve of my face, cascading the side of my throat. He watches his movements as he descends between the valley of my breasts, running along the underside of one before circling the outer ring of my areola, careful to avoid my beaded nipple. He does the same to the other before continuing his path downward.

He's slow.

Methodical.

I am completely enthralled in his reverent, purposeful exploration.

My eyes want to drift shut in ecstasy, but I don't let them. I can't look away. No one has ever done anything like this to me before, preferring to get to the main course immediately instead.

After a detour dipping into my belly button, he finally reaches my waxed mound. Goose bumps erupt all over when he begins to draw tiny circles. He moves slowly from one side to the other, coming close, although never breaching my slit. His attention stays glued to his thorough inspection.

I'm hardly breathing. My nipples tingle. My sex feels emptier than it ever has. I feel both exposed and embraced. This is an intimate moment, just like last week in Livia's kitchen, and I'm struggling to wrap my brain around *this* Luke. The real one he doesn't let many people see.

After what seems like hours, when he lifts his heavy gaze to mine, I fight to catch my breath and stop the sting I feel building behind my lids.

He looks awestruck.

"Addy," he breathes. My slowly drawn out,

softly spoken name is full of adoration that destroys me. "I have never met anyone like you. I want you. More than I've ever wanted another woman."

Oh God.

"Then take me. Please." Take me now so I can escape back to my room before I fall completely in love with this romantic, attentive Luke. *It's too late*, my inner self whispers. *It's too fucking late.*

As if cattle-prodded, Luke moves into action. Retrieving a strip of condoms from his nightstand, he tears one off, rips it open, and sheathes himself in record time. I try not to think about how much experience he has doing that.

Leaning his back against the headboard, he pulls me astride him, lining up his thick cock with my weeping opening. "This okay?" he asks. I swallow hard, nodding my head.

Stop it! I want to scream. Stop acting as if this means something more to you than conquering that girl who refused you months ago. I probably tarnished his perfect record and it's been a mocking blow to his ego ever since.

"I want to watch your pussy swallow my cock," he rasps thickly. He grasps my hips and lowers his eyes to where I hover. For the sake of my own sanity and keeping my heart in one piece, I push everything but the pleasure he's about to give my body to the back of my mind.

"Hands on my thighs," he commands.

I quickly move them back and balance myself, which opens my hips further, exposing me even more. I start to sink, when his grasp tightens, halting my movements.

"Slowly, fireball."

My eyes flick to his, which are still fastened intently on our groins. I watch his face as I lower myself inch by inch, ignoring the fire now burning my thighs in favor of the one now scorching my core and the one I see tightening his features in excruciating pleasure. Each low, agonizing curse that falls from his perfect mouth sets the blaze higher and hotter.

When he's fully seated, I hear him curse as my head falls back at the pure ecstasy I feel in the very center of my being.

My God, he's massive. He's thick.

He's perfect.

So damn perfect. *Too* perfect.

"Luke..." I gasp as I start rolling my hips slowly. My hands are behind me on his muscular legs for leverage. I can just imagine what I must look like with my breasts jutted out, my head thrown back, and my hips undulating in a slow cadence.

"So right," he grates. "Addy, you're fucking perfection."

His fingers dig into my hips, controlling my pace, controlling his depth. Controlling, period. In this position, *I* should be in control, but I'm not. Luke gave me that illusion, easily winning the reins back from me. Or I simply succumbed; I'm not sure which or that it even matters.

"You're a goddess. So fucking beautiful," he mumbles right before pulling me to his mouth, thrusting his tongue between my lips. His kiss is slow; it's deep and drugging. Dreamlike.

My world reduces to only the feel of his massive manhood sliding repeatedly over thousands of sensitive nerve endings. His pubic bone hits my clit in just the right spot with each unhurried thrust.

I'm lost in the clouds of euphoria as he slowly, skillfully brings our bodies to a fever pitch. It's painfully apparent he's wholly focused on me, my pleasure, my needs, wringing another climax from me before finally bringing us over the goal line together. We cry out in unison as we shatter, riding the waves and waves of pure bliss he's brilliantly crafted. For long seconds, our bodies quiver in tiny aftershocks.

"Addy..." he pants. "Christ."

I concur.

Quietly, I sag in utter satisfaction against Luke. My limbs are liquid, my breathing still ragged, my body covered in cool sweat. Strong arms band around me, one wound in my hair, one grazing lightly up my spine. He showers tiny kisses along my cheek, my throat, my shoulder. He holds me tight like he knows I might try to escape. He couldn't be more right.

Lying here, I realize I followed every roughly whispered command Luke gave me. I realize this is the single best sexual experience I've ever had. I am all too aware this felt like anything but a simple hookup with a random hot guy. Hell, this felt different from *anything* else I've ever experienced with *anyone*.

He made me feel cherished, and until this very moment I didn't even know I hadn't been before.

As I start the descent from my sexual high, the full force of what I just let myself do slaps me squarely in my stupid face. I'm scared as hell about the emotions flooding the girly parts of my brain.

There's a reason I haven't had sex in over eight months. I'm the typical female who can't separate sex from emotion. I get attached, and sleeping with Luke could have possibly been the stupidest mistake I've ever made since I already have feelings for him. *Strong* ones. Which is why it was so damn easy to give in to what just happened. I've been desperate for him for years, and trust me when I tell you, there's no way any sane woman would turn down Luke fucking Colloway. Or do I have that backward?

I want to slam my head against the closest wall. Despite Luke's gruffly whispered declaration as his lips lingered at my ear a few minutes ago, *"You're mine now, fireball,"* I know all I want will never be. Not with him. He's in love with another, even if she's not available. I've been the runner-up all my life. For once, I want to be the goddamned winner.

Good God...what the hell have I done?

Chapter 16

LUKE

It's three in the morning and I can't make myself fall asleep. The only woman I've imagined sliding my cock into for the last six months is wrapped in my arms, her naked body pressed tightly against mine. It feels as fucking perfect as it did months ago. More so, actually. But this time, my insomnia has nothing to do with the fact she almost drank herself to death and I had to make sure she didn't choke on her own vomit.

No...that's not it.

I'm fucking wrecked.

Her tight pussy strangled me.

Her heat burned me.

I can still feel her silky walls clenching around my cock when she screamed my name. *My* name. I want to climb on top of her, sink to the hilt, and pound into her hard so I can hear her hoarse cries again and again. I want to ride her raw. I've never not wrapped it up for a woman before, never not wanted to, but I'm fucking dying to bareback and feel each single ridge as I force her to take me slowly, millimeter by millimeter.

Watching myself disappear inside her tightness was hands down the most erotic experience of my life. And when she started moving? *Fuuuck. Me.* I had to take over or I would have shot my load like a randy teenager. That would have shot to shit my goal of bringing her more pleasure than she's ever known.

I never knew sex with a woman could be almost transcendent. *Silence, haters.* I guess that's how it is when you make love versus just fuck. I would guess that's the way it's supposed to be when it's with the *right* woman versus one who just opens her legs for anyone.

I feel myself falling for her. Hard. It's a surprisingly comforting feeling instead of one that makes me want to slit my wrists. *That's good, right?*

But as I lie here listening to Addy's even breathing and savor the heat from her body that seeps into mine, easing my inner turmoil and calming my soul, I have no idea how *she's* feeling. That scares the shit of out me more than anything. Hence my insomnia.

Unable to hold it in, I declared my intentions as our blood was still buzzing hard with dopamine. I made it clear she's mine, but she didn't respond and I'd be lying if I said my mood didn't plummet at her stubborn silence. At the very least, I expected an argument. I've no doubt that's coming later, in the light of day.

Case in point: When I could finally make my body obey my commands to move, I disposed of the condom and wet a washcloth for her, which

I've also never done for a woman before, I might add. When I came out of the bathroom, she was nearly out the damn door before I caught her around the waist, dragging her fine naked ass back to my bed, under her pathetic and fruitless protests. After cleaning her, I pulled her into me and haven't let go since. I fully expect her to rabbit on me—I also fully intend to roadblock her at each pass.

I have many scars on my soul. They're thick and ugly. They run deep. They've marred me for life. I thought they were impenetrable. Turns out I was wrong. For the first time since I was sixteen, I feel like I'm no longer bleeding out on the inside. Just being in the presence of this five-foot-eight-inch leggy beauty with a sassy mouth has staunched its constant flow. It's an unbelievably contented feeling to truly no longer feel alone.

But I don't have the girl quite yet, do I? I may have had her body, yet that's only a small part of what I want now. The rest will be far harder to pry from her tenacious grip.

I want *her*.

I want her heart, her soul, her mind, her obstinate will.

I want it all.

I want the Holy fucking Grail.

But I already see the signs. She'll fight this. She'll make it hard. She'll even deny her feelings. That's okay. I'm up to the challenge. I'm all in and I won't rest until she's mine.

You ever get the feeling that something's too

good to be true? I mean, if it's too good to be true, it probably is, right? I'm feeling that in spades right now. In fucking spades.

Being able to call this incredibly amazing woman snuggled into me *mine*? Winning her love? Is that too good to be true?

I fucking hope not, because I'm not going to give up until I have it. Until I have her. Every last shred of her. Then I will treasure each one, treasure *her* and the gift she's given me for the rest of my life, knowing I'll never deserve it, deserve *her*, but trying my damnedest to earn it each and every day anyway.

Chapter 17

Addy

I lazily blink my eyes open, taking in my surroundings. I'm in my room but not alone. Holding me tight like I'll disappear is Luke. I almost want to laugh; I don't, though, as I don't want to wake him.

I woke up around four a.m. and extricated myself stealthily from his arms, commencing the shortest walk of shame known to man. I counted the steps.

Twenty-five.

Twenty-five steps separate Luke's bed from mine.

Twenty-five short paces that can be covered in the span of a little over six seconds.

Yep...twenty-five. That's now become my most hated number because I'll never make that walk again.

As much as my entire being wanted to stay wrapped in everything Luke, I just couldn't wake up with him like we're some sort of couple or even lovers. That would have been too hard...*is* too hard. It was a one-night stand, it *has* to be and no matter how much I wish it were different, it's not.

Seeing him here, though, is even more confusing than last night was. I expected him to fuck me hard and fast, carrying his bruises like trophies for the next week. But he was unrushed and tender and attentive instead. Does he have a different view of last night than I did? Why did he pick my lock and crawl in bed with me after I'd purposely left? Did last night mean more to him than I originally thought?

Why does that conniving bitch, *hope*, have to constantly hover around the edges of my life, waiting for her chance to jump in and fuck me over once again? I've been in this position more times than I can count and there's no reason to think that this man will be any different from all his counterparts before him. In fact, he'll be far, far worse. I will never be the same after Luke Colloway, of that, I'm one hundred percent sure.

Riding the rails of hope is like being on a rollercoaster. The g-force is intoxicating for those few short seconds; then the ride is over and the rush is left behind on the ground far below. Each time you ride it, the thrill is short-lived, but damn it...you're addicted now and you want to do it over and over again just to get that heady feeling one more time.

Luke is hope. Luke is my rollercoaster. One I'll surely crash and burn on.

He has some sort of invisible hold on me, and I can't figure out why or find the damn elusive fishing line so I can cut myself free. This is heartbreak waiting to happen. It's inevitable. That familiar panic creeps back in and I suddenly feel suffocated under his weight. Taking a chance on waking him, I gently lift his arm and slide out from underneath, placing it back smoothly on his stomach.

I slowly scoot to the edge of the bed, grateful I put on a tank and some panties last night after I returned to my room. When I stand, I can't help but turn and ogle the human masterpiece tangled in my sheets.

The top sheet rides low on his hips, showcasing his elaborate markings and the splendid descending cut that makes my mouth water. I didn't get enough time to appreciate Luke last night, but *hot damn*...he's simply incomparable to anyone I've ever known. His body is unbelievably ripped, yet what makes him a work of art is, hands down, his ink.

Black and shaded grey tats adorn his arms, shoulders, and chest. Not a one of them is in color that I can see and I inanely wonder why. Does he see things in black and grey? Does he feel like he doesn't deserve even a splash of brightness? Am I being too philosophical? Somehow I don't think so. Not where Luke's concerned.

I stand stock-still, allowing myself to memorize his perfection.

His right shoulder has sunbeams peeking through cumulous clouds, which rain down on a crown that has the word *Faith* scripted underneath. Further down on his forearm is a dove in flight with an hourglass inset right above her, almost like she's carrying mother time on her back. The sands in the hourglass are impeccably detailed.

There are five pretty simple crosses in a beautiful abstract pattern on his right pec with a rosary woven in between them, the cross on the end of the prayer beads dangling lower than the others, making it an even six symbols. The sunbeams from the shoulder tat seem to illuminate the crosses. It's absolutely stunning. Farther down his torso, right over his ribs, are four various-sized seagulls in flight. At first glance, they seem like they're out of place with the rest of his art, but oddly, they aren't.

Moving my eyes to his left shoulder, I drink in the details of the strikingly beautiful mare with a hooded demon, or angel, riding her. I can't tell what she's supposed to be, although I do have my suspicions.

From this angle, I can't see the script, but last night, I couldn't help noticing he has writing in a foreign language going up the left side of his torso, from his hipbone right up to his armpit. I long to know what it says—it can't be anything but profound.

The thing that strikes me as most insightful, though, is the heart he has over his left pec. Over his very own. Tiny cracks run through the fragile, life-giving organ, which is wrapped tightly in thick chains. And if that doesn't say it all right there, I don't know what the hell does.

I want to inspect every inch of his body to see what else he's hiding. I already know there's not a spot on Luke that wasn't done without thought or meaning. Luke tries hard to close people out, only I don't think he understands how much he really tells the world through his adornments.

He's a walking billboard of pain and suffering.

I sigh softly, wondering how the hell I'm ever going to get this beautiful, complex, frustrating man out of my head or my heart. But I have to. I don't have a choice. I must or I'll end up with my own matching broken heart tattoo, except mine will be wrapped in barbed wire because it will perpetually bleed.

I'm turning to head to the bathroom when I realize Luke's opened his eyes and is watching me drool over his flawlessness. The smile he gifts me with when my eyes meet his is so utterly blinding, my knees buckle. I have to steady myself on my dresser.

In a casual move, his knee comes up, making the sheet fall to his groin, barely covering his impressive package. *God almighty.* Throwing a hand underneath his head, he rakes my barely clothed body, drawling lazily, "Morning, fireball."

His gravelly voice, sexy with the remnants of sleep, makes me want to abandon my plans with Madge, along with my clothes, and spend all day naked in bed with him instead. But that would only be getting myself in deeper. And I'm so fucking deep right now, I'm not sure how I'm going to get out.

And why does that asinine character name not

piss me off quite as much as it did last week? In fact, why does it now send shivers down my spine to my dark, now wet, thoroughly used girly parts?

His eyes break away from me to gaze around my room, and my cheeks sting with embarrassment. I'll admit it up front. I'm not the cleanliest of people. I'm not a total slob, but I'm no Nancy homemaker either.

I have a chair in the corner where I pile the clothes I peel off at night and I'll go through it once a week to sort what's dirty and clean. I have a couple of dresses hanging over my floor-length mirror and dirty socks on the carpet by my dresser. I have jewelry strewn all over my nightstand, along with a couple of glasses that need washing and a pile of books I keep hoping to get to, although I never do. If you walk into my bathroom right now, there are makeup and hair products all over the counter. Maybe even a towel or two on the floor.

"Looks like an EF-2 tornado struck your room," he quips. That damn corner of his mouth turns up and his eyes sparkle in amusement.

"You do realize that picking a lock is akin to breaking and entering, right?" I snap, irritated by the enjoyment he seems to get out of constantly mocking me.

"That's not a lock, babe. That's just a nuisance."

"Do you understand the concept of boundaries, Luke?"

If I thought my question would piss him off or

run him off, I should have known better. He lies there, like a goddamn king on his throne; his knowing, arresting grin widens. "I understand I need to do a better job fucking the obstinate out of you next time."

I gasp. This man has balls of steel and audacity big enough to overflow Wrigley Stadium. I spin, intent on escaping what is no doubt heading into another round of mind-melting sex. Despite how infuriating Luke is, it's excruciatingly hard to drag my eyes from him and how damn good— and *right*—he looks in my bed. But I manage. Barely.

I scarcely cross the threshold of the bathroom when I'm spun around and pinned to the closest wall. It's very déjà vu of not even ten hours ago and my sex readies herself to be completely owned again. She's clearly not on board with our decision to make this a one-night stand.

"Hit too close to home, did I?"

"Leave me alone."

"What are you doing, Addy?" His voice softens which makes mine harder.

"I think it's pretty obvious what I'm doing," I retort.

He surprises me by cupping my face and leaning down for a sweet kiss that curls my toes. His lips feel too good on mine. I need him to stop. I never want it to end. When he pulls away, he's looking so deeply into my eyes I feel like I'm unable to hide my thoughts fast enough.

"Yes, it is. I know exactly what you're doing, fireball."

See? I was right. "Is that so?"

"That's so. I've done it all my life."

I swallow hard, deflecting his insights. "Well, I'd hope so. You'd smell pretty rank otherwise."

He ignores my clever comeback, forging ahead into places I don't want to go. Places I can't even think about going with *him*. "I want you, Addy."

"You can scratch that off your to-do list," I murmur snidely, biting my lip. I can't let him know I want him to take me again and again, because once just wasn't enough. A million times couldn't possibly be enough.

Palms meet the wall on either side of my head and he leans even closer if that's possible. I expect another cocky grin; once again, he throws me off my game. The need I see in his eyes strips me bare, reminding me of last night when we were unmistakably *not* fucking, but making love.

"If we're talking about lists, you should know mine is so fucking long it will take us two lifetimes to scratch off every wicked and immoral thing I want to do to your body."

I'm speechless, my brain fighting between the images he's conjuring and trying to think of a witty comeback when his next words screech all thought to a grinding halt.

"But I want so much more than just your body, Addy."

I'm utterly confused. What else could a man like Luke possibly want from me other than a late-night booty call? "W—what do you want?"

He places his hand gently over my heart. "This."

Uninvited tears sting my eyes. A huge lump now sits in the middle of my throat and I swallow a couple of times to rid it. It's not budging. "You don't mean that," I finally croak.

"I've *never* meant anything more, fireball," he rasps. He searches my face, anxiously waiting for a reply.

I close my eyes and shake my head back and forth repeatedly, kicking myself for my lack of self-control last night. I've had a taste of something I can never have again and it would have been better to never sample the goods at all. Drawing in a deep breath, I blow it out slowly. "It can never work."

"I told you last night you were mine, Addy. Trust me, I don't say a damn thing I don't mean. Ever."

"Slipping your dick inside me does not make me yours," I snip. *Protect yourself at all costs, Addy.*

His eyes momentarily harden before turning molten again. His hands are back at my face. He surrounds me entirely, his thick desire for me pulsing into my lower belly. "Make no mistake, fireball. *No one* will lay a finger on you but me. You will only *ever* be mine."

"What if I don't want to be yours?" I breathe. I don't mean it. God, I *want* to be his. So badly, I can taste it.

He leans down until we're nose to nose, fiery eyes burning mine. "Liar."

"I can't be yours, Luke."

His lips lightly brush mine, feathering over my

jaw, melting my resistance into a puddle at his feet. His body heat warms me and his breath fights with mine. "Why, Addy? Why can't you be mine?"

I don't want to voice the words because it will make them real, and it's the only reason I'm holding myself back from him. It's the only reason I'm trying to pretend I don't feel a damn thing for him when even he can see it for the lie it is. "Because your heart belongs to someone else," I counter softly. "I've been down that road too many times before, Luke. I can't do it again. I can't be second."

He freezes, pulling back. Determination and passion have lit a fire deep inside him and it's blazing hotter than I've seen it yet, tightening every one of his facial features. "Regardless of what you think you know, you couldn't be more wrong. My heart became yours the very moment I set eyes on you, Addy."

He believes what he's saying. I know he does. But then I flick my gaze to his bare chest. To the heart that's clearly been locked away and is deliberately advertised as such. It might as well come with a flashing neon sign, *Want commitment? Move the fuck on.* I still feel the sharp pain that lanced through my own chest when I saw it, deflating the hope that was rapidly building, like a needle to a balloon. When my eyes lift, connecting with his again, he nods slightly, his mouth drawing into a thin line.

Yep, we're both on the same page now.

Dropping his hands, he takes a step back. Why

do I ache to have his skin back on mine? Why do I feel like the best thing to walk into my life is just about to walk out? *Because you're pushing him away, you dumb shit.*

"It's a fight you want then, fireball? Fine by me. It's a fight you'll get. But, know this. Nothing...and I mean. Not. A. Thing in my entire life has been worth fighting for more than you, Addy Monroe. Not. A. Fucking. Thing. You're my color."

On that note, he turns and exits the bathroom, softly closing the door behind him, leaving me to spin helplessly in my own thoughts and emotions.

"You're my color."

I'm not sure anyone else would know what those words mean, but they resonate deep inside me. Our pasts may be vastly different, but our present is exactly the same. People have hurt us and neither of us has been loved in the way we deserve, by the people we want. The difference between us is he plasters his hurts all over his body for the world to see while I've kept mine locked inside, hidden away.

"You're my color."

My legs give out at their implication and I slide to the floor. Those three simple, almost innocuous words punctured my already fluid defenses more than anything else he could have said or done.

I'd better prepare myself for the mother of all rollercoaster rides. That declaration may have pierced my defenses, but it's reinflated hope to the point where she's now almost bursting at the seams. I hear them ripping.

I now have two choices: stay away from any sharp, pointy objects for the foreseeable future, or stab *hope* myself so I don't allow Luke to deflate her for me.

I know which choice I *want* to make. I also know which is the right one, and that makes me ache with a deep sadness I know I've not experienced before.

Chapter 18

LUKE

She'll fight it. She'll make it hard. She'll even deny her feelings.

I called it. I fucking called it, didn't I?

When I woke up to an empty, cooling bed, I knew the fight had already begun. When her pain-filled eyes dropped to my tat, I knew the ante had just been upped.

I'm meticulous about my body art. Everything is with purpose, and I haven't regretted one drop of ink on my skin...until today. She thinks my guarded heart is about a girl, probably even thinks it's about Livia. That's the furthest fucking thing from the truth. It is, however, about the pain loved ones can cause and I regret the resigned look I saw as she tried to incorrectly decipher its meaning.

But this isn't about a tattoo. It's about convincing her I'm for real. That I'm in this for *her*. Making her mine is not about the chase or even winning for the sake of winning, although I love to win just like the next guy.

No...this is my fucking *future* we're talking about here.

My life.

My happiness.

My *color*.

I honestly never used to think about my future. There were no tomorrows, no dreams, no light at the end of my fucking suffocating tunnel. Hell, I wasn't sure I'd live to see another day when I closed my eyes at night. Those black days are gone, behind me, and while I may not be part of the underworld anymore, I still hadn't stopped looking too far ahead, mainly because that destination was a bleak and lonely place. For the first time ever, though, I'm looking at the future. Looking *forward* to the future. Greedily anticipating it with growing impatience.

And Addy's in it. Hell...she's *it*, period.

So I'll fight to the death to get her. I'll do anything and everything I can think of to make her believe I don't have feelings for anyone else but her. No matter what crap she tries to spew, I know she wants this too. Along with being a horrible slob, she's a terrible liar. She cares about me. More than she wants to admit. I see it plain as day.

What Addy doesn't understand yet is I play for keeps. Once I set my mind to something, nothing takes me off course. My path to destruction was powered by betrayal. My path to redemption ironically fueled by hate.

I've fought a lot of battles in my life. Some internal, some with real-life monsters.

Eventually, I won every single one of them, yet I intuitively know this thing with Addy is different. This is all-out war.

I think about the ink I ironically have scrolled in Latin on the left side of my torso: *Sed in bello confecto bello furit.* The battle may be won, but the war rages on.

I got that to remind myself that regardless of the battles I've won to this point, they came with a high price. *My soul.* My internal demons are still at war and they're a constant I fight. But my fireball has single-handedly calmed them, blinded them so they're shrinking in the shadows and I can finally breathe.

It hit me this morning, as I climbed into her bed and tugged her back into me, that all the battles I've fought up until this point have been to prepare me for the big one. The only one that really matters.

Getting the girl. *My* girl.

I want her. Hell, I *need* her. I intend to win this fucking war, win *her*, living the rest of my life in blessed peace with her by my side.

So settle in, fireball. You're in for one hell of a wild ride.

Chapter 19

Addy

Time got away from me. I don't know how long I sat on the bathroom floor before I pulled myself up and stumbled into the shower. I blindly went through the motions, functioning on autopilot.

Well...maybe not quite so blindly.

All I could think of while washing my hair was how Luke's fingers felt tightly wound around the long strands, positioning me so our mouths fit perfectly.

All I could remember when scrubbing my body was how his molten eyes singed me as they slowly traveled over each inch of me, his branding left behind.

All I could feel when my own hand dove between my legs and relieved the fevered ache that had built to unbearable proportions was Luke's mouth on my center when he had me pinned to the kitchen wall, writhing in unspeakable pleasure.

Once back in my room, I got waylaid for five

minutes when Cooper called. The conversation went something like this:

"Jesus Christ, Addy, I was seriously getting ready to call the fucking cops. I've been calling and texting you all goddamned night. Are you okay?"

Oh shit. Other than my fleeting guilt that I was about to fuck another man after being on a date with him, I didn't give Cooper a second thought, even though I vaguely recall my phone ringing repeatedly when Luke's fingers were inside me, working me to deliciously euphoric places.

"Ah, yes. I'm fine."

Silence.

Uncomfortable silence.

"Are you and he…?"

"Are we what?" God, Addy. Really?

"I didn't realize you were dating someone." Did I imagine it or did his voice just turn rock hard?

"I'm not dating anyone, Cooper," I sigh. True. A one-night stand does not equal dating.

"Then why was he there? He seemed pretty possessive for someone you're not dating."

"He's bipolar." I want to laugh at my joke because sometimes I wonder if it's true.

"How did he get in?" he hedges, still obviously trying to figure out what the hell is going on. Well, join the confusion club. It's swirling like fucking mad in here and I could use a friend.

"He, uh…sort of lives here."

"What do you mean, 'sort of'?"

"He's my roommate. It's a long story." One I don't even know myself.

"Okay." He draws out the word, making it more like a question. *"But you're not dating him?"*

"No." Why do I feel guilty when I say that?

"Well then can I ask you out again sometime?"

"Cooper—"

"No. Don't say no right away, Addy. I really like you and I had a great time last night. Just think about it and I'll call you sometime soon, okay?"

I'm quiet for a few beats before responding quietly. *"Okay."*

"You're sure everything is all right?"

No. Not by a long shot. *"Yes. Everything is fine."*

After I hang up, I stand there more confused than ever. Even though I repeatedly tell myself last night with Luke meant nothing, I was just sex-starved and Sin Personified himself propositioned me, I can't make myself believe it. Especially after what happened in the bathroom an hour ago.

Donning black yoga pants and a mint green pullover with my hair tugged haphazardly in a high ponytail, I finally pull myself together and rush out of my room. It's almost ten o'clock and by this time, I'm sure Mrs. Ruffalo will be minutes away from a stroke.

When I reach the end of the hallway, however, I freeze, almost toppling over at the abruptness of my faltering steps.

I'm not at all surprised to see Luke in the kitchen, acting all domestic and as comfortable as if he didn't just elbow his way into my home, my life, and my heart. While his sheer masculine beauty is enough to freeze every muscle I have—

except my inner ones—that's not what has me stopping in my tracks.

It's the fact that Madge, my eighty-five-year-old paranoid neighbor, is sitting on a stool at the kitchen counter with a steaming cup of coffee, chewing Luke's ear off like they're old friends.

Not once in the four years I've lived here has Madge set foot in my apartment...and it's not for lack of trying. I ask her every single time I take her out and she always politely refuses. She's somewhat of a recluse, actually, rarely leaving her dingy little apartment, except when I take her for an errand and an occasional weekday jaunt to the senior center to play scrabble. From the sounds of it, her kids don't even visit her all that often. It's sad how many of the elderly are forgotten, really.

I stand there like a party crasher, eavesdropping on their conversation. *Eavesdropping?* Hell...*I'm* not eavesdropping! I live here, dammit. If anyone's the interloper here, it's Luke, and now he's gone and stolen my date for the day.

Damn him.

"She sounds lovely, Madge."

Madge? Did he just call her *Madge*? I didn't even know Madge's first name for almost a whole year! I'm feeling irrationally jealous about the fact he's not only wormed his way into my life and my bed but now, he's stealing my little pet project, too.

Oh my God. A thought hits me like a ton of bricks as I stand here watching the laid-back interaction between the two of them. If Luke Colloway, the tatted, long-haired gorgeous man with the eyebrow piercing and perpetual scruff can charm the panties off my frail, skittish, little old neighbor, I don't stand a chance in hell against his sensual onslaught.

"I've only seen her once since she was born. If Milton were still alive, we'd see more of her, but I can't drive. Never even had my license, you know. It may sound old-fashioned to you, but in my day the men drove. Don't you be thinking that made me soft, though. I loved Milton, but that man couldn't find his way out of a paper sack if it were left wide open and there were flashing signs leading the way. He may have done the driving, but I did the bossing."

Luke laughs and the sound zings straight to my nipples, making them tingle. "I don't think a lot's changed between your time and now, Madge. Most women I know still have their man firmly by the balls, but I think most of them are okay with that if it's the right woman doin' the tuggin'."

My lungs seize as my mouth falls open. It's only in part due to what he said, as I'm not sure his saying "balls" in front of an old woman is appropriate. It's that he lifted his eyes to mine as he said it, and they are as full of fire and passion and steadfast resolve as they were an hour ago. It's so potent it almost knocks me on my ass.

I manage to unfreeze my feet and am charging my way across the living room when Madge swivels in her seat, facing me. "Oh, Addy, dear, you should have told me your boyfriend was moving in. He's an absolute treasure."

I stop between them, my brows drawn together in confusion. My eyes snap to Luke. "My boy—"

"Morning, beautiful," he interrupts. His smoky voice drips with want and potent hunger and even Madge would have to be stupid to miss it. And Madge may be old, but stupid she is not.

"Look, I don't know what he to—"

I'm suddenly cut off when I'm yanked into Luke's solid chest by the nape of my neck. His soft lips land on mine, pushing my protest back with his tongue. I'm momentarily stunned before my ovaries cheer wildly and I melt into him, blindly following where he leads.

He breaks the kiss and it takes my heavy lids a few seconds to catch up and open. When they do, my stomach free falls at the barefaced yearning swirling in his multifaceted speckled depths. I'm not sure how long we stand there lost in each other before Madge pipes up, breaking our thrall.

"Ah, young love. I remember when my Milton used to kiss me like he would die without his lips on mine. You two remind me so much of us at your age," she says wistfully.

I want to tell Madge we're not together, not in *that* sense of the word, but I don't. I want to deny that it's love I'm feeling, but I can't. And the satisfaction that I'm not refuting a word of what she says is written all over Luke's smug face. Bastard.

He leans down to my ear, grating, "You look

good enough to eat, fireball." My thighs clench, remembering it wasn't long ago he was doing just that. Then, pressing a lingering kiss to my temple, he drops his hold on me and walks back to the counter to grab his cup. With one hand tucked under the opposite armpit, he brings the steamy mug to his tilted lips and leans back casually like he didn't just ratchet my body temp up by five degrees.

"Your Luke is very handy, you know?"

Oh boy, do I ever. And why does it feel so good for her to call him mine?

"Is that so?" I ask, taking the cup of coffee Luke hands me, which I didn't realize he poured. I look down at the caramel liquid in my own mug to see it's just how I like it. When I taste it, it's simply divine. The best cup of coffee I've ever had.

My eyes lift to his. He smiles softly. I fall further under his enchanted spell.

"It's an organic Ethiopian blend," he offers.

"It's delicious. Better than Folger's," I mumble, before taking another decadent sip.

"Yeah, about that. I kinda threw that crap out. I figured since we'll be sharing a coffee pot, I'll buy the good stuff. If that's okay?" he adds quickly.

I cock a brow. "You're asking after you already threw it out?" Typical Luke move.

"It's better to beg forgiveness later than ask permission first, fireball."

That makes me genuinely laugh. "Yes, I'm figuring out that's your MO." Our gazes collide and hold. The sexual tension is palpable, the sizzle of it crackling on my skin.

"So, how long have you two been together?" Madge asks innocently.

"We aren't—"

"It's relatively new," he interrupts. He does that a *lot*. "But I knew when I first laid eyes on my Addy that she was the *only* one for me."

Oh.

"Luke," I whisper, barely audible.

"Addy, dear, did Luke tell you he fixed the locks on my door and my ceiling fan? That landlord is worthless. Your man has only been here a week and already he's fixed the light in the entryway and had the security system repaired. He even gave Elda's little Rachel a few tips on learning to ride her bike earlier this week."

I look back to Luke in utter shock and he actually looks a bit embarrassed. "No, he didn't tell me."

"Yes, he's very handy with a tool belt."

His embarrassment quickly morphs into cocky and I can't help but chuckle again.

"Yes, he certainly knows how to use his tools," I say, my face full of heat. At that, Luke full-on laughs and I swear I want to bottle the sound, so I can uncork it and listen to it anytime I want.

I shake my internal head at the way I'm acting. I need to get the hell out of here, before I do something really stupid, like feign sickness so Madge leaves and I can ask Luke to demonstrate his mechanical proficiencies on me. Again and again.

LUKE'S ABSOLUTION

I look at the clock and note it's now 10:20. I take one final drink of my delicious brew and set it down. "Luke, thanks for keeping Madge company. You ready to go?" I ask, looking at my sweet neighbor.

"Oh, I'm coming with you, fireball," he declares, setting down his own cup before closing the distance between us.

"Uh, that's not necessary, Luke. Madge and I have been managing for years on our own." Dammit, I need to get away from him, not spend the day doing "couple" things that will just draw me further into his sticky web. It's already clinging in too many places.

"It's already been decided. We need to stop by the hardware store and pick up a new sink stopper and a light switch for Madge's kitchen. The one she has keeps shorting out and is a fire hazard."

I stand mute.

As I watch him gently help Madge down from the stool, I start to realize Luke is a force to be reckoned with. One I won't be able to stop. I realize he means every heated word he spoke in the bathroom.

He intends to fight for me.

Standing close, my heart leaps when he leans down and whispers in my ear. "For the record, you look absolutely stunning when you blush."

Then he slips his hand in mine and pulls us toward the door like this is something we've done a hundred times over. I can't stop the feeling of completeness that rushes hotly through me.

With every new facet I learn about the mysterious Luke Colloway, I can't help the gnawing feeling in my very gut that I've finally found my someone.

Would it really be so bad to let go of my reservations and see where this sizzling chemistry between us leads? Can I possibly lay my heart on the line again when I'm absolutely certain no one would be able to destroy it like Luke? Should I give him a chance? *Us* a chance?

I don't know.

Everything inside me wants to, but I just don't know.

Chapter 20

LUKE

"Hi, Mom," I greet when she answers my call.

"Luke!" I hear the smile in her voice. It's contagious, my own lips turning up. "How are you, my sweet boy?"

There's rustling in the background and I wonder what my energetic mother is up to now. Probably in the kitchen making something for a church bake sale or the community center she volunteers at.

"I'm good, Mom. You sound busy."

"No, no, just baking some sweets to take to the community center, you know."

Bingo. God, I don't love anyone like I do my mother. She's an incredible, incredible lady and has been my strength to get through some very dark times, whether she knows it or not. I may have abandoned my family, but my mom never abandoned me. *Never*. No matter what I did or the vile things I said when I was a bratty teenager, she always forgave me. I've kept in touch with her regularly over the years, even though I didn't see her as much as I wanted. She epitomizes unconditional love.

"How's Chicago? Your business? Your brothers? Livia? Tell me everything."

I laugh at my mother's feistiness. Barb Colloway has a heart of pure twenty-four-carat gold, but she's not someone you want to cross or she'll come at you with both guns blazin' hot. God knows she put my brothers and me in our places more times than I can count over the years. She is the underlying machinery that keeps our family together. That one critical linchpin that, if lost, causes the whole damn thing to fall apart.

It hits me that Addy is a lot like my mom and my heart swells from the feelings I'm rapidly developing for her. Now, the reason I've been so drawn to her makes perfect sense. Addy's not only my color, she's my missing pin. I think about the intricate, interlocking gears I had her brother, Eric, tattoo on my back. I got them with my mom in mind, but it's applicable to Addy as well. Kinda strange how that works, just like the battle tat.

"I like it here. Better than I thought I would." Yeah, because the woman you're falling in love with is right within your grasp, living right under your nose. "Got a big contract signed last week with a local law firm and I'm so busy I've had to hire two more investigators."

"Fantastic! I'm so happy for you, Luke. You deserve success."

"Thanks, Mom."

"You find a church yet?"

LUKE'S ABSOLUTION

Our family grew up Catholic and we religiously attended church every weekend without fail. It may sound odd, but that's one of the things that's stuck with me all these years and it hasn't escaped my notice that my brothers did not follow in those footsteps our parents laid.

I fell away from the church for a period of time. Around twenty-one, I started going again as much as I could. I'm not a bible-thumping freak or anything, but especially when I worked for Peter, I almost never missed a week, sometimes going more than once a week. It was the only thing that kept me sane and grounded. It was the only thing that kept my faith strong that I would actually survive hell and come out the other side alive.

A faithful criminal. Could there be a more absurd oxymoron?

"Yeah, St. George's. Father Tim looks like he's ready to drop dead any day now, but he's a great guy."

"Next time I'm in town on a Sunday, we'll go together."

"Sounds like a plan."

"And your brothers? How are they?"

What my mom really wants to know is if we've mended fences. When I started getting tangled up with downright vicious sociopaths, the only thing I could do was exile myself from my family. I had to protect them from the vile people I had inadvertently brought into my own life until I could figure out how to get myself untangled. That took a hell of a lot longer than I thought or ever intended.

"Just had dinner a couple weeks ago with Gray, Ash, and the girls. Conn was on a business trip and couldn't make it. It was nice, actually. And Livia's doing well, although I'm sure you already know that, Mom. It's not like you don't talk to her or Gray probably two or three times a week."

"Just worried about my grandbabies, you know." My mom. Always worried about something or someone. "Did you hear that Alyse and Asher have finally picked a destination for the wedding?"

"We talked about that a bit at dinner. Sounds fun."

They picked some super fancy resort in the Caribbean. As surprising as it is, this will be my first trip out of the country and I'm really looking forward to it. I only hope by then Addy and I will be there as a couple instead of just as guests since I know she's also invited. She's become very close with Alyse these past few months.

"Are you okay with flying, Mom?" My mom's not terrified of flying; she doesn't like being stuck "in a flying tin can," especially over a body of water.

"Don't worry about me, Luke. Nothing a nice prescription won't cure. So, are you coming home for Easter?"

"Shit. When is that again?"

"Luke, language and it's in three weeks"

"Sorry, Mom. Wouldn't miss it," I reply contritely. All of us brothers have a little bit of trucker in us, but I seem to have gotten the mother lode. When we're all together, it tends to get worse, though we try to tamp it down for her sake. "Everyone else coming too?"

"Yes, yes. I know for sure Gray and Asher are coming on the Friday before because we're having Livia's baby shower the Saturday afternoon before Easter. Not sure what Conn's plans are."

Huh. Baby shower. My wheels are already turning. I'm quite sure Addy plans on being in attendance as she's Livia's best friend. I'm busy plotting and taking a drink of coffee when suddenly it's being spewed all over my desk by her next statement. "Why don't you invite that fiery girl of yours to Easter dinner?"

"Fiery girl?" I cough, grabbing a napkin to wipe up the mess I just made.

"Yes, that pretty little thing from the wedding. What was her name again?"

"What pretty little thing from the wedding?" I am mortified. I think back to when I cornered Addy at the bar and pray that my mom didn't see that little display of pure male aggression. At the time, I didn't give two shits who saw me. *Now*, I care. A helluva lot, if it was my mother.

"Luke, I don't know what it is about you boys that makes you think I don't have an eye in my head or two functioning brain cells to rub together. I see far more than you think. I see far more than even *you* see sometimes."

"I—"

I'm stunned silent when she practically screeches in my ear. "Addy! That's her name.

Addy. She's going to be here for the shower anyway so you might as well invite her to stay for Easter. Yes, she was quite smitten with you."

Smitten? "Christ, Mom," I chide, trying to suppress a laugh.

"Luke. Anyway, we'll have plenty of food. I'm sure Alyse and Livia would love to have her stay, too."

"What makes you think she's mine?" I ask softly. If I didn't know how devout a Catholic she was, I'd swear sometimes my mom is a fortune-telling witch with a crystal ball.

When I found out Addy has been taking Madge and a couple of other elderly people who live in our building on errands every few weeks for the last three years, I couldn't help but feel proud of her. She's independent, messy, obstinate, and by the charred smell in the apartment on Thursday night when I got home, can't cook worth a damn. She's also selfless and kindhearted and has a soul that shines even brighter than her outer shell. With each day that passes, I want her more.

In true Addy fashion, she's been trying to avoid me. I must admit I've been working some long hours myself. I miss her like hell. It's been a week and a half since I've touched her or been inside of her and I don't know how much longer I can wait to feel her again, to claim her again, to remind her she's going to be mine. She might as well save us both a helluva lot of trouble and just acquiesce now.

"It couldn't be clearer she's the fire to your ice, my dear. If she's not yours yet, you need work harder."

At that bold statement, I do laugh...and confess. "I'm working on it, Mom."

"I'm glad to hear it. Should I plan on her then?"

"Probably only if she's bound and gagged," I mumble. Jesus Christ, the thought of binding her to my bed so I can have my wicked way with her has my cock hardening in world record time. I wouldn't ever gag her, though. I love her smart mouth way too much to fill it with anything but my cock.

"What you do in the privacy of your own bedroom is your business, Luke. I don't need to hear about it."

"Mom, really. Stop. It was just a joke." But now that I've thought it, there's no way I'll be able to get the vision out of my head until I have it checked off the list. A list that grows longer every fucking day.

We talk for another ten minutes about inane things like Mom's volunteering, her run-in with a new staff member at the senior center over lemon bars (I know...are you as confused as I am about that?), and the neighbor's crazy-ass fifty-year-old son who she saw shoving the garden hose up his father's car tailpipe before turning the water on full blast.

Before hanging up, I ask my mom one final question. "Hey, Mom, do you know what a Louboutin is?"

Chapter 21

Addy

I stare at the calendar, the days blurring together. I shake my head, focus my eyes, and try again. The lines morph into one big blob. It's no use. I've been trying to get the kids' summer fun program schedule done for an hour now, a menial task that should have taken me all of fifteen minutes and it should have been done Monday. Now, it's Wednesday and I still can't manage to finish it.

Apparently, my brain has been hijacked as well as my libido. Or maybe my brain's been hijacked *by* my libido. In either case, I'm utterly useless today, as I have been since the carefree day I spent with Luke and Madge a week ago last Sunday. Tootling around town with Luke felt comfortable. He was fun and funny and lighthearted. And the way he fawned over Madge as if she was his precious grandmother almost brought tears to my eyes a couple of times.

The gift he talked Madge into getting her great-granddaughter, Kaelyn, almost did me in.

She was insistent on a stuffed turtle, but Luke talked her into an easel and watercolor set, complete with a paintbrush and little plastic apron. He convinced her not only will it help her learn her colors, it will develop the creative side of her brain as well. When she was worried about the paint getting everywhere, he pointed out that it was nonstaining, meant just for kids. How a thirty-year-old man with no kids would know that blew my mind.

As I stood back and observed him "selling" her on the paints, I half wondered if he was doing to it get into my good graces—and my pants again—but I quickly dismissed that idea. He was passionate about his rationale, talking about cause and effect and learning the arts at an early age instead of getting their noses stuck in a computer screen.

The depth I see underneath the rough exterior he uses to keep people out is thoroughly enthralling...and endearing. It's sexy as hell.

Darcy, my kids' activity coordinator, pops her head in my office. "Addy, hey class is about ready to start."

Wow. Is it seven already? I look at the clock and sure enough it is. Not only have I not finished half of what I needed to do today, I didn't eat dinner either. Sighing heavily, I stand and follow her into the studio, wishing I could get my head in the game and off the man I shouldn't want.

We have two main areas in my studio: One is for general painting and crafting, where I keep all the pottery and glass materials. Here, the walk-ins can sit at spacious tables, creating their one-of-a-kind works of art. The other area is where we teach classes. In one corner, I have a smaller table and chairs for the kids' classes and in the other, we have easels and seating for the adult classes.

Tonight we're hosting a one-hour session for kids to make their mothers a plate for Mother's Day, which is coming up in a few weeks. This session was so popular it's the first of three we have planned over the next three weeks.

We have a dozen kids here ranging from five to twelve. I've set out some light snacks and drinks in the main area for the dads or older siblings who will wait patiently for the hour to pass.

After getting the young ones settled with their supplies in front of them, I try to rein in chaos. It's like corralling wild animals. Or water. "Okay, everyone, you ready to hear what we're going to make for your special moms today?"

"Yah!" a dozen loud voices cheer at once and I smile broadly. God, I love my job. I pull out my example that Darcy made last week and hold it up. It's three simple flowers made by dipping a hand in paint and pressing it to the plate. Add a few stems and petals, and viola...a personalized flower garden for Mom.

"You have several plates of color in front of you. We're going to do a little finger painting today." After I explain how they're going to make their art, Darcy and I set about helping the younger ones dip their hands just right so they don't drip paint all over their plates. Not ten minutes into class, I feel the air electrify and all chatter virtually stop.

I follow the stares of even the youngest female in the room, five-year-old Jessica, and my breath catches. Sin Himself just walked into my studio and is watching me with a raw hunger that's tangible, and every other female senses it. Even Jessica.

Suddenly, I realize *that's* what I've been missing and I feel calm for the first time in days, my anxiety simply melting away like snow in the hot sun. Mother of God, I am so lost in him and the last of my reserves is waning fast.

"By all that's holy, who the hell is that?" Darcy whispers in awe.

"Trouble," I whisper back.

"Well, shit. He's trouble I'd invite into my bed every day of the week," she replies huskily.

I couldn't agree more. *So why aren't you?*

Not responding, I leave the table and close the short distance between us, not realizing he's holding a paper bag until I'm standing in front of him. The black beanie he has on his head makes him seem both younger and rougher at the same time. *Damn, he looks good.* I want to kiss him so badly my lips throb.

"What are you doing here, Luke?" I ask. I didn't even know he knew what I did let alone where I worked. I'm floored he's here. And impressed. *Very* impressed. In all the time I've had this place open, no man has ever stopped by to see me. Including Aiden.

"Thought I would bring you dinner, but I see you're busy." He nods toward the table, his heated eyes never leaving mine.

I look back at the kids, who have now lost interest in us and turned their attentions back to painting. Darcy is clearly torn between helping the little ones and spying on us.

"That's...wow. Thank you," I stutter, completely baffled.

Snaking an arm around my waist, he pulls me close, telling me quietly, "I've missed you, fireball."

Why do I have an almost irrepressible urge to respond in kind? Why can't I stop thinking about the fact I don't feel empty anymore when he's near? Why do I keep denying what's going on between us has gone far beyond physical? Why can't I just give in?

After pressing a soft kiss to my temple, his hold on me drops. I feel the loss of his warmth acutely.

"Have a place you can put this?" he asks, holding the brown sack between us. "It needs refrigeration if you can't eat it right away."

"Uh, sure," I say, taking the bag from him. It feels heavy. "What is it?" Unable to curtail my curiosity, I start opening it and notice a familiar Tupperware soup bowl inside. Familiar because it's from *my* cupboard.

"Asian lentil and kale soup. Homemade. I threw in a piece of French baguette and some butter, too."

"Homemade? As in...*you* made it?" He made soup? For *me*?

In the back of my mind, I've always known I dated the wrong kinds of men. Men who don't do shit for me. Not once in my dating history has a man done something as simple as make me a meal or have a steaming cup of coffee waiting for me every morning or written a sweet note to have a great day. Luke has done the latter two every day since last Sunday.

Every.

Single.

Day.

He smirks. "Don't look so surprised, fireball. I could give Emeril a run for his money."

Somehow, I don't doubt that. He could give most guys a run for their money. I have to stifle the sting in my eyes, biting my lower lip hard enough I'll probably leave teeth imprints.

"It drives me fucking crazy when you do that. I want these between my teeth," he rasps, tugging my lip free. His hooded eyes watch his thumb drag across its fullness and the low rumble I hear in his throat races like lightening through my blood straight to my clit.

My eyes feel heavy. Air is suddenly scarce.

My whole body throbs with want. I have to force my brain to tell my feet to take a big giant step back before I do something incredibly stupid like drag him back to my office and beg him to fuck me over my desk. I am keenly aware of our surroundings, but this second I couldn't care less I have a business full of people. Every cell in my body is begging to be joined with him again.

Right. This. Very. Minute.

My feet finally get the message and I step away from his touch, silently grieving its loss. A knowing smile ghosts across his lips when I clear my throat. "Well, thanks for this. I, uh, I guess I'll see you later then?"

"Sure."

I turn and walk toward the back, slowly at first, then picking up the pace as I feel his gaze burning a hole in my back. I don't even look at Darcy when I pass her. I can't. Once I reach my office, I shut the door, lean against it, and close my eyes, taking several deep calming breaths.

I don't know how long I stand there, trying to regain my composure, but I know it's too long. Darcy is handling a bunch of adrenaline-amped kids by herself while I'm fantasizing what it would be like to be taken rough and fast where I stand. After placing the soup in the compact fridge tucked under my desk, I head back into the fray, stopping short when I enter the room.

There, on his haunches helping a shy boy who looks to be about seven, is Luke. He's removed his black leather jacket and is wearing a navy-blue V-neck tee with white stitching around the edging. My mouth waters as I watch his decorated biceps flex and bulge with each movement. My eyes slide downward, appreciating the muscular thighs underneath his taut jeans.

I shift my gaze to Darcy and smile. She obviously doesn't realize I'm standing here because she's snared in Luke's magical spell, too.

It's virtually impossible not to get sucked into his sensual vortex.

Luke is a very intimidating man and not just because he's tall, broad, and imposing with his ink and piercings. He has this certain...*ambience* about him that's authoritative and dominant. Omnipotent almost. But when you start stripping away his layers upon layers of complexities, underneath he's just a man with vulnerabilities like the rest of us mere mortals.

As I watch how gently he interacts with this shy boy, pulling him slowly out of his shell, I swallow hard, knowing the battle lines are getting blurred and that I won't be able to reinforce my walls much longer against his constant assault.

I'm going to cave. It's no longer a matter of if, but when.

CHAPTER 22

LUKE

"Hey man, how you been?" I haven't talked to Eric since that night back in October when he called telling me Livia was in a bad way after her blowup with Gray. Addy, who was at her wits' end with no idea what to do, knew Livia needed me. She had no way to get ahold of me, so she called her brother, who knew how to get in touch.

I'll never forget how pale and fragile and lost Livia looked when I walked into her bedroom. I immediately knew what had happened. At that moment, I wanted to kill Gray for hurting her so deep, but I also wanted to spill the entire horror story so he knew what hell the woman he was in love with had endured. I'm glad she came to her senses and did it herself. Gray needed to hear it from her, not me.

"LC, haven't heard from you in a while. Same old, same old, man. You?"

"Pretty much the same. Moved my PI biz to Chicago a couple months ago."

"Your brothers are there, right?"

"Yep." And your sister, who I'm going to marry someday, like it or not.

This is the thing about Eric. He's highly protective of his family. Always has been. When he first hooked me up with Addy so Livia would have a place to live, he made it crystal clear she was off limits, even though she was a grown-ass adult. So unless Addy has said something to him—and I know she hasn't or he would've called to chew me a new asshole or shown up with a shotgun by now—he has no idea I'm now her new roomie. I want him to hear it from me first, and not over the phone, so my call is twofold.

"You talking to them now?"

"Yeah."

"Glad to hear it." I know Eric means it. He's a genuine family man. Despite the fact his background is similar to mine, he never cut ties with his like I did. But we've both pulled our shit together and are in far better places than just a few years ago.

"Say, I'm gonna be in town in a couple weeks for Easter. I'd like you to draw up some new ink for me so I can take a look at it. Then we can schedule some time to get it done."

Eric is an incredible artist and co-owner of a highly successful tattoo shop in Detroit called Inked On. He's created and inked all my tats except for the dove and hourglass I have on my right forearm. I got that done when I was living in hell on earth in Boston, so I'd have a constant reminder of why the fuck I voluntarily stayed.

In Egyptian times, the dove was a symbol of innocence. That represented Livia. The hourglass reminded me to have patience in my task to free her and do it right so neither of us would end up dead in the process.

I spend the next few minutes describing what I want in detail. "You think you can do it?"

He laughs darkly. "Who the fuck you think you're talking to, LC? I make gold out of shit."

"I'll start saving up, then. Do you make them into bars, too?"

"Fuck you."

"Hard pass."

I hear Addy stick her key in the lock and try to turn it. She shakes the handle, rattling the door when it won't budge.

"Say, gotta run. I'll hook up with you Easter weekend."

"Looking forward to it."

I rise from the couch and jog across the room. When I swing the door open she looks startled.

"Oh, sorry. My key wouldn't work for some reason," she says, sliding past me. I don't budge an inch, forcing her body to brush against mine. I almost sigh in blessed relief.

Don't say it. I'm pathetic. I'm pussy whipped. She already has my manhood securely harnessed in a cock cage. All true.

Ask me if I care.

"I changed the locks today. New keys are on the counter for you."

She turns toward me after setting her purse down along with her jacket. "Why?"

Today she's wearing a greyish-green short-sleeve shirt that says *Rain Rain Go Away*, along with painted on tan skinny jeans and bright green chucks. Her dark hair is in loose waves around her barely made-up face. She looks fucking amazing.

"Why what?" I ask, walking back to the couch, discreetly adjusting my hard-on. I sink down in the corner, spreading my legs wide, throwing my arm over the back. I watch her eyes lazily travel down my seated form and fuck I want to give in to the cocky smile begging to be set free, but I don't dare or I'll stoke her ever-present smoldering embers into a raging fire. And right now, I'd just as soon have a nice conversation than an all-out battle of wills.

"Why did you change the locks?" She leans that fine ass against one of the island stools. I wish she were sitting by me instead. Okay, *on* me.

"A blind five-year-old could pick the ones you had. They were unsafe."

She regards me for a few seconds, a small smile on her lips. "Lucky for me there are no blind five-year-olds who live in this building then, I guess."

"I guess." I can't help but return her infectious smile. Holy Mother Mary, she's magnificent. *Down boy. Down.*

"Don't you have a gun?"

Her question surprises me. I do have a gun, my trusty SIG Pro 2022. After the life I've led, I'm very comfortable using one, although I can say

I've never killed anyone with it (come on, you know you were wondering). I'd rather never see one again. Unfortunately, sometimes my job is dangerous, particularly the bounty hunting part, so I'm forced to have it. I only carry it when necessary, though. I also know for damn sure I've never left it lying around the apartment.

"Snooping, are we?"

She looks a little sheepish. "No. I just...I saw it on your dresser one day when I walked by your room."

I have nothing to hide from her. Hell, I want her to know everything she's getting into with me. That's why I always keep my door open, unlike Addy, who has her private space locked down so tight you'd think it contained codes to the country's nuclear warheads. Not that it's kept me out. That's one fucking lock I am *not* replacing.

"Does that make you uncomfortable?" Christ, I hope not. I'll never stand a chance with her.

"No. I—not at all. I feel safer, actually," she mutters, looking down.

"Really?" I hear the hope in my voice. I'm sure she doesn't miss it either.

Her eyes lift to mine. "Really," she replies softly.

The air becomes thick, pulsing with desire. Somehow I don't think she's talking about the firearm anymore.

I took Addy dinner on Wednesday. Today is Friday. While things haven't been as tense as they were and we've even come to some sort of weird truce, she's far from letting her guard down completely. Despite what my mom thinks, I'm working my ass off to obliterate it to dust so she'll let me in.

It's now been almost two fucking weeks since my cock has been denied entry into his rightful home and he's getting antsy. I can't tell you how badly I want to pounce on her, pinning her to the counter so I can fuck her into conceding to this insane attraction that's arching hot between us.

But as much as I want her to be, she's not ready and the next time I have her, there will be no fucking dancing around what we're doing. I won't give her up and I sure as hell won't let her walk away from me again. I realize I sound very caveman. Trust me, I feel like it too.

So instead, I clear my throat and ask, "Did you eat?"

"A protein bar."

My eyes flick to the round clock on the kitchen wall that looks like a sunflower. It's hideous, but that's beside the point. It's almost ten p.m. and she's just arriving home from work. I've already noticed Addy doesn't take very good care of herself. She doesn't eat well, she doesn't exercise—*not that she needs it, mind you*—and it hasn't escaped my notice she usually doesn't sleep through the night either. I hear her padding around on the wood floor frequently.

I stand and walk past her to the fridge, pulling out the leftover chicken fettuccine Alfredo I made earlier. Funny...I haven't really wanted to cook once in the past couple of years, yet after registering her emotional reaction when I brought her something as simple as soup on Wednesday night, I find myself wanting to cook for her again. For my entire life, even.

I dish some on a plate and stick it in the microwave, setting the timer for a minute thirty seconds.

"What's that?"

"Your dinner."

"I already had dinner."

"A protein bar does not constitute dinner, fireball." I can't help but notice she's not yelled at me about my pet name for her since the night of dinner at Gray's. I have to suppress a smile.

"I can't eat something that rich this late. I'll get fat," she protests.

I take a few steps until I'm standing in front of her. "First, you're fucking perfect and a few bites of pasta won't change that. Second, you don't eat well and I intend to fix that. Maybe if you ate better, you'd sleep better."

She looks surprised at my observation, although I don't know why she should be. I told her I would fight for her. How does she think I'm not going to pay attention to everything she does? Some days I feel like a goddamned stalker I'm so attuned to her.

The room grows silent except for the humming of the microwave warming her food.

"You did this with Livia."

She doesn't have to elaborate on what she means. I nod, remembering when I tried to get Livia to eat chicken noodle soup, which she promptly threw up because she was pregnant even though I didn't know it yet. It took me all of twenty-four hours after she came home from the hospital to figure that out. "Yes."

I don't know what I expect her to say, but it's not what she does. "Because you care about her."

Fuck it. It's time to address the pink polka-dotted elephant that's sucking the life, along with my chances, right out of the room. "This doesn't have anything to do with Livia, Addy. It has to do with my concern about *your* well-being. Since you brought her up, though, ask me what you *really* want to know."

The ding sounds indicating her food is hot. Neither of us moves for so long I don't think she's going to say another word...but she does.

"Do you love her?"

She doesn't fuck around. I love that about her. I *love* everything about her. I'm pretty fucking sure I'm in love with all of her, pigheadedness included.

"Livia and I share a unique history, Addy. It's complicated."

She doesn't blink. "You didn't answer the question."

"Who hurt you, fireball?"

"Who didn't?" she retorts flatly. My soul aches for her. For us. I don't want to be lumped into the category with every other man who's come before me, even though I should probably lead the pack. God knows I have no idea what the hell I'm doing. Pure instinct is driving me here.

"Do you love her?" she asks again.

I frame her beautiful, petite face with my mammoth hands. "You're like a dog with a bone."

"Says the Rottweiler."

I smile briefly. She's got my number. "I'm not in love with my brother's wife if that's what you're asking," I tell her adamantly. Not anymore.

"But you were."

Yes, I was in love with Livia. But I now understand that loving her brought me to the woman I'm supposed to spend my life with, so I will not regret it and I sure as fuck will not apologize for it. Sighing loudly, I say, "Addy, we all have a past. Don't hold mine against me. Please."

Her face falls and her eyes drop.

"Addy, look at me," I coax softly. "Please, baby." Watery eyes meet mine, and it couldn't hurt worse than if I'd been shot. And that hurts like a motherfucker, let me tell you. "I care about Livia. I always will. We went through something horrific together, something I know you think you want to know about. Trust me, you don't. And to protect everyone, including you, that's all I can say. But I meant every damn word I said in the bathroom. You've had me wound up with that clever tongue of yours for months. *You* are the only woman who has my heart. *You* are the only woman I want, Addy Monroe. There's no room inside me for anyone else but you. *Just you.*"

I lean down slowly, giving her a chance to protest. She doesn't. I hear the quickening of her breath, matching mine. "You're my color, fireball," I whisper against her mouth before I take it in a soft, slow kiss. My God, it's like nirvana to have my mouth on hers again. She's hesitant at first, but only momentarily before relaxing easily into me. My cock leaps, thinking he's getting in on the action. Fuck...he's not. Not tonight.

I keep my caresses intentionally light, tenderly worshipping her. I gently clamp her plump bottom lip between my teeth and suck. I live in her quiet moans I know she doesn't want me to hear. The heat of the palms she's now resting against my waist easily penetrates my thin tee, scorching me.

After a minute, I force my mouth from hers. I need her to burn white hot for me like I do for her. She's getting close, but she's not quite there yet.

"I'm not giving up until you acknowledge you're mine," I husk, pecking her mouth one more time.

"I'm not some prize for winning first place, Luke."

I pull back and stare deeply into her eyes. She looks scared and confused. I choose my words carefully, sensing she's balancing precariously on a wire and one stiff breeze will push her over. If I'm not careful, she'll be lost to me forever. "You couldn't be more wrong, Addy. You? Your love? They're the ultimate prize no man walking this earth deserves, especially me. But I want it all anyway and I'll work every single day to earn it."

K. L. KREIG

Her misty eyes, which look greener today, bounce back and forth between mine, seeking something. She must find it. I don't realize I'm holding my breath until I see the corner of her mouth turn and her mossy pools glimmer with...sheer happiness.

"Are you always so direct?"

"I see no reason to dance." I scoop up her hair and push it over her shoulders so it's cascading down her back like a waterfall. What I wouldn't give to grab a handful, directing her every move as she sucks my aching cock.

Her smile spreads. I have a feeling she knows exactly where my mind has gone. "So you don't like to dance then?"

She's not talking about the waltz here, which, for the record I used to know how to do once upon a time. My mom made all us boys take dance lessons when we were younger. She wanted "well-rounded" young men. You can imagine how that went over with a bunch of eleven- and twelve-year-olds. Our dance teacher pretty much banned us from returning after the first season—something about scaring the girls, blah, blah, blah.

Ah...good times.

"Not when my entire future is on the line, no."

"Luke..." she mumbles softly. She shakes her head and I can tell she doesn't know what to make of me right now. Hell, I don't know what to make of me either.

The semi I constantly sport these days starts to stiffen with the husky way she said my name and the doe eyes she's giving me right now. If I wanted to press the issue, no doubt I could have her underneath me in fifteen seconds flat. So instead, I take a step back.

"Is the air clear now?" I ask roughly.

She nods.

"Good. Now, how about that dinner?"

"Okay." She adds her qualifier quickly, making me chuckle. "But only because I'm hungry. Not because you're making me."

"Of course not. I'm pretty sure the only place I could make you do anything is in the bedroom. Only you'll try to fight me there, too, because you don't know how much pleasure I can bring you when you let me be in charge. Don't worry, though...I can already see you're a fast learner, fireball. You'll catch on pretty quick." I wink and her cheeks flush.

Did I tell you how much I really love the color pink?

I reheat the pasta for a few seconds and set it down in front of her, observing as she enthusiastically digs in. I've never enjoyed watching someone eat before, so what does that say about me? I'm a fucking goner for this woman, that's what.

"This is fantastic, Luke. Homemade?"

I nod. "Thanks."

The shy smile she gifts me tugs profoundly on my heart strings. I've known my feelings for Addy have been escalating at the speed of sound and I daresay before today I thought I was in love with her. Right now, the feelings of contentment and rightness and peace that race swiftly through my blood leave not one shred of doubt: I am unequivocally in love with Addy Monroe.

My color.

My fire.

My pin.

My future.

When I'm with her, things just make sense and I don't feel quite so soiled. Is it possible Addy could actually cleanse my soul? It feels a little less black each time I'm with her, so maybe. I just have to be sure that blackness doesn't rub off on her. If it does, although it would hurt like a mother, I'd let her go.

"You have plans tomorrow night?" I ask, knowing it's time to up my game to the next level. She's ready.

"No," she responds around a mouthful of creamy goodness.

"Good. Don't make any."

She hesitates. "Okay."

We stare at each other for a few seconds—not in challenge, unlike most of our interactions lately. This time, it's something entirely different. It's finally acknowledgment of what's been completely out of either of our controls since our eyes first connected months ago.

I think I have some new prayers to add to my list this week. For once, I'm going to be selfish and ask God for something other than absolution, because let's face it, sometimes that's the most selfish thing us sinners can ask for when we've committed an unforgivable wrong. Which I have.

This week I'll pray that if there's a speck of anything deep inside me that even remotely deserves a woman like Addy, it will shine through the darkness so she can see its glimmer.

This week and every week from here on out, I'll selfishly ask for *her*.

Yep. Complete and total goner.

Chapter 23

Addy

"Hmm, I wonder what could have caused that giddy, goofy schoolgirl look on your face?" Alyse jibes, a shit-eating grin on her own.

"I have no idea what you're talking about, Alyse." I turn my attention back to the double stroller Livia has on her registry. Seven hundred dollars for a buggy with four wheels and two seats? Good grief. The baby market is a damn racket.

"Oh, I think you do," Kam pipes up with a smile that matches Alyse's. "How's that new hunky roommate?"

Wow. That's a fully loaded question. *How much time do you have?*

"I wouldn't know. I don't see much of him. Our schedules don't really mesh." I intentionally keep my gaze down so my friends can't see right through the lies I'm trying to feed them. I'm utterly transparent when it comes to lying. Like tissue paper. Or Saran Wrap.

"Mmm hmm." Alyse doesn't believe me, but I

don't care. "Say, Asher has a business dinner tonight so I was thinking that maybe we could make a girls' night out. It's been a while since I could join."

Ruh-roh. "Uh...sorry, I can't. I have plans."

Wow, have you ever really noticed how tiny newborn socks are? I mean, they're like two inches long. And how long can they really wear them before they outgrow them? One or two times? So this little two-pack of Ralph Lauren socks for twelve dollars means it will cost like two bucks per wear. That's insanely stupid. They're socks.

I realize it's silent and look up to see Alyse and Kam exchange knowing glances. "Well change them," Kam insists. "Or do you have a hot date?"

Why yes. Yes, I do. *I think.* He didn't say so, but this feels very much like a date. A scorching one.

I put on my best Judas face, intent on not giving away the fact I'm going to be spending the evening tonight with my sinfully sexy roommate. "If you mean with a bunch of paperwork so I can get ready for my tax appointment on Monday, then yes, it will be downright steamy."

Kam studies me for long seconds. So long, I'm starting to squirm and my pits are sweating. I feel like I'm in an interrogation, eyes squinting under the bright lights meant to intimidate. This is stupid. I'm a grown adult, for Christ's sake. I'm just getting ready to tell her to stick it when she starts laughing. "Taxes, Addy? Really? That's the best you can come up with?"

Kam and I have been friends since college. She

knows me better than almost anyone, besides Livia and my brother.

"Just admit you're banging your new playmate so we can all sit around and gossip about how big his dick is. I, for one, really want to know if it's as impressive as it looks behind a pair of tight denims."

"Jesus, Kam! You're ogling his package?" I squeal. *Do I sound possessive?* I have no right to feel that way, but damn if the fact that my friend is checking out Luke's junk doesn't piss me the hell off.

"Can you blame me? Hell, if you're not doing him, hand him over. I'd be happy to take him for a ride or two."

Jealousy fogs over my vision. Kam is stunning, successful, and rich. A catch for any man, although I know exactly what she's doing. She's goading me into giving up the goods. Still, it doesn't stop me from visualizing her and Luke together anyway, even though he's not shown one ounce of interest in her.

"Piss off, Kam," I stammer, turning my back on her before I scratch her eyes out. No ogling with bloody retinas.

Judas would be so disappointed in me for losing my cool.

"God, did you see the balls of fire shoot from her eyes?" Kam laughs loudly.

"See it? It singed me," Alyse replies.

"You're a terrible liar, Addy. I honestly don't even know why you try. You're so doing him," Kam says.

Before I can come up with another denial, because I only "did him" once, my phone dings. When I dig it out of my purse, superglue couldn't have stopped the broad smile that splits my lips, followed immediately by a loud bark of laughter. I actually hear a huge chuck of my wall hit the ground.

Apparently, at some point, Luke helped himself to my phone. He's added his contact info, only not as Luke. His reference last night to no dancing comes racing back.

Tiny Dancer: do u like salmon, fireball?

I'm laughing so hard I can hardly type my response. Kam and Alyse must think I've lost it.

Me: I'm sorry. who is this?
Tiny Dancer: fireball…you're being a bad bad girl
Me: so bad spank me
Tiny Dancer: addy…you're playing a dangerous game here
Me: I thrive on danger. live for it. breathe it. I AM danger

What the hell is wrong with me? I'm goading the great white that's been circling me for weeks with fresh chum. I'm a clueless seal splashing merrily on top of the blue ocean water, completely unaware of what's lurking in the depths below. Stupid, stupid girl.

Tiny Dancer: don't start something you're not ready to finish yet

Me: I'm not sure you've figured it out yet but telling me not to do something has the opposite effect intended

Tiny Dancer: oh Addy...I know so much more than you think

Why do I believe that's true? For some reason, Luke easily sees past all my barriers no matter how hard I try to keep him out. They become translucent. He seems to know what I need even more than I do. Is that what they call a soul mate?

Tiny Dancer: now, salmon?

Me: yes

Tiny Dancer: k. ltr baby. have fun shopping

Me: ltr EJ

Tiny Dancer: u should brush up on your music, fireball. there are well over two-dozen artists who have various versions of that classic song. my personal fav is the electric guitar version by doug smith

Once again Luke has me speechless...and confused. He's acting as if we're a couple when we're no such thing. *Are we?*

I read his messages over and over. He's so utterly complex and has a wicked sense of humor. He's kind of mind-blowing all around. When I finally look up, Kam and Alyse are watching me, but the looks on their faces aren't smug or full of "I-told-you-so's." They look...happy.

"In the ten years I've known you, I've *never* seen you look like this over a man, Ad. You're glowing as bright as the Golden Gate Bridge at night."

Kamryn couldn't be more right. Guess my ruse is up. Not like it was working anyway. "I know," I confess softly. Leaning back against the closest wall I let my eyes float to the ceiling.

My God, do I know.

———————

Three hours, two cocktails, and a dozen packages later, I walk into my apartment to sounds of Elton John playing loudly through speakers I didn't even know we had.

I can't help but laugh.

"Hey, how was shopping?" a disembodied male voice yells from the kitchen.

"Uh, fine," I call back, dropping my purchases by the door. When I get to the kitchen, I think a grocery store may have exploded on our counters. There are boxes and bags and fresh vegetables and fruit everywhere.

Luke's hunched over the sink cleaning something green, a kitchen towel thrown over his shoulder. He hasn't given me a clue what we are doing tonight, but it looks like we're staying in. Does he know I would much prefer that to a fancy restaurant? My heart pangs with the domesticity of the scene in front of me and how much I like it.

I clear the frog in my throat. "What's with the music?"

"Thought you were a big EJ fan?" His gaze slides to mine and I don't miss the smirk tugging on his mouth.

I chuckle. "Not really, but if you haven't heard of "Tiny Dancer," you've been living under a rock."

"Want something else?"

"Okay." I grab a piece of celery that looks to have been cleaned and take a bite, leaning against the counter as I watch him.

He wipes his hands and whips out his phone, punching some buttons. A few seconds later Lifehouse's Jason Wade starts crooning "Falling In." Luke's sultry eyes sweep to mine. "Better?" He smiles cheekily, but I don't miss the undertone of affection on his face or in his voice.

Shit. He's good.

I gulp. You've listened to Lifehouse, right? So no, this is absolutely not better. "Sure," I croak, trying to ignore the lyrics Jason's singing about not being scared because it's love we're falling in. Stay calm and unaffected, Addy. Cool, calm, and unaffected. "So, ah, whatcha got going here?"

"That would be dinner. I know it's a foreign concept to you, fireball, what with your protein bars, Cup-a-Soups, and frozen waffles that you think a meal makes."

It sucks having someone so observant living with you, especially when that someone is who you're trying your best to guard against. Somehow the secrets you want to keep buried deep seem to bubble to the surface and you can't stop the fizz that draws their attention.

"I'm a busy gal."

He turns from his task, pinning me with a deliberate stare. It burns the truth right out of me.

"Fine." I throw my hands up in defeat. "I can't cook. Not everyone has a 'Leave It To Beaver' mother like yours, Luke." Mine was more like Courtney Love. I hate the sympathy I see in his eyes as he walks toward me.

Cupping my check, he says, "*I'll* teach you, then."

My eyes. They're stinging.

"Okay?" he asks softly like I'll blow away if he breathes on me too hard.

"Okay," I answer just as quietly. Leaning down, he places a chaste kiss on my mouth. I try to keep myself from melting, but fail. Luke is simply unlike any other man I've ever met or known. *He keeps telling you that, showing you that.*

Remind me why I'm fighting this again, because I've gone and completely forgotten.

"Here, put this on." He hands me an apron that he's retrieved from a drawer. *Huh. We had an apron?* Who knew. "Gonna put you to work."

"But I don't know what I'm doing. I don't even know how to chop an onion," I cry in a panic. Sad, but true.

His hand lands on my shoulder. "Take a deep

breath, Addy. It's an onion, not plastic surgery. I'll teach you, babe."

"Don't make fun of me or I'm outa here." I twist my head to look up at him and tremble a little at the amusement I see dancing in his eyes.

"Can't guarantee that, fireball, but we'll have fun."

"You're incorrigible, you know that, right?"

"So my mom used to tell me." He kisses the tip of my nose before clearing the space in front of me, setting down a cutting board and a huge knife that looks very sharp.

"Uh, I'm not so sure you should be handing me such sharp objects. I tend to hurt myself. Don't we have like a kiddie version of a knife somewhere? I know my brother got me one for Christmas two years ago. He bought it as a gag, but I seriously use it."

"You'll be fine."

"Luke, I'm serious here. I cut off the tip of my thumb once with a serrated knife. I still don't have feeling in the end of it."

"Then you won't feel a thing if you cut it again." He laughs and I slap his chest with the back of my hand pretending I'm really angry, although I don't stop the smile that pops out. "Fine, then I'll take you to the emergency room and you'll get stitches. You'll live."

"Maybe I could just wash vegetables or something like that?"

"Now I'm more determined than ever to make you cut that damn onion. You do realize you've dug yourself into a hole, right?"

Shit. Should have played that differently.

"Fine."

We have two onions that need dicing, so Luke shows me how to do it on the first one. Cut it in half, peel off the first couple of layers, then slice thinly and dice into small pieces. He demonstrates his fine culinary skills slowly with his pungent piece while I try to replicate it with mine. Doesn't seem so hard, until I look at the finished product. His pieces are all even and small; mine are large and irregular and look like the proud work of a six-year-old who used a butter knife.

I look up at him and he's trying to hide a smirk; it isn't long before he bursts out laughing.

"That's it," I growl, throwing down the knife and untying my apron. The knife bounces across the counter and falls off the other side. *Whoops.* Probably not the smartest idea I've ever had to throw weaponry around so carelessly.

"No, no. I'm sorry. I'm sorry," he sputters. He grabs my hands, halting my angry movements. "I'm sorry."

"You're not. You're still laughing."

Lightly chuckling, he pulls me close, careful not to touch my face with his now rank hand. "You're just so fucking cute, Addy. I'm not laughing *at* you. Really."

"Well, you're definitely not laughing *with* me, because that would require me to laugh and, clearly, I'm not."

"Baby, I'm sorry. I'm sorry. You did good. And no blood or fleshy parts on the cutting board."

"I didn't," I complain. "A blind five-year-old could do better."

Laughter—*not mine*—echoes off the walls, drowning out Lifehouse. Well...that's a plus, I suppose. "It all cooks the same, fireball."

"We have to cook it now?" I shriek, throwing my hands in the air.

Luke's body shakes as he tries to contain himself. "How about you pour the wine? Can you handle that?"

"Wine?"

"Yes, you know. The alcohol made from grapes."

"Smart-ass."

"We going down that road, Addy? Really?"

"Fine. Wine I can handle."

Wine? What the hell am I thinking? The last thing I need is more alcohol to lower my inhibitions—as if his intoxicating scent isn't enough to make me want to strip naked right here. The pheromones coming off this man constantly swirl in the air around him, making me lust-drunk and it's not even his fault. I think he was injected with an extra dose of sexiness when he was created.

I walk around him to the sink and wash the onion off me, internally panicking at how much I like this feeling of just *being* with Luke. When I take the towel from his shoulder to dry my hands, I'm nearly frozen with the look of heat and want I see blazing from him. Clearing my throat, I retrieve the wine from the fridge and take a few deep breaths while my back is turned, wondering how I'm going to keep resisting this incredibly sexy man for much longer. Or even why I'm trying.

He could have easily tried seducing me any number of nights this week, but he hasn't, which is confusing and endearing at the same time. We haven't spent a lot of time together since he threw down his battle words. We've watched TV together a few nights this past week, him on his side of the couch, me in the chair, so I wasn't tempted to crawl over to him like a cat in heat and rub myself all over his corded body. It was cordial, comfortable, actually, if I'm being completely honest.

We trade barbs because that's our thing, although it's with far less bite now than it was even two days ago. It's almost like a ridiculous mating dance that starts in grade school on the playground. Boy likes girl, pulls her hair. Girl likes boy, sticks out her tongue at him. Makes no sense, but it's how the game is played nonetheless.

Only this is no game and I already know that. Luke doesn't strike me as the type to play games; he plays for keeps. He makes me feel things I never thought possible. He makes me feel like I *matter*. Every layer of him I uncover, I just want more.

And regardless of how much I'm fighting this, deep down, there's that tingle low in my belly that's thrilled that *I'm* his target, that *I'm* the one he wants to keep.

Me. Addy Monroe.

Chapter 24

LUKE

Addy sets two glasses of wine down on the counter, a nice South African chardonnay I've picked out to pair with the salmon. I much prefer beer, but even though we're staying in, I admit I wanted to impress her. As I watched her cut that damn onion—or *attempt* to cut it—all I could think of was how *right* this all feels. I never thought I would like domestic, but shit, I do. A helluva lot.

She takes a seat across the island and her scent, a combination of perfume and her own uniqueness, hits my nose and my cock jumps. Fuck, maybe I should have taken her out instead of staying in. That way, I wouldn't be tempted to strip her down, throw her on the closest surface, and fuck her into admitting she belongs with me.

Who am I kidding? The setting wouldn't matter. I want to fuck her anywhere and everywhere all the damn time.

As much as I want to act out every wicked fantasy running through my head, I can't and I won't. Not now. She's still skittish, even though she's coming around, and I don't want to do anything to jeopardize the progress I've made with her the past few weeks.

"So what are you making?" she asks. She hums in appreciation when she takes a sip of her wine, making me smile. And harder, if that's possible. Since she walked through the door, I've been trying to discreetly adjust my raging erection to a place that's more comfortable. It's not working too well. Thank God for the apron.

"*We're* making pomegranate-and-orange-glazed salmon, Mediterranean rice, and steamed broccoli. Chocolate chip cannolis for dessert—I picked those up at a little bakery on my way home, because they take quite a bit of time to make."

"Wow. Everything sounds great. Except the broccoli."

"Not a big greens fan?"

"No, I like greens just fine, just not broccoli." She makes the cutest damn face, wrinkling up her nose. "It's stupid, really."

"Sounds like a story there," I say, chopping a few cloves of garlic in short order as she watches in fascination. My knife skills are impressive, I'll admit it. If that's all it takes to impress her, then hot damn. We'll be spending every fucking meal in this kitchen and she'll be mine by next Wednesday. *Why didn't I think of this before?*

"Yeah. So when I was seven, my dad was cutting up some veggies. I picked up a piece of raw broccoli and popped it in my mouth. Eric freaked, telling me it was poisonous and that I was going die, so, of course, *I* was hysterical. My dad finally had to get our neighbor, who was a doctor, so she could assure me I would be just fine. Eric got in a whole heap of trouble, but permanent psychological damage was already done. Broccoli equals death to me."

She laughs and I laugh along with her. Eric was always a prankster and it appears he started at a mighty young age. "Shit. That's cruel. Eric's played one or two nasty tricks on me."

"I'm not surprised. He's never lived it down. I've gotten him back tenfold, believe me."

"Why am I not shocked that vengeance lurks deep within your soul?"

"I don't know. You shouldn't be," she winks flirtatiously. Taking another sip of wine, she rolls her eyes slightly. Fuck...I want to be the one to make her eyes roll back in pleasure. Even though it's not intentional, she's making it very hard to keep my hands to myself right now.

Willing my dick down and trying to get my mind back on dinner, I set a grater and lemon in front of her, describing how to grate the lemon rind we'll need for the rice.

"You still want my help?" she asks, surprised.

"Can't learn if you don't do, fireball."

She eyes the grater as if it has spikes dipped in poison.

"It's fine, babe. This is easy, I promise."

"Okay, but no more dicing. And if you get any of my skin mixed in with the lemon, don't blame me."

I chuckle. She really didn't do *that* badly. "Fair

enough. We'll work on chopping again next time."

"Next time?"

The look of hopefulness on her face slays me. Has no one ever treated this woman the way she deserves? More and more, I'm starting to think the answer is no and while I don't think I'm good enough for her, what does that say about the other losers who have come before me?

"Yes, baby. Next time," I tell her softly.

Because there will be a next time. I think we both know there's only one way this thing between us is going. The forever kind.

We stand there for a few stolen moments, our eyes locked in silent conversation. I hope she gets what I'm telling her. I meant my declaration of war. I want her and I'll do anything to have her. I just need to convince *her* of that.

The next hour is spent working together side by side, talking about our businesses, our childhoods, our siblings. I don't miss how she speaks about her brother and her dad with affection yet doesn't mention her mom at all, even though I know she's still alive. And whenever the topic of my father comes up, I skirt it like the fucking expert I am. Guess we both have a fucked-up parental gene pool to some degree.

After dinner, I take her hand and lead her to the couch. Pulling her down beside me, I settle her in the crook of my arm. I'm not letting her slink away to the chair like she's done for the last week when we're in the same room.

In short order, I have a movie streaming. God bless technology. It just continues to make us lazier and lazier. Whoops, I meant easier.

"What's this?" she asks.

"You haven't seen *National Lampoon's Vacation*?" I ask, tugging her close, kissing the crown of her head.

"Not in its entirety, no."

"What? That's almost sacrilegious, fireball. Stick with me, babe, I'll open up a whole new world for you."

"I have no doubt you will." Her voice goes soft and her head tilts up. When I tilt mine down, our lips are mere inches away. Her eyes are glazed with such need, the urge to introduce her back to the couch, strip her down, and fuck her until she's a sated, sweaty mess is almost too overwhelming to ignore. But as much as I want her to be ready right now, she's not. And the next time I'm inside of her, the dancing she's doing will stop. She will be mine and there will be no turning back for either of us.

There's already no turning back for me.

"Stop looking at me like that, fireball," I growl lowly. "I'm trying to do the right thing here by following your cues."

"Sorry," she breathes, turning her attention back to the TV. I shove down my disappointment that I won't be inside of her tonight. Instead, I just enjoy the fact I'm holding her in my arms and she's not fighting it. It's progress.

We relax and watch the movie, and when she lays down, putting her head in my lap halfway through, I harden involuntarily. It takes several minutes to get in control of my body, but I finally wrangle the big guy down enough that I can touch her the way I want. I run my fingers hypnotically through her hair, lulling her to sleep.

I gently lift and carry her to her room, wishing it were my bed she was sleeping in tonight instead. As I lay her down she wakes, blinking up at me lazily. My God, she steals my very breath away sometimes.

"Guess I didn't make it to the end, huh?"

"Nope. We'll try again." I kiss her softly on the forehead, letting my lips linger too long, wanting to do so much more. I stand and look down at this beautiful woman I long to call mine and my heart swells with all kinds of new and different feelings.

"Thanks for dinner," she says softly.

"You helped," I remind her.

"I did, didn't I?" she replies with a smile so magnificent it could light up the night's sky.

Jesus, I am so gone for her. I want nothing more than to crawl in bed beside her and hold her all night long, but for once, I'm trying to do the honorable thing.

Unfortunately, my cock doesn't feel quite the same. He's ramming against my zipper, declaring outright mutiny, and has recruited the twins below, who are probably so blue they look like Smurfs by now. They're drawn tightly against him in a show of solidarity.

I'll deal with them later.

"Night, Addy," I croak.

"Night, Luke."

I force myself to turn and walk away, telling my feet to get a fucking move on, compelling them to take step after step. I'm almost to the door when she calls after me. "What's this?"

I look back to see she's holding the stuffed French bulldog I bought her as a surprise, leaving it on her bed earlier today. Yeah, that lock she uses to keep me out could use a lot of reinforcement, kind of like the one she keeps around her heart. And she thinks I'm closed off? Pot, kettle. All I'm gonna say.

"Well, I couldn't convince the supe to give in on the no dogs policy, so..."

I don't miss the water in her eyes before she looks back down at the fluffy white animal in her slightly trembling hands, studying it like some foreign object.

"You bought me a stuffed animal?" Her soft voice is barely audible. Full of wonder. I want to tell her I'd do anything for her. A stuffed animal is meaningless, but by the way she's looking at the damn thing, you'd think I handed her the key to immortality instead.

"Yeah. I know it's not exactly what you wanted. It's the best I could do for now."

"Thank you," she chokes. A lone tear runs down her cheek, which she unashamedly lets me see.

I want nothing more than to march back over and show her just exactly how much she means to me, but if I lay a finger on her now, I won't be able to stop myself. Addy's so much more lost than she lets people believe. I see through all the bullshit and it fucking kills me that no one has given her what she's deserved before.

I smile gently. "You're welcome, Addy. Night."

"Night, Luke."

I turn back toward the door, shutting it on my way out. Each step I take away from her is filled with pain. It takes every ounce of willpower I have to do the right thing, which is to leave.

My heart knows it's the right thing, but my cock wholeheartedly disagrees.

Chapter 25

LUKE

Two hours and one sad hand job later, I'm drifting in and out of a light sleep when I sense a presence in my room. I look toward the door to see Addy standing at the threshold. A crack of lightning, followed closely by a loud boom of thunder has her jumping a foot in the air. It's only then I register the sound of heavy rain battering against my window. Guess I was in a heavier sleep than I realized.

I sit up, holding out my hand to her. "You afraid of storms, baby?"

Another crack of lightning has her quickly crossing the room, taking it, and sliding into my bed. She presses tightly against me, throwing a leg over mine, and I don't miss the fact she's only wearing a tank and tiny panties. The feel of her bare skin against me is almost nirvana. I only wish there were more of it. I normally sleep in the buff, but tonight had the foresight to put on my boxer briefs instead.

Believe you me, I'm regretting that fucking decision right about now.

"Stupid, I know."

I shake off my lascivious thoughts, trying to remember what we were talking about. Oh, yeah. Storms. "Not stupid. Everyone's afraid of something."

Snuggling closer, as if that's even humanly possible, she asks, "What are you afraid of?"

Other than not making you mine? I'm not sure I've ever been so afraid of anything in my entire life than not having this woman.

"Sharks," I confess instead. I've not told a single person outside of Addy of my fear of sharks, except my twin of course.

She laughs. "Sharks?"

"Hey. I didn't laugh at you."

"Sorry, sorry," she chuckles lightly. "It's just a pretty weird thing for a landlocked person to be afraid of. What happened? You have a nasty encounter with a hammerhead at Sea World or something?"

"Nah. Nothing like that. You've seen *Jaws*, right?"

"Of course," she answers indignantly.

I chuckle, tightening my hold, enjoying her warmth seeping into me. "Well, you understand I had to ask. You haven't seen the classic Chevy Chase's *Vacation*, so I have to question your cinematic exposure."

She punches me in the stomach and it actually hurts a bit. "Ouch. You have a wicked left hook, fireball."

"You've met my brother, yes?"

"He's a good man."

"He is. He's also a good teacher of self-defense. So...sharks." She starts drawing little circles on my chest. Sheer grit is all that stifles a guttural groan sitting in the back of my throat. I reach up, taking her hand in mine before I do something stupid and she ends up underneath me, filled to the brim with my raging manhood. I don't think she has a fucking clue what she does to me. If she did, she'd be cowering alone in her own room right now, storm or not. If she moves her leg up about another three inches, she's going to feel firsthand exactly how her nearness affects me.

I clear my throat, hoping the thick lust that's lodged there dissipates somewhat. "Yes, sharks." Not quite, but I continue anyway. "When I was eleven, Gray and I spent the night with a buddy. It was summer and there were several of us. We had the run of the basement. Came across *Jaws* on TV. Everyone was stoked to watch it, of course, but I didn't want to. I was already irrationally scared of the ocean, even though I'd never been and *Jaws* scared the living piss out of me. I dreamed of blood and body parts for weeks. Honestly, weeks. I was even afraid to go in the pool for the rest of the summer, even though you could see clean to the bottom and logically I knew there were no sharks in there. Told my mom I had warts."

I feel her smile against my chest. "Have you been to the ocean?"

Lightning strikes again; this time, the thunder takes a few seconds longer to reach us and I hear the rain has lightened up a bit. Still, every time it cracks, her body trembles.

"Been there twice, but never got in. What about you? Why are you so afraid of storms?"

"You really want to know?"

"Wouldn't ask if I didn't, babe." I feel her chest expand against my side before I feel her hot breath drizzle over me. *Fuck*.

"Okay. Well, I was five and it was summer. My mom always insisted on putting me to bed early enough that it was still light out. She never let me stay up late no matter how much I begged. I had to lie in bed and listen to the other kids laughing and playing outside, so one night, I snuck out of the house. I remember it was incredibly easy and wondered why I hadn't done it before.

"Instead of playing with my friends, I walked to the park only about three blocks away. Even at five, I knew how to get there. Take a lefty loosey out of the driveway and keep walking until I see the park. I honestly don't know how long I was there before the storm rolled in, but I distinctly remember swinging on the swings and going down the slide so many times I lost count. I didn't realize it was getting darker and darker and it had nothing to do with the sun setting and everything to do with a bad storm rolling in.

"When the rain started falling, lightly at first, I did the typical kid thing. I held my head back and my arms out and twirled in a circle, hoping I could catch some stray drops in my mouth. But then the rain picked up and it started stinging my skin. I think in retrospect it was hail. Then I heard them. The sirens. And I knew what they meant. I was in trouble and instead of trying to run home, I took shelter in this circular cement tube on the playground. If you got enough kids in there and we all pushed with our legs, the momentum made it spin. I used to love that thing," she says wistfully.

She pauses, her body stiffening. "It's okay, baby," I whisper, tightening my grip on her. I palm her scalp and massage lightly, which relaxes her.

"The sound of the hail hitting the cement and sirens echoing off the insides, along with the thunder, was deafening. I was sure I was going to die. Then I heard my dad. He had come for me and found me huddled there, sobbing. We rode the storm out there together. I found out later a tornado had touched down only six blocks from our house. Killed three people."

Her voice drops so low I have to strain to hear the rest of the story. "When we walked through the door, all I remember is my mom screaming at my dad. She didn't want him to go out and find me. She was more concerned about something happening to him and what would she do without him, blah, blah, blah. I may have been only five, but I knew my mom was selfish, and that day literally broke my spirit. What kind of mother would voluntarily let her kid be caught in a storm? A dangerous one at that? As you can probably tell, I'm not close with her. She hasn't changed in the slightest all these years. And I think that was the beginning of the end for my parents. My dad was furious with her."

"Oh, Addy. I'm so sorry, baby."

"No need to be sorry. Luck of the draw, I guess."

"Yes, I know all about that."

"Who?" She doesn't have to elaborate. I know what she's asking.

"My father," I confess softly.

She doesn't ask any more questions and for that I'm grateful. Addy and I are more alike than she knows. We both had parents who were disappointments to us, who let us down. I realize parents are people too, with imperfections like the rest of us, yet some things they do are simply unforgivable.

I can't blame Addy for her animosity toward her mom, just like I can't forgive my dad for his indiscretions, for his affair.

We've fallen quiet before I notice it's no longer raining. There's only an occasional flash of light through the darkness, and I can't even hear the rumble of thunder anymore.

Addy must notice, too, because she pushes off me and starts to sit up. "Well, uh, I should...go. Thanks for letting me lie here with you."

"No, stay," I say, tugging her back down to me.

"I should let you get some sleep," she mumbles into my chest, her hot breath skittering across my skin.

"I sleep better when you're in my arms."

She snorts. "That can't be true."

Flipping her on her back, I hover above her,

balancing on my forearms so I don't crush her. Her hands are pinned beneath mine.

"What have I done to give you the impression I'm anything less than sincere in the way I feel about you?"

It takes her a few seconds to answer. "I've known guys like you my whole life."

Fucking pisses me off she's lumping me into the same loser category. See, this right here is the problem. She's projecting her past failures onto me and unless I can get her to see I'm not like the other assholes who've come before me, this is going to be over before it even has a chance to get started. If they were stupid enough to let an incredible woman like Addy go, they deserve to live a life in bland shadows of grey. *Me?* I plan on living my life in color.

"I can guarantee you've never met anyone like me, fireball."

"You're awfully arrogant," she retorts with a slight bite.

"Maybe, but it doesn't make it any less true." I choose to take a different tactic, hoping I can break through her stubbornness. "Look, I'm all in here. I got nothing left to hide and I've fallen for you, Addy, harder than a landslide. I could lose the game and I'd still be all in tonight. Hell, I'm all in for life."

When she laughs I know I've hit a home run. "Oh my God. That sounds like something from Lifehouse."

"Hmmm..." I scrunch my eyebrows together, feigning confusion. "I thought that sounded familiar." She shakes her head, but her grin doesn't fade. And her eyes? They glitter like starlight. "Maybe I did paraphrase, but I don't know a better way to make you understand how I feel about you. I'm genuine here in my quest to win you. I like you, Addy. A *lot*. Kill the shields, babe."

"Luke..." she whispers breathlessly. Christ, the sound of submission sounds sweet rolling off her usually spiked tongue.

Her smile is now replaced with acute longing and my cock hardens painfully. You know that honor I mentioned earlier? Suddenly he's become a very slippery fucker.

I may not be able to fuck her tonight, because of my perhaps misplaced honorable intentions, but I do plan on kissing her, pouring every emotion I'm feeling into it, and showing her exactly how much she means to me.

While keeping my hands pressed to her face, lest they wander somewhere hot and wet that will cause my nobility to evaporate, I press an unhurried, soft, and sweet kiss to her lips, which is in complete contrast to the way I want to take her right now. Hard, rough, and fast.

When I tease her mouth open, our tongues duel lazily as I deepen my strokes. Her hands, which are becoming more urgent with each passing second, are now roaming over my shoulders, neck, back, nails scoring me lightly, causing me to groan. She shifts under me, spreading her legs, and my pounding erection nestles smack dab in her hot center. He jumps up and down excitedly, thinking he's going to get in on the action. Once again, he's going to be sorely disappointed.

Our hips are now undulating and I am all too aware that only two thin scraps of fabric separate me from having her. I grab her pelvis firmly to halt her movements and drag my mouth to her jaw, her ear, and down her throat, lightly biting the sensitive indentation where her neck meets her shoulder. Her breathy moans almost completely unravel my good intentions.

With willpower I didn't know I possessed, I flip onto my back, bringing her with me and tuck her into my side. I try to get both my breathing and my cock under control as I blink up at the ceiling thinking of contracts and stakeouts and cleaning my gun. *Anything* but how much I want to be inside her right now.

"Is something wrong?" she pants.

Wrong? No, other than I want to fuck you into the next state. She's breathless just like me and sounds genuinely confused. Fuck me. Doing the right thing is excruciatingly hard sometimes.

"No. Nothing's wrong." That thick lust has relodged, causing me to sound almost hoarse.

"Don't you want to...?"

The words hang in the air like bubbles above her head waiting to be filled in with any number of things. I can think of a dozen carnal, wicked ways to complete that sentence in just seconds. If I take her now, though, I'll be undoing everything I've worked for these past two weeks. She'll think this was all a ploy to get into her pants again and while my entire body is aching for that release, I need her to understand—no, *believe*—there's so much more to what we've started.

I want it all.

Everything.

"Addy, fuck. I *want*. I ache with want. What I *need* is for you to believe that I'm in this for more than just sex. Don't get me wrong, I desperately want that, but I want so much more. If I slip my dick inside you right now, you'll question it. And I don't want you questioning my intentions. I don't want you questioning *us*."

I know I've done the right thing when she responds quietly, "You're not like anyone I've ever met before, Luke."

"I'm glad you're finally starting to realize that." I know she can hear the smile in my voice because she snorts. It's cute and endearing, like everything else about her. "Stay," I demand.

After only a brief hesitation this time, she gives in. *Sweet progress.* "All right."

"Addy?"

"Hmm?"

"Don't sneak out again on me or I swear I will redden your ass this time."

I don't miss the hitch of her breath and shit...Honor. Honor. Honor. Put it on repeat, fucker.

"I won't."

Is it wrong of me to feel disappointed in that answer now?

"Night, Luke," she tells me quietly, placing her small hand in the center of my chest. I grab it and hold onto it like a damn lifeline, my other feathering up and down her arm.

"Night, fireball."

Later, as sleep takes me, I don't think I would have heard her murmur softly against my chest if I hadn't felt her warm breath scatter over me. Falling into a deep slumber, I can't help the smile that curves my lips at her quiet confession.

"I like you a lot, too."

That night, I dream of us making wild, passionate love with bubbles containing her declaration floating to the ceiling, so many of them they almost suffocate us. Suddenly, the dream changes into a nightmare as the bubbles pop and the words drop all around us, morphing into venomous serpents. They coat every surface. The bed, the floor, the walls. I fight them off with my hands, blood pouring from my wounds in rivers. I fight tirelessly to protect Addy as the red-eyed reptiles slither around us, trying to sink their poisonous fangs deep into our happiness.

I wake with a start, my heart pounding. Addy snuggles beside me, burrowing deeper into my side and I tighten my hold. I lay there for a good hour, shaken by the dream, wondering if it's a premonition or a warning that I've latched onto an innocent woman and that one act alone handed me a one-way ticket to hell.

Even if it is some kind of omen, I decide I don't care. Bring it on. I'm battle ready and not even a showdown with the devil himself will make me give up my color now that I have her.

Chapter 26

Addy

"Thanks for meeting me for dinner," I say when Livia joins me at the table. After the last few days of swirling in a maelstrom of confusion, I need my friend and I need to put this misplaced guilt behind me.

"Of course. I miss you."

She takes a seat. A perky blonde comes over with waters and menus, leaving us to look over them for a few minutes. When our waitress returns to take our order, I actually get a good look at her. With her clown makeup and blinding lipstick, Wanda, according to her nametag, could almost pass as a fifties pinup girl. God knows the outfit fits. Skirt so short her lady bits almost hang out and the buttons on her blouse are stretched so taut those suckers could be projectiles if she takes too deep a breath. The only things she's missing are garters and high heels and I bet if she could get away with wearing them, she would.

"What can I get you?" she asks, chomping her gum loudly. *Ugh.* Unprofessional much?

"Salmon salad for me."

She turns to Livia. "And for you?"

"I'll have the falafel wrap," she replies sweetly, handing her the menu.

"For your side?" she asks, tapping her pencil repeatedly on her notepad as if she has a nervous tick. "Fries, please. Thanks."

As soon as she's out of earshot, Livia and I exchange knowing glances and giggle like mean girls.

"Warn me when you see her coming back. I'm going to need to put on my sunglasses. Her lipstick practically burned my retinas and her buttons could easily put out an eye," I tell her.

I don't know what it is about women that makes us so judgmental, but we all are. We do it in elementary school. We sharpen our skills as teenagers, and when we grow into women, we're practically Oscar winners at it. Sometimes, I think just having a vagina gives us a license to step into the ring of castigation, wielding caustic words and biting remarks like verbal weapons, while we keep the manicure we just spent sixty dollars on yesterday all smooth and shiny and unchipped. Men fight with fists. Women with words.

I'm not proud, by the way. Just want to make that clear.

"So how are things going with Luke?" Livia dives right in, a slight smirk on her lips. She takes a drink of her iced lemon water, watching for my reaction over the rim of her glass; now dripping condensation. I know her so well and exactly what she's asking.

"Great! Perfect, actually," I lie, a plastic smile plastered on.

Aaaand...Livia knows me just as well. "Mmm...I can see what Kam and Alyse are talking about."

Of course, my friends told her I was glowing brighter than the White House Christmas tree at the sheer mention of Luke's name. Is nothing sacred anymore?

"I have no idea what you're talking about, Liv."

Livia reaches across the table, laying her hand over mine. "It's okay, you know, Addy."

Is it? Really?

I want to ask her so many questions that are none of my business. Questions I have never asked before about her past, about her relationship with Luke. Not knowing what went on between them and if she's okay with this— this *thing* that's blossoming faster than I can stop it—is killing me inside. I need to know if she's all right with me being with a man who means so much to her. And against my better judgment, I'm going to ask the forbidden questions anyway, even though I very well may not want to hear the answers.

What's that saying? Curiosity killed the cat? It's a damn good thing I'm not a feline then.

"Did you sleep with him?" I blurt. I probably could have phrased that better, but I'm not usually one for discretion. I was somehow born with a 'what the fuck' attitude.

Livia barks a laugh. "Well, no one can accuse you of being indirect, can they?"

"It's a strength of mine."

"And you know I love that about you, right?"

"I do."

She studies me for a few moments and I start to get a bad feeling. "Did you? And don't tell me it's complicated, Livia. That's just code for it's none of your damn business."

"I didn't have sex with Luke. Our relationship wasn't like that, Addy."

"Then what was it like?" I ask, apparently unable to keep my damn mouth shut. "I know you're with Gray now and deliriously in love and you're going to pop Gray one and Gray two in just a couple of months, but I saw the way Luke was with you a few months ago, Liv. There's no way you'll convince me you guys don't care deeply for each other."

A pensive look crosses her face and she sits back in her chair. Lacing her fingers, she places them on a belly that's big enough to be used as a shelf. And I have told her that to her face, by the way.

"It *is* complicated, Addy," she says quietly, pain clearly evident in her voice.

I remember her telling me a couple of weeks ago she was running away from something when she moved here, which I'd already guessed. Suddenly, I feel like a piece of crap grilling my friend about her past when it's so obvious it's still like an open, festering wound. Wanting this man has made me so desperate, I'm doing things

I wouldn't normally do, such as treating my best friend like shit.

I suck.

"I'm sorry, Livia. You don't have to tell me. It's none of my business."

"I just can't talk about the whole story, Addy. It's too painful. Luke and I share a unique bond and I do care for him deeply. He literally saved my life. I made some personal sacrifices and they cost me dearly. Had it not been for Luke, I wouldn't be sitting here with you now and that's no exaggeration. I do love him, but I've never been *in love* with Luke. I've always been and always will be in love with Gray."

I look down at my lap where I'm anxiously twisting the cloth napkin laying there. I can't decide if I'm relieved to hear Livia and Luke didn't have that sort of relationship or devastated to know my best friend in the entire world has been through something so horrific that, years later, it's still clear the scars run deep and probably always will. Both, I think. And the guilt returns once again.

My eyes mist as I start spilling my guts.

"I've always wanted a dog, you know. When I was growing up, my elderly neighbor, Mrs. Kravitz, had a bulldog named Gerard. I loved that damn thing. A lot of people don't like bulldogs because they think they're ugly, but I love their sad little faces. I think I could always relate, maybe. Anyway, I pretended Gerard was my own since my mom refused to buy us a dog. Said she didn't want something else to take care of. I went over after school every day and walked him and played with him until he died when I was eleven."

Livia waits patiently for me to continue. "He bought me a stuffed animal. Luke did. Last week. During one of my many rants, I apparently told him I wanted a bulldog and our complex has this 'no dogs' policy, you know, so instead he bought me a toy one." I choke up on the last few words, still unable to believe he did that. I'm not sure I could ever make him understand how much that one small gesture meant. I'm not even quite sure I understand it myself. It's just a stupid toy.

I look up through blurry eyes to see Livia with a knowing, *pleased* smile and I immediately know I have her approval. My entire body relaxes.

"Outside of my dad, no one's ever done anything like that for me. No man I've dated has cared enough to bring me dinner or teach me to cook or make me coffee or buy me silly kid toys because I said something in passing."

I've been thinking back to that night, trying to remember what else I confessed during my tantrum. The only other thing I remember was that I told him I wanted to be first, and he's made that painstakingly apparent with his selfless acts, including denying my advances the other night. His rejection stung until he explained himself and I think at that moment, I fell completely, totally, and hopelessly in love with him.

"That's because you've been with the wrong men."

"Don't I know it," I mumble. "He let me sleep with him the other night when we had that thunderstorm." That was Saturday, three nights ago now, and every night since I've secretly been praying for another torrential downpour. Is that wrong of me to need a storm to drive me into his arms? Yes. Yes, it is.

"I was worried about you when that hit." We smile, remembering the times Livia let me stay with her during bad storms. We'd make an entire night of it and end up either eating ourselves sick or drinking until I didn't care anymore about the rain or the pain I still feel in my heart at my mom's indifference toward me. I will forever associate the lightning that cracks in the sky to the night my mother's insensitive words cracked my heart wide open. She later said she didn't mean it, but we all knew the truth.

"I think I'm in love with him," I confess quietly, wiping a stray tear that's escaped. I'm not being totally honest with her. I *know* I'm in love with him. There is not one doubt in my mind. The fear of being hurt paralyzes me, though.

"I know," she replies just as quietly.

"I'm scared."

"I know that, too, Addy. I'm going to give you some advice that a wise friend told me a few months ago."

"Why does this sound backwards?" I manage to chuckle.

"Because it is."

"Wise, huh?"

"Very." Livia grins and she's absolutely glowing. Pregnancy agrees with her. "Let's be honest. You've dated a lot of frogs and each one has left his little damaging wart on you somewhere. Let it go. Let *them* go. I think the man you've been looking for all along is finally standing right in front of you, Addy, so give him a chance. Look forward, not backward. Besides, I know Luke and he's just like his brothers. Once they set their mind to something, they'll stop at nothing until they get it. And Luke wants you."

"You think?"

"No. I *know*. Not one person missed the scorching heat between you two at dinner a couple weekends ago. He's different around you. He's different *with* you. He's softer and happier and lighter than I've ever seen him. He's in love with you, Addy. I can tell."

I hold her gaze, silently questioning, and she nods in affirmation. I don't know if he's in love with me, but there's absolutely no denying he likes me a lot. The fact that I was practically throwing myself at him in bed the other day and he did the honorable thing by denying me says more than his words ever could.

"So this...is okay with you?"

"My best friend and my brother-in-law? Hells yes."

"Thanks, Livia. I love you."

"Love you too, Ad." Livia glances up and mumbles, "Incoming," seconds before our waitress reappears and we fight to contain our laughter. I look down the entire time, just in case you were wondering. Gotta protect the eyes.

An hour later as I say good-bye to Livia, I now know the only person standing between me and Luke is, well...me. I think it's *always* been me.

Chapter 27

Addy

It's after nine p.m. when I get home from my dinner with Livia. I don't miss Luke's Ducati sitting in the lot, but when I walk through the door, I don't see him in either the kitchen or the living room. I try not to be disappointed. I need some time to get my head on straight anyway and his presence always fills my brain with a fog of sexual need.

After talking things through with Livia and getting her "blessing," I feel a little lighter as I head to my bedroom. I throw my purse on my bed, intent on changing into comfy clothes and vegging in front of the tube for a while, watching mindless, brain-cell-zapping reality shows. My skirt is halfway unzipped when I realize my shower is running. I stop what I'm doing and head toward the bathroom.

Once inside, I freeze like a deer caught in headlights.

My shower has clear glass doors, which are a pain in the ass—you have to squeegee them every single time you shower or they get hard water buildup that can barely be removed with anything except paint thinner. I hate those shower doors. *Every* day for the past four years I have cursed that clear glass. Every single day.

Now I am cheering those doors. Wildly.

I have no idea why Luke is in *my* bathroom, and at this moment, I couldn't care less. That stupid song about the roof being on fire and letting the motherfucker burn rings in my ears. I agree. Let her burn, burn, burn, because nothing short of the floor collapsing from underneath me could make me budge an inch.

As I stand here like the voyeur I didn't realize I was, but clearly am, I am in total and utter awe of the male perfection standing in front of me. A naked Luke is something magnificent to behold—a naked, wet, and very aroused *masturbating* Luke is literally mind melting. Like, commence total shutdown.

Eyes squeezed shut in pleasure/pain, he's leaning forward, forearm against the fiberglass, head hanging low, so his chin almost touches his chest. His legs are spread wide, butt cheeks clasped tight so that sexy indent is even more pronounced.

As hot water sluices down his rippling, cut, decorated flawlessness, I shamelessly watch as he fists his thick, heavy cock with the other hand so hard it almost looks punishing. He strokes slowly at first, circling the plum head with his thumb each time. His breathing and pace pick up as he edges closer and closer to the end, and I anxiously wait for the explosive finale, my core pulsing, my own breaths coming in short gasps.

When he reaches the pinnacle, I have no way of stopping my own low moan while he throws his head back and groans on a guttural curse as endless ribbons of milky white shoot onto the fiberglass wall in front of him.

Jesus, he is glorious.

I continue to look on as he starts the descent from his blissful high. I should leave, but I can't, and so I stand frozen like a statue as his head slowly tilts my way, his heated eyes snaring mine. His chest heaves with his recent effort as he watches me through steam or lust. I'm not sure which. It could go either way.

"Enjoy the show, fireball?" His voice is heavy with wickedness and thick with promise.

Yes, very much. Thank you.

I don't know how long I stare at him, mouth agape before I finally snap out of my desire-drunk stupor. It's not easy, trust me, and my girly bits are already cursing me.

"Your shower suddenly not good enough?" I croak. I am so damn turned on right now I can barely speak.

"Broken." Standing to his full height, he swivels to face me, indifferent to his nudity.

God almighty. I got nothing.

"Oh."

"Care to join me?" his gravelly voice drawls. *That damn drawl.* His voice alone tugs on your panties, but the silkiness of that drawl is like throwing gasoline on the raging heat flaring between my thighs. I feel like I'm burning up down there.

He stands proud, an arrogant smirk tilting a corner of his mouth, still palming his semierect staff, slowly stroking. His daring, cocky stare never drops mine. This whole scene is very distracting.

What was the question again? Oh yes...care to join me? There is a wrong answer to that question, right? Because I'm quite sure I'm about to give it. Guess I'm still standing in my own way for some stupid, very stupid reason. Not one sane woman would walk away from this sinful proposition, except apparently me.

Reaching underneath the sink, I pull out the cleaner, walk to the shower door, and open it, careful to keep my eyes above sea level and off the bobbing raft below. "Make sure you clean up before you leave."

He laughs loudly. Taking the bottle from my hands, his fingers purposely graze mine. Heat shoots up my arm and down to my core, joining the campfire below. "Your loss, fireball."

"Don't I know it," I mumble, turning to leave. "Don't I know it."

———————

It's 3:32 a.m. and the red digits on my clock mock me. Insomnia at its finest right here. I dozed off early yet have been lying awake for over an hour now, tossing and turning, unable to get the real-life porno shower scene I witnessed just mere hours ago out of my head. It's running on a continuous, torturous loop.

The first thing I did when I locked myself back in my room, like the chickenshit I am, was to strip off my embarrassingly wet underwear.

Okay, fine. So that wasn't the *first* thing I did, but it was the second because they were even wetter after the first...*thing.* No amount of self-pleasure has helped; my body still aches for something I've been stupidly denying myself.

Luke.

Finally, I give up and slide out of bed in a huff. Pulling on a light blue tank over navy lace panties, I quietly open my door. The apartment is dark, except for the blue rays from the full moon shining through the blinds. I easily find my way to the kitchen, not needing any additional light.

Opening a cupboard, I grab a glass and turn to the fridge to pour myself some milk. I take a sip and, deciding it's not cold enough, pull on the freezer door to grab a few ice cubes, plopping them into my cream. I stare for a moment at the Bomb Pops I saw earlier this week. I haven't had one since I was probably fourteen and yet here Luke is...enjoying them as a thirty-year-old man. Just another mystery that is Luke.

I lean my back against the fridge and sigh. Closing my eyes, thoughts of popsicles vanish. I once again replay the sight of Luke stroking himself to completion as hot water jetted over his perfectly formed physique. My chest constricts as I remember the throaty, purely male sounds he made when he neared his climax. Till the day I die, I won't ever forget how he threw his head back in utter euphoria as he released, groaning as if almost in pain. My entire body vibrated with need. It still does.

"Can't sleep, fireball?"

I'm so lost in my salacious memory, it takes me a second to register that the soft sound of Luke talking is actually real and not just in my mind. His presence startles me so much I gasp and drop the cup I was holding. Milk and shards of broken glass scatter everywhere on the linoleum floor.

"Shit," I mutter. I take a small step and wince loudly at the pain that stabs my sole.

"Fuck, stay still," he hisses as he rushes to me from the darkness. When he rounds the corner I notice two things.

First, apparently he was out here when I walked in because I see a barely eaten Bomb Pop in his hand, frost still coating the bottom layer.

Second, he's utterly mouthwatering in his dark grey boxer briefs, which are not doing a damn thing to hide his very rigid package. *God have mercy.* I cannot pull my eyes away from the cock I've just been caught fantasizing about.

I can hardly concentrate on anything other than the intense throbbing between my legs as he sets his popsicle down on the counter and starts toward me. I hold out my hand trying to stop him from coming closer. If he touches me right now, I'm a total goner. At this moment, he'll be able to get me to do anything he wants. *Anything.* "Luke, no. You'll get hurt."

"Steel's impenetrable, baby." He continues forward, heedless of my protests and regardless of the fact his feet are as bare as mine. He steps carefully, avoiding the largest pieces of glass and grabs me firmly by the waist, lifting me effortlessly as if I were a sack of flour. After depositing me on the counter, he hands me his frosty treat. "For safekeeping. This is one of my favorite sweets in the world. Don't you dare lick it, fireball," he says with a wink and a mischievous grin.

I don't know about you, but when somebody tells me not to do something, *yeah*...makes me want to do it all the more, so while I watch him walk to the hall closet, retrieve the broom, and begin to clean up the mess, I lick away.

I slurp.

I suck.

I make a big production out of eating his red, white, and blue popsicle, laughing the entire time as his gaze continually slides to me, a slight smirk upturning his lips. He turned on the overhead light when he got the broom, so there is absolutely no mistaking the heat in his eyes burns hotter each time they connect with mine. And definitely not in anger.

A few minutes later, he dumps the broken remnants of the glass in the garbage can, along with the milk-soaked paper towels. Leaning the broom against the wall and the dustpan on the floor, he turns, and the second his predatory gaze lands on mine, my laughter dies.

Uh oh.

When I was a kid, the thing I loved about Bomb Pops, as opposed to other popsicles, is that they're big. They're a good thick inch of tasty girthiness, so they take a while to eat if you know how to savor them instead of biting your way through. So although I've been eating Luke's frozen treat for the last few minutes, there is still plenty left for him.

I think at this point I should also confess when I was fifteen, my girlfriends and I used to practice our bj skills on Bomb Pops before we ever practiced on a real penis. And, for the last five minutes, I *may* have been reenacting my teenage days, except my skills are far more honed and refined now with "real-life" experience.

"You're awfully good at that, fireball," he husks, his eyes dropping to my mouth as I slide the melting delicacy out from between my probably now blue-stained lips. His voice sounds like it's been steeped in sex, then double dipped in raw decadence.

"That I am," I reply just as hoarsely. I don't even recognize my voice it's dropped so many octaves.

He's now standing between my legs, having wedged them apart with his hips. His hand winds around mine, the one with the popsicle, and brings it to his own mouth, smoldering eyes holding mine as he draws it slowly between his lips, tongue snaking out to catch the melting ice.

Oh God.

Air. I need it.

He pulls it out just as unhurriedly and sets it on the counter beside me. "You didn't follow directions, Addy."

He runs a hand slowly down my leg, goose bumps following his touch like starstuck groupies. Grabbing my injured foot he draws it back to take a look, gently extracting the protruding piece of glass stuck in my tender skin. Leaning over, he throws it into the trash and I hear a ping as it hits the other shards.

"What can I say? I'm a born rule breaker," I tease breathlessly. I try to laugh, but it comes out strangled.

I'm momentarily dazed when his tongue darts out, licking the injured spot that now mildly throbs. *Oh, fuck.* "Rule breakers usually need punishment to understand the err of their ways," he purrs between wet kisses up my arch to my ankle.

"You think?" I'm panting now. Actually panting with excitement and hunger.

"Abso-fucking-lutely," he mutters roughly, continuing his hot assault up my inner thigh to almost the edge of my panties. One slight turn of his head and he'll be in the Promised Land.

Turn, turn, turn, I silently beg.

I almost cry out when he does, his nose nudging my silk-covered sex. I hear him inhale before he stands up. He gently releases my leg, trailing his large hands up my bare thighs. The groupies are back, except this time they're all over in hot anticipation to get closer to the sex god standing in front of us.

My eyelids are as heavy as my head. "Luke..." His name is a hoarse plea, but I'm not sure if I'm begging him to stop or continue. My breath hitches when his thumbs reach the edges of my panties, his thick hands wrapped tightly around my hips, kneading my flesh.

"Stop thinking, Addy. Let go. I promise I'll catch you."

"Oh God," I choke as his lithe digits tunnel under the scrappy fabric. My head falls and my eyes squeeze shut when I feel the rough pads feather too lightly along my soaked, bare nether lips.

My heart is pounding so fast, had he not hummed the words directly in my ear, I'm not sure I would have heard. "Surrender to me, Addy. I've got you." Hot lips suck ravenously and at a maddeningly slow pace down my throat, which I've tilted under his sensual onslaught.

My heart and body are on the same page, and for the last couple of weeks, the two have been ganging up against my stubborn will. They've finally just won. The last of my resolve withers away like wilted lettuce under his touch, his lips and his rough, but heartfelt demands. I can no longer deny what I'm feeling for this man. I no longer want to.

"Luke, please."

My hips begin moving, trying to get what I now so desperately need, but the quick squeeze of his hands stops me, holding me still. With great effort, I pry open my lids to see him staring at me with the same look he had the last time we made love.

Awe. Pure and utter reverence.

My heart liquefies.

Then my face is in his hands and that determination I saw when he told me he'd fight for me is back in full force. "I want this. Us. Jesus, I'm...stop fighting it, *me*. Tell me you'll give us a chance."

I nod and feel him marginally relax.

"No more denying this. Say it."

"No more denying."

"No more dancing."

I shake my head. "I'm a terrible dancer."

A corner of his mouth briefly turns up. "Yes. You are."

His molten eyes search mine. He struggles for a few seconds to speak and it doesn't take me long to understand why. Being openly vulnerable is like flaying your own skin. "I—God, I've *never* felt like this before, Addy. About *anyone*." And I get what he's telling me. I also didn't realize I needed to hear it.

"Me either," I confess softly, raising my hand to stroke his jaw. Then I add, "Don't hurt me, Luke. Please."

His mouth drops to mine, branding it in a hot, passionate kiss. "Only in ways that feel good, baby."

Grabbing the hem of my top, he draws it over my head. His gaze snaps to my breasts, which are full and needy, aching for the suction of his mouth, the bite of his teeth. Lifting his smoky eyes back to mine, he stays silent as he hooks his fingers in my panties and pulls them down my legs, leaving me physically bare and emotionally vulnerable.

Taking my hands, which are wrapped tightly around the edge of the counter, he sets them behind me, so it appears that I'm casually leaning back like I'm lying out, worshipping the sun instead of about to be worshipped by him. Then he pulls on my hips until my ass is barely balancing on the ledge. I have to lean back farther to keep from falling off. Finally, Luke spreads my legs so far apart, I'm quite sure I look obscene from his angle, all splayed open for his searing perusal.

"Don't move, Addy. A single muscle or I promise you I'll make it so you can't." The lust that thickens his voice to the point it's gruff and husky sends hot sparks thundering through my blood. When he leans down and latches onto a pebbled nipple, sucking hard, I gasp at the pleasure and let my head fall back. My arms wobble and he winds one of his behind my back for support. I hope that doesn't count as moving a muscle. Or maybe I do. The thought of being tied up and completely at his mercy is exhilarating.

I suck in a sharp breath when I feel biting cold against my neglected nipple, a complete contrast to the heat currently wrapped around the other. I whip my head up to see Luke's grabbed the popsicle and is circling my areola. Cold, flavored water now runs in rivers down my breast and stomach. Luke's lips quickly travel over to the hardened nub and it takes only seconds for it to warm under his attention, the fiery sensation waning.

"Fuck, you taste good, baby," he murmurs against my sticky flesh, his tongue lapping at me like a cat. "Been dying for it."

He stands, the frozen treat still in hand. Delight dances in his hazel depths as he brings it to the other nipple. Repeating his earlier actions he ignores my breathy protests, except this time, he doesn't lean down to lick it off. He lets the syrupy goodness drip as he takes his time coating both of my breasts before running a path straight to my center.

When he reaches my open slit, he pauses, eyes snaring mine, daring me stop him. Daring me to move. Daring me to say no.

Daring.

"You wouldn't," I whisper, unsure if I want him to continue or stop. *Continue*. Definitely continue.

"Oh, but I would. This is number twenty-two on the bucket list, fireball," he hums. I almost laugh until he slowly pushes the ice cold frozen dessert into my hot, aching sex.

"Luke, fuck..." My hips buck, my mouth falling open in a silent scream.

"Don't. Fucking. Move," he growls, desire punctuating each syllable. He holds me firmly in place with one hand as he continues his merciless assault on my tender tissues. "So goddamn sexy," he mumbles.

"Ahhhh," I cry out when he pushes deeper. I've never felt sensations like the ones currently battering my core. Fire. Ice. Burning in my very center from the inside out. I want to escape and I never want him to stop. I feel unbelievably sexy and hedonistic as cool, melted water drips, pooling under my ass.

Then he's withdrawing it and the worst of the fiery feeling abates, coolness lingering in its place.

"Addy, look at me," he grates roughly.

My eyes flutter open.

"You're fire everywhere, sweetheart," he tells me before putting what's left of the Bomb Pop in his mouth and sucking. He closes his eyes briefly in pure rapture.

Fuck. That. Is. Hot.

"I'll never eat another one of these again without thinking about your pussy. In fact, I don't think I'll ever be able to eat another one of these again without taking a little dip first because this is the best fucking Bomb Pop I have ever tasted."

"God," I breathe. I'll never again be able to walk by the freezer aisle without my thighs clenching. Ever.

"I need to hear you moan. Scream. Writhe in pleasure under my tongue." He abandons the sliver of ice left on the stick and swoops down, his cool tongue meeting my still cool core, licking from bottom to top. Two fingers enter me on a hard thrust as suction on my clit has me shattering into a million brilliant pieces within seconds.

"Again," he demands against my now sensitive sex.

Now Luke takes his time. He circles my clit slowly, then flicks fast, ending with a tiny bite before starting all over again. His fingers push in and out on a quicker pace, setting a perfect rhythm like he's in time with a metronome.

Circle.

Flick.

Bite.

Again and again, until I'm splintering in two as I ride the wave of pure heat running through my veins. I burst free and float. I feel the flip to gravity switch off and I'm hovering aimlessly in space, never wanting to return to earth.

"You back, baby?" he asks huskily. I've been so lost in pleasure I hadn't realized his clothes are completely missing, but don't put out an APB. Trust me on this.

He's lying over me, our hands entwined and our arms stretched out over my head. I don't know when I laid down, but I now register the hardness of the countertop beneath me, and I can't make myself give a damn. Luke's hips are moving back and forth, causing his steely cock to rub along my wetness, coating himself thickly with me.

"You good?"

"More than," I pant, not understanding how just rubbing his shaft on the outside of my sex can feel so damn good.

"Are you on the pill, Addy?" he rasps in my ear before nipping my lobe hard, drawing a moan from me.

His question makes me nervous. I've never had sex before without a condom. I've never trusted anyone enough to do so, I guess, but so help me, the thought of having Luke be the first man inside me like that sends a fiery zing of eagerness rippling through me. All of a sudden my body is craving his seed on some type of biological level and there's no way I can deny its call.

"IUD."

Our eyes lock. "I want to fuck you raw, Addy. I need to feel my cock slide over each wet, hot ridge as I claim you, brand you. As I own your body and steal your soul."

"Luke..."

I realize his head has slipped shallowly inside as he was talking. Hand to God, it feels so damn good I think I'm going to come again. With each word, he slips inside further. "I'm going to come," I choke.

"Fuuuck," he curses long under his breath, teeth now scraping my neck. "Is that a yes, baby?"

"I've—I've never had sex without a condom," I admit.

He draws back and the look on his face can only be described as triumphant. "You haven't?"

"No."

His smile blinds me, rendering me speechless. "Me either. So I guess that means I'm yours and you're mine."

Hot sparks of yearning pelt me where we're about to be joined bare for the first time and I couldn't say no even if I wanted to, which I don't. "Fuck me, Luke. Please."

The words have no sooner left my lips than his mouth slams to mine, and he thrusts violently inside me, seated to the hilt in one long drive.

"Jesus, Addy. Fuck me. You feel so good," he grates, breath mingling with mine. He holds himself still as he stands and I can feel him pulse against my walls as he places my legs over his shoulders and palms the back of my neck with one hand while gripping my hip hard with the other. Strong fingers dig into my flesh and I know this time I'll have the trophies I craved last time.

"You're fucking mine now," he grits before withdrawing slowly and slamming back as quickly and brutally as the first drive. Withdrawing again, he repeats the same process. My eyes roll back. Jesus, the man is brilliant in bed. Or the kitchen. Whatever. "Don't close your eyes. I want to watch them glaze over. I want to watch you slowly unravel, baby."

And by slowly, he means excruciatingly *slooowly*. He brings me to the edge repeatedly yet doesn't let me fall over, changing his pattern frequently so my body has to readjust. As I near the high again, he pulls back and alters his cadence, his depth.

"I love the way your walls clench my cock, baby." I bear down again and he moans loudly, briefly letting his head fall. I delight in my feminine prowess to bring this man to his knees right before me. Turnabout is fair play. I do it again as he withdraws and his nostrils flare. "Fuuuck," he curses lowly.

"Stop teasing. Please."

"Please, what fireball?" he torments. The bastard knows exactly what I want. "Plead, Addy. Beg me to let you come."

Now, under normal circumstances, the last thing I would do is beg a man for anything, but right now Luke Colloway owns me. He owns my body, my mind, my heart, all of which have reluctantly been slipping away to him these past weeks. And now he's taking the last piece I have to give; I do it freely, which ironically is the hardest one for me to let go of.

He finally owns my will.

"Please, Luke. Please. I need to come."

"Fuck, I love it when you submit. It humbles me, baby."

Then he does what I so sweetly begged for and within five hard thrusts, lets me soar headlong into rapture, the white lights behind my eyelids temporarily blinding me. Pleasure so profound surges through me when he follows on a loud growl; I lose myself completely, forgetting even where I am.

When I'm coherent again, Luke's lying over me, panting, lips skimming along my jawline. *Huh*. I may have to rethink this begging thing. It turned out well for me. Very well indeed.

"Swear to God, I've never felt anything that good. Perfect, all of you," he mutters against my now goose-pebbled flesh, hands roaming all over me. Even with a good fucking like the one Luke just gave me, he's made me feel nothing short of cherished and cared for and maybe even loved.

"Utopia, right?" My voice sounds rough, like sandpaper. Could be the screaming I've been doing for the last half hour. I hope I didn't wake the neighbors.

"Fucking A, right. Come on. We're a mess."

"A good mess, though."

As he extricates himself from me, his gaze is still laced with barely controlled heat. "This is going back on the list."

I laugh. "Except next time, it's my turn."

A wicked smile spreads his lips. "If you insist."

Then I'm in his arms, being carried through the living room, down the hall, and into my bathroom. He sets me down and turns on the shower, steam filling the small space quickly.

Pulling me into the fiberglass compartment, he backs me up against the cool hardness, drawling before taking my lips in another scorching kiss, "I'm not nearly done with you yet, fireball. In fact, I'm quite sure I'll never be done with you."

Luke grabs my loofah and some shower gel, lathering the sponge until it's nice and foamy and drops to his haunches in front me. Picking up one foot, then the other, he starts to gently soap up my body. I can only lean against the shower wall for support as I watch him treat me like some precious piece of antique handblown glass. Once again, this is something no man has ever done for me. When I told Luke I wanted to be first, I didn't realize that I was setting a whole series of firsts into motion. My heart is so full right now it feels like it's going to burst.

Traitorous tears spring to life and I can't avert my eyes quickly enough when his gaze sweeps up my body.

"Baby, what's wrong?" he asks, almost panicked, completely forgetting about cleaning me as he drops the loofah to the shower floor.

I shake my head, unable to talk for fear of sobbing like a baby. Just what a man wants after he's fucked your brains out, a woman who goes into complete meltdown. Not cool.

Cupping my cheeks, he looks deeply into my eyes. "God, Addy, please tell me you don't regret this."

"No. I couldn't," I manage to say through a clogged throat.

"Thank Christ." Putting his forehead to mine, he closes his eyes, releasing a long, shaky breath. "You're scared, aren't you?"

I nod, my own eyes closed.

"So am I, baby. I've never given a woman the power to destroy me before."

I have, I want to say. Too many times. *And now I've just cracked open my chest and handed my heart to you to do with what you will.* But now doesn't seem like the time to mention that as we're standing bare and exposed in more ways than one.

"We do this together, yeah?" he says softly.

"Together," I agree.

He presses me into the now warm fiberglass, lips working their way across my collarbone as his hand works its way back to my sopping center. After the multiple orgasms he just gave me in the kitchen, I wouldn't think I could get aroused for a week, but that pool of desire starts to build again as his fingers dive in and he groans. His intense want for me pulses against my thigh.

"Addy, I need to fuck you again. Now."

"I need you to fuck me again. Please." I've never needed anything more.

Lifting one leg, he wraps it around his thigh and gently pushes inside. This time, there's no screaming and no frantic clawing. This time, there's only reverent words and sweet, slow but passionate lovemaking.

Thirty minutes later, we drop exhausted and clean into Luke's bed. Within only minutes, I fall asleep against the man I love, contented and truly happy for the first time in a very, very long time, wondering why it took me so damn long to let myself believe in him, yet still carrying that little grain of worry that he'll break my heart.

Chapter 28

LUKE

"I didn't realize you had a car, too. I mean I saw this beauty sitting in the lot and guess I should have known it belonged to you."

I look over and grin in response. We're driving down I94 in my black Audi RS7, heading to Detroit for Easter weekend. It's taken me the last two nights to convince Addy to drive together. We're going to the same damn place, for fuck's sake, but her stubborn-ass self makes things more difficult than they need to be.

It didn't take me long to figure out how to persuade her to see things my way, though and yes, it's exactly what you're thinking. It's incredible how pliable a woman, particularly Addy, becomes after you've sated her with several orgasms. And it's not a hardship either, let me tell you.

"I thought it was supposed to be nice this weekend. We could have taken your bike."

My laughter fills the car. "Then you should have packed a smaller bag, fireball. There's no way that damn thing would have fit in the saddlebag."

Besides, if I'd taken the bike, I couldn't have spent four hours looking at her beautiful face. Since she finally stopped denying that we have something real here, we've been nearly inseparable these last couple of weeks, and with every passing day, I fall into her even more.

"It's not that big."

"Not that big? I thought maybe you'd decided to move out, you packed so much damn stuff."

"Hey. Don't hate. A girl needs options."

"It's two fucking days, Addy. I'm quite sure your suitcase weighs even more than the airline allowance of fifty pounds. I'm not sure how you're going to make it to the Caribbean without sending clothes ahead."

"Whatever," she grumbles, although I can tell it's not in anger.

"I want you to come to my mom's for dinner Sunday."

This has been another bone of contention for us over the past few days. Addy refuses to come to my house for Easter, trying to use the lame excuse she doesn't want to intrude, but I know there's more to it than that.

She hasn't told her family about us yet. I know for a fact Eric will not take this little bombshell well, but he can piss off. I don't care how upset he gets or what kind of hissy fit he throws, *nothing* will keep me from my color now that I have her.

Eric's fiercely protective of his sister, just like her father is, so she wants to do this her own obstinate way. That brings me to another smoldering problem: she refuses to stay with me at my mom's, so I have to spend the next two nights away from her. Both my pride and my cock are less than happy about that development.

"Luke, we've talked about this."

"Yes, and I don't like your answer."

"You don't have to like it. You just have to accept it."

I am a stubborn asshole sometimes. I admit that. But my spitfire surpasses me in the obstinate department tenfold. I've quickly learned when I can't sex her into seeing things my way, a little *persuasion,* you might say, gets me what I want more often than not. I didn't live this long without having trapdoors buried all over the fucking place. "Baby, I want to spend our first Easter together," I coax.

She softens. *Bingo.*

"So do I, but..."

"Just think about it, okay? You're mine and I want everyone to know it." I bring her open palm to my lips, pressing a kiss in the center.

"Okay."

Her phone rings. I don't miss the guilty glance she throws my way when she fishes it out of her purse and silences it before she tries to throw it back in. I'm faster though, grabbing it from her fingers.

I look at the caller ID to see it's the camera man. My blood seethes black.

"Answer it," I grit.

"Luke, stop."

"Answer. It." Instead of giving her an option, I press the receive button and hand her the phone.

She throws daggers my way before answering sweetly. I can only hear her part of the conversation, but none of the words are "*don't call me again because I'm fucking taken,*" which, as far as I'm concerned, should have been the first and last words out of her mouth.

"Hi. Good. You?

"Headed to Detroit.

"What are you doing?

"Uh..." I can tell by the hesitation and the quick look she gives me exactly what the man who's trying to steal my girl just said. I grab the phone out of her hands, against her screeching protests. *Shit, that hurt.* I'm going to be deaf by the time I'm forty if she keeps that up.

Pinning her wrists together with one of my hands, I use the other to slide the phone between my cheek and shoulder, before taking the wheel again.

"Cooper, right?"

"Uh, yeah. Who's this?" he asks hesitantly. He knows exactly who the fuck this is. I raise my voice above Addy's who is howling like a banshee in the background.

"Look, Cooper, I think there's been a misunderstanding about Addy's availability."

"Her availability?" I don't miss the fact that his voice steeled. Can't say I blame the guy. He knows he's just lost out on the best thing to walk into his life.

"Yes, her availability. As in...she's not." Cocksucker.

Silence. He's silent for so long, I almost hang up on the asshole. Then he says, "Let me talk to her. I want to be sure she's okay."

Without responding, I hand the phone back to Addy, who rips it out of my hand. She spends the next couple of minutes assuring *Cooper* she's fine and that, *yes*, we're together, before disconnecting the call.

"You're an ass," she spits, throwing her phone back in her purse.

"You're mine."

"Cooper's a nice guy. He deserved better than that."

"He wants to fuck you. He's damned lucky that happened over the phone or I would be headed to the pen for second-degree murder. Be happy I was so congenial."

"Congenial?" she screeches loudly. I touch my ear, testing for wetness.

"Yes, congenial." There were a whole bunch of other choice words I could have spewed, but out of respect for Addy, I held my tongue.

"You're infuriating."

"Everyone has to excel at something, sweetheart."

Silence descends; it's not uncomfortable, at least not for me. She can be put out all she wants, but if the tables were turned and a woman who wanted to fuck *me* was calling, she'd have plenty to say and I can guarantee you my hellcat would be less than cordial.

Addy turns on the radio to some pop station. I much prefer alternative or rock music, like Five Finger Death Punch, but when I was growing up, shotgun always got to choose the station. I'd let her anyway no matter where she was sitting.

She looks out the passenger side window, giving me both the back of her head and the silent treatment. It's hard to stifle my laugh, but I manage. After a while, she begins to hum softly to the radio and half an hour later, when she starts singing the acidic words to "Black Widow" in my direction, I know everything is okay. I hold in my smile for fear of setting her off again. Oh...and having my balls twisted. She tried that last week.

When the song's over, she turns off the radio and shifts in her seat to face me, pulling her left foot up to her chin. Jesus, that woman is flexible, as she's proven many times over the past couple of weeks.

"What's the tattoo on your side say?"

I sigh internally, not wanting to make her mad again. Quite frankly, I'm surprised it's taken her this long to ask. I've been waiting. But I suppose I shouldn't be surprised she chose to do it in the car while we're driving seventy-five down the highway. I'm the definition of a captive audience right now.

I think about how I want to answer her question without revealing too much. My ink is intensely personal; each and every one has special meaning to me and me alone. They're like a badge of honor. A remembrance of who I am, who I was. Remember earlier when I said I was an open book? Well, I may have exaggerated a bit. My book's not fucking open to the pages that I've superglued together so no one sees that part of my life, especially the woman I love.

"It's a war cry."

"That's what it says? It's a war cry?"

"Pretty much."

"Pretty much or exactly?"

"Pretty much."

You would think with a vague answer like that, Addy would get the hint, but *nooo*. I've come to the conclusion that "no" isn't in her vocabulary. I should rephrase. It's in *her* vocabulary; she just doesn't hear it when it's spoken *to* her.

"What do the seagulls represent?"

I bark a laugh. "I like birds."

"And the horse and demon?"

"I like the wind in my hair."

"Mmm. What about the crosses?"

I sigh. "I grew up Catholic." The truest answer I've given yet in her dissecting interrogation, but she already knows this because she attended church with me last Saturday night.

Then she surprises me by asking, "Why no color?"

Addy's incredibly perceptive and I think that's one of the reasons I am so drawn to her. No one has ever gotten me like she has. I reach across the console, grab her hand, and bring it to my lips. "I already told you. *You're* my color, Addy."

Her eyes sparkle and a slight smile turns her beautiful lips.

"Why the third degree on my ink, babe?"

"Why the evasion?"

I release her hand as an uncomfortable hush falls like a wet blanket. I can't tell Addy about my ink without revealing more than I want her to know and I never want Addy to be exposed to the darkest parts of me. The parts of me *I* don't even like.

"I know more than you think I do, you know."

"Dog with a bone," I mutter under my breath. "Yeah. How's that?" I keep my focus out the front windshield, pretending that I'm paying attention to the road. I'm not.

"Well, for one, I know every tattoo you have is personal. They mean something to you."

"All ink is personal, sweetheart. Try again."

She sighs lightly and lays her head against the headrest. Out of my peripheral, I see she's chewing on her bottom lip. I've discovered she only does that when she's nervous or deep in thought.

I'm mentally bracing myself for a verbal spar, so her touch is completely unexpected. Electricity jolts through me as she lightly traces the scripted word *Faith* that sits underneath the crown on my right bicep. Next, she slowly outlines the sunbeams and puffy cumulous clouds that peek out from under my sleeve, pushing it up so she can get to all of it.

She leans over the console and I jerk, sucking in a sharp breath when her lips meet my neck.

Her tongue darts out, trailing a line up to my ear where she sucks the skin underneath. Then she surprises me by tugging on my tee, trying to remove it.

"Fuck, Addy. What are you doing?"

"I want to touch you. Feel you." Her hand travels down my stomach and cups my stone-cold-hard cock with firm intent. "Please," she murmurs between kisses.

What fucking idiot is going to deny his sweetly begging woman that request? Not this one, that's for damn sure.

I help her take off my shirt, careful to keep a hand on the wheel at all times. She throws it in the back and then her mouth is back on me, her tongue now tracing the crisp beams of light down my shoulder while her fingers skitter over the crosses on my right pec.

"Addy," I groan. *Sweet Jesus, I want her.*

I mourn the loss of her mouth when she leans back and starts quietly analyzing me. "I know that you're faithful. It centers you, grounds you. I think you feel you need absolution for something in your past."

My breathing picks up and my heart pounds as she moves to outline the hourglass on my forearm. "A dove represents peace or innocence and the obvious representation of the hourglass is the passage of time, but I think it means more to you than that. Patience, maybe."

Dancing down my abdomen, her fingers feather across my seagulls and she continues, undaunted.

"You want personal freedom but you think due to life's circumstances, you can't have it or don't deserve it."

"Addy," I breathe softly, now stroking her dark locks with my free hand.

Reaching across to my left shoulder, she continues, whispering, "As far as the wild mare and hooded monster go, I think you're the horse. You're trying to outrun your demons, but you feel like you can't ever get them off your back. You hope the sunlight breaking through the clouds banishes them to the shadows. I can see them lurking in the corners, behind your crown on the other arm."

My mind is buzzing when she finally grazes over my etching. She leans into my line of sight so she can snare my eyes, which are darting between her and the road. "As far as the decorations on your back, I don't know what they mean yet. I haven't had a chance to study them enough, but I hope someday you'll feel you can trust me with what the words mean. Regardless of what you think, Luke, nothing you tell me about your past can change the way I feel about you."

I swallow hard. She's been so spot-fucking-on with every insightful observation, it's unnerving. She can see right through me. Through all the masks I wear, hiding myself from the world. If it's even possible, I just fell more in love with this woman.

"Christ, Addy," I growl. With a hand on her nape, I yank her to me and kiss her hard and

LUKE'S ABSOLUTION

deep, pouring every ounce of emotion I have for her into it. I can't kiss her the way I want or I'll kill us. It's a promise of what's to come later, regardless of our sleeping arrangements.

When I release her, her hot mouth is back on me.

"You're so sexy," she mumbles. Pressing wet openmouthed kisses over my crosses, her warm breath washes over my pecs and travels south, swirling around my cock like a tornado where I feel my seed being tugged directly from my balls in a desperate need to explode.

My abs flex and ripple with each light nip. She doesn't leave an inch of exposed skin untouched before working her way back up, mumbling against my lips as she works the button and zipper on my jeans. "I want your cock in my mouth."

Before I can respond, my dick is sinking between her hot little lips, her tongue swirling madly.

"Shit, fireball," I growl. My head slams back against the headrest and one hand fists her hair, guiding her up and down my greedy shaft. My eyes want to fall closed so I can focus only on the feel of her suction, her wet tongue, her talented fingers as she fondles my balls. I force them open, focusing on keeping my vehicle between the white lines, so I don't send us both to an early grave. But what a hell of a way to go.

"Yes. God. That's it, baby," I croon. Encourage. Within mere seconds, she's brought me embarrassingly close to climax. I can already feel the telling tingling in my spine, the precursor announcing my impending explosion. To be fair, she had me knocking on ecstasy's doorstep before she even started, every light touch pushing me closer.

"I'm gonna come in your mouth, Addy," I warn. I tug on her hair to try to dislodge her, knowing I'm only seconds away from erupting, but she pulls against me, her pressure and pace increasing. I hardly get a chance to enjoy the euphoric feeling before my seed is being viciously ripped from my balls and shooting down her throat.

"Fuck yes. Yes." My hips buck so hard I hear her gag; she never stops sucking or swallowing until I begin to soften.

Yep, fucking fire everywhere, my fireball.

I can honestly say I've never received a blowjob while hurtling at breakneck speed down the highway. I can also honestly say that I hope it's not the last time, because... *Fuck. Me.*

That was brilliant.

Chapter 29

Addy

"Pull up on the left side there."

Luke does as I instruct, stopping close to the garage. He shuts off the car, which throws us into darkness except for the streetlight three houses down that barely illuminates us. A row of thick hedges lines our left, giving us privacy from the neighbors next door. We've pulled so far ahead that no one can see us from the front window or door either, which was my intention.

"Let me come in with you."

"Luke, stop. You said you'd let me do this my way."

Except I haven't exactly figured out what "my way" is yet. Eric will absolutely flip his lid. My older brother has not approved of one of the men I've dated and I have to wonder if he had some sort of sixth sense about them. He's tried to keep me away from guys like Luke my whole life. Hell, he's tried keeping me away from *Luke*, although he has to know by now I've met him since I'm best friends with his brother's wife. But he hasn't asked and I haven't offered.

My dad is almost as bad as Eric. He'll take one look at Luke and lump him into the same category as all of the other men I've brought home. To be fair...I did the same thing.

It didn't take me long to figure out, though, while on the outside Luke may look like the others, on the inside, he's wholly unique. I'm sure it will take all of two minutes for my dad to see how much he cares about his little girl. Eric, on the other hand, will be a tougher nut to crack. Luke has a tough road ahead to convince the men in my life, my protectors, that he's worthy of me. I know he'll do it, though. Just like he did with me.

"Addy," he pleads, grabbing me by the nape and helping me over the console so I'm straddling his lap. "You're my girlfriend. Call me selfish, but I want your family to know. Mine does."

My heart melts.

"Your girlfriend?" I can't stop the huge smile that pops out.

"You like that?" he husks, tugging on my bottom lip with his thumb.

I fucking love it!

"Ehhh," I respond, shrugging my shoulders nonchalantly.

"Little liar," he chuckles. He pulls me to him for a ravenous kiss. When his tongue touches mine, insatiable want detonates inside me, clouding my thoughts. Suddenly I need him buried deep in me this damn instant. I'm so worked up from the car ride, from touching him all over, I can't think straight.

Before we left, Luke took me hard and fast against my bedroom wall after he teased me about my suitcase, but it's not enough. I can't imagine going even a day without making love to him. Now, I'm regretting my decision to stay at my dad's house. I'd die though before I'd tell Luke, giving him the satisfaction.

I lift my hips and start to undo his jeans when he grabs my hands, halting my frantic efforts. "What's wrong?" I pant. Jesus, I'm panting and he hasn't even touched me yet. My body responds to this man like no other before him.

"Addy, I'm not fucking you in my car outside your father's house. That's disrespectful to both him and you."

"Why? He can't see us here."

One hand grasps my hips, stopping my movement. "Sounds like you have some experience with that?" he growls, his face turning hard and angry.

Whoops. *Maybe?*

"I plead the fifth."

"Jesus Christ, Addy. All the more reason I'm not fucking you here. You deserve better than to be treated like a two-bit whore who gets a quick fuck and then is sent on her way back inside like a good little girl. If those are the kinds of men you've been dating, then…"

That melted heart? Just hardened like slate. How dare he! I may have made some poor choices when it comes to men, but they're *my* choices. *My* mistakes. And I'm certainly no damned whore.

"Then what?" I grit, my voice full of venom.

"Then they're stupid fucking pricks who don't deserve an incredible woman like you, Addy. Christ, you should be revered, honored. Men should be kneeling at your feet, giving you jewels, and feeding you grapes and shit. I don't think you understand how special you really are."

I snort, but I'm starting to weaken and he knows it. Cupping my face, he continues. "Baby, don't ask me to treat you with anything less than the respect you deserve, okay?"

Sigh.

It's dizzying how I can vacillate between wanting to kick him in the balls one minute and wanting to crawl into his arms and never leave the next. I love this man so much already it hurts sometimes.

I kiss him nice and slow. Tasting, taking, giving. "You're like no one I've ever met before, Luke Colloway," I whisper against his lips.

"I keep tellin' you that, fireball," he drawls and I laugh. "Someday you'll believe me. Now, you'd better go in or you're coming home with me."

Chuckling, I give him another peck and open the door. He follows me out and retrieves my luggage and purse from the car, setting them in front of me before his arms secure me tight.

"You never analyzed my heart tattoo."

"No." Purposefully. I look down, unable to hold his intense stare for fear he'll see the doubt that's never too far away.

With a finger under my chin, he lifts it back up. "Do."

"Why?" My heart races. I'm not sure I want the answer.

"Do it, sweetheart," he cajoles, cupping my cheek. "Please."

I take a deep breath. "Okay. Well, that one's the most obvious. Someone you care greatly about hurt you deeply and you have your heart on lockdown to prevent you from being hurt again."

"All true," he says softly, lightly stroking my chin with his thumb. "But it's not a woman like you're thinking."

"It's not?" I whisper, searching his eyes.

"No."

I wait for him to elaborate and when he doesn't, I just ask, "Who then?"

He looks away quickly before reclaiming my eyes. "My father."

"Oh, Luke," I whisper. Kindred spirits, Luke and I. We're alike in so many ways.

"You've melted them, you know."

"What?"

He leans down, placing a chaste kiss on my lips. "The chains, sweetheart. They didn't stand a chance against your fire."

Oh.

Wow.

"I'll see you tomorrow?"

I swallow thickly, my mind still back on the melted chain thing. "Yes. Eric's bringing me."

"Call me if you can't sleep, okay?"

"Okay."

"Goodnight, fireball."

"Night, Luke."

We've said our good-byes, but neither of us moves for what seems like minutes, an invisible magnetic force locking us together. When I do finally turn and make my way to the front door, I not only have to force my feet forward, I have to force myself to swallow three words that want to come flying out of my mouth. Despite the fact that I've not ever felt like this about another human being, it's too soon to voice them, at least to Luke.

That doesn't stop me from saying them under my breath, though, once I reach the front door.

Chapter 30

Addy

"Can't sleep, Leenie?" my brother asks, padding quietly into the dimly lit kitchen. I smile at the childhood nickname he gave me after my full first name, Adeline, which is all my mother calls me, regardless of the fact I've asked her repeatedly to call me Addy.

"Nope. You?" Eric and I both inherited the insomniac gene from our father. I'm surprised he's not joined the party yet.

"Same. You know I heard yoga or meditation is supposed to help with insomnia."

Laughing, I tease, "And how exactly is it you know about yoga or meditation?" The only way Eric would know about either of these things is through a woman.

Eric and Luke are so much alike, in both looks and personality. Eric isn't quite as tall as Luke's six foot four frame, but he's just as built and ripped and decorated as he is. And with Eric's chiseled cheekbones, dark hair, and goatee, he could have almost any woman he wants, just like

Luke. I know he's had girlfriends, he just never stays with them long.

"I don't live in a cave, Leenie," he dodges.

"Mmm hmm. Right." Breaking off a piece of the oatmeal raisin cookie I'm eating, I pop it in my mouth and practically moan. Whenever my dad knows I'm going to be home, he always makes sure to have these from my favorite bakery. They're giant and sinful and worth every damn calorie. "I'm glad you're staying here this weekend. I don't get to see enough of you."

"Me too, squirt."

Eric has his own place, but it's almost forty-five minutes from his shop so sometimes when he works really late or doesn't feel like driving home, he'll crash with our dad, which is only five minutes away.

With a beer in hand, Eric leans against the kitchen counter, crossing his beefy arms, studying me. "So you're dating someone, huh?"

I choke on the bite I was just swallowing, coughing a little. "How...why do you say that?" I ask, my eyes now watering. Panic creeps through me. Does he know it's Luke? The adrenaline abates when he answers, making me shiver.

"Dad told me when I called him earlier to say I was coming. Said you were glowing. So?"

I spent a couple hours talking to my dad before he turned in, although we never talked about the new man in my life. My dad did suspect as much, and he hinted several times in his roundabout way.

"Glowing?" I hedge.

"Yeah. Glowing like a firefly."

"It's the males that glow. You know they glow because that's their mating call, right?"

"Mmm hmm..."

I laugh, shaking my head. "Yes, I am." This is my perfect opportunity. I should tell him it's Luke, but I don't. Yes, I'm chickenshit. *Balk, balk.*

"He treat you good?" he asks, taking a swig from his bottle.

"The best. He's a wonderful man, Eric. Not like anyone I've been with before."

He watches me for a few seconds. If he asks me who it is, I won't be able to lie so a big part of me wants him to so I can just get this off my chest. Another part of me doesn't want to have to battle about my choice of mates in the middle of the night. And honestly, the biggest reason I'm avoiding this discussion is I don't want to come between Luke and Eric's friendship and I fear it might if Eric can't accept it. He's just as stubborn as I am.

"I see what Dad's talking about. Your eyes are sparkling. I'm glad Leenie. You deserve it."

"Thanks, Eric."

He walks to the cupboard, snagging two of *my* cookies. "You'd better not eat all of those or you may find yourself on the receiving end of some nastiness, brother."

"Oh? Is this like the time you said you were going to prank me all day and didn't?"

"No, this will be like the time I set your alarm for three in the morning with the volume on max."

"Shit, Addy...that scared the piss out of me. Literally. I was so drunk that night, I actually pissed my bed."

"Serves you right. You ran off the boy I'd been crushing on for six months."

"He wasn't good enough for you."

"You don't think anyone is," I counter snidely.

"No one *is*, Leenie. You're...special."

See what I'm talking about?

"So, have you talked to Mom lately?"

"No," I reply quickly. And I don't plan on it, either.

"You need to, Addy. She's not doing well. Sam called me a couple of days ago and said she's been a lot more forgetful lately and she's retaining a lot of fluids. She's in a bad way, going downhill pretty fast now. I don't think she's going to make it much longer. I'm headed down to see her next week."

My mom has severe cirrhosis of the liver, diagnosed almost two years ago now. Although she contracted Hepatitis C during surgery when she was a child, her condition has been exacerbated by her abuse of the bottle. She's not a candidate for a liver transplant because she also has a heart condition and the doctors don't think she'll make it through the surgery. I also think that's due to years of alcohol abuse. The kicker is, my mom hasn't given up her drinking even with the death sentence she's been handed so I don't plan to sit around and watch her intentionally, slowly kill herself.

He adds, "Sam said she's been trying to get ahold of you."

She has. I've been ignoring her calls, preferring to live in my happy little bubble instead.

"I'll think about it," I reply. He knows I'm full of shit.

"You're going to regret it if you don't see her, Addy. She's going to die and it will eat you up to not resolve things between you two."

Eric is the typical middle child, the peacekeeper of the family. He's always trying to push my mom and me back together, but he knows better than anyone in our family how things were between us.

Sighing heavily, I spit, "What exactly would *I* have to regret, Eric? *She's* the parent, and a piss poor one at that. We both know how our mother feels about me, anyway."

I wasn't wanted in the first place. *Did I forget to tell you that?* I was an unfortunate accident, a mistake. A mistake she constantly reminded me of, especially when she was between boyfriends, because somehow that was my fault. She didn't want me, but she wouldn't give me up either, always refusing my requests to live with my dad. She had custody and regularly used me as a bargaining chip in her charade of selfish games.

I should have taken a lesson out of Eric's playbook and gone down the wrong road so she'd send me away; I just couldn't make myself do it. Instead, I strived for perfection in hopes I could eventually make her happy and proud of me. I now know it was a fruitless effort. I wouldn't admit it to Eric, but no matter how much I don't want it to, her rejection still stings.

"I'm going to bed." I stand, pushing the chair back.

"I'm sorry, Addy. I know you had it rough with her."

"Yeah, well, I had you and Dad."

"It's not enough."

"It never is," I say softly, kissing him on the cheek. I'm halfway up the stairs when I freeze midstep at the words that follow.

"Oh, by the way, Luke Colloway called and asked if we would come to Easter dinner at his mom's house Sunday. She's a mean cook. You've met Luke, right?"

Shit.

Why that goddamn infuriating, underhanded man! Going behind my back to get what he wants. Now I'm going to have to spend all day with him either pretending we're not a couple in front of my family or telling them before we go. Ohhhh...he's good. Very good.

"Yes," I answer, trying to keep my voice steady. I should confess now. He's mentioned Luke's name so I should just tell him I'm in love with his best friend and beg for his understanding. The door is open, only I'm standing on the threshold, paralyzed. I chicken out...again. "What did you say?"

"I said yes. Figured since you're friends with Livia and his brother that it would be okay and would be better than that shitty diner. Dad said he didn't care either way when I called him."

I think we all know by now that I can't cook and a home-cooked meal sounds better than dry ham and runny mashed potatoes from a restaurant, but still. It's the principal of how Luke went about it. You can be damned sure he's going to get an earful in about sixty seconds. "Okay. Fine."

"I can cancel if you want, Addy. It's no problem. I just thought..."

"No, it's fine. Really." He'll just find some other way to get what he wants. "Night, Eric."

"Night, squirt."

When I make it to my bedroom, I pick up my phone and text Luke. Who cares that it's after three in the morning? Not this pissed-off female. I am about to live up to my nickname right now. He wants fire? He's got a fucking inferno burning.

> Me: really, luke?
> Me: using my brother
> Me: to get what you want?
> Me: kinda childish
> Me: don't you think?

Yes, I intentionally sent multiple texts hoping to wake him up. Who's acting childish now? I proudly raise my hand. He responds almost immediately and when I see his text come through, I have to contain my squeal and remember why I'm pissed at him. My thighs clench in both desire and chilly remembrance. *Damn* him.

Bomb Pop: there are no rules in war, fireball
Me: is that what this is?
Bomb Pop: until I can call you permanently mine, yes. I won't apologize

I sit there staring at those words. Well, *one* in particular. Surely he doesn't mean...

Bomb Pop: can't sleep?
Me: no. my furnace is missing. you throw off enough heat to warm half of chicago
Bomb Pop: how did you ever live without me?
Bomb Pop: want me to come over?

How did you ever live without me? *I don't know*, I think. I honestly don't know. This entire revenge text is backfiring on me. *Big* time. I need to take control back. I choose to ignore his first question, answering his second.

Me: no. did I wake you?
Bomb Pop: shame and yes. your incessant pings did the intended trick. everything ok?
Me: other than I'm mad at you?
Bomb Pop: I'll make it up to you. thoroughly and repeatedly, maybe with a dash of wicked thrown in if you need more convincing

Well. Shit.
Winner: Luke.

Me: luke?

Bomb Pop: yes baby?
Me: you infuriate me, but...
Bomb Pop: yes...??
Me: I like you
Me: a lot
Bomp Pop: I couldn't like you more if I tried addy monroe

I swallow hard, trying not to read more into that than he probably means.

Bomb Pop: night beautiful
Me: night

Once again Luke managed to commandeer the reins from me, but I find myself not caring. It's fifteen minutes before I float down from the ceiling and more than an hour before I finally talk myself into going to sleep because the entire time I'm twisting and pulling apart his use of the word permanent.

Did you know there are over forty different ways to say permanent and they all essentially mean the same thing?

Existing perpetually.

Everlasting, especially without significant change.

Long lasting or nonfading.

In other words, forever.

Forever.

For keeps.

Till hell freezes over.

Permanently.

Chapter 31

LUKE

"Another round?"

Conn, Asher, Gray, and I were kicked out of the house this afternoon during Livia's baby shower, hence our hole up at Stubby's Bar. If it were up to me, I would have stuck around, if for no other reason than to stand in the corner and watch Addy. Mom shooed us out well before the guests arrived though, so now I get to spend the next two hours or so with my brothers, which isn't the worst thing in the world either.

Gray looks to me, brows raised, knowing two beers is usually my limit. I've had two already, but I'm not driving and decide what the hell. "Sure."

I notice Conn watch our perky, pretty, twenty-some-year-old waitress saunter away, checking out the ass she's purposefully swaying. She's good, I'll give her that. She immediately discounted Gray after seeing his wedding ring, but she's been trying to play to the rest of us every time she comes by, which is frequently. I think she's finally caught on that Conn's the only one possibly biting. I usually pay attention to that shit, but ever since I've met Addy, I just don't look at women that way anymore. They all look...dull compared to my fireball.

I've fucked exactly *zero* women since the night I laid eyes on Addy Monroe. That's right, you heard me. A big fat goose egg. I couldn't fathom that act with anyone other than her. Hell, I'm not even sure I could have gotten it up for another woman.

Now that I have the woman I want, I can think of nothing other than when I can be inside of her again. I honestly think I could fuck us both to death if she'd let me, so the fact I couldn't be inside that sweet, hot pussy more than one time yesterday does not leave Luke a very happy man. The fact I won't be able to have her today either is making me extremely irritable.

And now I'm being cockblocked by one of my best friends, unbeknownst to him, because Addy hasn't come clean yet. I keep waiting for Eric to show up on my mom's doorstep. The fact he hasn't says it all right there, so I just gave her the push she needed by inviting the Monroes to Easter meal at our house through her brother.

I never thought I was possessive; I guess I just didn't have the right person to be possessive over. She's mine, and I don't want her pretending she's not. But her silence makes me wonder what she's waiting for. Is she unsure about us? Is she mad about how I handled the camera man yesterday? Is she dancing again? Denying? Not ready to commit? Shit...that thought makes my heart palpitate, because there's no one else for me but her.

So yeah, long story, but...I could use the extra beer.

"You're quiet," Gray says, regarding me keenly. Although Gray and I may not have had the best relationship over these past few years, it's improving and he's still my twin. No amount of time or distance can erase that unique connection we share.

"Just thinking," I mumble, taking a long swig of my Heineken.

"About one pretty, leggy brunette?" Conn pipes up, wagging his thick brows.

My gaze shifts to my younger, pot-stirrer brother. "Careful of that one," I nod to "Candi," with an "i" as she pointed out when she introduced herself (like we can't read the nametag stuck right above the tit she's got practically popping out of her red-checkered half shirt). "Got crabs written all over her."

He throws his head back, laughing. "I may appreciate, but the women I bed have an IQ higher than eighty, dick."

"Wow, just eighty? You've lowered your standards a bit in the last few years," Asher quips.

"That's because I've picked the good ones over already."

I half wonder if it's true based on what Asher's said. I remember Conn liked a redheaded beauty in high school, Nora something or other, and I also heard she moved away at the end of their senior year. Mom told me that Conn moped around like a lost puppy for weeks on end. I sometimes wonder if Conn hasn't gotten over that woman and is using his escapades as blacktop. Blacktop may fix a pothole, but it's temporary. Concrete's more solid, the good stuff. Wouldn't be the first person to do so, won't be the last.

"So, Mom mentioned the Monroes are coming over for Easter tomorrow."

I look at Conn and think, *you're the last one to fall, fucker*. And I can't wait for the deafening sound when he does. I may have been absent for a while, but I'm pretty sure he's been fighting it the most of any of us, not even letting the sheets warm up before showing his "date" the door, patting her ass on the way out. The bigger they are, the harder they fall, right?

"You haven't changed a fucking bit, you know that?" I tell Conn laughingly. "You just dump shit in and keep stirrin' and keep stirrin' until you get some kind of explosive reaction."

"Is that a question or a statement?" he asks with a cocky smirk.

My response is to flip him the bird.

"On a serious note, I was wondering if I could hire you for a job?"

"Want me to scope out your next conquest? Make sure her intelligence is up to snuff?"

"Something along those lines."

Turns out it's not a woman but a company he wants me to research. We spend the next ten minutes talking about Steele Recruiting, a smaller-scale executive recruiting firm he's looking to add to Wynn Consulting's portfolio, the division of GRASCO Holdings that Conn runs. He wants me to do some due diligence work. It's something some PIs do although it isn't generally my thing. Yet, I think it would be just right for the new guy I hired a couple weeks ago. Conn's pretty far along in the deal and has met with the owner several times now, but he wants me to research a few of the top executives and recruiters the owner insists he keep on staff for a period of time as part of the deal. We agree he'll send me the details in the next couple of weeks.

"A hundie on pool?" Asher throws down pointedly to Conn.

"Happy to take your money anytime, Ash."

They get up and head to the tables, leaving Gray and me alone. We watch them rack and trade barbs for a minute or two. Jesus, I love my brothers. I have sincerely missed them.

"This is nice. Being with you guys," I confess quietly.

"It is. I've missed you, Luke."

"Me too, brother."

"So, things going well with Addy then I take it?" Gray asks nonchalantly.

I watch my younger brothers, remembering the highly competitive streak we all seemed to inherit from our father, deciding how to answer. Truth it is. "She makes sense, you know. With her, I can just...I don't know...*be*, I guess. It sounds like a chick thing to say, but I feel like the man I was always meant to be has stepped out of the shadows. Like she's unlocked some fucking invisible door or something."

I think back to her observations of my tats yesterday, particularly the sunbeams banishing my demons to the shadows, except she didn't get that one quite right. It was *me* in the dark and the demons had free rein of the light. Now it's as if I've traded places with them and she's solely responsible.

I slide my eyes to Gray to find he's looking at me with a slight smile and...understanding. "I get it. I felt exactly the same way about Livvy. Like I didn't know I was missing something until I saw her and then everything just clicked."

"Yeah, except I knew I was missing it, I just didn't know what 'it' was. I've never felt like this, Gray. It's fucking scary. Like I'm free falling without a parachute or something, but I don't want to stop."

He barks a laugh. "Love's fucking scary, Luke. With the right woman, it's worth every terrifying plummeting second."

We're silent for a few beats and I know he understands the whole meaning of this conversation without me having to come right out and say it. I may have had deep feelings for Livia, but not like this. Addy's in a whole category to herself, as she should be.

"I didn't say I loved her."

He shakes his head. "Yes, you did. Just not in so many words."

"I feel like I'm not worthy of her," I admit quietly a couple minutes later.

"Define worth, Luke. You're an honorable man."

I snort. "I'm the furthest fucking thing from honorable, Gray, and we both know it. I've done so many dishonorable things, I've lost count."

"No. I don't know shit. You overcame the odds, Luke. You sank low and you scratched and clawed your way out of your own personal hell. You saved my wife. You gave me a family. A future. That's honorable if you ask me."

"I've taken a life." I can barely hear my own confession, yet I know Gray hears it plain as day. I may have alluded to this months ago, but Gray never asked and I never offered. It's a confession I need to get off my chest to someone who won't judge me because God knows I do enough of that myself.

Yes, I killed a man. Peter Wilder. I didn't shoot him. I did something far worse. I betrayed his trust. I slowly poisoned him with a legal medication that was supposed to be lifesaving, so that when his black heart stopped beating for the last time, it would look natural and no one would question it. Everyone knew he had heart problems. Turns out too much nitroglycerin over a long period of time for someone who has a bad heart has quite the opposite effect. Probably shouldn't put that shit so readily available on the Internet.

"No matter how vile of a human being he was, I premeditated and deliberately carried out a murder. I played God, and that weighs heavily on me. How can I expect absolution from anyone else, especially an incredible, pure woman like Addy, when I'll never be able to give it to myself?"

"We're talking about the low-life maggot who murdered my baby and nearly killed my Livvy, yes?"

I nod sharply and we go silent, both of our eyes zeroed in on our younger brothers. When the waitress comes by, we order another round. After a few minutes, Gray speaks quietly.

"I think you need to flip this around, Luke. You premeditated to *save* a life. The life of an innocent woman who was being tortured and raped, slowly marching toward death's door every day. Every encounter with him could have been her last. Had you not done what you did, the life of an innocent would be haunting you right now instead, and that would be a hefty burden you'd never be able to shed, no matter how many Hail Marys you say or masses you attend. I know this has eaten you up, Luke, but the fact you even give two fucks about what you did to that piece of shit who was deserving of far, far worse says *everything* about your character. Your *honor*."

I finally slide my gaze to his as he continues. "It's time to bury this, to forgive yourself. It's time to let yourself be happy. You fucking deserve it. You're worthy of her, Luke. More than. And if she does find out about this, then I have no doubt she'll understand."

"She's my color." My voice cracks a bit and if Gray hears it, he doesn't call me out. Good brother, that. If he did, I may just have to reclaim my manhood and throw down some type of challenge.

"To blinding color," he says, holding up his own green bottle, a small smile turning his mouth.

"It's fucking brilliant," I reply, tipping my own bottle to my lips.

"Livvy wanted me to give you a message, by the way."

My brows cock. "Really? What's that?"

"She said if you hurt her friend, she'll cut off your balls."

"Wow," I snort. "Become violent, has she?"

"You have no goddamn idea," he chuckles. "Say, can I ask you something? You don't have to answer if you don't want to."

Our attention shifts briefly to Ash who is now whooping it up, making a big scene. He must have won the last game and I see they're racking another.

"Shoot," I reply, not at all sure where this is going. Could be any number of sinkholes I can't step into.

"How did you get hooked up with that sadistic murderer anyway?"

"Who? Peter?"

Gray's eyebrows rise. "There were more?"

Not like him. "He was the worst of the worst."

"So can you talk about it? Help me understand?"

Can I? I'm not supposed to speak of this. Ever. But if I can trust anyone to keep this secret, it's Gray.

"This stays between us."

He nods. "Understood." Gray signals the waitress for two more beers before I dive headfirst back into the underground.

"It was quite by accident, actually. I had some charges for drug dealing and second-degree theft pending back here in Detroit, so I did what every criminal does and skipped town, going to Boston with a buddy. Changed my name, as you know. Got some new creds, illegal of course. Worked some odd jobs, tried to straighten out my shit, stay out of trouble. Eventually got a job as a cook in a Greek restaurant and this guy would always come in. I'd heard he was a big-time mobster, but I had no idea who the fuck he really was. Over the course of a few months, he kinda took to me. Loved my Bougatsa and Galaktoboureko. Was a big foodie.

"One day I overheard a couple of lowlifes talking a little too loudly about how they were going to take him out. Few days later one of his bodyguards came in for a pickup and I warned him. Saved the fucker's life. If I only knew then what I would learn a couple years later, I would have gladly let him be fish food, but he had been good to me. Thought I'd repay the favor, not thinking much of it.

"Then, I was summoned to his house and essentially taken into the fold. Not something you're really at liberty to say no to unless you want to end up at the bottom of the Charles River, which I did not. Fuck, I've gone back and replayed that day a million times wishing I had kept my mouth shut."

"But then you wouldn't have been there to save Livvy."

"I know," I tell him quietly. It's a catch-22 of epically fucked-up proportions.

I finish the beer sitting in front me, palming the cold one and continue, wanting to just vomit it all now. "Six months later, the FBI, which had been watching Peter Wilder for well over a year, approached me. They managed to find out who I really was and in exchange for any inside intel that would help put Peter behind bars, they would wipe away all pending charges, plus I would have immunity for anything that happened until they could take that masochistic fucker down. Then I'd go into the WITSEC program."

"Shit. Are you serious?" I would laugh at the incredulous look on Gray's face if I thought any of this was fucking funny. As it is, I don't. It was sheer, torturous hell. A tightrope walk that I balanced every goddamn day. It took cunning and an incredible sixth sense to keep my ass alive and that of Livia's when she was brought into the sick, twisted game, changing the rules completely.

"Dead."

"They had to have known about Livia, then? If you were working with the FBI?"

I nodded, my stomach madly churning with a mixture of acid and hatred so thick it was cloying sometimes.

Gray's face was a mask of pure fury. "And they didn't do a fucking thing to help her? Save her?"

"No. It would have 'jeopardized years of undercover work and wasted hundreds of thousands of dollars of taxpayer's money.'" I lowered my voice and air quoted the death sentence the senior agent prick, Billings, essentially gave Livia when I asked for help. For some reason, this was an intensely personal vendetta to Billings and he wasn't going to let anyone or anything jeopardize his mission. Sometimes I thought he was worse than Peter.

"So you took matters into your own hands."

I hold his stare. This is where I step off. The exact details of what I did will never be known by another. "Official death certificate says stroke. Fucker had a bad heart. Ate like shit, smoked, drank too much, was under constant stress. It was all finally too much for his weakened organ to handle, I guess."

"I guess," he nods. "And the FBI?"

"They saved taxpayer money that would have been spent on a trial, but were able to take down over thirty men for various crimes and ended up with some very damning information on a syndicate family. I would say they thought it was a win. And they honored their end of the deal."

Quite frankly, that's all I fucking cared about. Billings was convinced I had something to do with Peter's early demise, but Dimitri, Peter's son, refused an autopsy so there was never any evidence. Dimitri hated his father with a passion, so if he suspected anything, well...he showed me his gratitude by making sure it was known I wasn't to be touched. Ever. His gratitude probably had something to do with the fact I also foiled an attempt on *his* life three years earlier. Along with our shared hatred for his father, it was enough to cement our bond. Either way, it didn't matter. I was finally fucking free for the first time in years.

"Jesus Christ, Luke. I had no idea."

"Not exactly how I had my life planned out, you know?" I tip my bottle, drinking about half of the contents in two large gulps. Fuck, I could use about a dozen shots right now. Oblivion is sounding more and more appealing, even at three in the afternoon. I don't like to think about those days, let alone talk about them.

For the thousandth time since I set my sights on Addy, I berate myself for being so fucking selfish that I can't let her go. Guilt and doubt mix together to corrode my insides, making me nauseous. I'm sick with worry that if she ever finds out about this part of me, she'll leave. Walk out the fucking door with her middle finger in the air and hate in her heart. It would ruin me. I would once again plunge into the darkness and this time, I'd have no hope of seeing the light ever again.

Gray's quiet for a few beats. "What happened to make you go sideways anyway? I could never work that out. I thought we were both on the same path to take over Dad's business. It's like some switch was flipped or something. One day we were best friends; the next, you were withdrawn from everyone."

Before I can skirt around a question I have

absolutely no intention of answering, my boisterous younger brothers approach the table. I see Ash pocketing a few bills. I chuckle, hoping that knocked Conn down a couple pegs.

"I'm ready to blow this joint. I miss my fiancée," Ash announces.

"She's got that string tied pretty tight, Ash. You sure the blood flow's not being cut off?" Conn teases mercilessly.

Ash takes it all in stride, not missing a beat. "Blood's pumping just fine, asshole. Sounds like jealousy talking, if you ask me."

"Jealousy? Not fucking likely. I like things just the way they are, fuck you very much."

Ash laughs. "Right. I'm counting the days until I meet the woman who will finally bring the almighty playboy Connelly James Colloway to his knees. It will be a humbling experience for you, brother, and you could use a good dose of humility."

"Not gonna happen. A wife and kids are not in my fifty-year plan."

"Wanna bet on that?"

"Fucking A. You're on. What do you want?"

"Deed to the land you own on the lake."

Conn actually looks shocked. "You want the deed to a piece of land in Lake Forest valued at over a million dollars?"

"Yup."

"Fuck off. I'm not betting that."

"You sound worried."

"I'm not."

"Then it's settled." Asher's hand is now

hanging in the air, eyes challenging Conn to accept.

"Fine." Conn grasps Ash's hand. "But just so you know, I don't plan on losing."

Antsy to leave, I finish my brew and stand, throwing two bills on the table that will more than cover our cheap drinks, plus leave *Candi* a nice tip.

"See, you're thinking about it all wrong, Conn," I pipe in, trying to give him some brotherly advice. "Your overpriced plot is just dirt and trees and rocks. Won't keep you warm at night, won't make you laugh, won't fill your soul with something that's indescribable. Finding that elusive woman who will plug holes you didn't know you had in ways you can't possibly comprehend is fucking priceless. And I guarantee when you find her, you'd give up every last thing you own to make her yours."

Then I turn and head toward the exit, trying not to laugh at the stunned looks on my three brothers' faces.

Don't look so surprised, either. I can be deep when I want to be.

Chapter 32

LUKE

The noise is almost deafening when we walk through the front door. I hear women laughing and talking, each raising their octaves to be heard above the others. Classic females.

When we walk into the kitchen, I immediately spot Addy sitting on the couch in the living room, but she doesn't see me because she's too busy oohing and aahing over all the baby stuff that's now littering the carpet.

For what seems like an eternity, I stand and absorb her stunning beauty, letting her mere presence calm my ragged soul. She's *so* exquisite, both inside and out, I sometimes feel a sharp pang in the center of my chest when I look at her, when I realize she's *really* mine now. I unconsciously lift my fist to my ribcage, rubbing back and forth.

Today she's wearing a short-sleeve pale pink dress with buttons that run down the entire center. She's kicked her shoes off somewhere and I notice she's painted both her fingernails and toenails a few shades darker than her outfit.

She's talking animatedly with her hands as she always does. Some days I wonder if she'll actually take flight because she's moving them so damn fast.

Somehow I managed to drink six beers in less than two hours, which has my mind fucking buzzing. The heaviness I constantly carry around has gotten denser, especially after Gray's and my downer discussion about years I would just as soon scrub from my mind. Another reason I don't generally drink much beyond a couple of beers. It just depresses the fuck out of me.

But just one look at Addy has me feeling marginally lighter. It's the exact same feeling I got when I first saw her. The heaviness dissipates just by looking at her. It goes away almost completely when she's in my arms and Jesus, do I need to hold her right now.

What Gray said earlier made a helluva lot of sense, although it doesn't take away the fact I made a conscious decision to end a human life. I'm not sure I can ever forgive myself for that, regardless of the reasons. But I try. Every day, I try.

I remind myself every single time I look at Livia and see her growing belly that I made the only decision I possibly could. When I see her laugh, her smile, her happiness. I remind myself every time I see Gray look at her with so much love in his eyes, it would almost be sickening if you didn't know their tragic love story.

I watch Asher and Gray go to their women, tug them close, kiss them. I watch Addy watch them before her eyes scan the room, searching for me. When they land on mine, I kid you not, I see sunbeams from heaven rain down on her at the brilliant smile she gifts me with.

Christ...I am so gone for her and I don't care who knows it.

I lean against the kitchen wall as everyone starts filing in, including Addy. It's chaos for a few minutes as the women attending the party start parading out two by two, like Noah's ark animals. Why is it women go everywhere in pairs? Makes no fucking sense to me.

Finally, the only people left are family. And Addy, who, for all intents and purposes, is family to me. It won't be too long before I make it officially so, either. I already know that. I simply cannot live without her.

Standing across the room, she looks at me thoughtfully, trying to split her attention between my mother and me, who's talking her ear off about something. Then I see her pat my mom on the arm, leaning in close to say something. My mother looks my way and smiles brightly before Addy heads in my direction.

She stops in front of me and I don't resist for another second. I yank her into me, squeezing tight, my hand palming her head. The tension I've carried since I saw her last fades and I feel like I can take a full breath.

I do.

I breathe deeply, taking her soothing scent into my lungs and holding it there before I slowly let it out. I do it again and again, each time feeling the pressure melt away more. I feel six sets of eyes on us, but I keep mine shut and my nose buried in her hair, which smells citrusy today instead of her usual vanilla.

"What's wrong, babe?" she whispers, holding me just as close, fingers caressing my spine. I don't think I can articulate how fucking fantastic it feels to have someone so in tune with you she knows something's wrong just by looking at you. I'm the master of emotional avoidance, but that façade just doesn't work with her and this is the only time in my life I'm glad for it.

"I need you, Addy," I tell her on a strained breath. I'm not talking about sex. Right now, I mean that statement in a much broader context than she realizes. I need her like I need fresh air or clean water. She's life.

"You have me, Luke," she replies so only I can hear. The shadows recede a bit more, my lungs feeling less constricted by the second. Pulling out of my arms, she twines our fingers together. "Show me around?"

My brows furrow until she winks, tugging my hand.

"Outside. Your mom was telling me about the grounds and the little lake over the hill."

"Ah, yeah. Sure. Okay."

Addy turns to my mom. "Is it okay if I steal your son for a while?"

My mom's eyes sparkle so brightly you'd think I just announced our engagement. I would laugh if I weren't wound so fucking tight. "Absolutely, dear. Take your time. Have fun, you two."

"Thanks, Barb."

We exit the kitchen, hand in hand, my siblings watching our retreating backs, and I decide that fate herself couldn't have picked a better woman for me—Addy knows exactly what I need.

And right now...all I need is her. Just her.

Chapter 33

Addy

It's a very nice early April afternoon in Detroit, with temps soaring into the upper sixties, so I leave my sweater on the coatrack, hoping it won't be chilly by the lake. I slide on my ballet shoes before opening the front door, never letting Luke's hand leave mine. I'm not exactly sure what's wrong with him, but I feel as if he may slip away from me without physical contact. I don't plan on letting go anytime soon.

We walk side by side in silence down the cobblestone path that winds from the front to the side of the massive Colloway estate. I have to say, I was stunned that Barb lives in a six-bedroom, seven-bath house by herself. When we stood alone on the porch in a stolen moment and I asked her about it, she said they'd have to drag her out of here in a body bag.

"This isn't just a house, my dear, it's a home. My husband's blood, sweat, and tears bought this home. We raised our family here, had countless

holidays and birthday parties here. My boys learned to fish in that lake over there.

"When he was thirteen, Connelly stood in that driveway, shooting hoops for hours, trying to perfect his free throw. Asher broke his arm when he was ten jumping off this very roof onto a trampoline. Stupid boy. Gray had his first kiss at fourteen right here on this front porch, and there's still a little dent in the garage door where Luke made his younger brothers stand while he threw a Frisbee at them. I think he was all of nine at the time.

"Laughter, tears, love, heartache, and memories are woven into the very fabric that make up this foundation and I will never let it go. They may not live here any longer, but it will always be my boys' home and I could never sell their childhood," she said.

She was so passionate, it brought tears to my eyes. I've never seen the love of a mother so strong for her family, her children, than Barb Colloway's and it shot a pang of envy through me that Luke has her. I want one of her for my very own.

"What's this?" I ask when we finally stop in front of a small house disconnected from the main house, about fifty yards away.

"The guest house," he answers curtly. Guess he's still in a mood. He bends down and picks up what looks like a rock; it's one of those fake ones you keep a spare key in. I admire the flex of his ass when he leans over. He looks deliciously edible today in his ripped, dark wash jeans and pale blue tee. He cut his hair last week and while it's still long, it's not long enough to pull back anymore. It looks more unruly than usual.

"You have a guest house?"

"I don't, but my mom does."

"Does anyone ever stay here?" I ask while he unlocks the door, ushering me in.

"They used to. My dad's brother and his family used to stay all the time when we were kids. Then for some reason when I was about sixteen, they just stopped coming, so it wasn't used a lot after that. Doubt it gets used much anymore, though. Mom probably has guests stay in the house."

He closes the door behind us and I look around. The space is relatively small but very nice. Very homey. To our right is a fairly decent-sized kitchen with bay windows overlooking the wooded backyard. Padded benches line three windowed walls and a square oak table sits in the middle. What a lovely place for breakfast.

Straight ahead is the main living area, with lightly used brown leather furniture and a big-screen TV mounted above a gas fireplace. The bookshelves are filled to the brim with what looks to be old encyclopedias. There are floor-to-ceiling windows in this room, letting in plenty of light. To the far right is a hallway where I assume there is a bedroom or two.

"It looks clean." And smells good. I expected musty if it doesn't get used much.

"Mom hires someone to care for the grounds and they make sure to keep this clean and air it out occasionally. She always wants to be ready in case she needs it," his tight voice replies from behind me.

I spin to see Luke leaning against the closed door, arms crossed, with a pensive look on his face. His eyes search mine as if he's expecting me to bolt any second. This is not at all the self-assured man who has pursued me relentlessly the past month. I see the pain in him as clearly as if he were standing here openly bleeding at my feet, the agony lapping angrily at my ankles like a rising tide. I wish like hell I knew what put it there.

His demons have escaped and I hate them. I hate what they're doing to him, how they're tormenting him. I want to slay them all so their black souls blanket the ground and burn to ash in the morning sun, leaving him with nothing but purity. Nothing but peace. I want him never to look like this again because it shreds my very soul to see him so clearly hurting and...doubting. *That's it.* It's doubt I see swirling in his distressed eyes.

It's then I know exactly what Luke needs and he couldn't have brought me to a better place. I don't know what happened to bring on this brooding mood; I do know how to get rid of it, however. This wasn't at all my intention when I left the house, but it's clearly what he needs.

Holding his gaze, I reach for the top button on my dress and slowly undo it before moving to the next one. His hazels drop to my hands, his jaw now ticking. I watch the bulge in his pants expand like one of those sponge animals dipped in a glass of water. I undo enough so my cleavage is exposed before I stop and drop my hands to my sides, causing his now heated eyes to snap back to mine.

"Change your mind?" he drawls, his eyes narrowing in challenge.

Oooohhh. Bad, bad Luke.

I ignore his sparring words, forging ahead with my plan. "No." Deep breath. "Tell me what you want. What to do."

"What are you doing, fireball?" he breathes, pushing off the door yet not making a move toward me. His muscles are tightly coiled. He's fighting his animal instinct to pounce and devour and claim. All three of which I want and will even encourage.

"Giving you control. Knocking those damn demons off your back, Luke. Let me help you carry them. Please."

Two seconds flat is all it takes for him to close the distance between us and slant his mouth perfectly on mine. He's not gentle and he's not loving as he spins me and shoves my back against the door he just vacated, pinning me tight, surrounding me. He wholly consumes me, taking what he needs, what I want him to have, his tongue demanding entry while his lips bruise mine. He harshly drags my plump bottom lip between his teeth and I gasp before he moves back in to swallow it, own it.

He tastes like beer and passion and desperation.

Then his mouth is dragging across my jaw, my

neck, nipping my ear. The harshness of his breath scatters over my heated flesh, making me dizzy with need, crazy with want. I pant as his hips thrust against my lower belly and I lift my leg to wrap around him, needing to align us better. Our bodies are writhing against each other like we're trying to crawl into the other's skin. I want to. I want to crawl inside of him so I can fight those rancid beasts for him from the inside, freeing him at last.

"Addy, Addy, Addy," he whispers brokenly as he makes his way across my collarbone and down to the swell of my breasts. "I love you. Christ, I love you so fucking much."

I still, my hands clutched in his hair. I'm breathless and clearly have a little wax buildup, because I couldn't possibly have heard what I just thought I did. "What?"

As if what he said weren't the most important three words ever said to another person in the history of life, my incorrigible man intentionally slows his movements, but keeps his mouth pressed to me, traveling back up the opposite side. I feel like it takes him an hour. All the while, I'm freaking out inside, trying to think of every word that could rhyme with love: glove, dove, above, shove.

There aren't many, at least that I can think of in the time it takes him to hum cockily, "You heard me, fireball. Don't pretend you didn't." My breath catches when his teeth clamp my lobe gently, tugging it through like he did my lip earlier.

"God, Luke..." We're both now perfectly still, except for our erratic breathing and my racing mind.

His lips hover at my ear as he pours his heart out and tears of pure joy flow. (Mine, of course). "I love you, Addy Catherine Monroe. I love every fucking thing about you. I love your clever wit and your wicked tongue. I love your crazy and your messy and your stubborn. I love your mad kitchen skills and your lack of movie knowledge. I love your big heart, your loyalty, and your blinding inner beauty."

I'm almost full-on sobbing now when he draws back and looks deep into my watery, blurry eyes. "I love the way your fire burns bright in your eyes and in the very depths of your being. But mostly I love how you *get* me, *see* me, *know* me. Know exactly what I need. I love how my soul feels at rest around you and *only* you and how everything that was dull before is brilliantly colorful now. And I love that you make me feel I can actually be good enough for someone like you even when I know I'm not."

It's hard to swallow. All the words I want to say back are stuck in the middle of my throat. He reaches up, wiping my trails of happiness away, and as we stare at each other, I'm sure I've never seen another person as vulnerable as Luke is right now.

I let a ghost of smile curve my lips. "So you love me, huh?"

Luke's eyes momentarily flare before he throws his head back and laughs. "Oh, Addy, I think we need to find something to do with that smart mouth of yours."

Before I know it, I'm being thrown over his shoulder and carted off like I'm being kidnapped by a medieval warrior to be used as his sex slave for the night. *Ooohhh*...I hope there are ropes involved.

Chapter 34

LUKE

I deposit her in the middle of the master bedroom, which, luckily for me contains a four-poster bed. The king-sized bed takes up the majority of the room, but that's okay. It has everything I need. A bed, a chair, but mostly her.

She wants to submit; I'll make her submit. Happily. And then I'll make her admit she loves me—I absolutely did not mistake that as I filleted myself open to the first woman in my entire life less than sixty seconds ago. I'd better make her submission worth my while because after I'm done here, she'll either beg for it again or she'll never offer again. I'll be perfectly fine with either as long as I have her.

She watches me as I walk to the bed and pull some of the long wispy translucent fabric pieces that hang down from the frame to make it look more sensual, I guess. Fuck all if I know. What I do know is they'll be perfect for what I have in mind later.

"What—"

"No talking, fireball," I growl, stalking to the

bathroom where I open drawers until I find a few things that will work. Actually, they'll work very well.

I shake my head as I walk back into the bedroom where Addy's gaze darts between mine and what's in my hands, now looking like an innocent little gazelle caught in the crosshairs by one very hungry king of the jungle. That metaphor couldn't possibly be truer.

Fuck, I want her with an urgency I'm not sure I've felt yet, even after she denied me for two straight weeks.

"What—"

"Was I not clear before, Addy?" I ask casually as I pull the maroon velvet captain's chair from the corner, positioning it perfectly toward the bed.

She opens her mouth to speak again and I cut her off, moving until I'm only inches from her, my finger to her lips. "Ah. Ah. I know this will be hard for you, fireball, but no talking actually means to close those beautiful lips of yours and don't let any noise escape. Moans, screams, and begging notwithstanding, of course," I smirk.

Her eyes widen right before I witness her intoxicating surrender. She wants this and I crave it from her. I love her lip every other place, except here. For some reason, I have this overwhelming need to control her in the bedroom, probably because I know she won't let me outside of it. Her submission takes work every fucking time, yet there's nothing like the high of her total surrender.

"Baby, I love your sweet submission," I croon

right before I take her mouth in a knee-buckling kiss. "I love that you trust me. I love *you*," I whisper, knowing she won't say it back since I've instructed her not to speak.

She stays silent as I leave her, walking back toward the chair. I know it's hard for her; she's working that bottom lip so hard, she may take off the first layer of skin. I see love swirling in her eyes as plainly as I feel it in my own chest, though I know I'll have to pull the words from her just like I do everything else. She's a constant challenge, but I'm very much onto her.

I set my things on the small nightstand I've pulled next to me and sit in the chair, legs spread wide. My jeans are so fucking tight right now, my cock is being strangled and is begging for mercy. He's going to have to wait for a while; I have other plans.

"Unbutton your dress. Slow, Addy. So fucking slow your fingers ache."

Her chest heaves and flushes as she silently obeys, bringing her hands up to the tiny white round disks. She does as I ask and it takes a good minute for the fabric to finally part.

"Take it off," I rasp, adjusting my throbbing dick. Licking her lips, her eyes track my hand before they sweep back up. She pushes the garment off her shoulders and straightens her arms, the cloth dropping to the floor in a heap.

"My God." I'm in awe. She stands before me in the same pink lingerie set she had on the night I walked into her room before dinner with Gray and Livia. I didn't get enough time to admire her then and I don't have the patience for it now either, but Hot. Damn. My woman puts Victoria's Secret models to shame.

"Lose the bra."

She does, without hesitation.

"Sit on the edge of the bed, fireball. Rest your feet on the frame." She slips off her shoes and once she's positioned, I give my next instruction. "Spread your legs. Wider."

"Fuck," I mumble. Her dark, wet tunnel glistens under the see-through lace and I want nothing more than to bury my face in it and eat her until she screams, but I don't.

"Fingers in your pussy, sweetheart."

She starts to tunnel them underneath the top, but that's not what I want. "No, move aside the crotch so I can see what you're doing. I want to see how creamy you are for me."

A harsh breath escapes when she does what I ask. I watch her fingers disappear inside before the shiny digits slide up to circle her clit.

"Slow, baby. Nice and slow."

"Luke…" she whispers in restrained agony.

"Play with your nipples. Pinch them hard like I would." She immediately obeys, moaning as she twists and pulls, her fingers disappearing again as she re-lubricates. I can smell the musky tang of her pussy from here. My mouth waters and my cock aches.

Fuck. Pre-cum now soaks my boxers. I'm hard as fucking titanium and my balls are drawn painfully tight. "Addy, baby, you turn me on so goddamn much," I croak.

She works herself up slowly, just like I want and I can tell the second she needs more. Her motions become faster, jerkier. I watch that delicious flush spread on her fair skin and the pulse in her neck race.

"Is your little clit hard, baby?"

"Yes." She's breathless and needy and poised on ecstasy's very sweet edge, her beautiful eyes silently begging me for permission to go over.

"Fuck yes, Addy. Get yourself off. Let go so I can fuck you. Love you." Her head falls back on a moan until I bark, "Eyes on me, fireball. Eyes on mine the whole time."

I unzip my constricting denim and pull out my throbbing cock, stroking it as I watch, needing the blessed relief, but restraining myself from coming outside of her sweet pussy. I have to give Addy credit; her eyes never leave mine the entire time until she enters that blissful place between time and space.

In all my days I will never forget the sight of the love of my life fingering herself to orgasm at my command. I will forever remember her breathy moans and *my* name on her lips when her body arched and convulsed in euphoria. And I will go to my grave never forgetting how her complete and total surrender shredded every beast I carried into this room with me, replacing them with nothing but her.

I fucking love her. I will never love another.

Chapter 35

Addy

I'm floating back from my happy, bright place when I'm being lifted from the bed and flipped onto my stomach. Before I know what's happening my wrists are secured behind my back and being bound together with scratchy fabric, probably the one from the bedframe.

"Feel okay?"

I nod.

Then my hips are being jerked up so I'm now lying on my cheek with my ass in the air, my panties roughly being pulled down my legs. I gasp as something cold and wet is poured on my lower back and drizzled in and down my crack, dripping through my slit onto the bed cover. Luke massages what I now know is the oil he brought from the bathroom into my ass, pushing it into my back hole, filling me, lubricating me.

"Luke," I moan, rocking back against him, his finger slipping in further. I know I'm not supposed to talk, but shit. I can't keep anything else inside. I want everything he's going to do to me, and then some.

"Silence, Addy," he growls. It's tight, restrained, almost feral.

When his hands fall away, I want to cry, until I feel something flat and smooth caress my ass cheek seconds before it leaves and returns with a crack, startling me more than anything. *The hairbrush.* I want to ask questions, but I don't. Luke needs this. *I* need this. He does it again harder this time, stinging my skin.

"Fuck, you're beautiful, baby." Fire and desperate need spread throughout each cell as he smacks then soothes with his palm time and time again, before breaching my empty sex with something hard and unyielding. It doesn't feel as good as he does, yet I can't deny that more wetness now coats my thighs. He pushes it in and out, cursing as he fucks me slowly with the smooth, thick foreign object while he adds a finger to my asshole. He increases the speed until I'm on the doorstep and then he slows, removing everything.

Bastard.

I whimper at the loss, mindless, needing to come again until I hear a hum and feel an abrasive, vibrating surface touch my aching, needy clit. *The electric toothbrush.* It feels coarse and alien and so fucking good the moan I've trapped in the back of my throat almost flies free. Holy balls, who knew a few household items from the bathroom could elicit such mind-blowing pleasure?

"Come, Addy. This time under *my* touch." He drops his faux vibrator and strums my clit with his fingers. Faster and faster until my vision darkens and pleasure coalesces with pain when he pinches my nerve endings hard, sending me soaring into subspace. This time, I can't hold it in. I moan, I scream, I try to squirm away, but Luke holds me steady as my limbs tremble with the force of my climax.

"My God, you're so responsive, baby. I fucking love it." Then he's driving inside me, his front molding to my back when he pulls me upright, my arms pinned between us. His hands palm my heavy breasts, rolling my nipples to tight points between deft fingers. My clit throbs with each strong tug, with each painful tweak. Luke is an incredibly talented lover, attentive, always pushing me to my limits. The things he does to my body feel too damn good.

"I'm in love with you, fireball," he declares in my ear between dominating, forceful stabs. "You're mine. Mine."

"I'm yours," I breathe, another orgasm building right behind the last. I can see it, taste it. I reach for it.

"You love me."

"I do," I admit. "I do."

"Tell me. Say the words. I *need* them, Addy." The hand he now has wrapped loosely around my neck turns my face toward him. "Fall with me, fireball."

"I already have, Luke. I love you," I cry, unable to hold in my heart's confession that's been

K. L. KREIG

itching to spill. "I love you, I love you. I'm in love with you, Luke."

Luke captures the last few words, kissing me slow and deep and long. He slows his thrusts and gently leans me back down, untying my binds and rubbing my wrists and shoulders. "Hands flat on the mattress above your head, baby," he gruffs. I readily comply.

Resuming his sensual assault, he spreads my cheeks wide. His fingers find their way again to my backside, dipping in. I go with it, encourage it. His other hand reaches around to rub my sensitized clit and I'm overcome with so many sensations I can hardly process them, barely hearing Luke's husky declaration, "I love watching my cock slide into you. Best fucking visual ever," before I fall headlong off the cliff into the warm ocean waters once again. Luke follows almost immediately. His body tenses and he swells and pulses as he releases deep inside me on a low grunt before falling on top of me. His pants join mine while we ride the last of our glorious high.

A few minutes later, after he cleans me with a hot cloth, we're lying on top of the comforter, buck naked, exhausted, and wrapped around each other. I would be cold if it wasn't for the fact Luke is like his own portable heater.

I have no idea how long we've been gone, but I'm in no hurry to get back. I'm sure it will be completely evident to everyone, including Luke's mother, that we were doing more than enjoying the beauty of the lake. Ugh.

"You're staying here tonight," he stubbornly announces.

"Luke—"

"No, Addy. I'm not giving in on this. I need you in my bed, in my arms. Last night was torture without you."

I tilt my head up to see him watching me.

"Please, baby. I *need* you here." *I know you do.* My weak resolve slithers away when he runs his finger down my cheek. It melts into nothingness every time he touches me and he damn well knows it.

"But your mom."

"Are you kidding me? My mom would probably drive to your dad's and pick up your shit herself." He laughs. "She's trying to marry us all off as fast as possible so she can fill this house with hordes of grandkids. It's fine. We can stay here in the guest house if it makes you feel better."

I don't answer (and I definitely don't let myself think about his marriage comment as if I didn't hear hope rip a few more seams), but I know this is the end of the conversation, because Luke has won again. Damn stubborn man has just gotten everything he's been bugging me about for the last week.

"What happened today?"

"What do you mean?"

I prop myself up on my elbow and glare down at him. "Luke," I chastise.

He gazes at me thoughtfully for so long I don't think he's going to speak. "I love you so much,

Addy." The devotion I hear in his tone undoes me as his reverent eyes scour my face. No one has looked at me the way he does. "I wish I could adequately describe how you've brought life back to me. Just being with you quiets my demons and brings peace to my soul. Don't cry, baby," he whispers, wiping away my happy tears.

His love is palpable, squeezing my heart. I've never felt anything like it. "I love you so much," I rasp. Love seems like an inadequate verb. The emotions rattling around inside me are burning and all consuming. Livia was right. The person I've been looking for all this time is right in front of me and I don't plan on ever letting him go.

Drawing me down, he worships my mouth for long minutes before tucking me back in the crook of his arm. Then he starts talking softly, each word more pained than the one before it.

"It's hard for me to come back here. It reminds me how good things used to be and how quickly they turned to shit in the span of fifteen fucking minutes. When I was growing up, our family was always tight-knit and happy. I loved my parents and my brothers. My mom stayed home and took care of the house and us kids while my dad worked hard building his company. We were well off. We were the envy of all of our friends. We went to church every Sunday. We gave to needy kids at Christmas. We took nice vacations. We were the all-American family. I thought my life couldn't get any fucking better."

I clutch him tightly as he pauses,

understanding how hard it is to purge your deepest secrets and feelings. "I had my whole life laid out since I was in middle school. I had acumen for math, like all my brothers actually, and together we planned to take over my father's company someday. Hell, he talked to us about it regularly when he found out we were interested. I started learning what a P&L and balance sheet were when I was in seventh grade. We saw how hard he worked, but we also saw what hard work got you. Money, a big house, a beautiful wife, respect.

"I loved my dad, Addy. He was my fucking hero. He could do no wrong. He taught me to ride a bike. To fish, drive, change the oil in my car. He let me help fix things around the house, so I learned how to be handy. Let me have my first drink of beer on New Year's Even when I was thirteen. Hell, he even gave me condoms. He was smart, he was handy, he was handsome. He was like a fucking God to me, which in retrospect was probably my fault. I thought he was perfect until I found out he wasn't. He was just human after all."

I prod him when he goes silent for too long. "What did he do?" I ask quietly, although I have a pretty damn good idea where this is now going and it breaks my heart.

"He cheated on my mom. Had a kid with someone else. I have a fucking half sister running around in the world somewhere who doesn't know us and we don't know her. I think about her all the time and wonder what her life is like.

K. L. KREIG

If she's happy. If she feels lost because she never knew her real dad, even though he was a cheating bastard."

"But your mom…?"

"Doesn't know. As far as I know, anyway. And neither do my brothers."

"But how?" I ask, now back on my elbow, gazing down at him.

"I caught him. Well, not in the act, but with the woman in his home office paying her off. I was sixteen, just two weeks shy of my seventeenth birthday, and it was a perfect fall day. I remember being pissed because I was sick and was going to miss the football game that night. I had a hundred two temp. After talking to my mom, the school nurse sent me home. I had my own car so I drove myself. Mom was helping at a church funeral and wasn't home. When I pulled into the driveway, I saw a strange car sitting there beside my dad's.

"My dad was *never* home during the day. Hell, a lot of nights he didn't get home until eight or nine o'clock. When I walked through the door, I immediately knew something was wrong. I could hear them yelling, even from the kitchen. My dad's office was right down the hall and I didn't have to take but a few steps to hear the whole sordid conversation.

"She said she still loved him, after all these years. He denied ever sleeping with her. Hell, he denied even *knowing* who she was. Who does that? I mean…did he cheat on my mom so many times that he didn't remember who he slept

312

with? I felt absolutely sick to my stomach that this was my father."

"What happened?" I ask softly.

"Long story short, she said the kid was his and she had pictures of them doing the nasty together and she'd be more than happy to show his wife, destroy his family, his business, his reputation. He asked to see them and they must have been pretty damning because the next thing I know he was asking her how much it would take to make her go away."

"You're kidding me?" I ask disbelievingly. I didn't know Luke's dad, but it's hard for me to wrap my head around this perfect family and how his dad would or could do such a thing.

"I wish I was. A few minutes later, I hid in the pantry so they wouldn't see me, but I saw them. I saw *her*. I will never forget the smug look on her tear-streaked face. A face that's forever singed in my memory. I honestly wasn't sure who I was more pissed with at the time. Him for cheating or her for extortion."

"Oh, Luke. I'm so sorry."

"Sometimes I wish I'd remained in the dark like the rest of my family. I wonder how my life would have turned out otherwise. I guess that wasn't how my cards were meant to play out. That was the turning point for me, Addy. I took everything I'd worked for and flushed it down the damn toilet. I was angry, disillusioned, and I acted out. I cut off my family emotionally. I distanced myself from Gray, my own goddamned right arm. I started not caring about school, started hanging out with the bad crowd and, no offense, that's when I met your brother."

I smile sadly. "No offense taken."

"Things went downhill fast for me and I got mixed up in a worse crowd, did a lot of things I'm not proud of. Things I wish I could go back and change so I could be a better man for you. A man you really deserve."

"Stop," I spit angrily. Straddling him, I take his face in my hands. "Just stop it right there, Luke. You *are* a good man. The best man I've ever known, so please don't say that."

He shakes his head, taking my hands off his face, gathering them in his. "That's the thing, fireball, I'm *not* a good man. I may be now, but I wasn't. For years, I was the furthest fucking thing from good. I have a criminal past."

"I don't care."

"You would," he says somberly. "If you knew some of the things I did, you would care. You're honest and pure of heart."

I sit up straight, dragging my hands out from under his and look at him for what seems like forever, not understanding where this conversation has suddenly headed. Minutes ago he was telling how much he loved me and now it feels as if he's trying to push me away.

"Are you trying to scare me away?"

"Fuck no. *No.* I may not deserve you, but I'm not letting you go either. The thought of someone else having you, I just...I can't even go there in my mind. I knew the moment I laid eyes on you that you were mine, Addy. The very second our eyes connected. I tried to be honorable and stay away from you, because you can do so much better than a guy like me, but I just couldn't. When I told you in the kitchen that I need you, I mean I *need* you. I don't have a life anymore without you in it.

"But I also just want you to understand the circumstances that have shaped the broken, flawed man you see before you and I guess…" He averts his eyes for a moment and when they return I'm gutted—every mask he wears is gone, and I swear I can see right into his life-ravaged soul. "I guess I want you to tell me that you'll still love him anyway because you're the first and the last woman I will ever truly love, fireball. If you choose to leave, well, then I guess I can't stop you; I'll never stop fighting for you either."

"This is war, huh?" I ask almost teasingly, remembering our text exchange last night.

I expect a cocky remark, but I don't get it. Instead, I get steely resolution. "Until the bitter end."

My heart hurts. I lean down, running my fingers through his long, dark hair. "Do you remember when you told me yesterday that I don't realize how special I am?"

"Yes," he rasps thickly.

"I think *you* don't realize how incredibly special *you* really are, Luke Colloway. You're honorable and loyal and amazingly perceptive. I've never met anyone else who has as much emotional and spiritual depth as you do or who has the sheer drive to get what he wants. It's just a bonus you're wickedly talented in both the kitchen and the bedroom."

He laughs, grabbing my sides until I squeal. "We all have a past, Luke, and I think we'd be hard-pressed to find a person who wasn't ashamed of at least some of it, myself included. Your mistakes don't make you undeserving. They just make you *you*. Human. Imperfect like everyone else. I've never loved anyone the way I love you and you're going to have to try a lot harder than this to get rid of me. I'm a stage-fifty clinger now."

I press my lips to his and sigh when his palm finds my head. I let him take over, slanting me so we fit perfectly. He increases the depth, sweeping his tongue over mine. I let him flip me over, spreading my legs with his. He fills me, completes me in ways I didn't know I needed. I let him take me, own me, and love me, both of us whispering our devotion on choppy, hoarse breaths as we reach that incredible summit together once again.

As we lie in each other's arms and I drift off, I feel truly and wholly loved for the first time in my life by someone other than my father and my brother. Luke's been showing me his feelings for weeks with his actions, but I've been pretending that wasn't really what he was saying. I've been protecting myself from heartache and despair, trying to convince myself I didn't need a man, need *him* to truly make me happy when nothing could have been further from the truth.

I now know I won't ever be happy again without him.

Even when I told him I wasn't dancing anymore, I still held a bit me of back, but no more. I'm all in. I believe and I will trust that what we have is pure and long lasting and real.

Today I finally gave him all of me, and I think he knows it.

Chapter 36

LUKE

I sit in the Monroe kitchen at the same scratched up table, looking at the same appliances and the same yellow-green linoleum floor with the same breadbox on the counter, memories rushing back like stage-five rapids. I don't know how many times we sat in this kitchen smoking pot or snorting coke when Eric's dad was gone, planning the next stupid thing we were going to do.

Addy's upstairs packing, having already talked to her dad who was surprisingly fine with the whole thing. Bob and I always did get along pretty well, even if I was just a fucked-up kid at the time. Call it parental intuition, but I think he knew I needed a father figure for a few years when I was little more than a lost boy.

Eric walked in just a few minutes ago and as far as he knows, I'm here to see my drawing. Addy wanted to handle this alone; there's no way in hell I'm letting her do that. We're a team now and we'll handle things as such.

"Beer?"

"Not if it's the shit you drink." For some reason, Eric hasn't moved past Pabst Blue Ribbon and I simply cannot drink that horse piss. I didn't even like it when I was drinking it years ago. I love Eric like a brother, but his taste in beer plain sucks.

"*You* used to drink that shit," he jibes, grabbing a can of utter crap from the fridge.

"*Used to* being the operative word. I grew up."

"Fuck off, LC. Sorry, man. Dad doesn't have anything else besides PBR."

"Don't sweat it. You got the drawing?"

Eric reaches into his art folder he carries with him everywhere, extracts a colorful piece of paper, and hands it to me. I look it over for a couple of minutes, completely blown away. "Wow. Looks amazing, Eric. You've outdone yourself with this one."

"You were worried. Admit it."

"Nah. If I could trust anyone with this, it would be you."

"So, ah...why the color? Why now?"

I look up from the sketch at one of my oldest friends, my girl's brother, and think on how I should answer his question.

I've intentionally never wanted colored ink on my skin and Eric knows this. With every tattoo, he's tried to talk me into something other than shades of black and I've refused. I don't think I really understood why until I met Addy. When I say she's my color, I don't mean that metaphorically. I mean she's literally changed the way I see things. It's as if I've put rose-colored glasses *on* for the first time and I don't want to fucking take them off. They're brilliant.

My eyes flit to the stairs, expecting Addy to bound down them like a five-year-old any minute. Her endless energy and zest for life are some of the many things I love about her.

She wanted to do this alone, I wanted to do this together. At this point, I think it's best if I just come out and say it now so he can get his fucking hissy fit over with before he sees Addy and upsets her.

"It's time."

"Uh huh." He takes a long drink of his brew. "Who is she?"

I knew that would be his natural reaction; he was the one who always told me my outlook would change when I met the right woman. I thought he was full of shit. Turns out he was right.

Well...here goes nothing.

I ease up from the table and make myself comfortable against the opposite countertop, crossing my arms. I need to be able to defend myself as I have no doubt Eric will be going for my jugular in five seconds. Probably would be if I were him too. "Addy."

Beer and spit spray everywhere, droplets hitting me from across the room. Probably could have timed that little announcement better than when he was taking a swig.

"You'd better be fucking talking about another Addy and not mine."

She's not yours; she's mine. She'll only *ever* be mine.

I don't answer. I don't have to. Eric can see the truth in my eyes. He slams down his beer, foam pouring out of the mouth. "You fucking son-of-a-bitch! I've only ever asked *one* thing of you, LC. Stay away from my goddamn sister and you can't keep your fucking snake in its cage?"

I say nothing. He's right.

He starts pacing the small length of the kitchen, back and forth, back and forth like a wild caged animal, growling under his breath. Only thing missing is the froth sliding out the side of his mouth. "No. No. You break it off with her right now, Luke. Right fucking now."

I stand taller. "I'm living with her. In the apartment."

"Fuck! Fuck! No. Nope. You're moving out first thing Monday."

"Name's on the lease, man. I'm not going anywhere."

Eric gets up in my face and I ready myself for a well-placed strike. Eric's one hell of a street fighter, just like me. "Well fucking break the lease or find someone else to take it over," he spits between gritted teeth.

Eric and I are pretty evenly matched in bulk and height. I may have ten more pounds on him, but if we come to blows, we'll both end up bloody and bruised. "Let's get something straight. I'm not asking your permission, bro. We're together and that's how it is. I'm in love with her."

"You're not good enough for her!" he shouts. "Jesus Christ, Luke, I've tried to protect Addy from guys like us my whole fucking life. She deserves better than us. Better than *you*."

"I know," I mumble. I fucking know all of this, but it doesn't change a thing. As long as Addy wants me, I won't give her up. Not even to preserve my friendship with one of my oldest buddies. A guy who knows more about me than my family ever will. I'm willing to sacrifice anything and everything for her, and I know he sees that determination burning hot in my eyes.

Eric backs away, stopping dead in the middle of the room. If looks could kill, I'd be fifty shades of dead right now. Yeah, I went there.

We're in a silent face-off when I feel *her*. As with ten years ago, I feel her eyes on me, warming me, breathing the very life into me. I feel her presence as keenly as if she's wound her body tightly around mine. My cock jolts. He knows his mate is near. My gaze shifts from Eric toward the stairs to see her standing at the bottom, suitcase in hand.

She is so damn beautiful. My pride swells that this exquisite woman wants me, loves me. *Me*.

She's changed into dark jeans and a pale yellow tee that says Old Navy on the front. Her hair's pulled back into a messy ponytail and I smile when I see she's wearing the stupidly— and I mean *stupidly*—priced designer heels I bought her and shoved in the bottom of her bag as a surprise. What a paradox. She's wearing a ten-dollar shirt and a pair of fifteen-hundred-dollar shoes, and if anyone can pull it off, it's Addy.

"What's going on down here?" she asks, worried eyes volleying between Eric and me.

"You tell me, Leenie," Eric grits.

I forgot about Eric's nickname for Addy. Hell, for years that's what I thought her name was. As I watch her stare down her brother, I wonder how much she's heard.

"Eric, stop it. Right now."

I guess enough.

"Stop what, Leenie? Stop protecting my sister from guys like him? Fuck no." Eric points his thumb my way and I want to use it as leverage to bring him to his knees and make him apologize for upsetting Addy.

"Guys like him?" she spits venomously as she sidles right up to Eric. "Luke is your friend. Your *best* friend."

"Was." Eric's jaw tics furiously. He may break a molar with how hard he's grinding his teeth.

"You listen to me, Eric Lawrence Monroe. I am twenty-eight years old and I don't need your protection anymore or your permission. What I do or who I sleep with is none of your damn business, so butt out."

"Leenie..." he grabs her shoulders, gently shaking her. It's taking everything in me not to rip his arms from their sockets. "He's not good enough for you."

She shakes her head furiously. "Why, Eric? Because he has a past, like you? Because he's made mistakes, like you? Because he doesn't deserve a chance at happiness since he made some bad decisions? Like you?"

323

He winces, starting to speak when Addy talks right over him. "No, Eric. Stop. I love you, but you're wrong about Luke and I know deep down you know that. He's been like a brother to you for almost half your life. And if he were standing here telling you about *any* other woman, I know you'd be happy for him. I know you'd be telling him he deserves *her* after the shit he's been through, after getting his life back on track. So why doesn't he deserve *me*? He's the best man I've ever known, the best man *you've* ever known. I don't give a shit about his past or who he was back then or what he's done. It's totally irrelevant to me."

She pauses, eyes cast briefly down to the floor before pinning her brother to the wall with her hot stare again. "Not one of the guys I've ever been with has treated me like I actually mean something until Luke. Not one, Eric. And it's not your decision who I fall in love with."

"Addy..." Eric sounds pained and I can't say I blame him. If I had a little sister, I'd do everything I could to protect her from me, too.

I go to her side and pull her close, sighing when her arm snakes around my waist and she lays her head against me. Eric's hard eyes find mine and fall to where my arm is wound around Addy, her body flush with mine. My lips find her hair. I press them to her, not caring that Eric watches on with fire and brimstone rolling out his ears.

"Leenie," he sighs heavily. "I just...I just want you to be happy."

"I *am* happy, Eric," she replies softly. "I've honestly never been happier. He's who I'm supposed to be with. I know it. I feel it in every cell of my being. You know it's true. Luke's my firefly," she says quietly.

Huh? There must be some inside story here.

"Fuck," he curses in pained resignation.

His angry pools bounce back and forth between us and I have to suppress a laugh every time they land on mine. While they are still very much full of vitriol, I also see reluctant acceptance creeping its way in.

"Does Dad know?"

"Yes," she clips. "He took it far better than you. Please be happy for me, Eric. *I'm* happy and isn't that all that matters?"

Eric's head falls against the white cupboards and the room becomes still. "You hurt her and I'll take great pleasure cutting off your dick, friend or not."

I nod once, fully aware that my manhood has been threatened twice today now. I feel a twinge and resist the urge to cup him in self-preservation. "Hurting her hurts me, bro."

He'd blow a lung if he sighed any louder. "Well, I guess that's that. I've failed as a big brother. All these years fucking wasted."

And that's when I know we have Eric's blessing. It will take him a while to get completely used to the idea, but we will get over this hump in pretty short order. Not only will I keep my best friend, I'll make a new brother, only official this time.

"Love you, Eric," Addy whispers into his chest as she catches him in a bear hug.

"Love you more, Leenie."

"Oh shoot, I forgot something. Be right back." She surprises me by stopping for a quick kiss, whispering, "The shoes are too much, but I love them," before I watch her disappear up the stairs. When she's out of sight, I turn to Eric and hold out my hand. He looks at it for a few seconds before grabbing it and pulling me in for a classic man hug.

His grip painfully tightens, keeping me there so he can whisper, "I mean it, Colloway. You break my sister's heart, there is no measure to what I won't do to hurt you back a thousandfold."

Breaking her heart would break me, period, so there's nothing that Eric could do to me that would be worse. "Understood."

Releasing me, we stand in silence, regarding the other. "She's my baby sister, Luke."

I know the instant I fell in love with Addy Monroe. I knew she was mine when I first saw her, though I can honestly say that's not when I took the hard fall. That would happen months later in the blink of an eye, and yet I tried to deny it was possible over the last few months. Love doesn't happen like that, does it?

When I overheard her sexy, drunk ass talking about a slice of hotness during Livia's bachelorette party, that was it. *I* wanted to be the man she desired. *I* wanted the right to touch her. *I* wanted to live every day making her happy because I could see the underlying sadness in her eyes and *I* needed to wipe it away. Those few seconds in time would forever change me.

"She's my entire life, Eric," I reply softly, never meaning anything more.

He nods.

I return it.

"Okay, ready," Addy says, back at my side and a little breathless. I can think of a dozen more pleasurable ways to steal her breath than running up and down stairs.

As if Eric is just noticing her suitcase for the first time, his eyes snap to mine and I just smirk; he knows she's coming back to my mom's with me. "It's not enough you're already stealing my baby sister, you're bringing your innocent mother in on your debauchery?"

"Not for long," I retort and now it's Addy's eyes that are snapping to mine, brows creased in confusion. She may not know exactly what I mean, but Eric sure as fuck does. His lips thin slightly before they curve, the smile reaching his eyes.

Yep. We're going to be one big happy family.

Chapter 37

Addy

I ate so much my pants are cutting into my waist, but I couldn't make myself stop. Barb Colloway is the all-around perfect woman. She's insightful, has a heart as big as Texas, and has a simply magnetic personality. The love she has for her boys shines as bright as a million suns and the selfless way she's already making me feel like a part of her family makes me want to bawl like a baby. It's just a bonus the woman clearly knows her way around the kitchen like a pro. I can easily see why Luke is an amazing cook.

Luke's mother is the role model you strive to emulate your entire life. You know you'll never achieve her perfection, but you try every day anyway to reach that elusive pinnacle, and in the end, you're a better person for it. I think that's what a good mom is and I give myself permission for a few moments to feel angry I didn't have that.

My dad is fantastic and never gave less than a hundred percent, yet at the end of the day...he wasn't my mom and through no fault of his own, he wasn't around much when I needed him most in my teenage years.

I think out of every bad relationship, you have to find the good. There's a lesson to be learned, even if it's one about yourself. And the good in my bad relationship with my mother is that I know the kind of mother I *don't* want to be. I will spend my life emulating Barb Colloway and if I can raise children half as wonderful as her boys, I will consider that a success.

"They seem to be getting along well, don't they?" my boyfriend (smile) whispers against my ear as his arms wrap around me from behind. He nibbles my lobe, making me shiver with desire.

"I was thinking the same thing," I reply quietly, watching my dad and Luke's mom gab away at the kitchen island. Every once in a while, Barb will touch my dad's arm and giggle like she's fifteen again. It's kind of adorable. "If I didn't know any better, I'd think your mom was flirting with my dad."

"If I didn't know any better, I'd say your dad is trying to pick up my mom," he chuckles. I join in.

My brows furrow. "That would be weird, right? I mean if they like started dating and got married or something?"

He leans against the kitchen wall, pulling me with him. The Colloway kitchen is huge, a good twenty-five feet in width, so while there are six of us in here, we're all in our own little bubble, our own little space, so our conversation can't be overheard. Still, we talk softly.

"I think you're getting ahead of yourself, fireball. I'm not sure my mom will ever marry again. Despite what she doesn't know, she was madly in love with my dad. Still is, even though it's been over three years since he's been gone."

"Would you be okay with it? I mean...not necessarily my dad, but if she got remarried?"

"Why wouldn't I be? My mom's only in her late-fifties and hopefully has a lot of life yet to live. I'd like to think there's someone else out there for her."

I think on that for a bit, knowing if what Luke and I have works out and we end up marrying and if I lost him at such a young age, I'd never remarry. No one else would ever be able to live up to him. Another man would always be my second and how would that be fair to him? "I couldn't," I mumble.

Turning me around, Luke scoops up my long hair, twisting it around his fist a few times before using it to tilt my head. His other arm hooks around my waist to draw me tight. My arms twine around his neck as he demands my undivided attention. "Couldn't what?" he asks probingly.

I'm completely aware of our surroundings and the fact that we are far from alone, even in this big house. Livia and Gray are sorting through their baby gifts, which are still sitting in the corner of the living room. Asher and Alyse are at the kitchen table talking about hors d'oeuvres and wedding music. And Eric and Conn are half asleep on the couch watching golf.

I'm also completely aware I should have kept my damn mouth shut, because, while we may have just declared our love for each other within the last twenty-four hours, I'm not sure how I'm going to get out of this conversation without intimating that I want to marry him. That's the kiss of death this early in a relationship. Not that I have personal experience with that, but I have plenty of friends who do.

Shit.

"Uh, nothing."

He searches my face before saying, "Has anyone ever told you you're a terrible liar?"

I try my level best to feign confusion. I'm good at a lot of things; subterfuge is not one of them, dammit. Even my white lies turn black. I forge ahead anyway. "I know not what you speak of."

He laughs loudly. Too loudly, because I feel lots of eyes upon us now.

"I want to marry you," he declares vehemently against my lips.

My stomach free falls, landing with a deafening crack at my feet. So loud was the sound, I'm not sure how the whole room couldn't have heard it. I try to pull back, but his grip is ironclad. "What?" I breathe.

"You heard me, fireball. Don't pretend you didn't."

Uh...does this sound like yesterday's conversation? Yes, except things just got fucking real. There's no way I mistook *marry* for hairy or bury or library. He definitely said marry.

M
A
R
R
Y

"Lu—"

He tightens his hold slightly on my long locks so I can't look away. "Don't speak, Addy. Just listen. I'm not asking you now—I'm making it known that's what I want. The only way this story ends is with you as my wife and the mother of my eight children."

I'm stunned momentarily as my brain catches up to his words. I can't believe how smooth this man is and not in a creepy used car salesman kind of way, but one that's utterly disarming.

"Did you say eight?" I chuckle.

"Six?" he counters.

I cock a brow.

"Four?"

I don't renegotiate and he beams with smugness, knowing he's hit the magic number.

Oh my God. What just happened here? Did I betroth myself to him and commit to having four kids while standing in his mother's kitchen with our family surrounding us?

It sure feels like it.

After several beats of awkward silence, I whisper, "I couldn't remarry."

"I know, sweetheart. I feel the same way."

Neither of us seems to care or remember where we are when he captures my mouth in a slow, seductive kiss, teasing my seam apart with his tongue. We stand in his mother's kitchen making out like teenagers until I hear my brother hiss his disbelief from across the room.

When we break apart, Luke gives me a cheeky grin and winks, holding my eyes, wordlessly reaffirming the conversation we just had.

"I love you," he mouths.

"I love you," I parrot silently.

Can someone pinch me? Is it possible I've fallen into a Disney movie where the perfect, handsome knight in shining armor steps out of the shadows, saves you by cutting down his foe with a magical sword, and swoops you up onto his snowy white stallion only to declare his undying love?

If I have plunged into such an enchanted place, please don't wake me.

Fuck the real world.

I want to stay right here.

Forever.

Chapter 38

LUKE

Today started out like any other normal day. These past few weeks since Addy and I returned from Easter weekend we've fallen into a routine, she and I, and I have to admit I like it. No, correction. I fucking *love* it.

On the days she opens her studio, we get up at the same time, around seven-thirty, and have breakfast together. I make the coffee and she cooks. I've taught her how to make eggs half a dozen ways and can even eat them now that she's learned there are more heat settings on the stove than just high. Patience isn't exactly one of my woman's virtues, in case you haven't caught on to that by now.

On the days she doesn't open, I wake her up anyway, except it's with my cock or my mouth instead of a smooth cup of coffee. I confess I may wake her up that exact same way on the other days too, but I don't hear her complaining. If she didn't like it she'd be sure to screech it loudly in my ear, so I know I'm on the right track. Although I love her, I've decided Addy should come with a decibel warning, kinda like one they give you when you walk into a rock concert.

Then we'll hook back up again in the evening for domesticated shit like making dinner together, watching TV, and massive amounts of fucking anywhere and everywhere until we pass out exhausted in my bed so we can start it all over again the next day.

I'm not sure we've left a surface or a wall untouched in our whole place, not that it's that big to begin with, but still. And bonus? Those ridiculously, stupidly expensive shoes look quite amazing when she's bent over the couch or my dresser or the counter in only those and nothing else. I make her wear them often so I can get my money's worth.

On Sundays, she doesn't work, so neither do I. And when we aren't running Madge or Mr. Neildorf from 2B around on small errands, we often stay naked in bed all day and eat and talk and read, or I introduce her to old classic movies she hasn't seen in between long, leisurely bouts of lovemaking. That's my favorite day of the week, the one where I get to hold her and touch her all day long. Makes for a hell of a withdrawal come Monday, but the aftereffects are worth it.

After my marriage declaration in my mom's kitchen a month ago, which I know took Addy by surprise, it hasn't been spoken of again. That doesn't mean I haven't been thinking about it every single day since. I sometimes wonder if I'm trying to rush things too much, too fast, but whenever I try to talk myself into waiting months or even longer to ask her, it makes me feel sick inside. Like blackness is seeping its way back into my soul, trying to drown out my brilliant color.

Marrying her is the only thing that feels right and I could wait five months or five years before I popped the question. We'd still end up in the same place.

With her as my wife.

So why wait?

I've become practically obsessed with the thought, so much so it's almost *all* I think about. I even broke down and over lunch a couple weeks ago, I talked to Gray and Ash about it. I knew they'd understand without giving me a rash of shit like Bigs would. They both told me essentially the same thing. "*When you know, you know.*"

Well, I know all right. I fucking know.

So I'm taking action. I've begun to ditch work for hours during the day looking for the perfect ring, but nothing I've found has even come close to being worthy of her, so I've started the process of designing my own with the same jeweler Asher used to buy Alyse's.

I don't have a damn clue what I'm doing, what I will like, what Addy will like, but the owner, Hank, is an absolute gem (pun intended). He's almost seventy years old and has fifty years of experience in the business, creating custom pieces for people from all over the world. He said, "*Finding the perfect ring is exactly the same as finding the perfect woman. When you see it, just like when you saw her, you'll know. It will hit you right smack in the middle of your chest."*

I wasn't sure about that, but he was right. Here I am, sitting at the kitchen counter staring at *The Ring*. This is the second set of designs Hank's created. I discarded the first set within fifteen seconds. Though I sort of felt bad because he'd gone to a lot of trouble; none of them hit me in the middle of my chest.

But this ring screams Addy. It's unique, just like her. It's multifaceted, just like her. And Hank said the cut would catch the light, creating a brilliant kaleidoscope of colors...just like her.

The stone is square with rectangular facets. It's so unique, the diamond actually looks like an upside-down pyramid when you stare down the center. Dozens of tiny round diamonds circle the centerpiece and run down the band. I lost my breath when I saw it, just as I did when I saw her, so there's no doubt it's the one. I'm lost in my thoughts when the front door opens and I scramble, slamming my laptop shut.

Fuck.

I look at the clock to see it's only four and wonder what the hell Addy is doing home already. It's Friday and she generally teaches that women's painting class Friday nights where they drink wine and try talking over each other. I attended a class one night. Let's just say it will be a while before I go back. I'd much rather stab a hot poker in my eye or have a vasectomy than go back to that again. If a guy tells you he wants to get his junk cut up over anything else, you know it's bad.

"What are you doing here?" she asks breathlessly as if she just ran up the stairs.

"I could ask you the same thing." I take her purse and the two bags of groceries she has in her arms, setting them on the counter.

"Landyn's coming today. Did you forget? She'll be here in an hour or so."

Landyn. *Shit.* Yep, it slipped my preoccupied mind.

When Addy first talked about her niece, I was confused. I knew Eric and Addy had an older sister, but I kind of forgot about her because Addy never once mentioned her name. Then, color me surprised to find out she's twenty-five years old. I didn't realize their sister was sixteen years older than Addy.

"No, I didn't forget, baby. She still staying here?"

Addy stops putting the food in the fridge and walks over to me. "Yes. Is that still okay?"

No. It's not okay and she knows it. Then I can't fuck her anywhere I want, anytime I want. *Can't she get a damn hotel?* I'll even pay for it.

"If that's what you want, but she's leaving Monday, right?"

She laughs knowingly, sliding her arms around my neck. "Yes, lover boy. She's leaving Monday."

"So we have an hour, huh?" I hum in her ear.

"A whole hour. Have any ideas how to kill sixty minutes?" she taunts, sucking on my neck.

"You know I do, fireball. I have a whole fucking list of ideas."

"The list will never go down if you keep re-adding things we've already done, Luke."

"Good," I reply, silencing her with my mouth. I have every intention of keeping that list perpetually long and adventurous. The more I have of her, the more addicted to her I become.

Her scent, her taste, her sounds, her fucking essence.

I love them all. Everything about her is tattooed on my very bones and runs thick through my blood.

In less than thirty seconds, our clothes are thrown in a pile on the kitchen floor and I have her sitting astride me on a stool bouncing on my cock when my phone rings.

"Don't get it," she moans breathlessly. "I'm so close."

Get my phone? She actually thinks I'd stop fucking her to answer my phone? There's no world in which that would ever happen. "I know, sweetheart. Your pussy's choking me. Christ, you feel so good, Addy." Like heaven. Like home.

I drive my hips harder and faster and just as Addy's crying out my name, coming all over my cock and quivering in my arms, *her* phone starts ringing.

"Fuck me. Really?" I grit angrily, ignoring it to latch onto a pert pink nipple that's dancing for me. Ten beats later I stiffen and release my seed deep into her on a low groan. Nothing on earth feels as good as being inside her.

We're panting and sweaty, our foreheads stuck together when I hear another fucking shrill break through our harsh breaths, shattering our post-orgasmic bliss.

"Jesus fucking Christ. Is someone dying?" I bark, reaching for my cell that's lying on the counter. I have to lean way forward to grab it and Addy almost slips off my softening dick in the process, which only ratchets up my ire further. Yanking her back on, because we have forty-five minutes left and I'm nowhere near done with her yet, I hit the accept button just as I see it's Gray.

"This had better be good, brother," I growl, still trying to catch my breath, except as soon as Gray starts talking I feel like a horse's ass.

"Livia's at the hospital in labor."

"What?" I lift Addy off of me, wrap my arm around her waist, and start ushering her toward the bathroom. By the panic in my voice, she knows something's wrong, so I have to keep shoving her forward when her steps falter. "She's not due for another five weeks."

"I know."

"Can they stop it?"

"I don't know. One of the babies is in a bit of distress so they want to watch her for a while. They could have to perform a C-section any minute. I thought maybe you and Addy would want to know. Maybe come down?"

Gray sounds anxious and very nervous. Fuck, *I'm* nervous and they aren't even my kids. "Shit, yeah. Of course, we'll be there. Rush University, right?"

"Yeah."

I turn the shower on, letting it warm. "We'll be there as soon as we can. Hour tops."

"Okay. Try to hurry. Oh, and can you call Addy? I tried and didn't get her either."

"She's with me. We'll hurry."

As soon as I hang up, Addy's peppering me with questions faster than an AK-47.

"Livia's in labor? Was that Gray? What did he say? Is she okay? Are the babies okay? Are Asher, Alyse, and Conn there with her? Did someone call your mom? She's going to be so upset she's not here for the bir—"

Dragging her into the heat and steam, I push her against the shower wall, palm her cheeks, and press my mouth to hers. "Addy. For fuck's sake. Take a breath."

"Sorry," she mumbles against me.

"Livia's in labor and they're trying to stop it, but one of the babies is in distress. They may have to perform a C-section, so we need to hurry. I'll call my mom on the way to make sure she knows. I assume my brothers also know, but I'll call them too. Did I forget anything?"

"No," she whispers. "It's too early."

"Everything will be fine, fireball. Okay?" I tell her soothingly. I don't know if it will be or not, but I see the fear in her eyes. I'm her rock and I want her to lean on me. Know she can count on me.

She nods. "I love you."

"I love you too, baby." I kiss her nose and we wash quickly. Ten minutes later we're out the door and halfway down the stairs when she comes to a screeching halt. "Shit! Landyn."

"Fuck." We stand there for a few seconds looking at each other while I try to work the problem. "Leave a key with Madge and text Landyn. Tell her we'll be back as soon as we can. I don't want to leave the hospital until I know everything is okay."

"Me neither. Landyn's a big girl. She'll be fine."

It takes five minutes for Addy to show several pictures of Landyn to Madge and convince her it's okay to let Addy's niece in without us there. Forty minutes later we're finally at the hospital.

When we get off on the fifth floor, I immediately spot Asher and Conn loitering in the hallway about three-fourths the way down.

"What's going on?" I ask looking around for Gray or Alyse when we reach them.

"The doctor is checking on her now." Ash nods to the closed door behind me.

A few minutes later a tall female in a long white coat and blue scrubs emerges, followed by a couple of nurses and Alyse.

"What did she say?" Addy asks Alyse anxiously, clinging to my hand.

"She's going to come back in another hour. The contractions have slowed, but one of the babies has a slightly elevated heartbeat. They'll decide what to do then."

"Can we see her?" Addy asks.

"I don't see why not."

We all file into the private room and I'm shocked by how large it actually is. It even has a couch and a coffee table on the far end, like they're just inviting spectators to pull up a seat and have a look-see. It's bizarre and makes me very uncomfortable.

Livia's sitting up in the hospital bed, all decked out in one of their pukey green gowns, her hair pulled back into a tight ponytail. Addy runs over and hugs her and everyone chatters at once. I'm able to gather they've been using some medication to try stopping the contractions It's not completely working. Another week or two baking would be ideal for twins, but the doctor says their lungs and hearts are all fully developed at this stage. If born now, they may spend a few days in the intensive care or they may be released to go home in a couple of days. Just all depends.

An hour turns into two and then into three and then finally into four before they decide they're going to take the babies today. Twice they thought they had things under control, but contractions started again. The good news is the delay allowed my mom to get here in time. And just as soon as I pick my jaw up off the floor that Addy's *dad*, Bob, is accompanying her, I'll be able to ask her what the hell that's all about.

At ten-thirty-three, baby boy one Colloway comes into the world weighing five pounds, eleven ounces and at ten-thirty-eight, baby boy two Colloway takes his first breath. At only four pounds, fourteen ounces, he's the runt of the two, just like I was. Gray and Livia have been very tight-lipped about the names they've picked out and it turns out we won't be finding out tonight because baby boy two has some issues breathing and baby boy one's heart rate is still elevated. Both are whisked off to the neonatal intensive care unit, or what they call NICU for short, and it's utter fucking chaos around here.

Finally, at midnight, Livia is back in her room, looking distraught and exhausted and Gray is down with the babies, checking on their status. My mom's sitting with Livia who is in tears. I don't know where Livia's mom is, if she's coming, and I'm not asking.

"They're strong, Livia. They'll be just fine," I tell her, pulling up a chair as I take her hand.

"I know. I'm just...I want to hold them," she sniffs. I hand her a tissue and she blows her nose.

"You will, dear," says my mom. "Just as soon as the doctors say it's okay. I remember when Luke here was born. He had to be on a feeding tube for a week. I was beside myself." I've heard this story a million times. A. *Million*. Maybe that's the reason I'm such a stickler about what I eat and why I have a love for cooking. I had to fight for my sustenance so early in life. I've had to fight for a lot of things in my life.

I look over at Addy sitting on the couch; she's lying down with her eyes closed and now I know why it's in here. Christ, birthing babies is a loooong-ass process. You'd think with modern medicine these days, they'd be able to come up with a quicker way to get them out.

The herd is thinning as everyone is exhausted. Asher forced Alyse to leave just a few minutes ago and Conn's out talking to the night nurse, waiting to take my mom and Bob back to his place. I'm about ready to do the same with Addy when Gray returns with a nurse in tow.

"Can I see them now?" Livia chokes on a sob. She tries to move, but winces at the pain from the stitches in her abdomen.

"Yes, angel. Let the nurse help you into a wheelchair and I'll take you to them."

And that's my cue.

I gather Addy, say good-bye to my family, and tell Gray, "Call me if anything changes, okay?"

"Will do," he rasps. He's beat, poor fucker. And he'll probably look this way for the next eighteen years. I may have to rethink this four kids idea and unless we have twins, I'm not sure I'll even be able to talk Addy into four kids now after what we've just witnessed. It's a damn wonder women have more than one kid, in all honesty. I have just that much more respect for my mother.

"Congratulations, Gray." I pull him in for a hug. "You did good, Dad."

"Thanks. I feel like today's been a blur."

"I think that's what the next twenty years will probably feel like."

He chuckles and stifles a yawn. "I think you're right."

"I'll talk to you tomorrow."

"Okay. Ready, angel?" he asks, turning his attention to Livia who's now comfortably positioned, ready to go.

"I think I'm going to fly into a rage if I don't get to see my babies within the next five minutes."

Gray kneels down in front of his wife, taking her hands in his. "They're perfect, Livvy. Absolutely, stunningly perfect."

She nods, water spilling down her cheeks in rivers.

I'm not sure I've witnessed a more poignant moment in my entire life and swallow the lump that's now formed in my throat.

Right now, I feel like a blessed man. I'm with the woman I love, witnessing new lives born to two people who mean more to me than almost anyone, with my family surrounding us.

Too bad shit's about to blow up in my face, throwing the perfect little world I've built into a fucking maelstrom of chaos and confusion, forcing me to meet my demons head-on or lose everything I hold dear forever.

I wish I could tell you I didn't fuck it up, but I can't.

I'm a man.

We fuck everything up at least once.

Chapter 39

Addy

Holy mother of all things unholy. *That's* what it's like to have a baby? And Luke wants eight? Screw that. Screw four. I'm not even sure I'll have *one* after what I just saw Livia and Gray go through. My emotions are completely wrung out, my body exhausted, and my heart feels like it's been sent through a shredder. And I didn't even give birth.

"You okay over there, fireball?"

"Peachy keen," I reply tightly, watching the lights blur as we fly past them.

He chuckles lightly. Grabbing my hand, his lips brush over my knuckles and my core spasms. I'm not sure if it's in lust or fear now.

"Did that scare you?"

My eyes find his, even in the dark. "Did it scare you?"

"Fuck yes. I'm terrified."

For some reason, that makes me feel better and I laugh.

"But not enough I guess. I still want kids with you, Addy. Loads of them."

My laugh turns into a cough because I now just swallowed spit down the wrong side when I sucked in a breath. We haven't talked about marriage, kids, or the future for over a month now. I'm not sure if that upsets me or relieves me. I think a little of both, actually.

"We aren't even married."

"I can fix that."

My heart's racing "Luke—"

"Hush, baby. When I ask, you'll know it. But I *am* going to ask. Sooner rather than later, so start practicing."

"Practicing what?" I ask, genuinely confused. Saying Mrs. Addy Colloway? Wow. I *really* like the sound of that. A lot.

"Saying yes, of course. That's not usually the first word out of your mouth when I ask you something."

My mouth hangs open for a second before I screech, "Oh my God! Seriously?"

"Damn that hurt," he says while laughing. His laugh is loud and boisterous and so contagious I can't help but join in. "God, I love you, fireball. So damn much."

My irritation melts. "I love you, too. When you're not pissing me off," I add. He smiles, knowing I'm teasing.

I lean my head back and just stare at the love of my life, trying to process these past few months, which seem like a whirlwind. I love him intensely and thoroughly, of that there's no doubt. I want to marry him and have a family (surrogacy is always an option, right?). I want to be part of *his* family, which I already love like my own.

Everyone thinks this in the beginning of a new relationship, a brand-new love, but I'm not sure there's anything that could happen that would possibly change the way I feel about this man. He's my someone.

Ten minutes later Luke and I are walking into my apartment when my steps waver. Landyn's sitting on the couch watching TV, as I expected. What I didn't expect was to see my sister, Sam, sitting right beside her. My gaze finds Landyn's and hers is chalked full of apology.

Fuck. A warning would have been nice. There's only one reason Sam is here and it's to guilt me into seeing my ill mother.

It's been two years since I've seen my sister and she hasn't changed a bit. Hasn't aged a bit. She looks like she did ten years ago. Hardly a wrinkle on her beautiful face, making her appear much younger than her forty-four years.

"Addy," she says, jumping up from the couch. "It's so good to see you."

"You too," I lie when she throws her arms around me.

"Who's your friend here?" she purrs. I want to scratch her eyes out for running them over my boyfriend, but I sheath my claws. For some reason my filter's wide open around everyone else; when it comes to my family it gets plugged up and not a single word of truth I want to speak will siphon through no matter how hard I try. I hate it.

When I turn around to introduce Sam to Luke, I freeze at the pure malice I see in his eyes. He's staring at Sam like he would literally take her head if he held a sword in his hand. His furious, fiery eyes are bouncing back and forth between my sister and my niece. I've never seen this look on him before and I know I never want to again because he looks downright lethal. My mind is a jumble trying to figure out what would cause him to act like this. Nothing makes sense.

"Luke, what's wrong?" I whisper, laying a hand on his arm.

He shakes it off like a hot coal and I stand there stunned when he cruelly spits in my direction, "Is this some sort of fucking joke?"

My gaze flits between Sam, who looks shocked, and Landyn, who is now standing just a few feet away clearly scared, and Luke, who is vibrating with anger. You'd have to be dumber than a box of rocks not to feel the hatred emanating from him right now and both Sam and Landyn take a step backward.

"What are you talking about?"

"I mean, what the *fuck* is *she* doing here?" *What is* she *doing here?* She? Sam? Why is he having such a violent reaction to the fact that my sister is here? I mean, I know it was a surprise to me, and Luke knows how I feel about my sister, but there is clearly something more going on here I am just not getting.

"I didn't know she was coming. I'm sorry. This is my sister, Sam."

"Jesus fucking Christ. *This* is your sister? Landyn's *mother*?"

"Yes," I mumble slowly, almost incomprehensibly. I watch his eyes land on Landyn now and see a plethora of emotions flash in quick succession.

Anger.

Shock.

Confusion.

Guilt.

Regret.

Sorrow.

He looks back to Sam, his eyes hardening to black slate. Then he turns and leaves. Walks out of the apartment without a word, leaving the three of us standing there looking at the closed door that he shut with a whisper, which is in such contradiction to the intense hatred I witnessed only a moment ago.

"What the hell was that?" Landyn breathes.

"I have no idea," I reply softly in utter confusion, a sick feeling forming in the pit of my stomach.

I have no fucking idea.

Chapter 40

LUKE

My lids crack open, my mind slowly churning to remember where the fuck I am and why my head feels like it's been split open with a sledgehammer. When I finally crawl through the thick sludge, the memory slams back into me with more force than my bike when I open her up, causing me to lose my breath and pray for oblivion once again. I hold my head in agony, wishing I was still passed out so I could forget how completely fucked this situation is.

My love's *sister* is my father's *mistress*. My woman's *niece* is my *half sister*.

How the fuck am I supposed to deal with this revelation? How am I supposed to spend the rest of my life with Addy knowing that her own flesh and blood screwed my family, literally and figuratively? Fucked me up to be the damaged man I am today? How am I supposed to cross paths with Landyn in the future and act like everything is peaches and fucking cream when it's not? How do I tell Addy her sister is a black widow who preys on innocent families, destroying them from the inside out? How am I supposed to keep the truth hidden from her and everyone else around us when I feel like it's written on my face in permanent black marker?

What am I supposed to do with this pile of stinking shit?

I don't have the answers. None. To *any* of the million questions swirling around me, which is why I'm still holed up in this hotel room trying to drink myself to death and forget.

How could the universe be so cruel as to take the one thing that nearly destroyed me and set it right in front me again like some sick taunt when my life is finally right for the first time in fourteen years? It's one thing to know she's out there, but to come face-to-face with her is entirely different. To have her related to my Addy is just plain evil. Addy has almost single-handedly locked my darkness down. Now, the door is standing wide open and every demon I possess has been let loose to endlessly torment and haunt me.

You're happy now, Luke? Well, fuck you, we'll fix that right up.

You're at peace now, Luke? Stupid prick. There *is* no peace for you.

You've finally found that one person who soothes your soul? Surprise! She's your half sister's aunt. This one-two punch has literally knocked me on my ass and I can't find any purchase to stand up again.

Fuck. Fuck. Fuck.

I want to slip back into the darkness, and

hopefully next time I wake this will all be just a horrific nightmare and Addy and I can laugh about it while we're lounging in bed on a leisurely Sunday afternoon.

I can't deal with this now any more than I could the last time I woke. I intend to fall again into oblivion, but first, I need to relieve myself before I piss the bed. After a few attempts to stand, I manage to make it to the bathroom. I finish my business and brush my teeth with the toothbrush the hotel gave me and turn on the shower because I stink like I haven't showered in days. Hell, maybe it has been days. Weeks. I don't know.

How long have I been here? I honestly don't remember and right now I can't make myself care enough to figure it out. All I care about is making sure I have enough liquor to put myself down again.

I take my time in the shower, letting the scalding water sluice over me, wishing it could wash away the beasts that have their teeth firmly planted in me, but it won't, so I embrace the pain instead. It feels good. Diverts it a little from my heart.

I wash my hair with the cheap shampoo and notice my scruff has grown into almost a full beard, so I must have been here a few days at least. After a good twenty minutes under the spray, I turn off the faucets and dry myself. Rather than put my reeking clothes back on, I wrap a towel around my waist and head back to the bed when I hear a knock on the door.

Glancing at the digital clock, I see it's after 2:00 p.m. so I assume it's housekeeping. I haven't let her in the last two times she's knocked. I'm feeling so sick at the moment, I couldn't give a shit if I was buck naked. I need my room cleaned so I can spend the next untold hours dirtying it again. I need my amenities refilled and my bed sheets and towels changed. The entire room smells like dirt, alcohol, and suffering.

I throw open the door but turn before I confirm it's housekeeping, which in retrospect would have been a damn good idea. The last thing I need is a fucking lecture that makes my ears bleed.

"What in the fuck do you think you're doing, Luke?" Bigs bellows from my open doorway.

My head drops and my eyes snag the nearly empty bottle of tequila that's lying on the matted carpet floor beside the rumpled bed. There's a wet stain around the mouth. *Huh.* That would explain the overwhelming liquor fumes I smell, I guess.

"Your woman is fucking beside herself with worry! Your family is ready to call the goddamn cops if you don't show your face. Jesus Christ, Luke, what is going on?"

I'm being selfish. I know this. I turned off my phone and haven't spoken to a single person other than Bigs since I walked out on Addy without one word of explanation. No one knows where I am, why I left, or what I'm doing. When I let myself think about it, I feel like a prick, so I just don't. Let myself think about it, that is.

"How many brain cells have you killed in the past four days?" he snarls, slamming the door with a loud thud that reverberates for several long seconds through my pounding skull. I deserve that, I guess.

Four days? I've been here for four days already? Time becomes meaningless when you're sucked into a quagmire of endless agony.

I sit on the edge of the bed, never looking my friend in the eye. I can't bear to see his condemnation right now. "How did you find me?"

He snorts, taking a seat on the second bed across from me. "Really, Luke? You do remember what we do for a living, right? Or have you forgotten that like everything and everyone else in your life while you have your little fucking pity party? You look like death warmed over, by the way."

I feel like it. "Get the fuck out. I'm not in the mood to hear your shit."

"I would deck you right now if I didn't see how much physical and emotional pain you're already in. Talk to me, Luke."

Not able to sit any longer, I lie on my back and blink up at the ceiling, wishing I could go back to a week ago when I was deliriously happy and the only thing I had to worry about was picking out the perfect ring for Addy.

Addy. God, I physically ache for her right now and have to push back the pussy tears welling in my eyes.

Another knock on the door sounds, along with

a disembodied light voice, "Housekeeping." Great. Now she comes.

"Not now," Bigs yells. *Yells*. As loudly as possible. Motherfucker.

"I told you when I talked to you that I'd reach out when I was ready, Bigs. Now that you've confirmed I'm alive, you can go."

Out of my peripheral, I watch him look around the room and I cringe at what he sees. Empty bottles everywhere. Dirty, stinky towels scatter the floor. My rancid clothes are strewn all the way from my bed to the bathroom.

His voice softens and his compassion hits me deep. "I'm not leaving until you tell me what happened to make you like this. I haven't seen you act like this, Luke, since..." He leaves his sentence hanging; we both know what he means. He hasn't seen me like this since I was a stupid teenager, trying to chase away my problems with drugs and alcohol.

Once I got my shit straightened out, I never touched drugs again. Didn't touch alcohol for almost three years. So being drunk off my ass for so many days that I've completely lost all sense of time is a big fucking red flag to Bigs. The fact I disappeared at all was the first one. Didn't take him long to track me down. Yesterday, I had to give the hotel my credit card because I'd run out of cash to pay for the cheap room.

"You've talked to Addy?" I ask instead of answering his question.

He sighs heavily, matching my position. "Couple of times, yeah."

"How is she?"

"How is she? Pissed as hell. Out of her fucking mind. Crying. Jesus, Luke. What the actual fuck, man? I thought you loved her."

"I do, but shit just got complicated."

"Complicated how?"

I take my time answering. Speaking the words out loud is hard. Makes them real. "Turns out her sister, Sam, is my dad's mistress. The one I saw that day leaving his office with a nice fat check in her hand."

Bigs jackknifes off the bed. "What? That can't be right."

"Ah, but it is. Fucked up, right? I mean the woman who helped destroy me is the fucking *sister* of the woman I love more than life itself. What exactly am I supposed to do with that?"

"Are you sure it's her, LC? I mean...after all these years, could you be *wrong*?"

I finally turn my head and look my friend in the eye. My head throbs and I could drink a gallon of water and still not be sated, but I can't; my stomach is revolting at even the thought of anything else being dumped into the roiling sea of toxicity.

"I wish I was. The woman in the kitchen that day had a very distinctive dark birthmark on her right cheek. I remember it almost looked heart-shaped, which I thought was ironic. What type of woman with a heart would let someone buy her child off? Addy's sister has that exact same mark, Bigs. That's not coincidence. And Landyn? Her niece? Definitely resembles my father. So, no. I'm not fucking wrong."

He goes silent for a few minutes before finally saying, "You should talk to Addy. Tell her. You're punishing her for something that's not even her fault."

"I'm not punishing her, Bigs. I just...I don't know what to do. I love her. I want to be with her for the rest of my life. I just don't know how I'm going to get over this hurdle. I need some time to think."

"Not sure how much thinking you can do when your head's stuffed in a vat of liquor. Drinking yourself dead isn't the answer, man. I've been telling you for years you need to get this fucking monkey off your back. It doesn't change the facts, but it spreads the load so you don't have to carry so much yourself. If you wait much longer, I can tell you that you'll have one less person to help with that and she's the best fucking thing to *ever* walk into your life. You fuck this up and you can just accept my resignation now because there is no way in hell I'll be able to be around your sorry ass after she walks away from you."

"You wouldn't."

"Fucking try me." I've never heard Bigs more serious than he is right now. After several beats, he adds, "I love you like a brother, Luke, but I've watched you suffer with this and what happened in Boston for too long. This shit is eating you up inside. Talk to your mom. Talk to your brothers. Talk to Addy. Fucking talk to someone other than your damn priest because that's obviously not helping."

He's right. I know he's always been right. Holding this secret in has gotten to the point where it's now absolutely deadly.

"I'll think about it."

Standing, he shakes his head. "You do realize that's how you always end this conversation. With that bullshit answer. If I don't hear from you within twenty-four hours, I'm personally coming back here for you and we're gonna have more than words, so be prepared to have some sense knocked into your sorry ass." Walking to the door, he turns to me, the knob in his hand. "You have a lot of people who love you, Luke. Who have *always* loved you. Unconditionally. It's about fucking time you trust in them, lean on them, or you will find yourself completely alone and that would be a travesty. Despite what you believe, you're a great man."

And with that dressing down, Bigs walks out, leaving me once again alone in my ocean of misery. I drift off, this time sans alcohol, and dream of the same dark, slithery, happiness-stealing reptiles I did weeks ago. I was determined to fight them then and resolve I'm determined to fight them now.

I just need to figure out how.

Chapter 41

LUKE

I feel her presence before she speaks.

I don't want her here.

I don't want to talk.

I don't want to think.

I don't even want to *be*.

I just want to wallow. At least I'm not drunk, so that's a start.

"How are they?" I croak.

She hesitates before answering. I know she's angry with me. Fuck, *I'm* angry with me. "They're doing well, actually. They're weaning them from the warmers and they should be able to come home in a day or two. Grant's doing a little better than Cash. He'll probably be released tomorrow if he can make it through the night without his body temp falling."

Grant. Only minutes ago when I arrived at the hospital and saw baby boy two's name had been changed to Grant, I had to choke back my emotions.

"He's a fighter," I mumble absently. "They both are, like you."

"Luke, what are you doing?" she sighs.

When I talked to Conn earlier and he told me the babies were still in the hospital, there's no way I could stay away. This part of the NICU has stars painted all over the walls and Grant and Cash have their own private little quarters. I stand at the thick glass door, unable to take my eyes from the tiny humans inside housed in their own little tropical bubbles.

My brother's boys.

Twins, like Gray and me.

Pure.

Innocent.

Beautiful.

Blissfully unaware of how life can royally fuck you over.

"I wanted to see my nephews. Make sure—"

"That's not what I mean and you know it," she scolds. "You've been MIA for five days. Five fucking days, Luke. How utterly selfish of you for so many reasons, but I'm too damn exhausted to start listing them off."

"Livia, don't." I snap. "You have no fucking idea what I'm going through."

"And neither does anyone else because you won't tell us. You just up and disappeared. We're your family, Luke. *Family*. And family doesn't do what you've just done to us. What you've done to Addy, for God's sake."

She's right. They don't.

But *I* do.

I run.

I hide.

I shove the pain deep so I don't have to deal with the anguish in my soul. The anguish that's blacker and thicker and even more acidic than it was before I walked out on Addy.

My color. My very lifeblood.

I miss her so damn much I can hardly take a breath; my body is oxygen starved. My cells cry out for more and I try to obey, but I can't. It's physically impossible to draw in any more air. Is this what it feels like to drown? A crushing, unbearable pain in your chest, your head, your organs? It's a slow, horrible, gut-wrenching death and I'm its prisoner, held tightly in its unyielding grasp. Unable to escape.

Livia stands beside me, quiet now. We both watch her children sleeping. Grant's starting to stir and I long to hold him and shield him from any suffering life may bring him. It's amazing how much I love these little beings who aren't even mine. I can't even fathom the love I would have for my own children, which is a chance I may never get given how massively fucked things are right now.

"I'm sorry," I tell her.

"I know, you know."

She doesn't know shit because I don't share my burdens. I shoulder them alone, protecting those I love.

"What do you know, Livia?" I'm tired. So tired. I don't have the strength to be an asshole right now. My head still pounds and my stomach still churns, courtesy of spending the last five days in a poison fog.

"About Peter."

My head whips to her; she doesn't turn my way.

I haven't seen Livia since the birth. I haven't seen her hold her children or coo to them or sing to them. I haven't seen the pure, raw, passionate connection she has with them. But as she continues to stare at her babies with unconditional love in her eyes and unfettered happiness shimmering around her, my twin's words slam into me.

I nearly break down and sob. *I* gave her this. I gave her life so she could create life and the soul-eating darkness I feel lightens somewhat.

I take a deep breath and it's a little easier this time. "Did Gray...?"

"Gray and I haven't talked about him in months, so whatever secrets you've shared with him remain safe. Even though we've never spoken of it, I've always known what you've done for me, Luke and..." She swallows, her voice cracking when she starts again. "I know how much it weighs you down. I know it changed you and I'm sorry for that. But I'm not sorry to be alive. I'm not sorry to have something of my very own that I thought I'd never have and if that makes me a horrible person, then so be it."

My eyes burn. "I'm not sorry. I'd do it a million times over for you, Livia. For Gray. For Grant and Cash."

She finally turns to me with watery eyes. "Then forgive yourself. Please, I beg of you. Let go of whatever guilt you're carrying around inside so you can be free. Happy. It's time. *Please*, Luke. Please."

Livia knows nothing of the last one hundred and twenty hours of hell and the fact that I am encumbered by more than one heavy burden, but I wouldn't be able to keep my tears from spilling if I tried. I pull her in for a hug, absently wondering where Gray is and if I'll get a fist to the jaw for touching his wife. I don't fucking care. I'll take it. Right now I'd even welcome it.

When Addy slept at my mom's house over Easter, we talked long into the night and she implored me to tell my family about the secret I carry like a two-ton boulder. Not just for me; for them as well. She said the only way to slay my demons was forgiveness and purging, but I was steadfast in my decision. Just like I have been for the last fourteen years.

Bigs was right when he called me out on my canned bullshit answer. I didn't mean it anymore yesterday than every other time I've said it, yet suddenly everything becomes so very clear to me. Like the sun peeking over the horizon at the start of a new day, casting its bright rays to light all that was dark only moments before.

I do need to purge.

Everything. To Addy. To my family.

I need to forgive myself for my own sins and let go of those that aren't mine to bear. I know what I need to do and it will be one of the hardest conversations I've ever had in my life.

"I fucked up."

"Big time," she retorts smartly.

I chuckle, kissing her head and wiping my face before I let her go.

"Will she talk to me?"

"I don't know, Luke. She's confused and angry and hurt and she has every right to be. When Gray left me for those few days, it was the worst form of torture. You *know* that. You witnessed it firsthand and yet you turned around and did the same damn thing to her. You know how stubborn she is. She's had a lot of people hurt her in her life and right now she sees this as almost an unforgivable wrong. You left without any explanation. Most of all, you didn't trust her."

"I know. It was wrong. I was just...*fuck*. There are things you just don't understand, Livia. Things about my past. Things I'm not ready to talk to you or Gray about yet. I know I need to. My past and my present kinda collided and it threw me for a loop."

"I don't pretend to know what you're talking about. What I do know is that you need to try to find a way to make this right with Addy. Then worry about your brothers. She's had a lot of guys screw her over. She's skittish and untrusting and she's more pissed than I've ever seen her, but she's also crazy in love with you. I know it. I'm sure you'll find a way to get through to her. Eventually."

"Right. Do you know where she's at now?"

"Probably her studio. I think she's been practically living there to take her mind off things."

I nod. "Thanks, Livia. For giving me the kick in the ass I needed."

"You're lucky I didn't take your balls." She smiles.

I chuckle lightly. "I think those babies have created a wicked streak in you."

"God, tell me about it. It's the pregnancy hormones. They're still making me crazy."

"About time you showed up," an angry grumble rains down on me from behind. "In addition to the stress of my newborns being in ICU, you've managed to make my wife cry every night by pulling your goddamn Houdini act, Luke."

I take one more look at my beautiful, tiny nephews before facing my livid twin, who now has his wife ensconced in his arms. "I have to go. I need to talk to Addy."

"You have some fucking explaining to do, Luke."

"You're right, but my woman is going to be the first to hear it. So if you'll excuse me, I need to go find her."

I'm halfway down the hall when Gray's voice halts me. "Luke." I don't turn. "Everything okay?"

I still don't know how I'm going to deal with the fact that my father's mistress will permanently be a part of my life, but I need to, because if I don't get Addy back in my arms, then no. It's not okay and I fully realize it will never be okay again. I could have completely ruined the best thing that's ever happened to me.

"I'm working on it," I call over my shoulder

before I push through the secured steel doors and head to hopefully fix what I've royally fucked up, praying the whole time that she'll find it within herself to forgive me.

Even though I don't deserve it.

Chapter 42

Addy

I sit at my desk, blankly staring at my computer screen. The blinking cursor mocks me. I'm not even sure what I'm supposed to be doing. It's another long, interminable day without Luke. Without talking to him or touching him. Without explanations. My voice mails and texts have gone unanswered. With every long minute that's passed my confusion and anger have grown to almost now explosive levels. I've cried, I've screamed, I've thrown things, I've stomped around my apartment like a bratty three-year-old. I've barely slept. I've barely eaten. I feel like a living, breathing zombie.

It doesn't make me feel much better, but I know I'm not in this alone: he's abandoned everyone else too. His new nephews. His brothers. His mother. Livia. The only person I know he's been in touch with is Bigs, who called me yesterday to say he's seen Luke and he's alive. Yet no matter how much cajoling or crying I did, he wouldn't tell me what was going on or where he was. I know he knows. His loyalty, while commendable, pisses me the fuck off right now.

I want answers. I deserve answers, but as much as I want to see Luke, I'm not at all sure I can stomach hearing them. At the moment, I'm so goddamn mad I don't think I can look at him. More than anything, though, I'm hurt. I can't even describe how much it hurts knowing he would just leave me and not look back. And I honestly have to wonder if I'll be able to build a life with a man who just cuts and runs every time his demons rise up from the ashes. I've done nothing but think about that since Friday night when he walked out.

A soft knock pulls me out of my reverie. I look over to see Julie sticking her head in my barely opened door. It looks like it's floating. It would be funny if anything struck me as such these days. "Addy, I hate to bother you, but there's someone here to see you."

"Who?" I ask, not wanting to talk to any salespeople or someone who's looking for a job today.

"Me," Luke's dark rumble answers right before he pushes the door open the rest of the way.

"Luke," I whisper. Never taking his eyes from mine, he walks in and shuts Julie out. He makes no move to come closer. Smart man.

I sit still, drinking in the sight of him. He looks like he's been to hell and back. His eyes are bloodshot. His clothes are rumpled. He looks exhausted. I think he's lost weight and it's clear he hasn't shaved since he left. For the hundredth time, I wonder what in the hell happened and what it has to do with my sister because she still claims to have no clue.

Two emotions hit me hard and fast: anger and relief. In a duel to the death, anger wins. I straighten my spine, sitting tall. My entire body shakes with my effort to hold back from slapping him. I wipe away the tears that are rolling down my cheek, pissed that they escaped.

"I'm busy."

"Addy, please. I need to talk to you."

Fuck his explanation. I can't listen to it right now and if I do, it will be on my terms, not his.

"I can't do this now, Luke," I say, turning back to my computer, pretending to type some numbers into a spreadsheet. I have absolutely no idea what I'm doing, but I'm not about to let him know.

"Baby, I am so sorry. There's no excuse for my actions, but please let me explain."

I fly from my chair, my vision clouded scarlet. "Sorry? You're *sorry*? Well, fuck your sorry!" I scream. "You just ran out the door with no explanation, no phone call, no text. *Nothing*. You abandoned me, Luke. I have no idea what the hell happened and I've been stumbling in the dark for five days wondering where you were. Five days! I didn't know if you were dead. If you were drunk. If you were fucking other women. I didn't know if you left me! I had to track down Ben to find out that you were even alive for fuck's sake! You called *him*, and you didn't call *me*. You cut me out completely, just like you did your family all those years ago."

He flinches, my words cutting him deep. I can't make myself care.

"You're right, Addy. About everything. I handled this poorly, but I can explain. *Please* let me explain."

"It's too late. You should have done that before you ever hit the threshold. Now it's too late." My voice cracks and I can barely swallow the saliva pooling in my mouth.

He looks devastated. The water I see in his eyes absolutely guts me and I feel positively sick because I may have actually meant the words I just said. I don't know if I can forgive him for doing this to me. To us.

"Please tell me I haven't fucked us up permanently," he chokes. He's trying to hold it together as much as I am.

"I can't," I whisper hoarsely. "I'm staying with Kamryn for a while, so you can go back to the apartment."

He nods and we stand there silently. I have nothing left to say, but I can't move either. I have to force my feet to the floor, pretending they're superglued because the urge to throw myself into his arms and forgive him is so overpowering. Every cell in my body is begging me to run to him.

I miss him.

I miss his kiss. I miss his touch. His laugh. His humor. I miss his arms holding me so I can sleep. I miss his heat. I miss his cooking.

I miss his everything.

His eyes fall to the floor. I let my tears flow freely, although I try to prevent myself from completely falling apart in front of him. I have far too much pride for that.

"The battle may be won, but the war rages on."

"What?"

His hazels lift. "My tattoo." I suck in a breath and my knees give out. Luckily for me, the chair is right there so I don't end up on my ass. "You wondered what it said. *That's* what it says. You're my war, Addy. You're the *only* thing worth fighting for. I'm not perfect. I fucked up. I know it, but I will never stop fighting for you. I love you, fireball, and I am so very sorry."

Then he turns to leave and it takes a minute for his next words to register. By the time they do, he's already gone.

"And war is my destiny until she is mine."

I put my face in my hands and sob.

Chapter 43

LUKE

Eric stares me down as I stride through the glass door, the tinkling of the bell announcing my arrival. Today he's wearing a ratty Lions hat backwards, black ripped jeans, and a black Godsmack concert T-shirt.

"Wow, you've got balls of steel showing up here like this," he spits venomously.

Guess that answers the question on whether he knows what happened between Addy and me.

"Thought we had an appointment."

"I didn't think you'd show."

"Guess you were wrong."

I stand my ground. I made this appointment two weeks ago and I am not fucking leaving Inked On until I have my new tattoo. The one I had him design with *her* in mind.

It's been over a week since I've seen Addy at her studio and every minute has been insufferable. I miss her with a raw ache that deepens with every passing second. If not for Bigs, I'm not even sure I'd make it to work. At least when I'm there I throw myself into it head-on so I can forget how empty I feel. I packed a bag and moved back in with him for a while so she could have her place back. She was there long before I was. When I texted her about it I didn't get a response so I don't know if she's living there or not. If she's anything like me, she can't.

I couldn't stay there without her. Everywhere I looked memories were woven into the very fabric of that place. Every surface. Every wall. Even the air. I walked by her room and could smell her unique scent. I slept in her bed that first night before I moved out, just so I could feel close to her. It tore my guts out to see that stupid stuffed animal sitting on top of the comforter, knowing she didn't take it with her. He looked lost and lonely and forgotten. A mirror of me.

I've called her daily, but she won't answer. I text her, but she won't respond. I had a package delivered to her this morning but haven't heard a peep. I know gifts won't fix things, but this one was special. It had meaning, a purpose, just like her. I know she digs that stuff.

I've decided while I'm back in Detroit for the long weekend to just let her be. Give her some breathing room. I'm not done fighting. I'll never be done fighting. Whether she takes me back or not, I at least need her to understand what happened and why I flipped out. Then maybe she can go through the process of forgiving me. I'm an insanely patient man when I want something bad enough.

Eric sighs in resignation. "I'm going to make this as painful as possible."

I nod, following him. "Was kinda hoping you would."

He leads me back to his private room, pulling the curtains shut. I take off my shirt and get comfortable on the table. Eric goes about getting the ink and his instruments of torture ready, eyeing me the whole time. He silently cleans the spot where my new tattoo will rest for all of eternity.

Pressing the transfer to my clean skin, he tests his tattoo machine, making sure the needle's working right. Eric uses the good old-fashioned steel tube instead of the disposable ones so many artists use today. Says it makes a huge difference in his end product and he's nothing if not proud of his art, as he should be. It's fucking incredible. Snapping on his black latex gloves, he looks at me with an evil grin.

"Ready, fucker?"

"Did you sterilize your gun?"

"Nah. I'm rolling the dice with you today." I'm not entirely sure he's kidding. I nod and he leans over to start. The familiar hum of the machine soothes me and I suck in a breath at the first bite of the needle but then settle in for a long session. We're silent for a good fifteen minutes before Eric speaks. I've already decided if he asks, I'll tell him, even though it should be Addy I tell first.

"You gonna spill?"

"You should lift the gun first." The last thing I

want him to do is fuck up my ink when he goes into shock. Which he will.

His gaze turns to mine and I cock my brow. He straightens and cuts the power, taking away the pain. I want it back.

"It's your sister."

"*What's* my sister?" He snarls.

"Sam."

"Sam? What does Sam have to do with this?" Ah, so Addy didn't tell him much beyond the fact that I hid for days like a pussy.

"She was the one at the house that day. With my dad." His brows pinch in confusion and I add, "She's the one he had a kid with. Your niece, Landyn, is my half sister."

"You're lying."

"I'm not Eric." I go on to tell him about the birthmark. I tell him how I wigged out when I saw Sam at Addy's. I tell him how I stayed drunk for four days straight. I tell him how I've tried to apologize to Addy repeatedly and win her back. I tell him I am ruined without her.

He sits in utter disbelief. I can see he's having just as hard a time wrapping his head around this shit as I did. *Am*, still.

"She's stubborn."

"As a fucking mule," I retort. "But I love her despite it."

A smirk flashes before it's gone. "You're good for her, Luke. I fought it because I didn't want her with guys like us, but I know now I was wrong. I see how much you love her. She'll come around."

"I hope so."

"You can't keep this a secret anymore, LC."

"I know. I'm telling my mom tonight."

He nods thoughtfully. "Don't envy you that conversation."

"Yeah," I sigh. "Neither do I."

Tonight I get to be the one to crush my mom yet again. I crushed her before with my actions. I'll crush her now with my words. That thought's been sitting hard and sick in the pit of my stomach for days. She just got home day before yesterday from Chicago after staying with Gray and Livia for a week to help with the babies and I didn't want to talk to her then. Now that she's here and I'm here there's no more putting it off.

Eric gets back to work. This time, we stay silent, both lost in our own thoughts at how small this world really is.

Chapter 44

Addy

Walking through my apartment door has to be one of the hardest things I've ever done. I've been standing in the same spot for I don't even know how long. Everywhere I look, I see Luke.

I see him in the kitchen dicing up vegetables or making coffee.

I see him on the couch, my head in his lap while he recounts why each stupid *Fast and Furious* movie is unique in its own way. He made me watch all seven of them.

I see him pushing me against the hallway wall before he sinks inside me because he doesn't have the patience to make it to the bedroom.

His entire essence surrounds me here, and my eyes well.

God, I miss him.

Tomorrow's the start of another weekend, which means another Sunday without him. I always loved Sundays even before Luke was in my life. I used to do nothing but sleep in and lie around all day, catching up on my stack of magazines or reading a steamy romance. Luke was more than happy to insert himself into my tradition, only we acted out the steam after he made me read it out loud first.

Now I hate Sundays. There's nothing fucking sunny about it.

Kam begged me to stay at least until Monday, but I can't impose on her anymore. Quite frankly, I'm tired of her asking me every five seconds if I'm okay. I'm tired of her telling me every hour to call him. I'm just tired, period.

After I'm changed into some pajama pants and a baggy tee, I pour myself a big glass of white wine, wincing when I see the Heinekens in the bottom of the fridge. I'll have to throw those out tomorrow. I don't even bother opening the freezer. Its contents will cause me to have a meltdown. I may have to call Kam to come over and help me purge.

Sitting on the couch, I turn on the TV, flipping until I find *The Breakfast Club*. I mute it. I can't stomach noise right now for some reason. Then I turn it off because I can't stomach even watching TV in here without *him*.

Lying down, I curl into a ball and pull the blanket from the back of the sofa over me. I can't seem to get warm. I've been cold for two weeks straight.

Frozen. All of me.

My blood.

My body.

My heart.

I feel dead inside without him. I wonder if I'll

ever be me again. *No. Because he's part of you now.*

Am I being too hard on him? Should I at least let him explain? Can I trust him not to run again? Can I trust him to trust me *instead* of running? I don't know. I don't really know anything anymore, I guess, other than I'm miserable without him, so maybe that's my answer.

"And war is my destiny until she is mine."

The whispered words he spoke have haunted me day and night. I run them over and over in my head. I dream them. I've written them countless times. He's been true to his word. Relentless but not pestering. There's a fine line there and he's butting up against it yet hasn't crossed it. Every time I see his name appear on my phone, I ache.

Restless, I sit up and look at the small robin's egg-colored blue box I'm holding in my hand. It arrived at the studio this morning. The deliveryman left before I could reject it. He was probably given very strict instructions to get in and get out before the crazy woman threw a temper tantrum. That sounds like something Luke would do. A sad smile tries to curve my lips but fails.

I flick it open, fingering the delicate silver olive leaf pendant inside. There are tiny filigree branches with even tinier leaves. There are no diamonds, no gemstones glittering back at me. It's simple, intricate, beautiful, and no doubt meaningful in some way. I remove the note that's tucked inside. The one I've been too chicken to read. The one I know will cut me to ribbons.

Taking a fortifying drink, I unfold the small piece of paper and begin reading. And sobbing.

My beautiful fireball,

An olive branch is traditionally associated with a peace offering. A way to win favor, reconcile, overcome distrust. In the bible, it's written that the dove Noah released brought back an olive branch to prove there was land, life, and all hope was not lost. It was a new beginning. But in ancient times, brides also often wore olive branches as a sign of their purity.

You're pure, Addy. You're pure of heart. It's magnetic. It draws people to you, including me. Especially me. Your innate purity brings me peace. It quiets my demons. It brings me life, color, breath. Clarity. A new beginning.

I fucked up. I lost my way, but I want you to know I'm working on things. Me. I want to be what you need, because you're the only thing that makes sense, Addy. With you, I can just be. You see the real, imperfect man and love him anyway.

You took a leap of faith on me the first time. Even though I don't deserve it, I'm asking you to do it again. Without you, I'm drifting. I have no purpose. I'm lost, fireball. So damn lost. But I'm holding on and I'll hold on until my very last breath because life doesn't make sense anymore without you in it.

I'm a patient man when I need to be and so I'll wait as long as it takes. I'm madly, deeply in love with you, Addy Monroe. Please come back to me. Come back to me, Addy. I am truly nothing without you.

"And war is my destiny until she is mine."

All my love,
Luke

That night I sleep in Luke's bed with his note in one hand, my stuffed bulldog, Gerard, cuddled to my chest with the other, and cry myself to sleep.

383

Chapter 45

LUKE

I pussied out last night and didn't talk to my mom. She's been gone all morning having coffee with her friends, so by the time she finally walks through the door at shortly after one my stomach is in forty different types of knots. I have absolutely no fucking idea how I'm going to start this conversation, because I can't just blurt out, "*Hey, funny story. You'd never believe that Dad's illegitimate daughter is also my woman's niece. Weird coincidence, right?*"

As it turns out, it doesn't take us long to get around to that conversation. My mom is *the most* intuitive person I know on the planet. It's almost like she has this creepy sixth sense, and as a child, that was damn unnerving, let me tell you.

"What happened?" she asks pointedly after grabbing a bottle of diet iced tea from the fridge. The lid makes a popping noise when she twists it off. When I said that I pussied out earlier, what I actually meant is I avoided her completely last night so this is the first conversation we've had since I arrived yesterday afternoon. This is actually the first conversation we've had since I came out of hiding.

I take a seat at the six-person cherrywood kitchen table. My mom slides in right across from me so I have no choice but to look at her.

"Can you be more specific?"

She ignores my contrived confusion. "You do realize your entire family was worried sick about you, Luke. Addy was a wreck. What you did was irresponsible."

I don't care how old you are, your mother's disappointment in you always cuts deep. "You talked to Addy?"

"Yes." I wait for more, but that's all she'll offer.

My sigh is heavy and long. "I know, Mom. I'm sorry. It's...complicated."

"Life is complicated, Luke. Every single day, each of us faces challenges and we have to figure out how to handle them. This time, you chose poorly. Your family has always been here to support you. To support each other. That's what family is. I can appreciate a sixteen-year-old not understanding what it means to handle what life throws at them with grace and maturity. A thirty-year-old man should know better."

Ouch. That hurts in the way it was meant to, each biting word another stinging slap. My mom is kindhearted and loving, infinitely patient and understanding, but when you cross her...Watch. The. Fuck. Out. Right now she is angrier than I've seen her in a long, long time.

"I was trying to protect you, Mom. Protect the

family. That's all I've ever wanted to do," I tell her softly.

Her voice relaxes, yet still holds a sharp edge. "What is this really about, Luke? Unburden your soul, son, because I promise you I don't sit in judgment. That's not my job."

I try to start saying the words several times, but they won't budge. Fuck, this is hard. Finally, I squeak them out.

"You probably don't remember this...I came down with the flu in the fall of my junior year and had to be sent home from school. We were supposed to play the Crusaders that night. I was mad I couldn't go because it was a big game and I had a hundred two-degree temp."

"I remember. You were sick with the flu for three days and could hardly get out of bed."

Moms. They remember every hurt, every wound, every tear.

"Yeah. Well..." I take a deep breath and drop my eyes to the dark wood unable to watch her face when I destroy her world. "What you don't know is that when I got home from school there was a woman here. With Dad." I sweep my gaze back up to see her watching me intently, confused at where this childhood story is going, so I continue.

"I overheard them talking, Mom. She said she had pictures. Proof. And then Dad asked her how much it would take to go away."

Her face hardens and you could have knocked me over with a feather when she speaks. "I am well aware of that situation, Luke. What I don't understand is what that has to do with why you just disappeared two weeks ago."

"You knew?" I ask disbelievingly.

"Of course, I knew. Your father and I didn't keep secrets from each other."

Standing, I start pacing, my mind reeling. "So let me get this straight. You knew your husband cheated on you, had another kid, and paid off the kid's mother to keep them out of your lives and you were *okay* with that?"

I am in complete and total shock. Never in a million years would I have believed *my* mother would be in on a scandal like this, let alone condone it.

"Is that what you think? That this was your *father's* child?"

"It's what I know. I heard the whole thing, Mom! As soon as he saw the pictures, Dad paid her off."

Her eyes water as she reaches for my hand. I take it and pull a chair close, sitting beside her. "Luke, my sweet boy. Is that what caused you to start skipping school and doing drugs and hanging out with delinquents?"

I don't answer, but I don't need to. She knows.

"Oh my. I should have known. I should have figured it out all those years ago and talked to you. Luke...Luke, that wasn't your *father's* child. It was *Fred's*."

"What?"

"Your uncle Fred. Your father's *twin*."

My shock just multiplied. My mom actually believes what she's telling me and that makes me hate my father even more. "Is that what he told you to cover his tracks? That this was Fred's kid?" I spit angrily.

"Luke, it's the truth. That wasn't the first time Fred used your father as an alias during his illicit affairs. He did it all the time in college. And that wasn't the first time your father had to dig Fred out of a mess he'd gotten himself into because he couldn't remain faithful to his wife."

"I—I don't understand, though. If this wasn't his kid, what pictures…"

"Identical twins, remember?"

I'm speechless. None of this makes sense. My mom goes right on talking, but I'm having a hard time paying attention.

"Your dad confronted Fred and found out that he apparently had a several month-long affair with this woman, who was twelve years his junior. She was young, in law school, and he met her at some bar. I understand he even set her up in an apartment for a while. He eventually broke it off and she moved away. Then she shows up out of the blue with pictures of her and Fred and pictures of her daughter. One look at the child and your dad knew she wasn't lying."

I know. I saw her.

Fuck. I am so confused and still not sure I believe this soap opera twist.

"Why would he pay off Fred's mistake? That makes no sense to me."

"Because your Aunt Carole had just been diagnosed with stage-four breast cancer only a couple months before that. She was dying and we all knew it. He did it to protect Carole so she could be at peace when she died. He did it to protect their kids. They were losing their mother. The last thing they all needed to deal with was a scandal like that. It may not have been the right thing to do, but your father thought the easiest way to handle it was just pretend he was who she thought he was and pay her off so she'd go away."

"But I heard her say she loved him."

"I have little doubt she was just here after money, Luke. If she really loved Fred, why would we never have heard from her again after that? And most of all, why would she just take the money and run?"

I stare into the thick woods behind our house. The leaves have started to fill in the sparse area that deadens each winter. Spring is one of my favorite seasons when everything comes to life again. It's kinda how I felt when I first saw Addy. Everything inside me just bloomed. Now, for so many reasons, I feel dead again. My beasts are threatening to take over completely and the visceral need I have to hold Addy in my arms so she can drive them away is excruciating.

"I saw them," I mumble.

"Who?"

"Both of them. The daughter, I guess she would be my cousin. Landyn is her name. And her mother is Samantha."

My mother's silence finally causes me to tilt my head her way. She's staring at me with as much bewilderment as I feel.

K. L. KREIG

"What do you mean you *saw* them? How do you even *know* them?"

So I tell her the entire story. I catch her up on the details of what happened that day I came home from school early. I tell her what happened when Addy and I got back from the hospital to our apartment and how I spent the next several days in a drunken stupor. I confess how Addy won't talk to me and how I may have completely fucked things up with her and when I'm done, we fall quiet for what seems like forever.

My entire adult life was built on a misunderstanding. An assumption based on overhearing a partial conversation. I made decisions based on false truths and half the facts. I've thought the worst of my father for the last fourteen years. I abandoned him, my family and completely changed the course of my future because I didn't have the courage to just talk to him about what I *thought* I saw. What I *thought* I heard.

I ran from a lie.

And I hate myself for it.

"Your father forgave you, you know," she says quietly, breaking our silence.

I laugh bitterly. "How could he possibly?"

I'll never forgive myself.

Never.

"Because your father was a good man, Luke. He was selfless, giving, and loyal. His family always came first. I know when you were gone and didn't come back all those years, you were putting us first in a different way—you wanted to protect us from your life, your choices.

"You are so much like your father it's uncanny sometimes. He constantly worried about you, your life, your safety. He hated the separation between you two and not knowing what put it there, but he knew eventually you would find the light. He *always* believed in you, Luke, even when you didn't believe in yourself. He just couldn't watch you destroy yourself until you found your way home. Even though it was hard for him, he would want you to forgive yourself. He did just that a very long time ago."

I left home at eighteen. My father was forty-two at the time and fifty-six when he died. I saw him approximately one time in those fourteen years. Twice, if you count the time I passed him on the road, me on my bike, him driving his fancy BMW. I attended his funeral, but at a distance. No one, except my mother, knew I was there.

I have carried unfounded hatred in my heart for nearly half my life and it's simply unbearable to think I'll never have a chance to make it right. My emotions swell until there's no place else for them to go.

I am wrecked.

"Mom," I choke on a ragged sob. Unable to keep my anguish at bay any longer, I hang my head and sob. My mom cradles me in her arms, comforting me like a mother will always do for her child, no matter how old or how big they get.

Chapter 46

Addy

I'm sitting outside the house, my car running. I'm nervous. I haven't been here in over five years and the house definitely looks worse for the wear. The peeling white paint is faded to almost a dull, flat yellow. The gutter hangs down on the left side about a foot. The bushes are unruly and overgrown and the cracks in the sidewalk and driveway have grown larger. A large tree branch from the hundred-year oak in the front yard lies on the too-long grass. It would have to be moved before the grass could be trimmed.

Sam's expecting me; my mother isn't. I told Sam not to say anything in case I changed my mind. It's not too late. I could turn around and drive back to Chicago. Forget I was ever here. I could tell Sam something came up at the studio and I couldn't make it. But just as I decide to leave, I remember Luke's words in his note about fixing things.

Fixing himself. For *me*.

And I know I need to do the same for him. I've

not acknowledged it before, but there are parts of me that are cracked. Parts only I can mend. Seeing my mom is one of those steps I need to take and it's something I need to do on my own. I think my bad relationship with my mother has affected all the others in my life more than I ever wanted to admit.

Steeling myself, I shut off the engine and step out into the cool spring air, making my way to the front door. Sam answers almost immediately, hugging me.

"I'm glad you came. She's lucid right now, so hurry," she whispers as she ushers me into the small, three-bedroom ranch house I used to call home.

Everything on the inside is exactly as I remember. The shag carpet is green and dirty white, matted in most places so you wouldn't even know it was supposed to be shag at some point twenty years ago. The walls match the outside; dingy off-white that's yellowing. When we pass the kitchen, I notice the peeling brown-and-gold vinyl floor and the same puke-green refrigerator that hums too loudly.

As we wind through the small house, memories assail me from everywhere, but the thing I notice now that I never did before is there are pictures of *me* everywhere. Baby pictures. School pictures. Recent candids that my mom must have gotten from Eric or Landyn. They didn't come from me.

They're everywhere.

On the walls.

In frames on the end tables.

Stuck with colorful magnets to the fridge.

And on the nightstand by the hospital bed that sits in the middle of the living room. It's a picture of me, Sam, and Eric three years ago at Christmas. It was one of the few holidays when Sam actually joined us at my dad's.

I'm speechless. And near tears.

"Adeline. My sweet Adeline. You're here," my mom rasps, holding out her shaky pale hand. I rush to take it.

My mother was officially put in hospice a week ago. She refused to stay in the hospital, saying she wanted to die at home, instead. Sam told me she didn't think she'd make it more than two or three weeks before she was gone. Seeing her now, I would agree.

I didn't plan on coming to see her, resolute in my decision that ours is a broken relationship and trying to fix it in the last few days of her life would be pointless. Yet, thinking about what Eric said weeks ago, I decided I didn't want to risk having any more regrets.

So here I am.

"Hey, Mom." Her hand is cold and clammy. Her skin is yellow, swollen, and stretched taut with excess fluid. She has several very dark, very prominent bruises on her arms, and it's easy to see how weak she is. She doesn't look at all like my mother. She looks like a woman who is close to death's door. Sam warned me what to expect, though I have to admit, I didn't conjure this picture at all in my head.

I pull up a chair that's close to her bed and take a seat. Sam quietly slinks out, leaving us alone.

"How are you feeling?" *Stupid*, stupid question to ask a dying person, but I don't know what else to say.

"Okay," she rattles.

"Can I get you anything?"

"No."

She weakly clings to my hand and we sit there in awkward silence. My mom and I were never very good at easy chitchat. We don't have much in common beyond surface stuff and even that's challenging most times. She never asks questions about my life, my business, my boyfriends. All of our conversations are always about her.

Except now, she starts asking questions about me. She has a hard time speaking and our conversation evolves slowly over the next half hour, yet she fires question after question. All about me, and I fight to hold myself together. Suddenly I wish I'd waited to do this until Luke was with me.

"Sam says you have a boyfriend." Sam told her that even after the crazy she witnessed?

I give her a sad smile. "Yes."

"Do you love him?"

"Very much, Mom." I tear up. I miss him so much I ache everywhere.

"Does he love you?"

"More than anyone ever has." I feel like that's a jab to my mother, but I can't deny the truth. I have never felt as unconditionally loved by anyone as I have Luke.

"I could have been a better mother, Adeline."

How does one respond to that? Do you agree? Do you assure her she was the best mother she could have been? Do you tell her it's okay when it's not? I don't know, so I say nothing.

We fall quiet for several minutes, the ticking of the clock the only sound in the room. The morbid thought crosses my mind that she must lay here and just listen to her life tick away, one second at a time. Suddenly, I don't want to waste another minute away from Luke, although I know I can't leave yet.

"I would do so many things differently given the chance." She pauses so long I'm sure she's fallen back to sleep. Her eyes stay shut, but she slowly continues. "I would have made sure you knew I loved you. I did, you know, even though I didn't show it like I should have. I should have been less selfish, seeing to your needs first like a mother ought to. I should have told you that you were wanted. I'm sorry, Addy."

Tears stream down my face for so many reasons. This is the first time in my life she's called me Addy. This is the first time she's *ever* apologized. This is the first time she's acknowledged she could have done better. Once again stillness reigns.

"You should rest," I tell her quietly.

But she doesn't listen. She squeezes my hand slightly before continuing.

"I loved your father, Adeline. Deeply. Truly. I

never loved another man before or after him, but I pushed him away like I did everyone else and I lost the best thing to ever happen to me. I've never spoken of this to any of you kids: my childhood was rough. There was abuse, neglect."

She pauses, gathering herself. I don't think she's going to say any more when she adds, "I always tried to deny the damage it really did deep within me. It's too late for me, but now, I do have clarity. Unfortunately, I think we see things too clearly when we know our time here on earth is about up and it's too late to fix our wrongs. I know I lived a messed-up life and I know how badly I screwed up the lives of so many of those in mine."

"I'm sorry, Mom," I croak through my thin airway. I have no idea what I'm even apologizing for, but suddenly I see her in a whole new light. I feel a twinge of empathy I've never had for her before.

"Not your place to be sorry, Addy." She glances at the new necklace I'm wearing, my olive leaf, before asking, "Are you and your man serious?"

I hesitate in responding. "I hope so. There are some...issues we're working through right now."

I haven't heard from Luke today. That worries me. Maybe he's given up. Maybe I'm too damn stubborn and this is too much work for him. After all, I've done nothing other than make the man constantly chase after me. I unconsciously push people away because I'm afraid of eventually being rejected. If I'm honest with myself, I've *always* done that. I'm doing it right now to Luke.

My God...I suddenly see so many similarities between my mother and me and I don't like them. Not one little bit. I don't want to be lying in a hospital bed in the middle of my home without the people I love surrounding me, comforting me.

"I have regrets, Addy. Too many of them. I know it's probably too late for motherly advice, but don't follow in my footsteps. Live life to the fullest with no regrets, sweetie. Go after what you want, when you want, with the ferocity of a mother bear, because our life is but a blip on the radar before our time is up."

My bitterness toward my mother is melting away with each word she speaks. She's not perfect. She clearly went through things I'll never know and they molded her into the person she is, like all of our own events do. Like mine did.

I am the woman I am today despite my mother, not because of her. I'm proud of who I've become, yet I have my own faults, my own imperfections, and apparently my own demons, which I've never acknowledged before. I need to let go of all my fears and put unconditional faith in someone.

And there's only one person I want that to be.

The only thing I can think about is getting to Luke. It doesn't matter what drove him away. What matters is that we love each other. And while I *can* live without Luke, I just don't want to. He thinks I'm his light, his color, his air. He's all those things to me and more. I need to talk to him before it's too late, but I have no idea where he even is.

"Go to your man, Addy."

"No. I—I just got here."

She brings up her other shaky swollen hand, cupping my cheek. Her eyes are filled to the brim with salty water; mine are overflowing. "Go. Whatever's wrong, make it right. Hold onto him tight with both hands and never let go. Then bring him to me so I can meet the man who put that sparkle in your eye before I have to leave."

My gut feels like it's being ripped from my insides. I nod, unable to speak. I wish we could have had these moments years ago. I wish I had more time to spend with my mother making good memories to replace the bad. I wish I had tried harder to mend our relationship before it was almost too late.

I kiss and hug my mom, sucking this moment in like a sponge, hoping like hell I'll get another one.

"I love you, Adeline Catherine Monroe. So, so much," she breathes in my ear.

I can count on one hand the number of times my mother has said those words to me. But at this second, I don't care; for the first time in my life, I really *feel* them. "I love you, Mom," I whisper on a broken sob.

After I leave, I just sit in my car. It's quiet, except for my sobs of anguish with the realization that I'm going to lose my mother before I even get to know her. Eric couldn't have been more right. I am overflowing with remorse right now.

I think back to all my failed relationships and my perception that no one ever put me first. Perhaps I still believe that's true, but I also didn't put them first either. I was always waiting for the other shoe to drop...always waiting for them to decide they didn't want me anymore or to figure out I wasn't good enough.

But not one day in the last couple of months with Luke have I felt like that. From the time he busted into my apartment, he put me first. He's always made me feel like I was wanted, like I was good enough. Like I was truly, deeply loved.

And I'm not going to let that feeling go. I'm not going to let *him* go.

Finally, I pull myself together and make a phone call. I have to get the love of my life back.

I hope it's not too late.

Chapter 47

LUKE

When I pull up in the driveway that curves in front of my mom's house, surprise and elation rush through me. I see her shitty little car before I see her sitting on the front porch steps and *my God*...she's breathtaking.

Today she's wearing a simple light blue sundress and sandals with straps that wrap around her ankles like a Roman goddess. Her dark hair is pulled off to the side, cascading down her right shoulder like a waterfall. She's never looked more fucking beautiful. Ever.

She stands when she sees me approaching. I feel like I'm walking in slow motion, unable to get to her fast enough. When I get close, I see she's been crying. Her eyes are bloodshot, her face tear streaked.

She looks sad. Lost.

Exactly like me.

"Hi," I say quietly, stopping in front of her. She's standing on the first step, which puts her at my exact height.

"Hi," she replies just as softly.

401

Both of us are frozen, unmoving. Unsure. My heart is pounding and my fists are literally balls right now. I'm fighting every instinct in me that screams to yank her into my arms and tell her I'm not letting her go again, but I didn't know she was coming and I don't know why she's here. Is it to say good-bye or that she's as fucking miserable without me as I am without her?

I have to be honest...if it's to say good-bye I think I'm gonna lose my shit. I will never accept that things are over between us.

"I didn't know you were coming or I would have been here. My mom is out for the evening, I think. Have you been here long?" It's just past six and since we're in daylight savings, it's still very light out.

"About an hour. Where were you?" she asks tentatively.

Fuck, I hate this awkwardness between us.

"I was at the cemetery. Visiting my father." I've been there all afternoon. It was cathartic, actually. I didn't sleep at all last night, replaying my childhood, my life, my decisions and I came to the conclusion that, while I wish they were different, things played out exactly the way they were supposed to for me.

Had I not gone down the path I did, I would never have been in a position to save Livia. She would have died. Gray would be dead inside, my nephews would be but a wish. Most importantly, I'd never have met Addy because I would never have met her brother.

My father's selfless actions set a series of events into motion that would ultimately save and change the lives of so many. My biggest regret now is I'll never get a chance to tell him that in person. But I told him today and I know he was listening. I told him all of it. It felt good. I was able to let go of a lot of the guilt I've carried for years. About him, about Livia, about the life I took that wasn't mine to take. I know it will take time for it all to dissipate, but I already feel a lot lighter.

"I'm glad, Luke," she replies sadly. "You look tired."

"I am, fireball. I'm so fucking tired." *I'm tired of being without you. I'm tired of fighting you, me, my beasts. I'm tired of doing it all alone.*

My eyes lower to her neck where the pendant I gave her lays right below the hollow of her throat. I finger it, almost moaning at the feel of her warm skin underneath my pads. Her chest rises and falls rapidly and a light pink flush starts its ascent upward. When I sweep my gaze back up to her, she's raptly watching my face, my reaction.

"You wore it," I whisper. *God, why does that make me want to weep like a child?*

"Yes."

"Addy—"

Whatever I was going to say dissolves as a fog of lust settles thickly around us when she leans forward. Her lips touch mine, tentatively seeking, asking permission.

Permission fucking granted.

My restraint snaps, my animal nature taking over in unrestrained fury.

Claim.

Brand.

Own.

She is *mine*. She'll always be mine and I'll do or say anything she needs in order to make things right between us again.

Palming her nape, I deepen the kiss. I invade, I dominate, I take. I tell her with every sweep of my tongue how much I've ached without her, how much my heart hurts with love for her, and how I can't possibly live another second without her in my life. Our breaths and moans and sighs mingle until we're creating our own sweet symphony.

With my other hand, I pull her body flush with mine, pressing my now stiff cock into her lower belly. The need to sink inside her wet heat this instant is so intense, I want to strip her naked and fuck her right where we stand. I could. No one would see. Instead, I lift her so her long legs wrap around me. Carrying her up the remaining five stairs, I have no choice but to leave the warmth of her mouth as I fumble for the house keys.

Her lips don't leave me. They travel all over my jaw and my neck. Her teeth nibble my ear, making my cock furious that he's not inside her yet. Her hands never stop roaming and my tee is already halfway up my torso in her quest to rid me of my clothes as fast as she can.

Once inside, I slam the door shut and her up

against the wall before reaching under her dress. I rip off the panties she's wearing, dropping them to the tile floor. Then my fingers are plunging inside of her, my thumb circling her already hardened nub. She's so wet, so tight and feels so fucking good, I think I could come from this alone.

I *always* think of Addy first. I always make sure she comes before I release, several times, in fact, but I've been outside of her for too many days in a row now that if I don't fuck her this instant, I will most undoubtedly embarrass myself.

"I need to fuck you, fireball. Right now. Right here."

"God, yes, Luke. Please. I ache so much without you."

In seconds, my jeans are around my ankles and I'm driving brutally inside of her.

It's rough.

It's passionate.

It's fucking bliss.

The instant I feel her wrapped around my cock, all my suffering for the last two weeks melts away.

"Look at me," I command. I need her eyes. I need to see into her soul. I need my light, my *color*. I've fucking missed my color so damn much.

I haven't been able to touch my cock in weeks, so the last time I got off was the night Grant and Cash were born. Already feeling the tingling in my balls, I know our race to rapture will be lightning fast, but it's only the first of many tonight. The only way my cock will be outside of his rightful place for the next twelve hours is if she begs me to stop.

"I love you, Addy. So much. So damn much."

"I...love...you," she replies brokenly between forceful thrusts. "Harder. Please."

"My pleasure, sweetheart." I pump with intent now, harder, faster, rougher. My thighs burn and sweat covers me, but it's all worth it when I feel her slick, velvety walls clamp down on my cock, taking me over the edge with her. We both plummet headfirst into one hell of an intense orgasm, crying out the other's name in sheer joy. Her entire body shakes. I can't tell you how much I've missed feeling her shudder in my arms and breathe my name.

I continue to hold her up against the wall as we catch our breaths. I scatter kisses across every inch of flesh I can reach while staying firmly planted inside her. I'm already growing hard again. With every touch of my lips, I whisper, "I'm sorry," over and over again. She holds me tight, fingers feathering my spine, whispering back, "It's okay."

I need to feel her completely. Skin on skin. I need her slow and soft. I need to swallow her whimpers and moans of ecstasy. I need to know she's mine again, forever.

Wordlessly, I carry her up the stairs and into my room. I strip her and divest myself of my own clothes before crawling on the bed, taking her in my arms and making unhurried, sweet love to her until we're both exhausted and sore.

I know I need to apologize for my epic screwup. I know we have a lot of talking to do and I'm certainly not looking forward to telling her about her sister. All that can wait until later. Right now, I tug her as close as I possibly can, entwining our limbs so she can't escape and allowing myself to truly relax for the first time in over two weeks.

"I'm never letting you go," I mumble as darkness pulls me under. I don't want to follow, but I'm so damn tired I'm helpless against her call.

"Good, because you're stuck with me now. Sleep, baby," she encourages. "I'll be here when you wake up."

I do let go then, falling asleep with my woman in my arms, a smile on my face, and blissful peace in my very soul. I've never felt more content.

Chapter 48

LUKE

When I wake, I'm momentarily confused as to where I am and what time it is. I'm so fucking tired, I have to fight from slipping under again. A look at the digital clock with its blue lights shows it's 11:32 and dark outside, so it must be night. I blink my eyes open to see I'm in my childhood room and the evening's events come rushing back to me.

Addy.

She's here, but she's not, because her side of the mattress is empty and cold. I panic, wondering if she changed her mind. Flying out of bed, I throw on my jeans and bound down the stairs, taking them two at a time. I'm getting ready to rip open the front door to see if her car is gone when I hear low voices in the kitchen and then I hear *her*. Laughing.

Fuck. She's still here. She didn't leave me. I'm so relieved that I sag against the cool wood and wipe off the cold sweat now dotting my forehead and upper lip. My eyes drop to the floor and I snicker. Her torn panties are lying in the open for anyone to see. I snatch them up, stuffing them in my pocket and take a minute to gather my wits, calming my heart rate before I walk into the kitchen.

When I see her standing at the island, talking to my mother and *her dad*, I am struck breathless anew.

Jesus, I love her. I never knew it was possible to love another person so much. I want to beg her to marry me, but I can't. I don't have a ring yet and I realize I haven't asked her father or Eric, all of which I plan to remedy in short order.

"You're up," Addy says with surprise when she sees me quietly standing there watching her. Her smile is bright and brilliant, although it drops when her eyes fall to my chest and she sees my new ink. We were all over and in each other for hours earlier, but I have blackout blinds in my room. We didn't explore each other in the light, so she hasn't seen my new tribute to her. Well, one of two. In addition to this new tat, I had Eric quickly ink my new war cry underneath the old one so I would remember that every day I lived without my Addy was one too many.

I've told her repeatedly how she's changed my world. This was the only way I could think to really show her I'm sincere; she knows how personal my ink is to me.

She walks over to where I'm standing and runs a trembling finger over the fireball I had Eric draw around my heart tattoo. Now my broken heart is engulfed in colorful red, yellow, and orange flames and my chains are nearly covered. Except for one row, which I purposely left showing.

Her eyes finally lift to mine as she traces the remaining links. Tears spill down her cheeks. "You have one left." Her voice is soft, shaky. Almost inaudible.

"Because I'm chained to *you*, fireball. You've melted the rest, but this one remains for you. *Only you*."

"And you have color," she says in wonder.

I cup her cheeks, uncaring that our parents are watching. "Because of you. *You* are my color. I love you, Addy." Then I kiss her, lift her in my arms, and turn to carry her out of the room, back up to my bed where she belongs.

I need sleep. These last two weeks without her have been utter hell. I can't sleep without her by my side anymore. I don't care that I'm being rude or a Neanderthal, but I do call over my shoulder, "You can explain to me later what you're doing with Bob Monroe at eleven-thirty at night, Mother. I'm taking my woman to bed now."

Addy tries to fight me, screeching at me to put her down and Bob's laughter follows me all the way upstairs.

Everything is now right in my world. Just about perfect, in fact.

Just about.

Chapter 49

Addy

"I'm sorry for your loss."

"Thank you," I mumble.

"She was a good woman."

"Thanks."

"I'm so sorry for your loss."

"Thank you for coming," I reply, trying to vary my lame responses.

I feel like a fake standing here, greeting people as if I actually knew my mother. Obviously, *they* did. More people turned out than I expected and what does that say about me for thinking that horrible thought? There was so much I didn't know about her and will never get the chance to. There's so much she didn't know about me, too, and that's something I will have to live with. Including the fact she didn't get to meet Luke before she died, just two days after my visit.

Usually, the after-funeral reception would be held at some sort of church, but my mother wasn't religious. We didn't pray or read the bible or go to mass on Sundays. The only thing she ever worshipped was the man she was currently with and the drink.

So here Sam, Eric, and I stand in my small childhood home, in a nice little line, greeting people as they come in the door like some damn wedding reception or graduation party. And while I want to pay respects to my mother, anywhere near my sister is the very last place I want to be. Eric feels the same way, but we're doing this for Mom because it's what she would have wanted. And it's the right thing to do. Sometimes doing the right thing is really, really fucking hard, though. Today has been an excruciating example.

Sam and I weren't close before. Now, the tension is so thick and toxic between us that I'm feeling claustrophobic and having a hard time catching my breath the longer I stand beside her.

I mumble to my siblings I need a minute and head into the guest bathroom, shutting myself inside. Loud voices immediately muffle and I can take a full breath for the first time in an hour without inhaling anger and resentment.

After what Sam did to the Colloway family and her own daughter, she should be appalled. She wasn't. She was unapologetic, saying it was the right thing to do for Landyn's future. I wholeheartedly disagree, as does Landyn, who hasn't spoken to her mother in over a week. They already had a strained relationship but I think this is the straw that broke the camel's back. Well...more like a giant evergreen that was uprooted during a tornado, destroying the house it fell on.

A soft knock on the door startles me and I yell, "Occupied." I'm not ready to rejoin the fray. In fact, I might stay in here for the next couple of hours until everyone leaves.

"Open up, fireball," a deep, rumbly voice rings from the other side. I immediately yank the door open and am engulfed in Luke's arms. "You okay, baby?"

"No," I mumble into his chest. "But I'm better now."

He steps in, shutting us back in our cocoon and holds me close.

"Thank you for being here." It's almost as hard for him to be here as it is for me. In fact, the entire Colloway clan, including the matriarch, is outside of this four by six room in a show of solidarity for me and for Landyn. When they all started showing up, I cried.

"Where else would I be?"

"I know it's hard for you to be around her. I'm sorry."

"This is about you, baby. Not me. And you have no reason to be sorry. Your sister made her own decisions. You had nothing to do with it."

We've talked about this numerous times over the past week since we reconciled. We drove home early on Sunday morning and spent the rest of the day naked in bed, surprisingly mostly talking. I ran through the full gamut of emotions that day, completely wrung out by the time we fell asleep.

Elation and relief we were back together.

Disbelief and anger my sister could do such a horrible, callous thing.

Sadness for Landyn because she was deprived of a fatherly relationship.

Heartbreak and devastation at the fact Luke never had a chance to make amends with his father. It made me all the more thankful I was able to do so with my mom before her last breath.

"I'm just still so angry with her."

"Understandable."

"Landyn wants to move to Chicago. She needs some space from Sam for a while."

"Then we'll help her. Whatever she needs. She's family."

I smile into his chest. "Thank you, Luke."

"No thanks necessary, fireball," he replies, squeezing tight.

I sigh, sinking into him further. His strokes on my hair are hypnotic. I'd give anything right now to just sit on the floor in here and talk to him for hours. As if reading my mind, he slides his back down the door and settles me comfortably between his legs, my back to his front.

I lean my head against his shoulder and breathe an audible sigh of relief, entwining our hands together. The space is small and with Luke's big frame, he has to bend one leg up so as not to hit the toilet, but I don't care. Right now all I care about is this much-needed break from sadness with the only person who has ever made me feel whole. With each minute that passes, I feel more relaxed.

"What's going on between our parents?" I ask. My dad is here, supporting his children even though he and my mom have been divorced for over two decades. It hasn't escaped my notice that he and Barb have been kind of joined at the hip. The two of them have worked in tandem today to be sure food and drinks are filled and the garbage is picked up.

He chuckles, the vibration echoing through my body. "I can't get a word out of my mom, other than she says they're just friends. But I think that's a load of bullshit. There's no doubt they were on a date last Saturday night."

"I think so, too. And he came to Chicago with your mom."

"I know."

"My dad denies they're anything but friends, too."

"I've seen the way he looks at her." I hear the smile in his voice.

"And I've seen the way she looks at him." I laugh.

"Huh."

"Yeah. *Huh.* Kind of a weird twist of events, isn't it?"

"I was thinking the exact same thing," he says with wonder. "I think my dad would have liked your dad, Addy."

"Thank you for saying that."

"You want to get back, sweetheart?" he asks, kissing the crown of my head.

I huff a laugh. "Do I *want* to? No. But I guess I probably should." Neither of us makes a move. I take a deep breath, readying myself. There are things I want to tell Luke that I haven't yet.

"You've given me things no one else has," I say softly.

He's quiet for a few seconds before responding saucily. "Which things, baby? A stuffed toy? A pair of stupidly expensive shoes? A dozen orgasms a day?"

I chuckle lightly. "No. Don't get me wrong, I love all of those, especially the orgasms, but that's not what I'm talking about."

He tightens his hold from behind. Kissing my temple, he encourages, "Tell me."

"You make me feel cherished. Special. Like I'm the most important person in the world to you."

"That's because you are, Addy," he whispers in my ear. Chills race down my arm at the feel of his breath on my skin.

"No one has ever done that."

"No one?"

"Just you," I whisper.

"Well then, we have a lot of firsts together, don't we?"

I nod, trying to hold in my sobs.

Hooking a finger under my chin, he tilts my face up to kiss me softly. "You'll always be first to me, Addy. Always. Don't cry, baby." He wipes away a stray tear, a happy one this time. "Just a couple more hours. Then I'm going to take you home and make love to you all night long."

"All night?"

"Hell yeah." He smiles, his eyes bright with

love. Every time he looks at me like that I have to pinch myself that he's real.

"Can we pick something from the list?" I ask sheepishly. Luke's pretty damn creative, I'll give him that. Some of the things he's thought up for us to try make me blush just thinking about them.

A wicked grin curls his sexy mouth. "We can do whatever you want, fireball."

"Whatever?"

"It's your world, babe. I'm just living in it now."

"That you are," I tease. "And you're okay with that?"

The devotion shining in Luke's eyes would buckle my knees if I were standing. "I wouldn't want to be anywhere else, Addy. Thank you for giving me a chance. For coming back to me."

"Thank you for waiting for me."

"You're worth waiting for." He steals my breath every time he says sweet words like that. He closes the scant distance between us, touching his lips to mine. His kiss is long and sweet and at our angle, it's a little awkward, but I couldn't care less.

"I love you, Luke," I mumble against his wet lips.

"I love you, too, fireball. Now come on." He stands, pulling me off the floor. "The sooner we get back out there, the sooner we can get home and start checking off the boxes. I'm thinking maybe we try number thirteen tonight."

I think for a minute, trying to recall what that

one was. When it hits me, my eyes snap to his. I feel the blush crawl up my neck to my face. "You mean the one with the..."

"That's the one," he winks, a wolfish smile eating up his handsome face.

"Wow. Okay," I breathe, anticipation now making my nipples and core tingle.

Clasping our hands together, he walks me back to the front of the house until we're standing next to Eric, who is talking to Mrs. Kravitz, my elderly neighbor who had the bulldog I was in love with. She's ninety-one and still going strong. Sam stands on the other side looking extremely uncomfortable, particularly with Luke close by.

Good.

I expect Luke to leave, going back to be with his family. Instead, he stays planted beside me, my hand still in his. When I look up questioningly, he tells me, "I'll be by your side, okay?"

This is the last place I want to be, but as long as Luke is with me I know I'll be able to get through absolutely anything life throws at me.

"Always?"

Smiling softly, he cups my cheek. "Always, Addy. Always."

Epilogue

Two and a half months later...

LUKE

"It's gorgeous here, isn't it?"

"Yes," I agree, but I'm not looking out at the shimmering greenish-blue ocean waters or the sun that's setting behind it or the powder-fine sand beneath our bare feet.

I'm looking at her.

She looks angelic in the glowing light with her hair twisting in the light breeze. We've been in the Caribbean for the last three blissful days. Tonight is Asher and Alyse's rehearsal dinner. Tomorrow they get married in front of their family and friends.

The past few weeks with Addy have been, dare I say, magical, and if all goes well, after tonight Addy and I will be the ones planning a wedding. I do have one more heavy weight I need to get off my shoulders before I can get down on one knee and ask the woman who has me completely tied in knots if she will do me the honor of becoming my wife.

It's a conversation I should have had weeks

ago. I've had plenty of opportunities to come clean. I haven't because I've been afraid of losing her. The thought she may take this knowledge I'm about to give her and run scares the living shit out of me. Being without her for just those two weeks was agonizing. But being without her for life? Unfathomable.

However, if I'm going to ask her to tie herself to me for the rest of our days, I feel I owe it to her to make an informed decision. She needs to know exactly the type of man she's marrying.

As we watch the last sliver of sun fall under the horizon, the sky turns a pink and purple hue. It's beautiful, mesmerizing. Serene. A complete contrast to how I'm feeling inside.

I wrap my arms around her waist from behind. It will be easier to say what I have to if I'm not looking at her face. I embrace the shroud of darkness falling all around us and start. "I need to tell you something."

Her fingers feather my forearms, her light touch setting my blood on fire.

"Sounds serious," she teases.

"It is."

My tone conveys my seriousness and she tries to turn, but I clamp my arms tight, holding her in place.

"Luke—"

"No. Stay like this."

"Don't say it," she pleads. Her voice is shaky and unsure; her body now tense. "Whatever it is, I don't want to know."

"Addy, please. I have to say this."

"No, you don't. I don't want to know."

"You do."

"Stop it. I'm happy. Don't ruin things. Please." Her broken begging almost undoes me, but I steel myself against changing course. I have to get this fucking weight off my chest and if I don't do it now, I'm going to pussy out again.

"It's about my past," I continue undaunted.

"I don't care about your past," she tells me softly, trying to squirm away. I hold fast.

"Do you care if I killed someone?" I ask lowly. I didn't intend to blurt it out like that, but I'm not exactly sure how you tell the person you're in love with that you're a killer. Not really a lot of good advice floating around on the Internet for that convo starter.

She freezes. My heart is pounding so hard there's no way she can't *not* feel it.

"Did you?"

"Yes," I confess on a whisper.

"On purpose?"

"Yes."

Silence. *Jesus*. I feel absolutely sick not knowing what's running through her mind.

"Why?" she finally asks softly.

I almost sag in relief. I don't hear judgment or condemnation in her voice and she has no way of knowing, but that's the only possible way I could continue this conversation. Had I heard either of those, I know I would be leaving here alone.

"To save Livia."

"What?" she breathes, drawing out the word in disbelief. I don't blame her. It's hard

421

for me to wrap my head around it most days still.

We stand on Grace Bay Beach on the island of Turks and Caicos, over fifteen hundred miles from home, lulled by the waves of the ocean while I tell Addy about the worst period Livia and I ever experienced in our lives. I talked to Livia about this yesterday, because I didn't want to divulge her secret to Addy without her consent. She gladly gave it, knowing how important it was for me to share this part of my life with Addy. For that, I will be forever grateful.

After I finish, she turns in my arms and I let her. Wrapping her long limbs around my neck, she looks me in the eye and says tersely, "Is that it?"

I nod, confused by her reaction.

"Good." Then she puts her lips to mine, kissing me with purpose. She's clearly in control here and for once, I let her be, simply enjoying the fact she wants to put her mouth anywhere on me after what I just admitted. She scatters kisses along my jaw murmuring, "You're an honorable man, Luke Colloway."

I'm not really sure what I expected, but it wasn't that. "How can you—?"

"Don't," she scolds, pulling away so our eyes connect. "Now it's *your* turn to listen, so you're not going to say another word until I'm done. Got it?"

I smirk at my woman, yet remain quiet, nodding instead. Always so full of fire and I fucking love it. God, I love *her*.

"You're a selfless, giving man who's made

mistakes. You've also made unimaginable sacrifices for those you love at great expense to yourself. You try to make it seem like nothing affects you, like you don't care how the world sees you, but I'm onto you Luke Colloway. You do care. You care more than you want to admit. You are not undeserving or tainted or damned or damaged or broken or any other adjective you want to use to protect yourself. You're pure and selfless and loyal and imperfect and worthy. And mine," she adds.

I try to respond; she puts a finger to my lips.

"I accept who you are, who you *were*. You saved my best friend. You gave her a life with her husband and children, so I don't think less of you or judge you, Luke. The fact you are even giving this vile person a second thought only reaffirms I was right about the incredible man you are. I love you, every perfect and imperfect part of you, but I want us to leave the past where it belongs. Let this last shackle go, Luke. Please. For me."

She stops talking. I'm not sure if she's done yet, so I say nothing.

"And the proper response to that is, 'yes, Addy,'" she quips, smiling.

"Yes, Addy?" I laugh, tugging her closer.

"Or maybe, 'God, how did I ever get lucky enough to fall in love with such a wise and wonderful woman?' I'd take either of those, or something else along the same lines would also suffice."

"I think the better response would be: How

did I get lucky enough to have such a wise and wonderful woman fall in love with me?"

Even in the dark, I see her face radiate with pure happiness. "I think I fell in love with your sexy stubborn ass the minute you asked me how my day was when you barged your way into my apartment and my life."

I grin smugly. "I thought you wanted me to move out."

"I lied," she shrugs nonchalantly. Oh, my lovely Addy. So hard to pull the truth out of her sometimes. Every day it gets easier. I know she'll always be a challenge. I also know I'll happily rise to it because everything about her makes me a better man.

An overwhelming need strikes me down. I don't want to wait a second longer for my future to begin. With Asher's blessing, I'd planned to get down in front of our entire family tonight, only this feels like the right moment instead. I nuzzle her ear. "I want to marry you."

She goes rigid. "Do you now?"

"Have you been practicing like I asked?" Her breath catches when I suck the delicate skin right below her ear. I can get her to agree to anything when I nibble on this exact spot.

"Yes."

"See? That's not so hard now, is it?"

"No." She's breathless. I feel how fast her heart is pounding against my chest as if she knows exactly what's coming next.

"Good." Dropping to one knee, I hear her suck in a sharp breath, her tiny hands flying to cover her mouth. I pull out the small box that's been burning a hole in my pants pocket for the last two hours.

"Oh my God," she mumbles. Her watery gaze flits to it briefly but lands back on mine.

Jesus, I'm nervous. I've been planning in my head for weeks what I'm going to say to her, but it all just evaporated the moment my knee touched the sand, so I speak from the heart instead.

"Marry me, Addy Catherine Monroe. You saved me. You fix all the broken inside me. You fill me with color and light and fire and hope and more love than I ever thought possible. You've seen the darkest parts of me and love them anyway. Without you, I'll never be even half the man I could be. I never used to think about the future until I met you. Now, I can think of nothing else but making you forever mine. Marry me, Addy. Have babies with me. Grow old with me. Be mine? Permanently?"

The moonlight reflects off her tears, making her eyes look as deep and fathomless and mysterious right now as the ocean behind us. She is all of those things and so much more. There's so much to love about her.

"This is where you say yes, fireball," I prod at her silence.

Her head nods, causing her overflowing tears to spill and run down her cheeks.

"The words, babe. Just like you practiced."

"Yes," she croaks. "Yes, yes, yes."

Smiling, I open the velvet box and pull out the

ring I had designed for her. It's a one-of-a-kind, just like she is. I slip it on her finger and stand. Cupping her face, I kiss her trembling lips until we're both breathless. I want nothing more than to return to our room and fuck her blind for the rest of our vacation, but we're probably already late to the rehearsal.

"You're mine now. Forever," I whisper against her lips.

"Yes."

"I like hearing that word roll off your tongue. You need to say it more often."

"Don't get used to it," she laughs between pecks.

My own laugh echoes in the dark. "Wouldn't dream of it, fireball."

After one last passionate kiss, I grab her hand and lead her back to my family, hoping like hell they aren't waiting on us. "Come on, let's tell everyone the good news. My mom's going to wig."

"So is my dad," she beams, skipping along in the sand. Her dad won't wig, he already knows, but I don't want to spoil her surprise. She holds out her left hand admiring the new sparkler that will rest on her ring finger forever. "I still can't believe your mom invited him."

"Yeah. 'Just friends' my ass."

"I know, right? They seem happy, though."

She's right. They do. There's a melancholy about my mom that's vanished. Regardless of what's really going on between her and Bob Monroe, I'm happy for her. She deserves to have someone care for her outside of her children, even if it is just a *really good friend*. "That they do."

"I'm going to dance with you all night long," I say a few moments later. I missed out on my chance to sway with her in my arms at Gray's wedding. I won't make that mistake again.

"I thought you didn't dance," she quips back.

"Fireball, I dance very fucking well when it suits my purpose." She stops walking and I swing her around in my arms.

"What if I want you to make love to me all night instead?"

I palm her head, kissing her long and deep, my cock jumping up and down at that idea. "I think that can be arranged."

"Good," she whispers saucily before tugging me along once again.

As we make our way back to the resort, Addy babbles the whole time while I just listen, absorbing her enthusiasm. I fully realize that I'm the luckiest son-of-a-bitch on the planet right now. I'm positive there is no one happier at this very minute than I am.

I now have everything I never dreamed I would.

A woman who loves me unconditionally.

A soul that's finally at rest.

And a family I will never leave or doubt again.

I fucking have it all.

Now everything in my world is perfect.

~ *THE END* ~

My musical inspiration for writing
Luke's Absolution

"Not Broken Anymore" by Blue October
"Black Widow" by Iggy Azalea
"Send the Pain Below" by Chevelle
"Goodbye Agony" by Black Veil Brides
"Wrong Side of Heaven" by Five Finger Death Punch
"Not Coming Home" by Arson City
"Break Me Down" by Red
"Angel" by Theory of a Deadman
"Bleed Out" by Blue October
"Drown" by Bring Me The Horizon
"Whatever It Takes" by Lifehouse
"My Demons" by Starset
"Fight Inside" by Red
"I'll Follow You" by Shinedown
"Cold" by Crossfade
"Falling In" by Lifehouse
"The Ever" by Red
"Secrets" by One Republic
"Face Everything and Rise" by Papa Roach
"Of These Chains" by Red

Other works by K. L. Kreig:

The **Regent Vampire Lords** series

Surrendering
Belonging
Reawakening
Evading (releasing April 2016)

The Colloway Brothers series

Forsaking Gray
Undeniably Asher
Luke's Absolution
Destination Connelly (releasing summer 2016)

Turn the page for a sneak peek at *Destination Connelly*, the final book in the Colloway Brothers series. Release date June 2016.

Destination Connelly

by K.L. Kreig

coming June 2016

Chapter 1

Present Day...

Conn

"Harder. Fuck, yes. That's it, doll." My fist grips her long bleached-blonde tresses hard, setting the pace I want her to take. Right now it's slow and steady because her mouth is pure sin and I'd let her drag me into the depths of hell as long as she kept it wrapped around my cock the whole way south.

I met Lorna at the gym a month ago in the building where I live. She'd just moved in and hadn't been warned about me yet, so I took advantage of the situation. I'm a cunning guy like that. As soon as she stumbles across the wrong woman in the locker room shower, she'll lock her abundant assets down tighter than Fort Knox. Good thing I didn't miss my chance.

I wanted Lorna the minute I set eyes on her. She's absolutely fucking stunning and has a rack I've contemplated sliding my cock between, but her lips are full and pouty, so it was a toss-up. The mouth won. And Jesus, am I glad because she's sucking me off like a professional. Hell, she should take out insurance on her mouth. It is *that* damn good.

Prying my head from the back of her couch, I look down at the woman on her knees in front of me. She's beautiful, yes. She has great tits and a smokin' body, no doubt. She can string a few decent sentences together in a row, so she seems halfway intelligent. Regardless of what my brothers think, I don't just tap anything with a pussy. I am a *little* more selective than that.

But I already know this first encounter with Lorna, as lovely as she is, will be my last. She's like all the others. Maybe she has a personality, maybe she doesn't. Maybe she could be long-term relationship material; maybe she'd turn out to be a whiny bitch and eating a bullet would sound far more appealing. Maybe she's my perfect "Match.com" life companion. Who knows? I don't—I won't give her a chance to get that far. I feel nothing for her other than intense physical pleasure as she works me expertly closer to one hell of a climax.

Her eyes sweep up to mine, looking for encouragement. She doesn't need it and she knows it, though I give it anyway. "You're doing great, baby," I rasp thickly. She holds my gaze, trying to see if there's something there. A spark.

Hope. Maybe I changed my mind about seeing the inside of her apartment once and once only? I may be a manwhore, but I'm no bastard. Before I let you anywhere near my dick, you know the score, and so does Lorna.

I don't do seconds. Ever. It's too messy for everyone involved.

Nope. No emotional connection whatsoever. No burn in my gut. No music in my ears. No racing of my heart—other than the fact I'm getting closer to spurting down her throat.

That emotional switch was flipped to the off position eleven years ago when the girl who managed to brand her initials on the soles of my feet and the palms of my hands got on a plane and never looked back. After the way she fucked me over, you would think I'd hate her. In many ways I do.

But it doesn't matter how deeply she's wounded me, I still try to picture *her* face in every woman I take. I still try to imagine the taste of *her* nipples on my tongue and the feel of *her* pussy embracing my cock for the very first time.

Getting the hint, Lorna's eyes flutter briefly before dropping again, going back to the task at hand. Sensing she wasn't quite truthful that she was really okay with this one-time thing, I decide it's time to reach the goal line. I guide her up and down my shaft quicker, fisting the base so I can squeeze hard, the way I like it. She gets the clue, sucking harder, moving faster, running her tongue perfectly around and under my crown until my hips buck. On a growl, my seed is ripped fiercely from my balls. Proving this isn't her first rodeo, she swallows every drop, not spilling a one.

My head is tipped back, eyes shut, and my chest still heaving with the effort of the last few minutes when I feel her crawling up my body. She straddles my lap, the warmth of her silk-covered pussy bearing down against my semierect shaft; her bare tits press against my still shirt-covered chest. Scattering kisses up my throat and jaw, she latches onto my mouth, thrusting her tongue inside. I taste myself on her and while it doesn't repulse me, it's not a turn on for me either.

Suddenly, I'm not in the mood to take this further. The vibe I'm getting from her is like epoxy: Elmer's glue. She's trying to fasten herself to me and I am the anti-adhesive. I'm a slippery fucker, like glass.

Again, I'm not a bastard. I may not feel like fucking her, but I'm not going to leave her with the woman's equivalent of blue balls either. So I reach between us, her pelvis now writhing, and pull aside the crotch of her white silk panties, slipping my fingers through her drenched folds.

"God, yes," she moans in my ear. Once I slide two fingers inside, she rides my hand like she grew up spending hours a day on a stallion. Feathering my thumb over her clit, I bring her to a quick orgasm, enjoying the feel of her womanly softness under my fingertips. I let her kiss me and, for not the first time, have a twinge of guilt that I can't feel anything for a woman beyond the physical pleasures they bring me. That part of me has been on lockdown for over a decade.

"Gotta go, babe," I say as I lift her off my lap. I linger too long on her generous tits and she notices. *Damn.*

Her face falls, her lips turn down, and disappointment is etched over every beautiful feature. Yep...this right here is why I don't do seconds. Technically, I didn't even do firsts with Lorna, and my spidey senses were spot-on. She wants more than I'm capable of giving.

"But we didn't get to the good part," she whines.

Ladies, I'm here to tell you, sticking your bottom lip out like a four-year-old child to get what you want is not attractive. Have a little more self-respect than that for God's sake.

"Have some work stuff I need to take care of." It's true, I always have work to do, even though that's not the reason I'm now anxious to make my getaway. I should have seen the handmade wedding invitations and 2.5 babies floating in her clear blue eyes well before I ever walked into her apartment, but I was too focused on getting her undressed, instead. I tuck myself away, zip my jeans, and make my way to the exit. I mean door.

"I want to see you again," she says pleadingly, grabbing hold of my arm.

I stop and take her face in my hands, enunciating my words clearly and slowly so she'll get the message. "Lorna, we talked about it. This was a one-time thing."

LUKE'S ABSOLUTION

She looks like someone just ran over her puppy and left it for dead in the middle of the road. It makes me feel like the hit-and-run professional I've become. That's not a great feeling, by the way, and I'm not proud of it, but *c'est la vie*, as the French would say. I am what I am and I don't foresee that changing anytime soon.

Lorna's actually a nice woman. She's funny, takes care of herself, and holds an executive VP of marketing position at some local media company, which is more than I want or need to know about her. She deserves to be someone's special girl. I'm just not that someone.

"But why?"

I know my smile will come across as sad and I'm not doing it to garner sympathy from the woman whose talented mouth was just wrapped around my cock and who I'm about to heave-ho. It's a genuine emotion that I try my damnedest to stifle. "I'm simply not capable of more. I'm sorry." And I am. Sorry. So fucking sorry to leave another victim in my jerky wake, but not sorry enough that I won't do it again and again and again.

Kissing her temple, I drop my hold and silently make my escape.

Lorna lives on the eighth floor. I live on the thirty-fourth. It would be much quicker to take the elevator, but I need to blow off some excess energy and make my thigh muscles burn a little since I missed out on my cardio just now, so I take the stairs instead, two by two. By the time I reach my floor a few minutes later, I feel better, despite being a sweaty mess, my tee sticking to my chest and back.

Just as I'm unlocking my door, I see Ella walking toward me with her arms full of bags. I run over to her, taking them from her grip.

"Why didn't you have the guard help you up with these?" I scold. She does this all the damn time and it drives me fucking crazy. She's the most stubborn, independent woman I have ever met. It's alluring and infuriating all at the same time.

"Because I don't like to be dependent on anyone. You know that. Now shut the fuck up."

"Jesus, you're a pain in my ass, Ella."

"That's why you love me, hun."

"You're right." I kiss her cheek and we walk a few steps down the hall until we're at her door.

Ella is my next-door neighbor. If there were any woman I could remotely envision myself with, it would be her. But I don't do emotion and I don't do commitment, much like Ella. We are simply the best of friends, although we've almost crossed the proverbial line several times late at night when we've had too much to drink and the moon is bright, throwing some sort of carnal spell through the windows.

As if she's just noticing the clothes sticking to me, along with the beads of water running down my forehead, she teases, "Make another getaway, did you?"

I laugh loudly. "Something like that."

She unlocks her door. I follow. Her condo is

exactly the same as mine, except the layout is flip-flopped with the spacious kitchen and open main living area on the left and two bedrooms down the hallway to the right. She has a bay of floor-to-ceiling windows that mirror mine, except I have a corner space, so my windows span two sides.

"When are you going to learn not to shit where you eat?" She shakes her head in mocking disapproval. "You're going to bang the wrong woman and she's going to know where you live and go all stalker on your ass. Not smart, Connelly. Not smart at all."

I shrug. She's right. "I'm a slow learner." I drop the bags on the counter and start helping her unload her groceries.

Ella and I have been neighbors and friends for the last year. Originally, when I saw her, of course I wanted to do her, badly. I even considered breaking my "one-and-done" rule because this woman is something incredible.

She's beautiful, both inside and out. Petite, probably only five foot three. Tight, fit body. Average tits, but they're all natural and I'd rather have a smaller, malleable handful than rock-hard fake ones any day. She's smart, witty, and successful. You can't have a three-thousand-square-foot condo in downtown Chicago that overlooks Navy Pier if you're not doing something right with your career.

But the more I got to know her, the more I discovered there's just something extraordinary about her heart that I don't want to ruin. Like we all do, she tucks a part of herself away that she should only share with that one special person when he comes along. I'm not that guy, so I don't want to take that away from whoever he is.

I sincerely like Ella and if we cross that sometimes-wavering line, I will lose her as a friend. I don't want that. Outside of my brothers, she's one of the few genuine people I have in my life who's not after something of mine, whether it be my contacts, my power, my money, or simply riding my coattails until they find something or someone better. When you are a young, attractive, wealthy, single man, trust me...you have a lot of sharks circling your boat, hungry for what you have, trying to take a bite no matter how small.

"When are you going to settle down?" she asks after putting the last of the fresh vegetables in the crisper.

"When are you?" I retort.

"You know the answer to that." At thirty-three, Ella is three years older than I am. I know she's been married and divorced. Other than that, she refuses to talk further about that relationship or any relationship for that matter. In fact, she doesn't talk about her personal life at all. Ever. "Besides, we're talking about you, now. Not me."

My lips curl. "This is a tired conversation." And one we have all too often. Ella thinks that by the age of thirty, I should be settling down, having babies, and building a six-thousand-square-foot house by the lake. Yes, she's hypocritical as well.

I wholeheartedly disagree.

"Well someone needs to make you see you have more to give of yourself than just your dick. As impressive as I'm sure it is."

My smile grows wide. "Impressive, huh? Want a demonstration?" I joke, wagging my eyebrows up and down.

Laughing, she answers, "As tantalizing as that offer is, it has to be a hard pass for me, cowboy."

"Hmmm. Your loss."

"I don't doubt it." She winks playfully.

This is what I love about hanging out with Ella. We flirt, we banter, we play around and it butts right up to the edge of sinful, but that's where it stops. Because as much as I don't want to ruin what we have, neither does she.

"How's that big acquisition you're working on?"

"Almost sewn up, actually. Did you secure that big marketing campaign?"

"Sure did," she replies with a shit-eating grin on her face. The small digital ad agency that Ella co-owns was going against a big-time, well-known large firm for complete redesign of a multimedia marketing campaign for a Fortune 50 firm. It's a campaign worth over ten million dollars. Annually. She's been working on it for months and it's been an all-out dogfight.

"Did you have to sell your soul?"

Her perfectly shaped brows rise. "Pretty damn close. I had to give up my first-born."

"I didn't think you were going to have kids."

"Exactly," she winks.

I spy a box that has brightly colored cartoons on the front and after leaning over to inspect it, I see it's a design tablet.

"Take up drawing?"

"It's for my niece. She loves photography and drawing. Really has an eye for a ten-year-old." She offers me a beer and I take it, popping off the top with a hiss. "I need to get it mailed."

"You have a niece?" I've known Ella for almost a year and this is the most I've gotten out of her about family.

"What are we? Girlfriends?"

"Well...yeah. I thought so." I laugh.

She chuckles. "Well, we're not, hot stuff. You talk about your conquests, I berate you, you ineffectively defend your manwhore actions, and then we veg and watch a movie or stuff our faces with your sinful home cooking."

She's right. We do. We've never really talked about the secrets we hide under the covers. Yet I find I want to know more now that she's opened that door. "So, a sister or brother?"

"Sister." I get the evil eye like she knows what's coming next.

"She as beautiful as you?"

"Oh, no you don't, Conn. Don't even ask about my sister."

"Why? Isn't she my type?" I take a long pull of my hops and barley. "Is she a butter face?"

"A butter face? What the hell is a butter face?"

"You know, everything's smokin', *but* her face."

"Oh my God. No, she's not a butter face, you fucking asshole. She's stunning. And smart. Exactly why she's not your type."

"Ouch, that hurts," I say, pointing my bottle at her. "And I'll have you know the women I date are smart."

"Date?" She asks mockingly, dragging out the word unnecessarily.

I shrug, wondering why that stings more than it should.

"See? That right there is why you are going to stay away from my sister. Now, have you eaten?"

"No. You offering?" I ask, finishing off my drink.

She smirks. "No. I thought maybe you would offer this time. You're a better cook than I am."

"True that." We both laugh. One of the very many lessons that was forced on me by Barb Colloway, my fan-fucking-tastic mother. "Okay. Give me twenty minutes to shower and change, then pop on over. I'll leave the door open. Fish okay?"

"Sounds perfect. I'll whip up some rice."

"You mean that bagged crap?"

"Uh...is there any other kind?" Her nose wrinkles and I know she's sincere. Ella eats processed food like it's about to be banned. It should be—it's poison in a bottle or box or can or whatever else they put it into.

"Yes. The good fucking kind."

"Fine. Then I'll bring some wine."

"Now you're talking. You have excellent taste in wine. See you in a few."

"Okay," she calls after me. I walk to the front door and let myself out.

As I slip inside my condo, strip off my clothes, and step under the hot spray a few minutes later, I think about Ella's question regarding the acquisition. I let my mind drift to the business meeting I have in two days with the owner of Steele Executive Recruiting, SER for short, which is the executive recruiting firm I've been doggedly pursuing for the last several months.

At first, it was only mild interest on my part. I'd heard he was looking to sell and I almost dismissed the acquisition after our first meeting...until I found out who he was, that is. From then on, I have been actively pursuing the company, upping the stakes repeatedly when Carl Steele has gotten cold feet, which has been several times.

With only one hundred fifty employees, SER is a relatively small organization that works with smaller to mid-level sized clients. They are highly successful and have a fantastic reputation in the industry, but don't place even a third of the executives that my company does. So, it's not like they are a huge competitor I need to gobble up. And they could merge with a number of other smaller firms or simply dissolve. A competitor would easily scoop up their best and brightest.

No, I don't need Steele Executive Recruiting to round out my business plan or fill a competitive hole. I don't need them for technology or their talent or their paltry 5.7 million dollars in annual net revenue to add to my own bottom line.

There's one reason, and one reason only I want to acquire them, adding them to Wynn Consulting's portfolio, the human resources consulting company I run as CEO.

Nora fucking Cantres.

Do you know how many Nora Cantreses there are in the US? Surprisingly, too fucking many. I could have pulled a Gray and hired a PI to find her like he did with Livia. I could have, but my youth at first and, as I got older, my pride prevented me from doing it. Even though I haven't hired a professional to find her, I've always kept my ear to the ground and my eyes peeled for her, nonetheless.

And this is the thing about my line of work: human resources. It's a relatively small and incestuous community. And the subspecialties within HR? Even smaller. So a few months ago when I started hearing rumors of a "star" executive recruiter who worked for SER by the name of Nora Cantres, my interest was piqued. And when everything about her fit *my* Nora to a "T," I knew this wasn't coincidence. I had finally found her.

Some men would do anything to scourge the woman who callously trampled their fragile masculine ego from their memory banks without a backward glance, especially one who whispered promises of love and devotion only to coldheartedly break them weeks later.

But I'm not like other men.

I still think constantly about the woman who devastated me eleven years ago. Do her eyes still sparkle like emeralds when she laughs? Does her voice still drop low and throaty when she's turned on? Will her moans of ecstasy still dive right into my chest cavity, squeezing my heart like a gentle fist?

I hear her whispers, her whimpers, her moans, her laugh, her very heartbeat. I feel the silk of her hair under the pads of my fingers, the kiss of her breath on my cheek, the brush of her lips against mine. I imagine her sweet taste lingering on my taste buds.

Her memory has endlessly echoed inside of me since the last day I saw her. Yet as much as it's haunted me, there was a part of me that always held fast to that echo anyway. When it would fade, I'd sit quietly and listen until I could hear it again. I couldn't force myself to let it go, let the ties sever. If I let her memory fade, it felt like none of it was real and I had to believe it was. It was real to me, anyway. Now I have to find out if it was real to *her*.

It's time for Nora and me to meet up again, but this time, we're all grown up and in much different places in our lives. And this time, *I'm* pulling the strings. I am going to reel her in and tie those fucking strings in so many damn knots she won't know where to begin to free herself. With any luck, she'll just give up and give in.

I've gotta hand it to my mom about now. Because she wanted "worldly," well-rounded boys, my brothers and I were in just about everything under the sun, including Boy Scouts, and I became very fucking proficient at tying knots, even earning a Knot Master patch.

Tying a physical knot isn't much different than tying an invisible one. You simply take the tools you have to work with and bend them to your will. You play, you twist, you curve, you angle, you loop, and then you pull tight. You pull so damn tight, you know whatever you've bound won't come undone without a big fucking razor-sharp Ginsu.

So while I started out tying physical knots in my youth, I mastered the invisible ones in adulthood. Now I'm the motherfucking king of loops and turns and angles, bending everything and anything to *my* will, *my* benefit.

And I've already expertly started weaving a combination of them to get what I want. I started the day I heard her name. And finally, two days from now I will come face-to-face with Nora Cantres for the first time in eleven years. It's a meeting I have requested, *required* actually. On top of Carl Steele's demands, I have a few of my own before I ink this acquisition, which hopefully will be after this next meeting.

The thing is...I really only give a shit about *one* of my demands.

Just one.

When I said earlier that Ella was the only woman I could possibly imagine myself with, that's not entirely true. She's the only one since Nora, but from the time I met Nora at age seventeen when she transferred to my high school in our junior year, she called to me on every level. Nora is the only woman I have had both an unholy physical attraction to and a bone-deep emotional, almost spiritual, connection with.

So I make no fucking apologies for what most people would consider extreme, possibly even unethical, measures to get to the woman who's always had my balls firmly in her grasp. She's managed to avoid me for more than a decade, but she can't run anymore and I've made damn sure of that.

Other than the fact she now lives in Cincinnati, Ohio and works as a top recruiter for SER, I don't know a thing about Nora nowadays: about what she's done the past eleven years, about her life now, if she has someone special. Does she still play golf? Is she still fascinated with ladybugs? Does she still volunteer at the animal shelter? Does she own enough animals for her home to qualify as a small zoo?

I realize that while in just two days I'll come face-to-face with the only woman I have ever loved outside of my mother, I know nothing about her now or how much she's changed. Eleven years is a long time. People mature, evolve, and change whether we want them to or not. I know I have, and as I wipe off the steam on the bathroom mirror from my hot shower and look at the reflection staring back at me, I have to wonder if Nora will like the different man she will see standing before her.

Not likely, I muse. Hell, even I don't like the emotionally aloof man I've turned into most days.

LUKE'S ABSOLUTION

So, I may not know a lot of things, but I do know this: now that I've found her again, I will not rest until I own Nora Cantres, thoroughly and completely.

And once I possess her, only then will I decide what I'm going to do with her. Because along with the deep-seated love that I've never been able to squash, I also have a whole fucking boatload of anger and resentment being thrown around in that noxious sea. I'm just not sure which emotion will bubble to the surface once I see her again.

Anyone will tell you I'm not a vengeful person. I'm not exactly a graceful loser, yet I don't maliciously retaliate either. However, the need I have to hurt her so it's a permanent scar to her psyche that will never heal, the same way she did to me, keeps trumping everything else I feel for her. And with eleven years to gather steam, right now I don't know if I can stop acting on the revenge brewing inside me, waiting to be unleashed, waiting to blow.

Or if I even *want* to.

Prologue

Five years earlier...

Livia

"Do you, Peter, take this woman, Livia, to be your lawfully wedded wife? To have and to hold from this day forward, for better, for worse, for richer, for poorer, in sickness and in health, to love and to cherish, till death us do part?"

"I do," he responds. Smugly.

"Do you, Livia, take this man, Peter, to be your lawfully wedded husband? To have and to hold...."

Every little girl dreams of her wedding day. That magical moment when you pledge your undying love to the man who makes your heart beat a little faster, who makes your panties a little wetter, and who you think will make the most handsome salt-and-pepper-haired ninety-year-old ever to walk the earth. Your father will walk you down the aisle, arm in arm, in a wedding dress so beautiful, your childish vision couldn't do it justice and he'll struggle to hold back the tears of both happiness at giving you away and sadness that you're no longer his little girl.

Every young woman dreams of the honeymoon that will quickly follow. Will he whisk me away to Paris, where we'll live on wine and cheese and each other for two weeks solid? Or will we fly to a secluded island, sit on the beach, soak in the sun, and drink pina coladas that our private butler delivers every hour on the hour? Or maybe we'll decide to cruise the Mediterranean, visiting exotic stops such as Istanbul or Rome or Santorini. But at the end of the day, it really doesn't matter where you go, because you'll be together.

And every girl, young or old, dreams of being married to a man who worships the ground she walks on, puts her on a pedestal, and would give his life for hers without thought or hesitation.

I was every girl. Except, instead of the fancy wedding, complete with tears of joy, I'm standing in a courthouse in front of a justice of the peace with tears of heartbreak welling in my eyes. Instead of the elaborate gown, complete with a long, beaded train that I picked out with my sister and my best friends, I'm wearing a simple black sheath and matching pumps, which fit my somber mood perfectly. And instead of marrying the man who I love to the depths of my very soul, who will love and cherish me all the days of our lives, I'm marrying a monster...

"You may now kiss the bride."

...who will make the next one thousand two hundred and twelve days of my existence a living nightmare from which I cannot wake.

Chapter 1

Livia

I see him across the room. I'm utterly breathless.

My heart races.

My stomach flutters.

My soul disintegrates into a pile of scattered ashes once again.

I'm a complete fucking mess. No muscle will obey my command to move, even my eyelids. They refuse to take away his image for even a second.

Why is he here?

I shouldn't be taking this risk. I shouldn't be openly ogling him, but I can't look away. Holy mother of perfection...he's everything I remember and more. As breathtaking as the very first time I laid eyes on him. He's every woman's fantasy, probably men too. I see other women watching him and I want to scratch their eyes out. Some blatantly stare, as I do. Some sneak sly glances so their spouses or dates won't notice.

Foolish.

Of course their dates notice a textbook male specimen such as him in the room. All other men are busy pissing in a circle around their women to ward him away.

As if sensing my weighty stare, his eyes lock with mine. Neither of us moves.

The woman dripping off his arm, hanging on his every word, seems oblivious to our connection. Every sound fades away as we stare into each other's eyes from across the ballroom. Eyes I'm all too familiar with but haven't seen in what seems like a lifetime. Eyes that haunt me.

God, I miss him with a raw ache that intensifies daily.

"Wow, look at that fine piece of ass. He's fuckable," whispers one of my best friends, Kamryn, following my stare.

The best of my life.

He starts across the room in my direction, his date all but forgotten as he leaves her in his dust. She's calling after him, but he simply waves his hand in dismissal, not bothering to look back. His angry eyes never leave mine, his full lips drawn in a tight thin line.

Oh shit. Time to go.

"Kam, I'm not really feeling well, sweetie. I'll call you in the morning after my interview." I'm frantic to escape. I turn to leave, heels clicking as I quickly walk toward the exit. Kamryn practically runs to keep up.

"Let me call my driver for you, hon."

I call over my shoulder as I race toward my escape. "No, no. It's fine. There are plenty of cabs out front. I'll just hop in one and be home in no time. Really, it's fine."

Her grip is like an iron fist around my arm as she maneuvers me back to face her. Kam frowns, clearly not believing the blatant lie I threw her way. Whatever. Over her shoulder I estimate he's just fifty feet from where we now stand and moving at a clipped pace. As if by divine intervention, he's stopped by a buxom blonde whose nipples are ready to fall out of her slutty dress any second. One deep breath and pop, they're free. He shakes her off, heading in my direction once again. Can't blame her for trying.

Crap, Livia. Get. Out. Now.

"I think I may be sick, Kam. I'd really like to get home before I lose those little shrimp thingies I just ate." Not so much of a lie this time. My stomach *is* doing somersaults.

I turn and flee. I hear Kam call after me, but keep going this time. Making it to the safety of a cab before *he* reaches me is paramount.

Damn Kam and her insistence that I wear her four-inch Louboutin heels. So what if the fire engine red is a perfect complement to my also borrowed black leather strapless sheath. The shoes are still half a size too small and pinch my feet, making a hasty escape nearly impossible.

I should ditch the damn things like Cinderella. I bet she didn't even 'lose' her glass slipper. She was no doubt trying to escape this supposed Prince Charming because he was an arrogant asshole, and it fell off in her urgency to get away. In traditional antifeminism fashion, a man weaved an elegant story about how much better a girl's life would be with a boy in it. He would swoop in and save her from her persecuted life and they would live happily ever after.

Bullshit. All of it.

There is no happily ever after. Not for me anyway. That childish fantasy was ruthlessly shattered over five years ago.

I make it out of the ballroom, down the stairs and have the front hotel door halfway open when a strong hand clamps down on my shoulder, effectively stopping my forward movement. An electric current runs through my body and I feel him everywhere. His hand may as well be between my legs for all my body cares.

Damn you, Louboutin and your impractical shoes.

"Hello, Livia," a deep sensual voice drawls behind me. His voice and touch combined almost make my knees buckle. After all these years, he still has the same effect on all of my senses like the day we met. He sounds the same, albeit a bit more grown up. And a *lot* more sexy.

Jesus, I don't think I can do this.

You can do this, Livia.

You have *to do this.*

Be cold.

Be unaffected.

Lie.

I take a deep breath, will the tears back, and steel myself before turning to face him.

"Hello, Gray. Fancy seeing you here." *Holy...breathe, Livia, breathe.* I am almost taken aback by how utterly gorgeous he is. He had been stunning across the room and he was always beautiful, but up close he's like a golden angel sent directly from heaven—or hell—to tempt me. His face is no longer boyish, but all man, complete with the sexiest scruffy whiskers I have ever seen. This is more than a five o'clock shadow, but not quite a full beard. I'm a sucker for scruff. Especially on Gray, but he's never worn it like this. It's downright sinful.

Double damn.

"What are you doing here Livvy?" *Livvy*. I haven't heard that name in over five years. It sounds so damn good I want to weep.

Dig deep, Livia...maintain the façade you've perfected so very well.

"I came for the same reason you probably did: the animals." Bravo for me. I sounded very confident...and very *stupid*. My internal head is shaking at me sadly.

He says nothing, remaining stoically silent, his eyes searching mine for the truth.

Subject change, before he asks too many more questions, for which I'll have to build lie on top of lie. I've told so many lies I need a cheat sheet to keep track of them all. "So, why are you in Chicago?"

His penetrating gaze makes me even more nervous than I already am, and I start to squirm. I never intended to run into anyone I knew here, let alone him. I would have never let Kam talk me into this stupid fundraiser otherwise.

Shit. Shit. Shit. This is so not good.

"I took over my father's company, and we moved the headquarters from Detroit to Chicago last year."

He lives here? In Chicago? My mind is spinning. I'm trying to process the fact that my ex-fiancé lives in the same city as I do and that he took over his father's company already. I didn't remember Frank being that old. I shouldn't be engaging him in conversation, but I can't help but ask, "Did he retire?"

"No. He died." I gasp and my heart sinks.

"God, I'm sorry Gray, I had no idea. Your dad was a wonderful man." He was like a father to me, more so than my own, who essentially sold me to save his own life. I loved that family. They were like my own until they weren't anymore.

"Of course not, Livvy. How could you possibly when you fucking disappeared over five years ago, without a trace, without a call, without a forwarding goddamn phone number?" His retort is ripe with barbs, and it stings the way it was meant to. I deserve some of his ire yes, but not all of it.

Gray has no clue the living nightmare I've endured. What I did for my family or for him. And it will stay that way. I have to get away from him before I do something stupid, like spill my guts. He is my past, and as much as it deeply pains me, he has to stay that way. Too much has happened in the last five years that I simply can't overcome. I am damaged goods now, and Gray would never want me if he knew the truth. I need to get the hell out of here before I break down. I can't keep the tears back much longer.

"I have to go. It was nice to see you again, Gray." I need to get out of here before I throw myself at him and beg for his forgiveness. Because even though I don't quite deserve it, a small part of me desperately craves it. Gray is my first love. The only man I will ever love. And that young, naïve woman now buried deep inside me will hold tightly to the memory of her first love with her last dying breath. It's all that has gotten me through the worst days of my life.

And it's all I have left.

I spin to leave when a strong hand pulls me back once again. Every time this man puts his hands on me, I bend to his will, and right now I feel like a torch has been set to my bones and they are far too pliable. My eyes flit between it and his ever-so-handsome face. He gets the gist and lets go.

Although his voice has softened, his annoyance clearly rings loud when uttering his next words. "How can I get ahold of you, angel? I'd like to have dinner. Catch up."

My heart skips a beat. I haven't heard that endearment in so long, I have to blink back the tears threatening to fall. I *want* to agree. I nearly do. But then, common sense slams back into my frontal lobe at a hundred miles per hour. If I spend time with Gray, he'll pepper me with questions. Questions he has *every* right to have answered. But those are answers I won't give. I can't. He can never know.

Gone is the young, naïve, rosy-colored glasses woman he fell in love with. Gone is the carefree, idealistic woman he asked to be his wife. What stands in her place, instead, is a cynical, horribly used, and hopeless one. Shattered beyond all repair.

"I can't," I whisper. Then I do turn and flee. Luckily, there are several cabs waiting out front and I hop in the first one, yelling at him just to drive. As I turn around, I see Gray standing on the sidewalk, breathing hard, watching me drive away. Déjà vu cuts me like a sharp knife and I begin to sob silently. These are the first tears I've allowed myself to shed in four and a half years.

Once again, I am leaving the only man to ever make my stomach flutter and my heart race. The man who pursued me relentlessly for that first date by returning for six straight nights to the pizzeria I worked at until I said yes. The man I dreamed of having children with. Growing old with. The only man I have and ever will love.

All because of *him*. Always because of *him*. As with every day for the past five years, I curse the day Peter Wilder set foot into my life. And I curse my father for bringing him there.

Excerpt of

Undeniably Asher

by K.L. Kreig
Available Now

Alyse

A quick glance at the clock shows it's almost noon. I ready myself for my next meeting, wondering what the hell Asher Colloway thinks he's trying to pull and why he didn't just put his name on my calendar instead of his holding company. Clearly he's trying to surprise me.

Well, the surprise is on him. Not only do I know it's him I'm meeting with, I know that he asked for client references, and I know he's already called each and every one of them. We're a small office and Heather keeps nothing from me, not to mention we like to give our clients a heads up when we know they'll be called by a potential customer.

The thing is, I have no idea what he would possibly want to hire my small firm for, but since I'm desperate for revenue, I can't *not* take the meeting. I have more to think about now than just my pride. I have three employees counting on me to feed and clothe themselves and their families. That's a heavy burden.

I thought about having Al sit in, but decided

K. L. KREIG

against it. I already know Asher and he knows me, so having another male in the room isn't a necessity. Besides, a little part of me is thrilled to spend a few hours alone with him, even if we are just discussing business. *Okay, a* big *part of me.*

I managed to close one deal earlier this week and am waiting to hear back from the other client, hopefully by the end of the day. That one doesn't look too promising as we're a bit apart on pricing for our services. I have a small office and can't afford to be quite as flexible as other, larger firms that have more capital to work with. Another thing I did not take into consideration when I jumped into this dream of mine headfirst. *Ugh.*

My speakerphone squawks, and Heather's voice floats through. Her normally quiet, soft demeanor has clearly been ratcheted up a few degrees, because she actually sounds excited. I can hear the smile in her voice. Yes, Asher Colloway will do that to a woman, at least any straight one. "Ms. Kingsley, your noon appointment is here."

Ms. Kingsley? Heather hasn't addressed me as Ms. Kingsley since our first interview, and even at the end of that meeting she was calling me Alyse. I keep the laugh from my voice as I respond, "Thank you, Heather. Please send Mr. Colloway in." Once I disconnect I do chuckle. Heather usually has me on speakerphone when she buzzes my appointments in, so Asher's little surprise has just been turned around. *Ha! Booyaa!*

I'm still laughing when Asher opens my door. The moment my eyes land on him, though, it stutters a slow death. My gaze slowly travels down his insanely fit body and I realize he's watching me watch him, but I don't care enough to stop.

He's absolutely breathtaking in his fitted charcoal suit and crisp white shirt, which he's left open at the throat, sans tie. And the tiny bit of chest hair I see peeking through against his golden skin makes me water in more than one place. I've never seen him in anything but jeans and henleys or polo shirts, but *hot damn* if he doesn't look even more mouthwatering when he's dressed up. My entire body feels warm and tingly, inside and out.

I gravitate toward men with dark looks.

Dark hair.

Dark whiskers.

Dark eyes.

Dark personality.

Asher Colloway fits that bill to a perfect "T". At a little over six feet, he's tall, at least for me since I hover around the five-foot-four mark, give or take a half inch on a good day. And he's downright beautiful. All of the Colloway brothers could effortlessly grace the cover of a magazine, but Asher is different. He's a guy you could easily get lost in before your brain catches up to remind you why you shouldn't. He has an aura about him that's nothing short of magical and when you look at him, a spell is woven that you can't escape. You don't want to.

When I met him for the first time at seventeen, I thought he was the best thing since sliced bread. I even thought I was in love with him, but we were in very different places in our lives. Then I met Beck and I moved forward instead of looking back. Now, though...now, I can honestly say that at twenty-nine, Asher *is* the sexiest man I have ever laid eyes on, hands down.

I want him. Desperately.

And desperation makes you do stupid, stupid things.

"Get your fill yet?" A smug smirk turns up one corner of his kissable mouth.

Damn him. I have absolutely no snarky comeback to that, because I've been openly ogling. I only hope I don't have drool dripping down my chin. I nonchalantly reach up to check, faking a cough.

"Why the secrecy?" I ask, changing subjects, not taking my eyes from him.

He closes the door before taking a seat in the chair across from my metal desk, throwing one foot onto the opposite knee. He steeples his fingers in front of his chin. The arrogant glint in his dark eyes makes me want to drop to my knees in front of him, unzip his pants, and wipe it off.

"You knew it was me."

I knew Asher had taken over as CEO for his father's company—I *may* have asked Livia what the Colloway brothers were up to after she'd reunited with Gray. In preparation for this meeting, when I researched GRASCO Holdings and found that CFC fell under them, I was irritated at first that Asher wanted to catch me cold. I never attend a client meeting without doing my homework first, especially since I'm fighting for the very existence of ARK Consulting. But then I quickly decided to turn the tables on the self-assured SOB.

Knowing that I would be meeting with Asher today, I've dressed particularly sexy in a short nude pencil skirt paired with a sheer royal-blue blouse and a matching low-cut cami underneath. Definitely not how I would dress for a normal client meeting, but I went all out for Asher. I let a slow smile turn my lips as I sit back in my black vinyl chair and casually cross my legs.

Asher's eyes follow my leisurely movements and widen at the expanse of bare thigh I'm now showing. He may have even seen a flash of the nude thong I'm wearing from his position. His heated gaze rises, capturing mine, and I have to actually talk myself into breathing, trying to remain unaffected by the intense desire he clearly wants me to see. It's not working too well.

"It may surprise you to know that I do know how to use the Internet," I finally manage to bite sarcastically.

"You haven't changed a bit, Alyse."

"I beg to differ," I retort, knowing full well life has made me more cynical and closed off.

He rewards me with a small smile, which almost melts me on the spot. He's like the sun.

Warm. Inviting. Only more deadly if you spend too much time in his presence. He's quiet for several beats, his eyes assessing me deliberately. "I like a woman with fire."

"Do you?" I cross my arms, unsure where this conversation is headed, but it's not about business anymore. I don't miss how his eyes linger too long on my now-exposed cleavage.

"Yes." He uncrosses his leg and leans forward, elbows on spread knees, hands clasped. His want-filled gaze burns my cocky attitude to ashes. "It makes her complete submission all the sweeter."

A flash fire of heat scorches my lady parts. My mouth drops open temporarily before I think to close it. Asher is so good, so smooth, and I am *waaaay* out of my league trying to trade barbs with him.

"What are you doing here, Asher?"

He leans back again, resuming a casual position, a slight smirk on his face. His eyes twinkle like stars and I find myself getting lost in them again. "Besides getting you wet?" he drawls roughly. Even though he's spot on, his assumption angers me. I open my mouth to protest when he interrupts. "You still with Popeye?"

Huh? It takes me a minute to figure out what he means. *Finn.* I stare at him in complete and utter shock for several moments. Then, I can't help it. I laugh. I've never been around a man who has kahunas as big as Asher Colloway. He was always direct, but in the years since I've seen him, he's sharpened it considerably. It's refreshing and unsettling at the same time.

I shake my head, still chuckling, but he's stony silent. His desire has now clearly morphed into annoyance, which makes me laugh even harder. "And if I say yes?"

"Are you?"

I almost decide to lie just to see how he'll react. Anger isn't the type of response I want from Asher, though. I'm not really sure what I do want, but I know it's not that. "No."

As fast as his annoyance came, it went with my admission.

"Did you come here to question my relationship status? You could have just hopped on Facebook for that, saved yourself the drive." I uncross my legs and lean on my forearms, the coldness from the steel desk seeping into my exposed pores through the thin fabric. It's November in Detroit and very cold, but I still can't regret my choice of wardrobe after seeing the appreciation in both Asher's eyes and slacks.

"Because it's not official until it's Facebook official, right?"

"Right," I drawl. "So, back to my original question. Why are you here?"

"I want to hire you."

I assumed when he was calling references that was his angle. I'm thrilled, but at the same time, disappointed. I need this job, but I also want Asher, even though that's not the best of ideas. And I can't have both.

Why?...a little voice whispers.

Because it's kind of a faux pas to sleep with your clients, I tell that little slut.

"For?"

"There's someone embezzling within my company. I want them found and stopped and prosecuted." He pulls an envelope out of a folder he set down on the edge of my desk earlier. "Our outside audit firm completed our annual audit and found a discrepancy in the books, but they aren't equipped to take it further. We need someone who has expertise in ferreting out things like this, whose techniques will hold up in a court of law. I know you've worked on cases before where your work has supported a legal case."

True. I live to bring down white-collar thieves. My dad was a thief; he just stole our childhood from my sister and me instead of a corporation or business. I think that's one of the reasons I went into this field to begin with. "Is this a past or ongoing issue?"

"I have reason to believe it's ongoing, but of course I can't be sure."

"Do you have any suspicions?"

"Yes. Unfortunately, nothing solid, though."

I look down, unsure of how I should approach this. I don't want to talk myself out of a job, but I want to be up front as well. I don't doubt my ability in the slightest, but CFC would be, by far, the biggest client I've worked on, and this project could possibly take months, given my small staff depending on how deep the embezzlement is buried. "You do know I haven't worked on a project for a company your size yet, correct?"

He nods, staying quiet.

"Okay. Let me look this over and work up a proposal and a timeline for your review. I can have it to you by mid-next week. Then we can meet again, discuss any questions you might have, and negotiate terms."

"No."

My brows draw together in confusion. "No, what?"

"No. I told you I want to hire you. *You*. I've already done my research. I don't need to review anything."

I'm taken aback for a moment. "I could rob you blind. My fee may not even be competitive with the other firms you're considering."

"I'm already being robbed blind. And you won't. Whatever your fees, whatever your terms, I'll agree to them. I want the best, Alyse." He pauses before he adds, "I hear that's you."

Huh? This is by far the weirdest client prospect meeting I've ever had. I have to wonder what the catch is, because this seems too good to be true. "Uh, oookay."

"I want you to start on Monday."

It's the Wednesday before Thanksgiving. I think for a minute, cataloging our current projects. I was planning to take this new client I just secured, but I can give that to Al. Tabitha still has at least two weeks on her current project, and I'll have to come in now on Friday to wrap up a few loose ends and do some paperwork. "I can make that work."

K. L. KREIG

He's silent, studying me. "One more thing. And it's non-negotiable."

I smirk. "I'm not sleeping with you." *Even though right now I can think of nothing else but your hot, wet tongue worshipping every inch of me.*

Laughing, he leans forward, his forearms on my desk, his face mere inches from mine. I want to lean back, yet not at the same time, so I don't. Once again, Asher invades my personal space. I can't stop the big breath I take, inhaling his manly, spicy scent. It's all I can do to keep my eyes from rolling back in my head.

He doesn't miss it either. I'm getting the distinct feeling he doesn't miss any of my bodily reactions to his inebriating presence. When he finally speaks, his voice drops several octaves to panty-melting sexy. "Good. Because I'm looking forward to fucking you instead."

Holy balls. His blistering stare and egotistical words light a blaze deep within my belly. If I was wet before, I'm positively drenched now. And mute. Very, very mute. On account of the fact that my mouth is now bone dry and all thought has fled my desire-clouded brain.

His next words pull me out of the sexual haze he has trapped us in. It's a place I could imagine myself staying. Forever. "I need you at headquarters during the audit. In Chicago."

I blink a few times to clear my mental fog, letting his words register. Being onsite during an audit is pretty standard, at least part of the time, but this will be a big audit and could take months. I bill for lodging and meal expenses, but the thought of spending months in a hotel and shuttling back and forth on the weekends to Detroit is less than appealing. On the other hand, it gets me closer to Livia. Hell, who am I kidding? I'd shuttle back and forth to San Francisco if there were a paying client there.

"You have offices here in Detroit, right?"

"Yes, but I need to keep this as quiet as possible. CFC is not all that big, so the fewer people who know about you, the better. I need you in Chicago. There's a secluded office available on my floor."

The thought of being near Asher daily does funny things to my insides. More than it should. More than I want. "That's going to be pretty costly for you," I murmur. *And me*, I think, in more ways than one.

He leans back slightly and I'm able to take a deep breath for the first time in long minutes without inhaling him. His unique fragrance is clouding my mind, my judgment.

"I have another proposal."

I roll my eyes, leaning back in my chair. His magnetic pull makes it hard to do even that.

I am in so much trouble.

"I'm not staying with you, either."

"Now, Alyse, why do you insist on ruining all my fun?" he quips, winking.

I smile, but remain quiet. Even if he would be so bold to suggest it, he would have to know I'd never accept.

"Okay. If you won't stay with me, then we

469

have an executive apartment that's not being used. It's fully furnished and close to the office. The building has a nice gym and a couple of restaurants. It's not terribly fancy, but it's better than a hotel."

"I—I don't know, Asher." I'm hedging, but the second his proposal left his mouth I already made up my mind. If I had a place that felt like my own, I could stay there most weekends instead of driving back to Detroit, where there was really nothing left for me except bad memories and ghosts from my past that won't seem to let me out of their unyielding grip.

He gets comfortable again before continuing his sales pitch. "It's in the same building as Livia and Gray, so you'll also be close to your sister. I know you're helping with their shotgun wedding and wouldn't it be convenient to be able to hop in the elevator and pop in on her? Of course, I would probably call ahead first, because..."

He leaves his insinuation hanging and we both laugh, lightening the mood.

As I pretend to think about it for a couple of minutes, his intense gaze never leaves mine. I can feel him willing me into acquiescence. I almost break a smile, but that would be giving him too much and right now I need to hold parts of me back, because I can already tell Asher will demand everything from me. And then some. Certain girlie parts are already begging me to submit, submit, submit.

Seeing Asher again a couple of months ago triggered something inside me. Made me remember my girlish dreams when I was eighteen and in love with Beck. Dreams that have been too painful to remember, but now that I do, I want them desperately. To be honest, it made me remember what I felt when I almost gave myself to a young Asher Colloway.

I want bone-deep love, a family, happiness, and a man that will worship me. I thought Beck was the man who would give me everything, but he's dead and apparently wasn't the man I thought he was at all.

Finn certainly wasn't that man.

And I don't think Asher Colloway can give me any of those things either. I'm not sure he can give *any* woman that.

Pleasure? No doubt.

A future? Not likely.

He's nearly thirty, never been married, and is clearly a player. I want more than that now. God knows I *deserve* more than that. As much as I'm attracted to him, sleeping with him is probably the dumbest idea to ever cross my mind, yet my conviction not to needs a lot of reinforcement.

I refocus on the reason we're having this discussion in the first place. Keeping my business afloat. "Okay. I accept your terms."

His smile blinds me, and all thoughts I just had about why I should stay away from this man float out of the room on a cloud of pure lust.

Yep, my conviction needs a lot of work.

A. Lot.

Babbles...

I absolutely LOVED writing this book and I hope you enjoyed reading it as much as I did getting these two souls on paper. Luke and Addy have probably been my favorite and easiest couple to write so far. Each word just flowed effortlessly and I could have made this book so much longer than I did!

I know Luke has been a fan favorite, and his story was supposed to be the last and the hardest, but that honor goes to Connelly, and I can't wait for you to really get to know him. Connelly's complex and tortured and he'll have to dig deep for his happily ever after. His and Nora's story is gut-wrenching to read (and to write), which is why he had to wait until last.

I love these brothers, I love this series, and no matter how many books I write, these characters will always hold a special place in my heart.

Now on to my thanks and gratitude. Friends, family, bloggers, authors, betas, editors, formatters, proofreaders, pimpers, and most importantly MY READERS: if you had a hand in this, if you supported me in any way, shape, or form, you know who you are and you know I thank you from the bottom of my heart. I am nothing but sincerely, eternally grateful for your belief in me.

Finally, after forty some years, I have found my true passion in life. I may never be a best seller, I may never win writing awards, I may never be able to make a true living at doing what I love, but I don't even care. Every message and each email I get from someone who wanted to personally reach out to me and praise me for how my work touched them in some way is *truly* a surreal feeling and *that's* why I do this. Because you all encourage me. For that, I thank you.

Even though I know they will never read this, I can't thank my favorite band, Red, enough for their musical inspiration to write this entire Colloway Brothers series. I always find inspiration in music regardless of my writing, but it's really incredible that each of their songs spoke to me exactly as if these characters did. If you haven't heard of them, you should check them out or at least listen to one or two of the songs I've written this book to. "The Ever" is one of my favorites and describes how Luke feels to a "T".

Thanks for taking this journey with me, for buying my book, and for supporting an author you love. Whether that's me or not, your support of your favorite authors cannot be overstated.

If you like this book, ***please*** tell your friends, your neighbors, shout it from the rooftops. Hell, tell people you don't even like! The best thing you can do to support an author you love is word of mouth and LEAVE A REVIEW on Goodreads, Amazon, or wherever. Even one or two sentences or simply rating the book is helpful for other readers. Reviews are critical to getting a book exposure.

About the Author

This is the hardest part...talking about myself.

I'm just a regular ol' Midwest girl who likes *Game of Thrones* and is obsessed with *Modern Family* and *The Goldbergs*. I run, I eat, I run, I eat. It's a vicious cycle. I love carbs, but there's a love-hate relationship with my ass and thighs. Mostly hate. I like a good cocktail (oh hell...who am I kidding? I love *any* cocktail). I'm a huge creature of habit, but I'll tell you I'm flexible. I read every single day and if I don't get a chance...watch the hell out, I'm a raving bitch. My iPad and I: BFFs. I'm direct and I make no apologies for it. I swear too much. I love alternative music and in my next life, I want to be a badass female rocker. I hate, hate, hate spiders, telemarketers, liver, acne, winter, and loose hairs that fall down my shirt (don't ask, it's a thing).

I have a great job (no...truly it is) outside of writing. My kids and my husband are my entire world and I'd never have made it this far without them. My soul mate husband of over twenty-eight years provides unwavering support and my two grown children know the types of books I write and they don't judge their mom anyway (and my daughter is a beta reader even...yes, that can be awkward...very).

I'm *sincerely* humbled by each and every like on my Facebook page or sign-up for my newsletter or outreach from someone who has read and loved my books. I still can't get over the great support. The romance book community is a wonderful and supportive one. I've made more friends since I started this journey than I've made in my life and I'm a pretty affable person. It's surreal. I'm pretty sure it always will be.

In short, I am blessed...and I know it.

If you're a stalker, the first step is to admit it. After that, you can find me in a lot of places, all of which I use with irregular frequency.

In this day and age, with so many great authors and so many new releases, it's challenging to keep up with it all, so if you don't want to miss when my next book is releasing, sign up for my newsletter found on my website. Promise no spamming and you'll only get it when I have something important to say.

Website: http://klkreig.com